Una Brankin is a journalist and media consultant. She lives in Dublin.

HALF MOON LAKE

Grace grew up in the shadow of her widowed mother and her superstitious, overbearing neighbours in the remote town of Preacher's Bay, Northern Ireland. One summer evening, a stranger knocks on their door, desperately seeking refuge. As Grace helps to nurse him back to health, she experiences at last the love that she has so innocently yet dementedly craved. Now, two decades later, Grace thinks back to her childhood and that steamy summer of 1976. And finally, the truth behind her lifelong reclusiveness, her relationship with her mother, and her first and only love, is revealed.

UNA BRANKIN

◆

HALF MOON LAKE

Complete and Unabridged

ULVERSCROFT
Leicester

First published in Great Britain in 2003 by
Pocket/TownHouse, an imprint of
Simon & Schuster UK Limited, London

First Large Print Edition
published 2004
by arrangement with
Simon & Schuster UK Limited, London

The moral right of the author has been asserted

This book is a work of fiction. Names, characters,
places and incidents are either a product of the
author's imagination or are used fictitiously.
Any resemblance to actual people living or dead,
events or locales is entirely coincidental.

British Library CIP Data

Brankin, Una
    Half moon lake.—Large print ed.—
    Ulverscroft large print series: general fiction
    1. Mothers and daughters—Northern Ireland—Fiction
    2. Recluses—Northern Ireland—Fiction
    3. First loves—Northern Ireland—Fiction
    4. Large type books
    I. Title
    823.9'2 [F]

    ISBN 1–84395–287–4

Published by
F. A. Thorpe (Publishing)
Anstey, Leicestershire

Set by Words & Graphics Ltd.
Anstey, Leicestershire
Printed and bound in Great Britain by
T. J. International Ltd., Padstow, Cornwall

This book is printed on acid-free paper

For Anne Maguire, Ruth Arigho
and Kathleen Doherty

Thanks to: Declan Murphy, Bridie Turley, Treasa Coady, Hugh and Sheila Brankin, Owen Hillis, Maggie Deas, Sue Booth-Forbes and all at Anan Cara, Writers' & Artists' retreat.

PART ONE

1

I wanted to die there. By summertime my flesh would have melted into a mush in the rushes, and the rain would have washed it from my bones and driven it into the water. A good feed for the eels. Then the winter frosts would have pounded my brittle skeleton into the ground, snow blanketing the indecency of it.

It was quite blissful while it lasted, that swirling sensation and shimmering light. Utter peace. I saw the most dazzling azaleas . . . if they'd left me alone, I believe a string section would have whipped up an adagio. What odds if it was a trick of the brain — my soul might not have been going anywhere, but it would have been silenced, at last.

Instead, here I am, under stiff white sheets, encased by yellowing walls; the sour whiff of sickness in my nostrils and six tired eyes trained on me. I can see my cousins vaguely through my lashes, but I cannot lift my eyelids nor shape my mouth to speak to them. I cannot move a hand, or even a finger. The boys, Bobby and Ignatius, are grizzled men now. Four fat knees under stained *school shorts, that's how I remember those two. The girl, Georgina, is beautiful. I have not seen her since she was a baby.*

I succumb to the weariness, but Bobby's big stupid whisper stirs me.

'Do you reckon she's a virgin?'

'Sure who'd have her?'

'Aye, but there was talk . . . '

'Shut up, both of you. She might be able to hear you.'

'Don't care if she does. And I don't care if she rid the country. As long as she's no bastards to claim the home place.'

God, my head's sore.

'What the hell was she doing walking into the reed bank anyway, and her so ill? Nobody ever goes down there nowadays.'

Right, until Jimmy Burns's poor confused brain decided he needed reeds to make a St Brigid's Cross, way past her feast day.

'She's walked the Preacher's Bay shore path all her life, every single evening, talking away to herself the whole time. Sure what else has she to do?'

. . . The garden . . . my books . . .

'They say she's as odd as two's even, always was. Real oul'-fashioned. Maybe that knock to the head will wise her up, if she ever wakes up. According to Burns, if you could believe him, she was face down at the edge of*

4

the water, blood running out of the side of her head. Must've hit it on an oul' stump or something. Doctor said she could've lost oxygen to the brain — '

'Look, Bobby, why don't you go and get us a cup of tea from the machine. Hospitals make me thirsty.'

'I'll go with you. Stretch my legs.'

Don't hurry back, boys. You hurt my ears.

A small squat nurse pads in, her rubber soles squeaking on the linoleum. She looks at the monitor and scribbles on the chart at the end of the bed. My cousin Georgina turns to her.

'Is there any improvement?'

'She's comfortable, but she's not quite out of danger yet.'

My cousin comes closer and lightly brushes my cheek with her crooked fingers. The nurse watches.

'Nice complexion, hasn't she? I must say, there's a strong family resemblance between you.'

'She used to wash her face in rainwater . . . her father and my father were brothers. She's my godmother, you know. I never knew her, though.'

'Look, she's in good hands, dear. Why don't you and your brothers go home and get some rest while you can?'

5

'Well, it is my birthday, my thirtieth actually. Supposed to be having a party later on, although it doesn't feel right.'

'You should go and enjoy yourself. I'm sure she would want you to.'

'Yes, I suppose so . . . God, I wonder what she's thinking . . . '

'Hopefully she'll be able to sit up soon and tell you.'

'I hope so.'

No you don't, Georgina Kane. No you do not.

★   ★   ★

I never really liked summertime in Preacher's Bay. The road gets invaded by swarms of bloodthirsty midges. They hang in the hot air like dirt clouds and itch the head off you. There are some dreadful creatures flying about the place. I have also been eaten by very stubborn woodlice, and once, as a girl, when I was riding my old bicycle at high speed along the shore path, a massive bee hit me smack in my eye like a plastic bullet and left me with a shiner for a week. At least it didn't sting, Mother said.

The flies gradually disappear in the first days of September, when that uncomfortable stillness gives way to a luxurious creamy breeze. I can only describe the way it skims my pale face and arms as sensuous. I always get a little lift from the sight of a weakened sun slanting along the sweep of the bay — the milky air of early autumn is such a relief after the glare of high summer. The sun at full strength makes me panicky. It makes my body feel too solid, a big sweating nuisance. When I studied a French novel at school, I perfectly understood how the sun made the protagonist kill the Arab. It was something I couldn't bring myself to articulate in front of the class, however. Sister Joan, a wee small fat black crow of a woman, wasn't interested in me anyway. Too dazzled by little Ivy Best, sitting beside me. Looking back, I suspect Sister Joan had a crush on her. 'Oh, what delicate little sneezes!' she admiringly exclaimed one morning when Ivy's hay fever erupted in class. I'll never forget the way she smiled down at her. Sickening. I attracted no such attention, but then my parents weren't the biggest landowners in the parish and I didn't have black shiny ringlets and baby blue eyes.

Post-adolescence, my blossoming, such as it was, had been all too brief. There's only so much you can do with strawberry blonde hair full of kinks and with a big cow's lick in the front, and I never really lost all the puppy fat, much to the consternation of my petite and glamorous mother. The only thing I'd inherited from her good genes was a pair of full lips.

I quickly became accustomed to my invisibility, yet I was still relieved when I had the shore path to myself in the evenings. The curious teenagers, so comfortable in their numbers, who littered the roads all summer long, usually disappeared with the flies. A walk is so much more pleasurable when it is unfettered.

★   ★   ★

Yes, cousin, I do talk to myself all the time, but I'm addressing my soul, or God, if you like. I don't suppose I will have much else to do here, while I wait. Maybe I could tell you my story. Can you mind-read? Oh, and I'm afraid my memory is haphazard. If memory is interest, then my detachment is excessive. The majority of the years of my youth have blurred. Bar one. The time there was talk. That year was the only one that mattered a damn, and, dotty or not, I remember everything about it, Georgina Kane. It would indeed be of advantage to you and your brothers to know what happened that summer, but you won't find out the whole

8

truth from anyone but me.

Anyway, it all began when my brother Frank and I turned 18. Our birthday falls in May. It was just another day to me. When we were born, he evacuated the womb a whole 27 minutes before me. I'd been in his shadow ever since. There was no party for our coming of age, of course, and only a couple of cards. But God, or fate, or some bloody thing, sent me a strange and very unexpected gift . . .

Too tired now. Maybe I'll talk to you later . . .

★   ★   ★

Georgina's birthday cards lay in a small heap on her kitchen table. The punchlines were not to her taste. She couldn't bear clutter on her white fireplace, or anywhere else in her spare, white-walled apartment. Nor did she wish to be reminded of her fading youth; the encroaching frown lines and the slight hardening of her features, which she saw every morning and every night in the bedroom mirror, were proof enough for her.

Two days after her party, she was still hungover. The morning-after cure had developed into a reckless boozy lunch with her friend Elaine in a wine bar next to her office in the centre of Belfast. The wine had energised her, then muddled and dulled her, and she'd broken her abstinence from cigarettes. The result was burning stomach ache worse, she thought, than her adolescent menstrual cramps, and a heavy head that felt like it was being pierced with red-hot knitting needles. Worse than the physical symptoms, was the hideously altered worldview brought on by her excess.

She huddled on her sofa and plundered the black recesses of her mind for tormenting fodder, with the persistence of a gambler pumping coins into a slot machine. A familiar list of thumping guilt, starting with the drinking and moving on to the negligence towards her job, played itself out it bursts of cold torture.

And now there was a new addition to her list. A faint but growing awareness of her innate greed had elbowed in from her subconsciousness, where it had been shoved out of the way while she considered the facts and figures of her cousin Grace's estate. However, while the accusation of avarice was still in its embryonic stages, she was just about able to summon the mental resources to quash it. For she and her brothers had, she told herself, a cast-iron justification for laying claim to the Kane land.

The clipped beeping of her mobile phone broke into her thoughts. She ignored it, lacking the mental energy to open her mouth and form coherent sentences. Earlier, she'd phoned the office to say she'd work from home, but as she swallowed two painkillers and willed herself to keep them down, she knew her local tourism project would be ignored until Monday. She waited until the ringing stopped, then checked the phone for messages.

'Georgina, would you get down here as quick as you can — she's taken a turn.'

Ignatius's voice was urgent, almost excited. Georgina closed her eyes and pressed the back of the phone against her stinging temples. To drive to the hospital was out of the question, even if Grace was on her deathbed, she decided, and tried to recall a local taxi number. She slowly punched in the digits as they came to her and ordered a cab to the hospital, in a voice hoarse from smoking and talking too much.

Nausea suffused her as she got up from the sofa and lurched into the hall. She rose too quickly and for a few seconds went into a walking faint. A slighter girl would have succumbed and collapsed on to the floor but Georgina's tall and strong physique fought off the loss of consciousness and kept her upright until she reached the wash-hand basin. She wasn't strong enough, though, to quell the tumult in her gut.

The retching was violent and compulsive, wracking her body until the nerves around her mouth convulsed and her hands quaked. Such was the force of the eruption inside her, she momentarily feared her heart would stop under the strain of it. She clung to the edge of the wash-hand basin until the involuntary spasms abated.

When it was over, she quivered like someone spat out by a hurricane. She looked in the mirror. Her stricken eyes streamed uncontrollably. Her pale lips had set rigidly against her teeth. Her skin had taken on the hue and texture of putty, her tangled hair hung limply around her hunched shoulders.

'Oh God I'm going to get cancer,' she thought, imagining the poisons racing through her bloodstream. She leaned down and rinsed her face with cold water and scrubbed her teeth until her gums hurt. The intensity of her vomiting had the converse effect of clearing her head and putting the pain away, and the merciful hiatus allowed her to quickly dress in a trouser suit, the first thing she put her hand to in her walk-in wardrobe, and to rub some colour into her wan face before the taxi arrived.

The local drivers had got to know her quite well since she moved to the exclusive apartment complex just south of the city a year ago, but she dreaded having to make small talk on the ten-minute drive to the hospital.

In her hurry out, she slammed the front door of the building, kick-starting the return of her headache. The brisk February air whipped her hair back and forth as she opened the door of the taxi and lowered herself into the back seat. Cloying boy-band music was playing on the radio and the driver, an overweight, pensionable part-timer with a wheeze, was looking at her in the front-screen mirror.

'Visiting somebody at the Royal, are you, love?'

'Yes. My cousin,' Georgina replied, flat-voiced and dull-eyed.

'Serious, is it?'

'Could be.'

The driver pulled up at a set of traffic lights and glanced over his shoulder. 'You must be right and worried about her, by the looks of you.'

'Mmm.'

'Ah sure she'll be well looked after. Those doctors and nurses have plenty of time for people now that there isn't the same trouble on the streets.'

Georgina couldn't get her voice beyond listless. 'I suppose that's right.'

'Aw yeah. You know, I seen people scalped from the bombs on Bloody Friday, back in seventy-two. The skin pulled right back off the head like the lid of a tin of beans. Desperate it was, desperate.'

Georgina slid a little further down into her seat and stared out the window. Out of the blue the taxi swerved sharply to the right, jolting her across the back seat. Another car flashed by in a blink, having switched lanes as the lights turned to green.

'What the — ? Fucking asshole! Bastard! Jesus Christ — did you see that?' The driver slammed the flat of his hand on the horn and let fly a guttural splurge of invective at the car. His fleshy face contorted, his eyes deadly and his tone becoming uglier with each exclamation of abuse.

Georgina's despondency grew. She had long despaired at the ungraciousness of the people she came into contact with, day in and day out. Growing up with two charmless brothers and a gruff father had led her to seek out polite society when she was old enough to leave home, and ugly talk and crude mannerisms still left her cold. A hangover made the brutishness worse, and underlined the knowledge that she could be as low-down

14

crude herself. She put down her occasional lapses to job stress and PMT, but the lurking fear of bad genes would always quietly join the queue of neuroses that came with fatigue and dehydration.

Nodding in pretend agreement with the driver's relentless diatribe, Georgina swallowed back the gathering saliva in her mouth and silently prayed she wouldn't have to get out and throw up on busy Great Victoria Street. She fixed all her concentration on the cheery pizzerias and pubs passing by, and closed her eyes in relief as they got past the Europa hotel without incident. The driver had moaned on into a history of the worst traffic incursions he had witnessed in his thirty-four-year career and by the time they'd reached the hospital, he had come to the emphatic conclusion that everyone should be made to redo their driving test every three years.

Georgina paid him and got out without waiting for the change. Again the wind mussed up her hair but once she'd got through the hospital's swing doors, she hadn't the energy to root in her handbag for a comb. She headed straight for the creaky lift and leaned against the mirrored back wall, relieved to be sharing it with only two preoccupied nurses, whom she recognised from intensive care. She followed them out at the third floor and hurried along the disinfected orange-walled corridor to Grace's room. Her brothers sat on a bench outside the room, drinking from plastic cups.

'No champers yet. Your woman's hanging on,' Bobby said.

Georgina put her handbag on the floor and sat on the bench opposite. 'Did she come round at all?'

'Kinda. Mumbling all sorts of nonsense, she was. Something about something on Matt's Island. Couldn't make her out, like.'

'The doctor said it was too late for a bone marrow transplant, not that we were volunteering,' Ignatius said.

'Did she see you?'

'Nope — she wasn't really looking at anything. Eyes were sorta wild, like.'

'Sounds like she's on her way out.'

'You don't look so great yourself, them bags under your eyes.'

'Thanks, Ignatius. You're not exactly fresh and sparkling either.'

'Hard to be, when you haven't two shillings to rub together.'

Georgina raised an eyebrow, surprised to see a hint of offence in her brother's crusty-rimmed eyes.

Time has made them even more alike, she

thought to herself, taking in the two long, unshaven faces and dirty fingernails, the cheap nylon jackets and baggy-kneed jeans. She had seen her brothers only a handful of times since she returned from London, and each time the yawning gap between the siblings grew wider.

'Suppose you're going to tell us we're not the height of fashion neither,' added Ignatius, catching Georgina scrutinising his scuffed boots. 'Well, Daddy, God rest him, never give a damn about the shirt on his back as long as there was enough to feed us. And I'm damn sure I'm not going to dress up for Grace Kane's dying. As long as we get the place back, that's all that matters.'

Georgina felt a deep loneliness take hold of her, and was suddenly aware of how everything was made hard and ugly under the strip lighting on the ceiling. She shrank away from her brother's bitterness and recoiled into the murk of her hangover. Is this the absence of God? she asked herself. When is He ever here anyway? Why can't I feel Him, or see Him in anyone? Are they evil? Am I evil?

'Ah, pay no heed to him, Georgina,' Bobby said. 'Sure we're all in this together. Isn't that right, Ignatius?'

Ignatius gnawed at the rough skin around

his fingernails. Georgina imagined he was plotting out new boundaries on Grace's land. In the ensuing silence, fatigue replaced her anxiety and muffled her racing thoughts. She leaned her head against the wall behind her, envying the patients the comfort of their narrow beds. The lingering enmity between herself and Ignatius prickled the atmosphere and she was relieved when he went to the gents.

No sooner had he gone than a nurse emerged from the room and beckoned Georgina and Bobby to the door.

'We've stabilised her blood pressure but she's still critical,' the nurse said, looking at her watch. She was a new one, younger than the last one. 'She can't have disturbance of any kind — no raised voices or anything like that.'

'Can we go in?' asked Georgina

'You can have five minutes, no longer. Dr Murray's just finishing with her.'

'I'll go and get Ignatius — you go on in, Georgina.'

Georgina followed the nurse into the room and stood at the end of Grace's bed. The older woman's face was as white and ethereal as a mountain mist. For the first time in as long as she could remember, Georgina said a prayer for someone other than herself.

* ★ ★

You wouldn't be familiar with the Preacher's Bay of my youth.

A lot has changed since I was a girl in that forgotten little hinterland of Antrim. Not one of the fishermen's cottages leading down to our farmhouse is the same as it was. Every house in the row used to have white-washed walls and outside toilets; now they are samey, ugly bungalows.

Old Josie and Dalloway Moore still live next door, but the McNicholls beside them are long gone; some to Belfast, some to Australia. They sold their house to a bunch of red-headed orphans who were burned out of Belfast. All on the bureau, or the dole as they call it now. Next to them are the Mulhollands, second cousins of ours. Big Molly Doherty's next. She's lived on her own since her husband Turlough fell out of his boat and drowned. That old breed of lough man never did learn to swim. Molly used to be the local hairdresser, and the only one I ever knew who really did use a baking bowl to get hair cut evenly. The Mullens still live at the top of Bay Road, beside the bus stop. Arthritis has made bumpy beef sausages out of Nelly and Mary's fingers, but they're still running the nets for their cousins, the only fishermen left in this neck of this woods. They sit outside untangling for hours, and fiddling with those tiny bait holders, and they don't miss one thing that goes on in this country. Oul' Yella Mary they call Mary Mullen, on account of her bad liver. Nelly has a face like the Pope's, wide-set hooded eyes just the very same.

The row's one saving grace is the view of the lough behind them and our five-acre spread in front of them. They call our bit of the lough Half Moon Lake, because of the curve of the shore and the way Matt's Island runs straight opposite it. Everyone still complains about the atrocious bus service into town. Nine miles is too far to walk, but Preacher's Bay village is only half a mile from our house, ten minutes if you turn left along the shore-path shortcut.

Only our place and its outhouses have been untouched by time, apart from the usual wear and tear. The pebble-dash walls and the veranda have taken a hiding from the winds and rain sweeping off the lough, and the white paint is peeling off the window frames at an alarming rate, but it's my house, and I like it anyway. Mind you, there was a time when I couldn't bear to be in it, and that's when I started walking.

★   ★   ★

On the day I turned eighteen, I couldn't wait to get out for my walk. As a child, I would have turned back at the point where the shore path led on to the main road, but as I grew older I ventured a little further towards the village, eager to soak up as much of that soft amber light before going back home.

I wore a knitted waistcoat — all plucked it was — over a blue cotton dress, and a pair of suede loafers Dalloway's dog had chewed. As usual I was pretending I owned the bay. In my own silent world, I was a very different girl to the one the world saw. In my silence, I could think and say whatever I liked, and that was often a whole lot different to the odd utterance that came out of my mouth, I can tell you. In the real world, of course, the years of being seen but not heard eventually take their toll.

So there I was, a birthday girl taking a leisurely stroll before dinner at a candlelit supper club with Gershwin songs being played by the in-house orchestra. For a little while I forgot where I was, and when I came to the turn for the shortcut home, I walked on towards the village.

I rarely shopped in Preacher's Bay village. There were too many people I might have to speak to, too many people who would nudge their companions and whisper. I preferred the anonymity of the market in town, very early on a Friday morning when the good plaice came in. My mother always complained that the flat white fish was an extravagant luxury when there was a world of eels and pollan to be had from the lough. But she ordered it anyway, once a month without fail.

I slowed my pace as I approached the chapel at the mouth of the village. I thought about turning back, but it was nearly that time of the month and the lure of O'Mahoney's sweet shop, opposite the chapel, was almost as strong as it was every Sunday morning of my childhood. I fumbled in my pocket for change and took my place in the small queue at the back of the tiny cluttered premises, waiting as the gaggle of small children at the counter argued and procrastinated.

Mrs O'Mahoney's niece sat hunched behind the counter, her sheet of blonde hair falling on to the pages of a glossy magazine. She had clean fair skin with tight pores and a pinky sheen, and a neat frame. When it came my turn, I asked for a quarter of sugared almonds, and was immediately struck by the girl's effortless grace of movement as, on tiptoe, she plucked the glass jar from a high shelf and weighed out the sweets, stemming their flow with her delicate fingers. Then her aunt came in from the stockroom, with a curling pin between her dry pinched lips, her bleached hair pulled so tight into prickly blue rollers that you could see the follicles on the scalp, her face roasted by the overhead hair-dryer. I almost felt sorry for Mrs O'Mahoney having to watch her niece bloom while she faded.

The girl's high voice cut through my distraction and brought a quick flush to my cheeks.

'Eighteen pence, please.'

I looked at my change and saw I was short. The stinging colour deepened furiously. Flustered and cringing, I stammered some-thing about putting some of the sweets back, but the girl, smirking, said I could leave the rest of the money next time. I took the bag and fled the shop, feeling the horrible colour sear my neck and chest and the top of my back.

The inner rebukes began in earnest as I half ran towards the pathway, and, on the way home, one irrevocable fact presented itself. There was no doubt about it, I was sure to redden painfully again in that girl's presence, especially if it was in the shop. Once I lost my composure in the company of an individual, the stinging memory of it would leave me dangerously vulnerable to a reoccurrence on the next meeting. I had to rely on a person's good grace not to comment, while cursing my own extreme gaucheness. In the aftermath of such embarrassment, I felt unnerved and jangly. The foxgloves that splashed the hedges lost all their charm and became common weeds, and the setting sun was suddenly blinding, and the path stretched interminably ahead. I plunged on, my eyes fixed on the mocking ground. My feet felt big and ugly, my ankles bony yet thick.

By the time I reached home, spared from meeting anyone else, the annoyance had taken all the good out of my walk, leaving me deflated and fatigued. I longed to go straight to bed and escape into the world of my novel, but two empty coal buckets awaited me on the doorstep.

I carried them to the coal bunker at the back of the cottage. Turning the corner I felt a sharper than usual breeze lifting off the lough, which bordered my father's low meadow. I couldn't look at this stretch of land without thinking of him. I tried to recall his face in his last days, watching the pleasure boats sail to and from Matt's Island, and the fishermen hauling in their catches in the evening. But seven years on, the last image of him, bloodless and waxen, still banished all others.

I filled one bucket with coal, the other with slack, and hauled them into the kitchen. Frank dozed in the fading light beside the range, his sturdy auburn head resting on the wing of the tweed-covered armchair. Mature beyond his years, and brown from daily labour under the sun, he looked strong and warm. His newspaper lay beside his reading glasses on the scrubbed pine surface of the kitchen table. I wanted to take my sketchbook out of the cupboard and draw him, but I knew Mother would be waiting for me to replenish the fire in the sitting room.

She didn't take her eyes off her magazine as she spoke.

'What kept you all this time?' She didn't wait for a reply. 'Stack up that fire with plenty of slack — not too much coal, it's far too dear. And make your brother a cup of tea, would you? He has to wait up on a cow calving. There's an apple tart in the bread bin. I'll take some too. With a bit of cream.'

★ ★ ★

A violet-tinged darkness was spreading rapidly when I finally closed the bedroom door behind me. Frank had taken his tea out to the byre with him and hadn't returned. I knew that the following night the cow he was calving would be standing alone in the field behind the house and I would be kept awake by its pathetic baying. No matter how many calves were born on the farm and immediately sold, the trauma of the mother was something to which I could never become inured. To witness that emotional pain, from a thing with supposedly no soul, was even worse than watching her eyes roll in stupefied agony as a slimy long-legged calf was hauled out of her with a rope. My father had snorted when I had once enquired if the cow could be put asleep during the horror of the birth. Later I decided that if animals had no souls, then neither had human beings.

The field was empty and peaceful as I closed the bedroom window. Peering out, I could just about make out the faint outline of Matt's Island and the Tyrone mountains rising beyond it. Closer by, the night light at the sand depository bathed the vast mounds in a artificial pinky orange hue, like a fairground ride.

It had begun to rain lightly and the air had become fresher than it had been for months. A freak low from the east, the weather forecast said. I shivered as I drew the curtains and switched on the bedside lamp. This was my favourite part of the day, propped up in my narrow bed, with a hot-water bottle and a good read. Nothing else mattered for the next few hours. I read urgently that night. I turned page after page until my eyes began to sting and I drifted into the jumble of vague and easy thoughts that precede a deep and all-enveloping sleep.

★　★　★

At first, my subconscious must have integrated the incongruous sound into the fabric of my dream. It became the wind, then a bassoon, then a cat. Gradually the insistence of the noise filtered though the layers of fug inside my head and woke me up. Then there was nothing. Silence. I rolled over on my side, hoping to slip back into my unfinished dream. It was 3.45 a.m. That meant a slow mind and grey skin in the morning.

A few minutes later the sound came again, a strange unearthly howl. As a child, I would have been convinced it was a banshee. I would have clenched in fear underneath the blankets, too afraid even to reach out and switch on the light in case something grabbed my arm. Grown men swore blind that a small hooded wraith was seen and heard outside Phelim Greer's house the night before he had a heart attack in his fishing boat. The image had chilled me and sometimes at night it was all I could think about.

A sudden rush of wind and slap of rain on the windowpane drowned out the howling. I swung my legs out of the bed and stepped across the cool floorboards to the windowsill. But like the frightened child of my past, I was afraid to look outside.

I reasoned that it was probably only a dog, and slowly lifted one of the curtains at the hem. I could see nothing in the darkness, but the weird yell suddenly became louder, jerking me back against the side of the bed. I reached for my dressing gown on the back of the door and went out into the hall to call Frank. His door was ajar and I could see that his bed hadn't been slept in. I thought he must be still out in the byre, yet I was loath to wake Mother, who always slept soundly. I crept past her bedroom door and tiptoed through the front vestibule and opened the kitchen door. The room was in darkness but in the hall that led from the scullery to the back door, I could see Frank's lofty silhouette and hear his angry voice.

'What are you doing here? Are you drunk? For God's sake — where are your clothes? Get away from there . . . ' He paused. 'What? Are you a soldier or what?'

I went into the hall. 'Frank, what is it? Who's there?'

He spun around. 'Away back to bed, Grace,' he snapped, pushing me back along the hall. 'Don't be looking at him . . . '

He stopped and glanced back over his shoulder. 'Wait, right, Stay there a minute — I'll go and ring the Mulhollands.'

He disappeared into the vestibule. I was as frightened and intrigued as a child in a ghost tunnel. I inched along the wall to the doorway.

A figure stood against the wall in the dark cold porch, shaking and wavering. I peered out from the door. He was naked and bloodied, a bit like Jesus on his way up Calvary. Even had a light beard. His hair was longish and plastered around his face in wet strands and he was moaning. In fact, he reminded me of one of the Moores' mutts after a fight with the pack up the road.

Then he saw me.

'Help me,' he rasped, one trembling hand reaching out to me, the other attempting to shield his groin. 'Please, *hide* me . . . '

I hesitated. Did he mean hide his nakedness? I looked around, then took off my dressing gown and held it out to him, not wanting to go too close. But as he lurched from the wall to take it, he fell down hard, on to the granite tiles. I watched transfixed as the blood from his head darkened the tiles and his flailing hand grew still. His face blanched, his mouth hung open.

But as I knelt down beside him, I knew he wouldn't die, for I knew he had come for me.

2

A thumb bears down below my eyebrow and raises my eyelid. Light blazes into my eye. The doctor flexes my arms, one by one. There is an uncomfortable and consistent tension under the skin of my left hand. A needle hitting a nerve, I think. I wish he'd shift it over a bit.

'She seems to be focusing all right, but she's not responding fully. I'm afraid her spleen is enlarging. I'll come back to see her again at the end of my rounds.'

The door opens and shuts. One of my visitors turns a page in his newspaper.

'Maybe she doesn't want to wake up. Maybe she was going to walk right into the lough and drown herself.'

'Sure it's shallow for half a mile. She would've got stuck in the glar like a right eejit. She'd have taken Moore's oul' boat out and jumped over the side if she'd really wanted to do herself in.'

'Or gone on ahead to the island and let the rats at her.'

'Supposed to be she was an awful one for that island when she was younger. Not right

31

in the head, you know. Throwing them dirty oul' fits. Probably spent hours talking to all them trees.'

There is sniggering.

'I'm going to the solicitor fella when I get a chance. We'd need to find out if there's a will. You know I'd say she could've left the lot to the chapel.'

'Don't think so. I hear she quit going years ago.'

'Sure we could always say she wasn't right in the head at the time, you know, if she's done us out of it.'

'What if she hasn't made a will at all?'

'Well, we'd be the next of kin, wouldn't we? Sure Frank's not coming back.'

'First thing I'd do with that place is pull down that oul' farmhouse an' build a nice new bungalow.'

Oh God.

'She'd probably come back to haunt you all your days in it, 'Natius. Aye, she'd be slipping into bed beside you at night, trying to get rid of that oul' lough chill. Then she might get a bit frisky and go for your tackle — '

'Shut the fuck up, for Christ's sake. There's somebody coming.'

Two nurses bustle through the door. Their conversation is drowned out by the clanking of my bed as they manoeuvre it towards the door. I keep my eyes shut. The sensation of movement is unnerving at first. How long have I lain here?

I am clanked into another room. When the nurses leave, I blink open an eye and see trees through a window to my right. It's that time of the evening when the sun hits one side of the leaves and makes them psychedelic. They sway a little and I sigh with them. Then I hear something that sounds like a gurgle. I look slowly to my left. A woman lies there sleeping, her slack mouth slightly open. She has a ludicrous mauve rinse in her thin permed hair. Her skin hangs in loose folds over her horsey profile and I think, as if things weren't bad enough . . . She's snoring through her throat like Daddy used to.

When his body was laid out, I stared at it so long I imagined I could see the rise of his breath, but of course no matter how hard I strained, I couldn't hear the snore. Mother used to say she missed his snoring. Right, and I saw Elvis in the hay shed.

⋆ ⋆ ⋆

They put the boy in the bed Daddy died in. He never opened an eye for the first couple of days. Mother and Josie Moore took it in turns to watch over him. I wasn't allowed to. The

33

men had decided not to move him. Dalloway reckoned he was about my age and Catholic, on account of the silver Lourdes medal around his neck.

'Could be in trouble, this client,' Dalloway had said, a self-important look in his turf-brown eyes. 'Could be on the run from the police or the tartan gangs, or God knows who else.'

Mother stitched the boy's cut with the needle she used on the turkey at Christmas. She had trained as a nurse in her teens but had the bedside manner of a civil servant. She had given up her job when she got married but was always called upon to clean up the dead for wakes. I think she preferred to look after corpses than the living, same as she preferred babies before they could talk.

The fuss over the boy was short-lived. The day after he landed on us, Florrie McNicholl had a heart attack right in the middle of getting her hair done up at Molly's. Molly left her leaning over the side of the bath and raced down to our house to get help. She could hardly breathe by the time she'd got to the door.

Josie had gone into town, so I had to take over in Daddy's room.

'Don't go near him, mind,' Mother called over her shoulder as she ran down the yard.

She was only a slip of a thing beside the rotund blousy Molly, not a hair out of place on her ash blonde head, nor a hint of a crease in her fitted collared dress. 'Shell those peas and mind your business. If he stirs, run and get Frank.'

It was the first time I'd been properly alone with the boy. At first I sat by the door and shelled the peas, digging the sides of my thumbnails into the crisp green pods. Then I drew the chair closer to the bed and stared at him.

My, what a beauty he was. Hair the colour of bitter chocolate, with red gold glints in it, a swarthy complexion and two black eyebrows that couldn't have been drawn better. The ugly gash on his forehead was taking its time to heal. I hoped the needle had been clean.

I reached out to touch the wound but the click of the back door latch sent me flying back against the chair. I dragged it back to the door and looked out to see Dalloway's burly frame in the hall. As always he sported a thick moustache and wore a striped tie over his checked shirt. No matter how warm the weather, Dalloway liked his little bit of sartorial formality.

'Well, Florrie's a goner,' he announced, turning his peaked cap over in his agitated hands. 'Cowped and died with her head all

35

suds, big Molly lathering away at her. Your mother's sorting things out, so you may keep an eye on things here.'

'I . . .'

Are you all right there?'

'Eh . . . yes, yes — oh, poor Florrie — '

'Desperate altogether, God have mercy on her.' He stood in the doorway, looking around the room. 'No signs of life out of that one yet?'

'Not a squeak.'

'Right, well, I'll be off. Be seeing you.'

I watched Dalloway stride out of the yard. Tall and broad, with a dependable-looking sanguine face, he was good in a crisis, and eternally pleased with himself. My heart didn't stop pounding for a full five minutes after he left.

Florrie lying dead, and there's me mooning at some fella half dead himself.

I felt so conspicuous in front of the figure in the bed, even though he lay there oblivious. All of a sudden the room was unbearably stuffy. I opened the small window to the right of the bed and followed the progress of a small plane flying low across the lough. The breeze shimmied in through the window, making tiny goosepimples rise on the boy's shoulders. I drew the eiderdown up higher, and noticed that the medal he wore was hollow, with hinges on one side. I gazed at it, wondering if he had some sort of devotion to Our Lady. I went out of the room and opened the front door. No-one was about. From the kitchen window, I could see Frank on the tractor up at the silo, but then I remembered the peas.

Back in the bedroom, I pulled the chair closer to the bed to look at the boy, and continued the shelling. A bluebottle landed on his neck and wandered casually along his thinly bearded jaw, and his forehead. I envied the fly his cheek. A ghost of a twitch of the lips was the boy's only reaction; he was still too far away.

I wondered how he'd feel waking up in the gloomy blue of this dour room. It had a vague whiff of damp and a loud tartan carpet. Mother had bought a remnant in a bomb damage sale, despite the fact that it didn't co-ordinate with anything in the house.

When he opened his eyes, the first thing the boy would see was a soppy Child of Prague regarding him from the cherrywood dresser at the end of the bed. The stumpy statuette had always reminded me of the village schoolmaster's spoiled and effete youngest son, and thus could not inspire any religious conviction in my already doubting soul. I preferred St Martin, whom I imagined as a grown up version of one of the black babies we saved for in school, or St Anthony, who helped you find things.

He'd saved my neck when I lost the money Daddy got for selling the donkey. After hours of beseeching his help, Anthony had reminded me that I'd stuffed the cash in the laundry basket when I was in an awful hurry to get to Friday-night Mass, and had to leave the house empty.

Strange, I felt no compulsion to pray for the boy. Something told me he didn't need it. When the pot was half full of peas, I stood by the bed and stretched. The boy's breaths were shallow, despite his deep unconsciousness, but Josie said he could be out cold for a week, given that terrible thump to the head, and the hypothermia.

A dusty shaft of pale sun glanced off the medal around his bruised neck, and I bent over to look at it. It lay just under the hollow of his neck, on a silver chain fine enough for a girl to wear. Impulsively, I picked up the chain and turned the medal over. He didn't stir, and I felt a detached sort of recklessness coming over me, the kind when your body seems to rush ahead of your mind. I pressed in the catch with my thumb, but it was stubborn. I drew down closer to inspect it and my hair brushed against his chin. I jerked my head away, but still he didn't stir.

I tried the catch again and it snapped open. Inside, folded into a square in the centre of the locket, lay a piece of lilac-coloured paper. I wondered if it was a segment of a love letter, but prying into the stranger's jewellery was oddly intimate, like sticking my finger into his ear. I was about to close the locket, when my fingers slipped and overturned it, and the paper fell out, down the side of the eiderdown and on to the floor.

I strained to hear footsteps and voices, but the house was silent, and in the distance I could still hear the steady whine and trundle of Frank's tractor at the silo. I reached down to pick up the piece of paper but the breeze from the window swept it under the bed.

The recklessness gave way to a mild panic, but I reassured myself there was no-one about. That scrap of paper could give a clue to the boy's identity, I figured, though a distant voice scoffed.

I knelt down on the floor and lowered myself under the bed. The red and yellow tartan was even more extreme in there, and the dust made my eyes burn. The paper had blown against the top left leg of the bed. I ducked down and snatched the paper, and was ready to crawl out when I took a fit of sneezing.

I should have known what was coming. How many times had I been watching a perfectly innocent film on television, only for Mother to walk in right in the middle of a love scene and catch me glued to it?

Her voice, from the doorway of the bedroom, now held the same accusing disparagement.

'What's going on in here?'

I almost laughed. How I wished she could have. I shoved the piece of paper into my apron pocket and scrambled out from under the bed, blowing into a hankie to hide my twitching face. I racked my brain to think of an excuse.

'Well?'

'Eh . . . my hankie blew under the bed . . . I opened the window to let some air in — '

'You opened the window, and that fella lying there with God knows what in his chest?'

She hurried over to the bed and put her hand on the boy's head. I willed her not to see the open locket, but as usual she missed nothing.

'You've been interfering with him, haven't you?'

'I was sneezing, you see . . . it's a bit dusty — '

40

'Get into the kitchen and get the potatoes on. Should have been on half an hour ago. Hurry up, would you.'

I slunk out of the room like a chastised dog as she pulled the eiderdown up to the boy's chin. I hurried into the scullery and filled a basin with big soil-encrusted potatoes. I peeled them at the sink in the kitchen, my humiliation turning to anger. I knew exactly what she was thinking. She was imagining me pulling the boy's bedclothes down and ogling his nakedness. Oh, the *shame* of it. I cringed until my toes curled, and took a lump out of my finger with the peeler. The blood mingled with the muddy and starchy water, but I peeled violently on, splashing the running water from the tap all down my front and on to the floor.

Mother came into the kitchen and complained. Then she sat at the table, smoking in silence. I hated anyone behind me when I was working in the kitchen. It made me drop things, but somehow I managed to get all the potatoes into the pot and on to the stove without incident.

'Get that wet dried up,' she said.

I already had the rag in my hand to do it. Suddenly I remembered the bit of paper in my pocket, and prayed it wasn't soaked.

'Put the peas on when the potatoes start to

41

boil. There's no meat in the house. The peas will have to do.'

She said the same thing almost every day in the summer, as if it were something new. I got down on my knees on the floor.

'I heard about Florrie,' I said. 'Terrible, isn't it? I didn't think she — '

She sat forward abruptly. 'Wheeest — is that somebody at the front?' she rasped, peeping out through the kitchen door. 'Christ, it's Father O'Loan — go and let him in and remember, not a word about the fella. Go on — hurry up.'

I dried my hands on the sides of my trousers and went to the back door. The parish priest stood in the porch, his nose like an over-ripe strawberry pressed up against the glass panel. How some people were blind to their blackheads was a mystery to me.

'Ah Grace, is your mother in, dear?' he asked as I opened the door.

'Hello, Father, come on in,' Mother said, suddenly brushing past me to usher the priest into the sitting room. 'Grace, make Father O'Loan a cup of tea and a nice sandwich.'

I looked at her in dismay. She was too proud to offer him potatoes and peas. I was saved, however, by Father O'Loan's next appointment.

'Oooh no, dear. I'm just on my way to the

McNicholls and they'll be coming down with tea and sandwiches. A wee nip of brandy wouldn't go amiss, though.' He walked over to the fireplace and stood resting his arm along the tall mahogany mantel. 'Now Elva, what I need to ascertain from you, is whether poor Florrie's soul had left her when you arrived at the Dohertys', in your opinion, dear?'

Mother closed the sitting-room door behind them. I'd heard her talking about the flight of souls before, when she attended the Greer boys after they'd drowned two summers ago. The shore was crowded but no-one had noticed them missing for an hour or so, and it was so long before their skinny white bodies were fished out that Father O'Loan deemed it too late to give them extreme unction. Their souls had already left them, he said. How Mother could know the whereabouts of Florrie's soul was beyond me.

They fell silent when I came in with the brandy. I handed them a glass each and scurried down to my room to examine the scrap of paper. I closed my eyes with relief when I saw that only one corner was damp. I unfolded it and as I was putting it on the windowsill to dry, I noticed something printed across it in indigo ink. NIRVANA. It meant nothing to me.

I watched as the edges began to curl up in

the sun. Putting it back in the boy's locket would be too much of a risk. Instead I flattened it on a page in the middle of the book I'd just finished and locked it in the bedside drawer. I put the key on top of the wardrobe, imagining I was withholding important evidence in some crime thriller. I cocked my chin and flicked my hair over my shoulder in an imitation of Veronica Lake, casting a challenging eye at myself in the dressing-table mirror.

More like Barbara Stanwyck, I thought to myself, sensing the impending doom of spinsterdom. A more immediate crisis was presenting itself, however. From the hall came the unmistakable salty pong of potato skins burning in the bottom of dry and blackened saucepan; and from the front door, the reverential tones of my mother bidding Father O'Loan goodbye.

★ ★ ★

They took the other woman away this morning. The room is silent again but the ringing in my ears persists, a high relentless hiss like the electrical snap in the air when a television set is switched off. And whatever medication they're administering, it's giving me a cotton-wool tongue, so even if I could

44

speak, it wouldn't be a pleasant sensation.

My goddaughter comes into the room, talking into a mobile phone. The light is sparking up her auburn hair.

'Nothing much to report so far. The doctors say she's comfortable but she's not out of danger yet. They've taken the old doll beside her away for blood tests. Yes . . . right. Look you'd better check Dalloway Moore's tenure on the low fields. We could run into complications there if she's let it to him indefinitely.'

She comes closer.

'God, do you know I think she's getting some colour into her cheeks. What? All right. Better go — bye.'

Well, bully for you, old body. Defying me again, this temple of the Lord. I will offer up my physical suffering for penance for the pleasures my young body gave me. My mind had nothing to do with it. And you, Miss Kane, I'm quite sure your exquisite temple has been defiled on a regular basis since you swore chastity at your Confirmation. I saw your picture in the paper. You had a gap in your teeth then. Must have had it fixed. You know, I think you have my eyes. Daddy's eyes, and your own father's, I suppose.

But I was never as good-looking as you. Only two people ever told me I was pretty.

45

Florrie's wake went on for the usual three days. I was sent up on the last day to help with the tea, while Mother kept an eye on the boy. At the wake she had been peeved when mourner after mourner said they'd never seen a better-looking corpse, and wasn't Molly a powerful hairdresser altogether to have a dead woman's hair looking so well. Mother didn't like to share the glory over her dead bodies. Since I was a toddler, she'd brought me to wakes to say a prayer for the dead. She'd be patting the corpse on the head or holding its hand, and once she nearly had me giving my Great-Aunt Greta a kiss on her cold forehead. She was a fright and a half, with her white streaked black hair hanging lankly on either side of her mottled face. They didn't bother with make-up in those days. Uncle Sean saved me by taking me into the garden to see his chrysanthemums.

Florrie didn't look so scary with her fresh curls, but they couldn't shut one of her eyes properly, and I could see the cotton wool in her nostrils.

'Sorry for your troubles, Mr McNicholl,' I muttered to Bear, Florrie's ashen-faced husband when he wandered aimlessly into their hot poky kitchen. What hair he'd left had gotten whiter overnight. Short and stocky, he had a baldy face: scant eyelashes and sparse eyebrows, a flattish nose and indecipherable lips receding back from a jutting chin. His stature belied the size of the feet, which long ago had provided the inspiration for his nickname. Local legend had it that he'd walked up the road in his sleep one snowy night, leaving footprints like a grizzly's all the way up to the bus stop.

He stood by the window, glassy-eyed, staring at nothing. I began chopping up the nettles Josie had brought in when we ran out of scallions. She stood beside me, a fine-featured little wisp buttering mounds of white pan bread as if there was no tomorrow, her wrists half the width of mine. If Josie was a sparrow, I thought to myself, I was a starling.

The widower broke the prickling silence.

'That young fella down at your house come round yet?'

I kept chopping. 'No, not yet, Mr McNicholl. He's just lying there, but he seems to be breathing all right.'

Bear sighed. 'God's taken Florrie instead of him, you know. It wasn't his time, you see, but poor oul' Flo wasn't ready. Sure she hasn't been to confession in an age . . . '

'Ah now, don't go upsetting yourself, Bear,'

Josie soothed. 'Sure don't they say tragedy comes in threes? That fella could be a goner too, and God knows what else could happen before the summer's out. But don't be annoying yourself. Florrie's in a better place.'

Dalloway appeared at the doorway, fixing his cap down over his thick greying thatch. 'Josie's right, Bear. Don't be getting yourself all bitter now.'

Bear turned from the window. 'Bitter? I'll never be through the chapel door again. What's gonna become of those wee children out there? And Florrie's soul lost in Purgatory, and us without a shilling to give her a headstone . . . '

The sight of a grown man in tears repelled me. Josie put her arm around his stooped back and led him out into the garden.

Dalloway came into the room. 'Poor oul' Bear. Peculiar when you think of it, mind you. A young fella coming to your door in that state and managing to stay living, while Florrie croaks with no warning at all.'

'Have . . . have you any idea where the boy could've come from?' I asked, as casually as I could muster.

'Aha, taking a wee fancy to the stranger, eh? Just thought you were taking powerful good care of him,' Dalloway teased, taking a sandwich from the table.

I held on to my crumbling composure by blinking rapidly and concentrating on chopping. Dalloway chuckled, his even false teeth just visible under his chunky moustache.

'I'd say he's either a Tyrone man or Belfast man, maybe out looking a bit of work,' he said, his mouth full. 'Definitely not from about here. Looks like he'd been out on the lough but there's no sign of a boat nor nothing. Strange, that. No doubt we'll hear all when the critter wakes up.'

Josie reappeared on her own, her tiny hands on her apple cheeks. 'Bear's taken a notion to weed the rosebeds, imagine. Oh, and Grace, your mother's sent word for you to go home and to tell Willy and wee Charlie Mulholland to come too, and do you know, it'll thin out the crowd here a bit. I'll go in and get them and you head on down the road.'

Glad to escape, I took off my apron and smoothed back my hot hair.

'Mind how you go, Grace,' said Dalloway, butter smeared on the side of his chin. 'Make sure and treat that boy well, girl.'

I put away the chopping knife and fled.

Outside it was dusk. The birds were making a racket and two of the Moores' mutts chased me for a few yards until they realised I wasn't an intruder. I wondered why they hadn't as much as raised an ear at our unexpected visitor's arrival in the dead of night. They usually kept guard on the whole row. Dalloway's teasing over the boy had been innocent enough but it unnerved me, particularly in the aftermath of Mother catching me under the bed. I resolved to show no further interest, yet, as I headed into our yard, I was irresistibly drawn to peep through Daddy's window on the way past. The curtains were drawn but they were slightly too narrow and I could see the boy lying there, unchanged and still as ever. I walked on ahead and paused at the back door to look at the roaring red sky above the water.

'Who's that?'

Frank never failed to hear a footstep in the yard.

'It's me. I'll put the kettle on.'

★　★　★

Willy and Charlie arrived soon afterwards and joined Mother and Frank at the kitchen table. Willy was Daddy's cousin, and as stout as the Kanes were lean. Charlie, Willy's teenage son, was a miniature version of his father, from his dimples to his ambling, hands-in-pockets walk. He was the only person I knew as quiet as me.

50

Frank poured brandy for Mother and Willy, and lemonade for Charlie. I stood by the sink with a mug of tea, wishing I could slip off to bed. Like her mother before her, Mother had lit the ancient gas lamp she kept in the window to mark the passing of a soul. Very apt it was too, for the flickering gaslight made ghosts out of all it fell upon. Even the fat and merry faces of the Mulhollands assumed eerie shadows around the eyes, and the handsome high cheekbones shared by Mother and Frank took on a severity that couldn't be seen in daylight.

It took three refills of the glasses on the table to get through the life and times of Florrie McNicholl. Then the drink loosened Willy's tongue sufficiently for him to reveal that Daddy once had a schoolboy crush on Florrie.

Charlie glanced up at me and giggled in his childlike way.

'Away on with you, Willy Mulholland,' Mother scoffed, a smile tugging at the corners of her coral pink lips. 'James had much better taste than that.'

'Now, I'm telling you,' Willy retorted. 'He had 'I love Florrie' written on his jotter for all to see. Nice wee girl she was too. Lovely fair curls, a bit like Charlie's there.'

I couldn't imagine my father as a tender

youth with an innocent infatuation. Yet that boy was no less a stranger to me than the man he became. Mother feigned disapproval at Willy's teasing and I could see the phoniness irking Frank. Unsmiling, he went outside to bring in milk for the morning.

Willy watched him with a raised eyebrow.

'Don't mind him,' Mother said, shifting in her seat. 'He's worried about all that milk we had to throw out 'cause of the big strike. It'll make some difference to the milk cheque at the end of the month.'

Willy tutted. 'Never saw a sorrier sight than the road turned white with that good milk flowing down it. Just shows you the harm that Paisley's done to the country,' he said, flicking cigarette ash into the turn-up of his trousers.

'Ach, I'm sick hearing about that oul' cod — Charlie, go on give us a tune,' Mother urged, nodding at father's fiddle, gleaming high up on the wall.

Charlie blushed and looked down into his glass. His mother, Sadie, had made him take lessons since he was six, when the schoolmaster said he was slow but musically gifted.

'Go on, boy,' Willy chimed in.

'Grace, get the fiddle down for him,' Mother ordered.

I took it down and handed it to Charlie. He

slid his stubby fingers along the bow and after a couple of stuttering false starts, launched into a searing lament, all traces of his embarrassed reluctance gone. Willy leaned back in his chair and folded his arms, his head cocked to one side, and when the tune ended and Charlie effortlessly segued into another, his father's big Santa Claus face turned serene with pride.

Charlie was finishing his third lament when Frank came back, his face sour.

Mother held her hands out and clapped, Frank opened bottles of stout.

'You know, our Grace has a nice way of reciting a poem,' Mother announced when she'd caught her breath.

I shook my head and looked away, secretly pleased. She persisted.

'Go on, do one of those sorrowful ones you like — go on. I didn't pay all that money for books for nothing.'

My throat constricted and I wanted to bolt, but I knew there was no way out. Willy joined in the bullying and I reasoned that it would have been more embarrassing to flee. I stood in the corner, fixing my eyes on the wall in front of me. The words came easier than I thought they would.

'When you are old and grey and full of sleep — '

'Speak up, Grace — speak up!' Mother interrupted, loudly.

'When you are old and grey and full of sleep, and nodding by the fire,' I continued, 'take down this book and slowly read, and dream of the soft look your eyes had once, and of their shadows deep. How many loved your moments of glad grace, and loved your beauty with love false or true, but one man loved the pilgrim soul in you, and loved the sorrows of your changing face; and bending down beside the glowing bars, murmur, a little sadly, how love fled and paced upon the mountains overhead and hid his face amid a crowd of stars.'

I glanced up quickly but there were no eyes to meet mine. They were all staring straight past, at the doorway behind me. I turned around to follow their gaze and there he stood, gaunt and pale, and wrapped in the scarlet eiderdown. I looked into that unforgettable face, and felt nothing would ever be the same again.

3

'Jesus, if it isn't Lazarus up from the dead,' Willy said.

Mother, fogged by the brandy, sat speechless.

Frank rose from the table and gestured towards his armchair beside the range. 'Take a seat there, boy. You're an awful colour . . . here, lean against me.'

I watched uneasily as my brother held out his brawny arm to the stranger. Slowly, he took a wobbling step into the room, his eyes cast downwards and lank hair obscuring his face. Frank guided him towards the chair, then opened the door of the range beside him. The fire threw out a blast of heat, its ochre light glancing off the glasses on the table.

'You've got the shivers, boy,' Frank remarked. 'Not a bit of wonder, the state you're in.'

The stranger leaned back into the chair and scanned the room, his wide-set dark eyes moving from one curious face to the other. The flickering firelight accentuated the hollows under his cheekbones and the shadows under his eyes, making him the most spectral of us all. I followed his gaze to the other side of the room, where it fell on the picture of the Sacred Heart, with its red candle-bulb glowing brutally in front of it.

He closed his eyes, as if in relief.

'What is your name, son?' Willy asked him, sympathy softening his gruff tone.

The stranger didn't answer straight away, and in the awkward silence, Mother motioned to me to give him some water. I half filled a glass and tentatively handed it to him. The eiderdown slipped to reveal a stiff, skinny shoulder as he reached out for the glass. I looked away quickly.

'Thank you,' he croaked, and drank deeply from it.

Willy scratched his head, and Mother raised her eyebrows at Charlie, who looked scared.

'My name's Saul.'

The boy's voice had an unfamiliar intonation, but it was too quiet to reveal an accent.

'Saul? You weren't struck by lightning by any chance, were you?' Willy challenged him facetiously. 'You were in a desperate state when you landed here the other night.'

'I don't remember much about it, I'm afraid.'

Mother found her voice.

'What on earth happened to you, anyway? Scared us half to death you did, turning up half dead in the middle of the night, and not a stitch on you.'

'I'm sorry. I don't know how I ended up here . . . I think I must have passed out in your field.'

'You're not from around here, are you, boy?' Willy asked.

He took another sip of the water. 'I'm from Belfast, the Free State originally.'

'Well, tell us this,' Willy interrupted. 'What kind of trouble had you got yourself in the other night?'

The dark eyes turned to me. I looked away.

'I have absolutely no idea. I have been lying in there for the past half hour trying to remember, but there's nothing — '

'Lost your memory, have you? Sure how do you know your name and where you're from, then?'

'It's just how I got here that I don't recall. I walked out from Belfast the other day, looking for a bit of summer work. I always wanted to see the island out there . . . ' He paused and rubbed the knuckle of his thumb down the side of his nose. 'I met a couple of guys by a sand place and we drank some whiskey, really rough stuff. Next thing I

57

know, I'm in a field, no clothes ... no rucksack, and it's raining, and I make my way towards a light — here, I think.'

Willy shook his head and tutted loudly. 'Somebody's filled you full of poitín and robbed you, more than likely. It's desperate the kinda villains you run into nowadays. It's funny, Dalloway could've sworn you'd been in the water, by the state of you.'

'No. No, I never made it that far.'

I caught the boy's eye. I knew he was lying. Having had years of practice, I could spot mendacity a mile away. There had been fear in his eyes that night on the porch and whatever he was hiding from, it wasn't a pair of poitín-filled thieves.

Mother stood up, scraping her chair along the hard kitchen tiles behind her. 'Is there anyone you want to phone?'

'No ... there's no-one. We were burned out of our house and the family has all moved to England to get way from the trouble. Thanks all the same.'

Mother stifled a yawn. 'Well, you can stay here until you get sorted out. You've had a knock to the head — you shouldn't be up at all. Frank, get up there and help him back into the bedroom. Grace, make him a hot-water bottle and something to eat. I'm away to bed; can't keep my eyes open.'

58

Willy opened the door to the hallway for her. 'Good night, Elva. Don't worry, we'll sort him out.'

I went to the sink while Frank helped Saul up on to his cut feet. Charlie glanced at me furtively and went out of the back door. He never liked strangers about the place.

Frank led Saul to the door.

'Oh, miss — I really couldn't eat anything but my feet are dead cold,' he said on his way out.

I glanced at him over my shoulder as I filled the kettle. A heaviness dulled his eyes and made his expression blank. I was used to such a reaction, yet my spirits drooped. I'd made no impact on him at all.

'All right, go on ahead.'

The industrial reek of boiling water on the cheap rubber hot-water bottle mingled offensively with the slops of stout and brandy from the dirty glasses in the basin. I opened the window above the sink and breathed in the night air, and as I tightened the stopper on the bottle, the thought of those deeply grazed feet on the rubber made me wince. I opened a drawer and took out an old cotton drawstring bag used to hold clothes pegs. I slipped the bottle into it and tightened the strings, pleased with my inventiveness.

Frank's curly head appeared around the

door. 'That's him settled. I'm away for a dram with Willy — never a word, mind.'

I waited until I heard the front door close, then wet my fingers and straightened my eyebrows. My fingers smelled like car tyres. I closed the kitchen door and walked into the hall.

The door to Daddy's room was slightly ajar and the bedside lamp was on. I knocked lightly and heard the boy mutter something. I peeped in and he beckoned me over.

'I remember your face,' he said quietly, as I walked into the room. He lay on his side, watching me intently.

I put the hot-water bottle on the side of the bed where he could reach it.

'It was the last thing you saw before you hit the ground out on the porch,' I whispered. I looked him squarely in the eye. For once in my life I felt I had the upper hand over someone. What I couldn't tell was whether he knew that I knew he was lying.

'Oh . . . right. What is your name?'

'Grace. After Grace Kelly.'

The second I had the words out I regretted them. The irony of being named after such a beauty was a perpetual thorn in my side.

'That's nice.'

He shifted on to his elbow, and the black eyebrows knitted into a wing on his forehead and his mouth tensed. I took two pills from the bottle on the bedside table and poured a little water into a cup and handed them to him. He propped himself up and swallowed the pills without the water.

'I could never do that,' I remarked, screwing the lid back on to the bottle.

He didn't answer, and I took it as my cue to leave. The lamp went off as I reached the door.

'Good night, Grace. And thank you.'

★   ★   ★

I couldn't read that night. The words were crowded out in my head by the teeming possibilities of a real story unfolding, right under my roof. I watched the sun roll up over the still black water and for the first time felt the newness of it.

★   ★   ★

The hospital clock says 4.30 a.m. Terrible, lonely time to wake up, in that limbo between night and day. It's been my pattern for many a year. I always hear the milkman stopping at the cottages, at least those who don't get their milk from me. Then I hear him slowing up past the house to throw the newspaper into

61

the yard. If it's wet, he gets out and puts it through the letterbox. I don't like getting up in the dark — it's too much like a gloomy continuation of the night before, rather than beginning of a new day. So I lie there, making a list of what I have to do, things I have to buy. I go over this several times until I'm bored with it. Then I might say a prayer, depending on what mood I'm in. The lack of sleep usually makes me deflated, but if I've gone to bed early enough the night before, I awaken as contented as a baby, and when it's light enough, I read for an hour before getting up. I put on the kettle and light the stove, no matter what the weather's like, because it heats the water. I'll take a boiled egg for breakfast. Never get fed up with a good egg. The newspaper stays on the floor or in the yard until I've washed up. Reading was always frowned upon at home until the chores were done. Indeed, being able to look at the paper before midday has been a luxury for me since I've been on my own.

There's no book or newspaper on my bedside table in this place. Mind you, even if there was a paper, I couldn't hold it up. No, I'm trapped within the limitations of my imagination. Can't even make a list. They brought Blue Rinse back yesterday and she's awake too, but I keep my head averted and look out the window. At least she doesn't make any noise when she's awake, apart from the odd grunt.

The only good thing about being awake at this hour in this joint is hearing the birds outside wake up and rejoice in the new day. I saw a wag-the-tail wake up once on the branch of a tree outside the scullery window. It had covered its head with its wing to sleep. I saw it give a couple of shudders and stretch back its wing, and look around. Then it put the wing back over its head and took another little nap. A few moments later, back went the wing. Then it stretched out its spindles of legs, just like a person would, and wobbled up on to its pronged feet. Wag-the-tails aren't the most powerful of singers but it's hard to resist such cheerful twittering from a thing that hasn't even had its breakfast yet.

City birds sound different. Not as perky, for a start. No, there isn't much to think about here. So I go back in my mind and begin to remember the time when there was something to get up for.

★   ★   ★

Frank drained his mug of tea in four gulps. He was always thirsty and baggy-eyed after a night with Willy Mulholland. Mother, her china blue eyes cool as a larder tile, watched him overturn his scrambled eggs. I wasn't in a much better state. Extreme fatigue had rendered me useless and clumsier than usual. I'd already dropped an egg on the floor and the disgusting slimy mass in my hands as I tried to clean it up had put me off eating. I could only tolerate the look of eggs when they were cooked. Raw, they seemed to me far too intimately female and primeval.

I forced myself to eat some toast, for it was Friday and I had to make the trip to the market before 8.30 a.m.

'You'd better get a bit of extra fish,' Mother said, writing a list on the back of a used envelope. 'That fella's bound to be weak from no food and he'll be starving when he wakes up.'

Frank pushed his plate away from him. 'Odd being, isn't he? Probably good for nothing, wandering about the place like a nomad.'

'When you've finished that, get out some of your old clothes and leave them in to him,' Mother ordered. 'He's nothing to put on him. You never know, you could get him to give us a hand with the peas and beans.'

'Looks too much like a townie for that. Wouldn't have done a decent day's work in his life. I'd say. Probably sits around with his nose in a book, like Grace.'

'You'd better get a move on,' Mother chided me. 'What sort of a face is that you've on anyway? I suppose you couldn't be bothered going, and me with God knows what all to do before Florrie's funeral.'

The worm had turned early today. I prepared for a quick getaway. 'I'm just tired, that's all. I'll go now.'

'Do you not think I'm tired, waiting on him coming in till all hours. Where were you till that time anyway?'

Frank was already halfway out the door. He was long past giving explanations for his actions.

'Bloody ungrateful . . . aach. Here, take that list and hurry up, would you. And don't forget my cigarettes.'

★ ★ ★

Normally I enjoyed getting jiggled about on the bus. It gave me a very private and guilty thrill. But that morning it made me nauseous and irritable, just like I used to feel travelling to school. I knew I had to be grateful that Mother would get up every morning to get Frank and me out, when other mothers lay on. Her moods, however, made those early hours tense and fraught, and the panicky rush for the bus exhausted us. I found it hard to be fully alert in the very early morning, and my sluggishness infuriated Mother.

I sat in the front seat of the bus and peered out at the whizzing hedges through the downpour I'd just escaped. I always took the front seat, to avoid having to make small talk with anyone further down the bus. I rubbed the steamed-up window with the cuff of my sleeve and imagined the soaking Florrie's mourners were in for. Relentless, vertical rain with no wind to blow it into your face was much more appropriate to a funeral than flippant sunshine anyway. Especially if the deceased had died without the solace of a last confession.

I was just beginning to enjoy huddling in my seat, with the intense wheeze of fusty heat from the bus's crock of a radiator roasting my legs, when we lurched and juddered to a halt opposite the market, a cavernous tin shed on the edge of town. Out of habit I thanked the driver as I dismounted. He never replied — why should he expect to be thanked for a job he was paid to do? As Josie said, you don't go about thanking the bin men for taking away your rubbish, or the road men for painting white stripes on the roads.

Charmless urban noises assaulted my ears the minute I stepped on the footpath and tried to cross the road. I hated the hiss of the halting bus and the squeal of the automatic doors. The new rain made the din worse. On the sodden roads, the urgent ugly traffic slooshed by in the continuous searing crescendo created by speed and a hard wet surface. Wipers waved in desperation across front screens and horns honked in fuck-you bursts. Rows of dimmed car lights in daylight, even under darkened skies, made the atmosphere surreal. I waited for a lull and darted to the other side of the road, glad of the hood on my raincoat.

The market was unseasonably cold and quieter than usual. I headed straight for the fish stand and selected four fine plaice from the fresh gleaming flesh on display, then wandered along the aisles, pausing at the stalls selling cheap jewellery and hair accessories. I was drawn to sparkling things, the more colourful the better, and, like a magpie, I was compelled to snatch them.

A row of hair slides studded with glass gems caught my eye. The wiry, freckle-faced stallholder was busy dangling a handful of gold chains in front of an elegant old lady, dressed entirely in black, at the other end of the table. They paid me no heed. I browsed casually, picking up the slides, then a brass bangle, then a watch with white leather straps. I noticed the stallholder bend beneath the table to pull out a box, while the old lady tried on a chain. I had a split second to decide between a sapphire blue slide and an emerald green one. I would've preferred the blue slide but thought, reluctantly, that the green one would better match my eyes. I reached out quickly and slipped it off the display card. A quick glance around assured me that no-one was watching, but instead of slipping the slide into my pocket, I kept it in my hand.

When I was twelve, I'd been caught with a set of colour felt-tip pens in my pocket at the village post office, and rather than learning the error of my ways, I'd learned to be as obvious as possible when stealing. If I didn't conceal the stolen thing, then I could claim that I was going to pay for it. I wouldn't, therefore, take anything I couldn't pay for.

I took my time to walk on, even running my fingers through the silk scarves that hung at the side of the stall beside the old lady, who was driving the stallholder mad with her fussing. Brazenly, I stopped at the next stall, which sold rosary beads, and asked the young lad there if he had any made of mother-of-pearl.

'No, love, sorry. Try Tierney's up on Marley Street — just as cheap to tell you the truth,' he said helpfully, and for an instant I felt abashed, for when I saw his mass of freckles, I knew he must be the son of the wiry little man from whom I'd stolen.

My shame was short-lived. A rush of sneaky glee replaced it as I stepped out into sunshine, no hand on my shoulder. I giggled into myself, simultaneously marvelling at how I could get such a kick out of a pathetic, insidious act.

Oh, to hell — they can afford it, I told my other self. She was such a self-righteous pain at times.

The bus home had better suspension and more chattering occupants. As I got on I recognised the butcher's wife from the village and nodded at her. She gave an unsmiling nod back without halting her conversation with the man beside her, who was a lay preacher at the chapel and the biggest gossip in the parish. He delighted, in particular, in being the first to spread the news of unmarried girls' pregnancies, with an indulgent gleam in his eyes which betrayed his outward condemnation.

I sat in the front seat behind the driver and looked at my reflection in the glass panel. Two blank dishwater eyes gazed back at me. I planned how I would sweep up the unruly hair with my new sparkly slide and pin it on the right hand side, and maybe take some of Mother's lipstick and rub it into my pasty cheeks. The skin on my face didn't take the sun, no matter how long I cooked in it. I would never put lipstick on my mouth. My lips were too big and tarty with colour on them, and mother's black mascara would have been too obvious on my cursed fair-tipped eyelashes, passed down by my father.

The bus driver dropped me off at the top of the row of cottages that led to home. The rain had abated and given way to white diamond sunlight. A shiny black hearse was parked outside the McNicholls'. Everyone in the parish enjoyed the drama of funerals and the mini-receptions afterwards. I liked the smell of the incense and the 'Abide With Me'. I blessed myself to show respect as I hurried past the hearse.

'Angel of God, my guardian dear/ to whom God's love commits me here/ ever this day be at my side/ to light and guard, to rule and guide/ Amen.'

I'd forgotten to say my morning prayer earlier. It seemed a selfish sort of thing to be saying, with Florrie lying there dead, so I told God I'd offer up the day's work for the repose of her soul.

Frank was hosing down a manure-splattered tractor when I turned into the yard. We never said hello to each other. Greetings seemed far too contrived and trivial amongst close family.

'Any word of the order?' I shouted over to him, raising my voice against the whoosh of the hose.

'Not yet. Don't go too far away from the phone and see if you can get any sense out of your man in there while you're at it. I've asked him to stay on to give us a hand out, seeing as he's after the work.'

In the kitchen, Saul sat at the table, lost in one of Frank's old checked shirts and a pair of worn jeans. The sore feet were covered by darned socks. It was the first time I'd seen him properly in daylight and the exotic effect unnerved me. He had navy blue eyes and he'd had a shave. He had a mug in his hand, and all of a sudden he was real.

'Hello, Grace.'

His voice was clearer and more townie than before. Now that he was up and about, and seemingly no longer in a state of collapse, I retreated back into the shadow I inhabited in the company of everyone else.

'How are you feeling today?' I asked him quickly, putting away the groceries.

'I'm a little better,' he said with an easy smile that revealed good even teeth. 'How do you like my new duds?'

I had no idea what he meant.

'The clothes, I mean. Your brother loaned me them.'

He raised the mug to his lips and I noticed a slight shake in his hand.

'Oh, yes. They're a bit big on you . . . but they're better than nothing at all,' I blurted, immediately affronted by the possible implication that I'd seen him naked.

I felt the telling colour rising into my cheeks and fled into the scullery with the fish.

I dithered, waiting until the blush had seeped into my chest before going back into the kitchen. He was standing beside the sink, gazing out at the lough. Somewhere beyond my self-consciousness, the thought occurred to me that Frank hadn't given him anything to eat.

'Would you like some breakfast . . . some toast or something?'

His eyes stayed intently on the water as he leaned closer to the window. 'No thanks. Frank gave me a big Paris bun. Delicious.'

'God, that's a funny sort of a breakfast for anybody,' I said, nerves making my voice squeaky.

He turned from the window and put his hands in the big baggy pockets of Frank's frayed jeans. 'I was thinking, I might take a little walk to get my whereabouts, if you'll show me.'

I'd just thrown some coal into the range and the dust had blackened my hands. 'Oh, but surely you couldn't be . . . up to it?' I spluttered, putting the coal scuttle back in the corner.

'I'll be OK if I don't go too far. I just need some fresh air, I think.'

'Well, all right,' I complied, reluctantly. 'I'll just wash my hands first.'

I left the room in an exaggerated rush and locked the bathroom door behind me. I always hurried too much when I was ill at ease, and had numerous small accidents in the process. Cups would be dropped, tea would be spilled, vases would be knocked over.

I snatched the slab of carbolic soap from the side of the sink and rubbed it around my hands under the hot tap. The masculine workhouse pong of the soap infected the plume of steam arising from the sink, and clung to my pores. I thought of our guest coming into the bathroom to wash and felt ashamed of the ugly maroon bath and sink, and sickly pink tiles on the walls and floor, and net curtains the colour of slush. Although Mother kept it scrupulously clean, the room reminded me of gums and old teeth and bad make-up, and women's bits. Even the soap was an unbecoming purple. I poked in the hot-press and took out two fresh towels, grateful that Mother insisted on buying new ones every January. And, I reasoned, at least we had a shower and an electric toothbrush, sent over from Australia.

Saul was still standing by the window when I came back into the kitchen. He didn't seem to notice me. I struggled not to babble, tugging at the hem of my tartan blouse before I spoke.

'I'll get you a pair of wellies — the grass is still damp and it gets a bit mucky around the shore.'

He nodded absently and I went into the cloakroom beside the scullery. Mother could never bring herself to throw out anything, and all the junk ended up in the cloakroom. The shoe cupboard held not only ancient boots and mismatched sandals, but biscuit tins full of nails, jam jars, lids of jam jars, clothes pegs and old plugs.

I pulled out a pair of Frank's old Wellington boots from a shelf and took a patched-up anorak from a hook on the wall. Saul was waiting in the hall when I came out.

'This is very good of you,' he said, taking the boots from me. 'God knows where mine are now.'

I cleared my throat, a habit I'd had since I

was a child. I wasn't used to this politeness. 'Would you recognise the ones that got you, if you saw them?' I asked him.

'I'm not sure. It was dark and it seems like a dream now.'

He pulled on the boots and reached out for the anorak. Instinctively I held it out for him to put on, as I used to do for Frank. He slid his arms into the sleeves in one easy movement and in the close confines of the hall I suddenly felt claustrophobic at the nearness of him. He was only slightly taller than I was and he smelled of the carbolic soap. I side-stepped him and opened the back door.

'Better hurry — can't be away too long. I've to put on the dinner soon and there might be a call for an order,' I prattled, stepping into the yard.

He followed me out, his feet clumping in the too-big boots. I shielded my eyes from the brittle sun with my hand and pointed to the field behind the house, which led down to the shore.

'Is that the way you came, do you think?' I asked him.

'I think so. I think I came round in a field at some point. Can we get down to the water from here?'

'Yes, this way, down the side of the field.

We have to get under that electric fence, You're lucky it was off the night you came or you'd have got a nasty shock, being all wet and all.'

His low-pitched chuckle took me unawares. 'Jesus! That's all I would've needed — getting frazzled in the nuddy,' he said, looking at me with amusement in his inky eyes.

But joking, especially of an intimate nature, didn't come naturally to me in the company of strangers. 'Oh yes, and your feet would have been hurt walking over those sharp stones behind the house,' I replied with a frown. 'We were supposed to get the yard tarred but you have to pay far higher rates, or something, when you get that done.'

I slunk under the fence, glad that I'd practised how to do it in one movement, on one of those long moodling Sunday afternoons when there was nothing else to do. I expected him to follow suit but instead he fell awkwardly to his knees and scrambled slowly under the fence on all fours.

'I'm afraid I hurt my back at some stage during my adventure,' he said apologetically as he got up unsteadily to his feet.

'Oh God, I'm sorry — I forgot all about . . . do you want to go back?'

'No, no way. I want to get my bearings,' he insisted, walking on ahead of me.

76

Despite his limp, we crossed the field purposefully, passing rows of waving scallions on the other side of the grazing patch. I felt an odd sense of adventure, as if I was on a childish exploration, yet I knew every ruck and ridge in the ground. In the clean open air, the sparkiness of this stranger's presence was diluted and I was comfortable on my own territory.

I held back a fraction and stole a glance at his profile. In the new clear post-deluge light, his skin looked dingy and for the first time I noticed a slight hook in his otherwise tidy nose. I cringed at my mother's crude stitching on his forehead, and flinched when he turned around and caught me looking. I quickly pointed to a clearing in the hedge ahead and told him it would take us out on to the top of the bank, which led down to the shore. He nodded and quickened his pace.

A fresh breeze zipped over us as we reached the clearing, and I paused to do up the buttons of my raincoat. Saul walked to the edge of the bank and stared ahead, his long fingers cupping his brow. I expected him, as most people did, to admire the view, but he fell as silent and still as a stone. I asked him if he'd like to rest for a moment and he nodded. He eased himself on to his hunkers while I perched on the edge of a rotting tree stump that used to be a huge elm. Frank had cut down a dozen of them along the boundary of the field, so Mother could have an uninterrupted view of the lough.

From our vantage point at the edge of the bank, Matt's Island seemed even further away than it did from my bedroom window. A wild and forlorn slew of trees rising above an undulating weedy surface, the island was a playground for duck shooters and curious townies.

Twirling smoky clouds swallowed up the spiky sunlight and threatened to leak. I pulled my raincoat around my knees and yawned widely behind my fingers. The fatigue was creeping up on me again. I didn't like this part of the shore, this poor man's beach of nettles and stones and bad yellow tufty grass. Even when the sun transformed the lough into a ribbon of quicksilver, underneath it was a murky manure-green soup of tangled weeds and muck, commandeered by long fat brutal eels like varicose veins, and plagues of disease-carrying water rats.

This stranger was the only person I'd come across who seemed as unimpressed as I was by this part of the world. I followed his gaze from the water, across the shore, to the rickety brambled bank below us.

'The sand depository's just a few hundred

yards up that way,' I told him, pointing to my right. 'If you wandered down this far that night, you could have sprockled up there to get into the field. That would explain why the legs and feet were cut off you.'

He narrowed his eyes in the direction of the depository.

'Yeah — I remember crawling up something in the dark, and God, it was cold. I never thought a place could be so cold at this time of year.'

He scratched the side of his neck and turned his head to follow the sweep of the shore towards the pier.

'If you want to go down on to the shore, we better get a move on,' I said, the old anxiety to hurry niggling at me.

He nodded absently. The bank had a steep drop and was impossible to descend gracefully. I ploughed on ahead, taking it sideways and sliding on the wet earthy surface. He followed close behind me, in much the same manner, but landed on his backside at the bottom. I expected to hear him chuckle again but his mouth was tight and his eyes vexed. It was the kind of look I knew all too well from home, so instead of helping him up, I proceeded on the short walk to the water's stony edge and feigned interest in a family of grey swans circling nearby. If I'd been alone, I would have waded out to the duck shooters' look-out hut and spent a while there daydreaming. The hut was a crude, roofless box of a thing, made from scrap tin and wood, with holes in the walls to shoot through. I liked to stretch out on the slatted floor and watch the sky. On a hot day, I'd strip off and dream that I was floating on the Mediterranean. It would be heavenly for a while, then I'd start to feel funny about being half naked and would have to put my bra and top back on. Still, it was the most private place in my world and I didn't want to share it with a stranger.

'How deep does it get out there?'

Saul stood up on a small rock beside me, squinting at the water. The thin sunlight had returned and revealed a semicircle of tiny lines around his flitting eyes.

'Well, the fishermen say it's bottomless in the middle. There's glar at the bottom, you see. Mucky stuff that goes on for ever. You can swim here but not too far out.'

The swans had drawn closer and when the mother spotted us, she butted out her neck with a shrill heckle.

Saul threw a pebble at her and she bolted, the cygnets flapping in her wake. 'Swans give me the creeps. Vicious things, you know.'

'Oh I know,' I agreed. 'I can't stand the

look of their snakey necks and their beady
eyes. Even the white ones. One tried to bite
Frank when he was wee and he's been scared
of them ever since.'

'You're not, I take it?'

'Eh . . . no. I'm more scared of eels. I stood
on one once when I was paddling and it
slithered around my ankle. I've never got over
the shock of it.'

He raised both black eyebrows and hawed
with loud unafraid laughter. I'd never seen
the funny side of the incident before but I
automatically joined in with an eejity giggle.
But the deviation of uninhibited laughter with
a stranger threw me completely. It was too
heady and I had to avert my eyes from his.

His laughter stopped abruptly. 'What's that
boat doing out there?'

A small fishing boat had appeared to the
left of the island.

'That's probably Dalloway or somebody
out for the afternoon catch. They cast their
nets out around there most days. You could
go out with them some time, if you like, if you
want to see around, I mean.'

A distant look in his eyes stopped me from
waffling on about my own fishing adventures
on the lough. Instead I suggested we return
home, and he turned slowly to retrace his
steps.

I paused to pull up my hood against the returning rain and a vague consternation overtook me. He'd been lying again. I knew it. It was obvious to me, from a mere dart of his eyes, that he knew more about this place than he was letting on. I couldn't fathom his switch in mood and it irked me. But as I watched him plod ahead of me, letting the skittery raindrops wash over his upturned face, the strange affinity returned.

What it was based upon, I had no clue. But it was there, sure as the hook in his nose.

★ ★ ★

Georgina drove slowly into Preacher's Bay village. She'd planned to get there earlier to attend Sunday Mass in St Luke's and to seek out Josie Moore, but she'd slept in. She had stayed late at the hospital the previous night, in the belief that Grace was coming round. For a moment or two, she could have sworn that her godmother was watching her, though she hadn't attempted to speak, and Georgina badly wanted to be the first to communicate with her.

Bobby and Ignatius might scare her off, she reckoned, whereas I could give her a smile. She imagined how she would comfort the dying woman and made a resolution to be

82

sweet to her. And if there's a few quid in it for me, she thought, that'll be a nice bonus. The tiny village was deserted. Inside the two neighbouring pubs, staff were preparing to open at midday but the doctor's surgery and the hairdresser's were closed for the weekend. A sharp pinch of early spring frost was keeping Teasie O'Mahoney from the doorway of her antiquated sweet-shop-cum-newsagency, where, for as long as Georgina could remember, she would await her regular flood of Sunday morning customers, and watch who went into the supermarket opposite.

Georgina looked at her watch and realised that the locals would still be in the chapel. She pulled up behind the row of cars outside the gates of St Luke's and freshened her lipstick in front of the windscreen mirror. She resented the unflattering light coming in from the sunroof; it made her face look drawn and showed up the odd stray grey hair in her parting. Tutting, she plucked one out and marvelled at how white it was. But in the bonhomie that comes with a good night's sleep, she was able to set aside regret for her fading youth and get on with living in the present.

Unhurriedly, she got of the car and strolled

into chapel grounds. From the limestone archway she could hear the faint burble of the Lord's Prayer. The heavy oak doors were closed against the cold air and Georgina had no wish to make a loud creaking entrance through them. Instead she wandered into the sloping graveyard behind the church, pausing at the headstones bearing the names of those whose deaths she remembered. Petey Walshe — leukaemia . . . Thomas O'Shaughnessy — drowned . . . Sean Ruddick — suicide . . . Mary Gallagher — drowned . . . Raphael Mulholland — murdered . . . Vinnie Burns — cancer . . .

A large railed plot with a tall Celtic cross caught her attention.

'Other and tamer methods they will leave to other and tamer men,' she read aloud. She shivered, pulled up the collar of her coat and made her way to the Kane family plot at the far end of the graveyard. Her grandfather had seen to it that he and his family would rest for eternity under the shade of a cypress tree, but it had grown too tall and was too sparsely foliated to offer much shelter. She looked down at the green marble stones covering the grave, imagining what lay beneath.

'Wondering who's next?

Georgina spun round in surprise. Dalloway had read her mind. She put her hand on her mouth and shook her head.

'God, Mr Moore, isn't it? You scared the life out of me. Where did you come from?'

'Aw, the chapel's awful stuffy. Got the heat turned up a tara. Haven't seen you in a while. Sean's girl, aren't you?'

'Yes, that's right . . . actually, I was hoping to run into you or Josie. I wanted to get the key to Grace's to check on the house.'

'How's she doing?'

'It's hard to tell. Looks like she's dying one minute, then she rallies again.'

'God help the critter.'

Dapper in his Sunday best and peaked tweed cap, the old man blessed himself as he joined Georgina at the edge of the grave.

'You know, your father didn't want to be buried in there,' Dalloway said, pushing out his bottom lip. 'He certainly didn't want in on top of James, his own brother or not.'

'Oh I know. Unless the dead can forgive.'

'Damn all your da had to forgive, if you ask me, miss.'

Georgina flinched. 'What do you mean?'

'I mean what I say. Your grandfather knew what he was doing when he left James the land. Sean was no farmer, no harm to you, miss.'

'Daddy was the eldest and he worked

terribly hard on that land when he was young. He never got the chance to show what sort of farmer he could be.'

'He could never have farmed the land like your Uncle James, God rest him.'

Georgina felt her hackles rising. She sniffed and shoved her hands in the pockets of her coat. 'Well that's all in the past now anyway. What's important now is that Grace does the right thing.'

She waited for a reply but Dalloway turned away, hobbling slightly on the narrow path between the row of graves.

Ignorant old carn, thought Georgina, falling into the vernacular of the dead beneath her. She thought of charging past him, but hesitated, remembering she needed his and Josie's co-operation to get into Grace's house. The old man stumbled. Georgina hurried up the path to aid him, and felt the lurking cunning within her reawaken.

'Let's not fall out over this, Mr Moore,' she said, linking his arm. 'Sure you know, we all care far too much about the land. It's bred into us.'

'Aye. And where there's a will there's a war.'

'Isn't that nearly always the way it goes? And you know Grace would want to know that the place was being well cared for.'

'Aye.'

'So, is it all right to borrow your key?'

'Call up to Josie and ask her. She's in the house.'

'Oh thanks, Mr Moore. Thanks a million.'

They walked back in silence to the gates of the chapel. The congregation was starting to spill out and Georgina wanted to get away.

'Would you like a lift home, Mr Moore?' she asked as they reached her car.

'Naw. I'm going for a dram.'

'OK. Well, thanks again.'

'You've nothing to thank me for, miss. And you know when it comes to the forgiving, it's Grace who has that to do.'

'Grace? I don't know how you make that out.'

'I've held my tongue all these years an' I'm not going to loosen it now.'

Her irritation creeping back, Georgina slipped into the driver's seat and closed the door without bidding the old man goodbye. But as she turned the key of the ignition, he tapped his thickened gnarled knuckles against her window.

'Go easy on Grace, will you? She's not to blame for what happened.'

Georgina lowered the window. 'I don't know what you're talking about, Mr Moore.'

'Aye, well maybe you're safer not knowing, miss. Good day to you.'

Georgina pulled away quickly to avoid the chattering worshippers. She determined to ignore what Dalloway Moore had said, relegating whatever it was to old gossip. She glanced in the windscreen mirror, saw him watching her from the side of the road, and cursed him for taking away her goodwill. Then a bull-headed compulsion came over her, a yearning that she had not felt in three days. She wanted a drink.

*   *   *

Last night I dreamt my father came back and forgave me. I asked him if Mother did too, but he didn't hear me. He disappeared and I couldn't find him.

They say you start to hate your mother as an infant, soon after you realise she's a separate entity and not an extension of you. Hating your father, I presume, would not be so instinctive. Sometimes it takes a long, long time to know that love and hate can co-exist quite comfortably in the soul, but I learned quickly.

*   *   *

Frank put down the phone in the hall and came back into the kitchen.

'We've sixty bags to pull before five o'clock. I'd say that'd finish out what we've left on the hill. Better get a move on, there. Ma's going to be up at the McNicholls' till all hours.'

'I could help you out if you need an extra pair of hands.' Saul looked expectantly from Frank to me, and back to Frank.

'Well if you could manage — '

'Sure I can. Grace has me walked the length and breadth of your shore and back again. The legs are in full working order now.'

I grinned down into my bowl of porridge.

'Right, well I'll go on ahead then. The two of you can follow me up in the Land Rover.'

I stood up to clear away the breakfast dishes, overly conscious of every single wooden movement I was making and ashamed of my terrible Crimplene trousers. I had spent most of the previous day with the boy, but he was still too new, his presence far too unsettling. I wished he would disappear, yet I wanted him never to go away.

'I've never done any crop harvesting before,' he said, helping to clear the table. 'Should be fun.'

'Eh . . . yes, but are you sure you're . . . up to it?' I replied.

'I don't feel too bad today.'

'Well, all right,' I said, rushing from the sink to the breadbin. 'We'll go now. I just have to make some sandwiches and change my clothes.'

'I'll make the sandwiches. You go on and get changed.'

He took the loaf from my hands but I couldn't bring myself to meet his eyes. I opened a cupboard and took out a can of corned beef, butter and a pot of plum jam, set them on the worktop and fled to my bedroom, muttering an awkward thanks.

My work clothes lay in a heap at the bottom of the wardrobe. They were so ugly and worn, I could never be bothered to fold them. As I pulled out pairs of paint-splattered trousers and old school shirts, I went over every tiny detail of the rushed encounter in the kitchen, relieved that I hadn't blushed like a moron. I undressed quickly and pulled on a pair of jeans I always felt comfortable in, only to find the zipper broken. Panicky anger shot through me as I pulled off the jeans and threw on a pair of brown cords and a baggy off-white T-shirt. Halfway up the hall I remembered I hadn't combed my hair and ran back to fix it. An absurdly over-stimulated pair of eyes looked back at me from the mirror. I shook my head and slapped my cheeks, took a deep breath and went back to the kitchen.

Saul was putting the sandwiches into a biscuit tin on the table. 'I put the kettle on, in case you wanted to make a flask of coffee.'

'Oh, sorry, we always have tea.'

I cringed. Coffee was so much more sophisticated.

'Great, fine,' he shrugged. 'Where are the tea leaves?

'Oh, don't worry about that — I'll do it. Look, there's a pile of old shoes and boots in a chest in the shed outside. Why don't you go and choose a pair? The ground's dry.'

'OK.'

He wandered outside in his sock soles. I made tea, scalding my hand with boiling water in the process. My hand stung and throbbed but I tried to ignore it. It was just the latest in a long series of accidental self-injury.

I put the flask and tin into a plastic bag and went into the yard. Saul stood by the Land Rover, tying the laces on a pair of Daddy's old cattle dealer boots, the type with stretchy panels up the legs of them. They looked ridiculous.

'Cool, aren't they?' he said as he climbed gingerly into the passenger seat beside me.

'Great leather in them. Perfect fit too. Do the farmers around here wear these instead of cowboy boots?'

His interest in something so mundane and familiar amused me, and I was glad that he was examining the boots instead of my jerky driving. Frank had given me a few lessons but I wasn't allowed to drive the car and I'd had very little practice.

'Yes . . . well, they wear Wellington boots a lot of the time. They wear those kind of boots to the cattle markets.'

'Does your brother rear cattle to sell?

'No. Daddy used to. He's dead seven years.'

'Oh, I'm sorry.'

I felt his eyes on me and didn't know what to say. My mind raced in search of something to change the subject. 'You know I've never seen a man make sandwiches before,' I ventured.

'Really? I always made my own, for my lunch at school.'

I turned into the rough laneway that led to the field on the hill where the beans grew. The Land Rover lurched over a pothole and threw us up in our seats. He rubbed the back of his neck and fell quiet. I pulled up at the gate at the top of lane and switched off the ignition.

'It's just a short walk through the gap in the hedge to the left,' I said glancing over at him. 'Are you sure you're all right?'

'Yeah, I'm fine thanks. Just a bit stiff.'

He eased himself out of the seat and walked behind me on the short pathway to the field. I hurried on self-consciously into the field, then realised he wasn't behind me. He'd stopped short, at the bottom of the path, looking at the view I'd so long taken for granted. Through his eyes I took in the wide-open ploughed field, lush with rows of beanstalks and wild brambles laden with pea pods, sloping down on to a shorn blond meadow with bails of hay stacked like wigwams across it. Beyond the meadow ran a tall and deep bank of straight, sturdy khaki and white reeds, standing stoically along the edge of the shore. Above the rolling gunmetal water, a hazy white sky promised a sunburst in the afternoon, with no breeze to scatter its rays.

I took a tall plastic bucket from underneath the oak tree in the corner of the field and brought it over to the bean patch. Frank worked at the bottom of the first two rows, in the unspoken understanding that he would be met in the middle.

'Hi there,' Saul called to him, as he strolled into the field. 'It's going to be a beautiful day.'

'Aye,' Frank nodded at him without pausing in his labours. 'Better get as much as we can done before we're roasted.'

The beanstalks had grown to over six foot tall that summer and were laden with long chunky pods full of fine meaty beans, nestling in a moist velvety white cocoon under the thick green skin. I showed Saul how to uproot the stalks and pull off the pods.

'Throw what's left in the furrow behind you as you go along,' I explained, glad of something to do with my hands.

The stalks were strong and stubborn to uproot, but despite his weakness, he managed to keep up with me. Before long we'd fallen into an easy rhythm, pulling and plucking and filling the bucket in tandem.

'Isn't it crazy what a few tiny seeds can create?' he remarked as he filled his third bucket.

I began to relax a little, even though I knew that I must look like the most unfeminine lump, working like a man in my dowdy get-up.

'The soil's good here,' I told him. 'The slope gives it natural drainage and the vegetables grow like mad.'

'Yeah? Soil fascinates me, the way it renews itself. And it has to put up with all this growing and pulling and hauling at it. See how we're disturbing it? It was lying there real peaceful and now we've come along and raped and pillaged it.'

I nodded, but I'd never thought of it like that. Soil to me was just wormy dirt. He raised an eyebrow at me and chuckled mildly.

'I'm only kidding, Grace.'

I forced a tight smile and missed when I threw a handful of bean pods at the bucket between us. The rhythm was broken.

He bent down to pick them up.

'Did you ever listen to the earth? You know, really get down there and listen?' he asked. I thought I saw him smirk.

'Oh, *very* funny.'

'No seriously,' he protested. 'If you lie down there and put your ear to the ground, you'll hear all sorts of stuff. Real busy sounds. I'm telling you — you can hear the wheels of nature actually churning around.'

'Eh . . . I'll take your word for it.'

'Aw go on, try it. Not on top of the dead stalks — try that good flat bit over there,' he urged, pointing to a bald patch nearby.

I shook my head. 'No, look — we haven't time to be messing around with such a big order in. And Frank would think I'd gone mad, lying down in the middle of the field and all this work to be done.'

He grinned and shook his head. 'I thought

you country people believed in taking time out to stand and stare. You've gotta live for the moment, you know.'

'That's all very well when you're not busy. I don't think you understand how important it is for us to get rid of these beans. They'll be past their best this time next week if it gets hot.'

The animation slid off his face. He nodded and went back to work. I hadn't felt like a bigger killjoy since I refused to kiss Paddy McKeown in a game of spin the bottle when I was fourteen.

'Maybe when we've finished I'll give it a go,' I continued hurriedly.

The easy grin returned. 'You're a funny one, Grace — oh! Don't move.'

He stepped over the furrow towards me and brushed my neck with his fingers. I froze rigid as a broom handle.

'This little mama was about to get lost in your hair. Cute, isn't it. What do you call these things?'

'It's a ladybird. They . . . they're harmless enough but I wouldn't like one creeping around my head, right enough.'

He let the tiny plastic-like creature crawl from one hand to the other before dropping it on to a leaf. I watched him from the corner of my eye and my heart sank when I saw Frank approaching. He'd think Saul was idling.

'Grace, would you get out the tea. I'll take mine under the tree. The sweat's blinding me already and the sun's not even out yet.'

For an instant I thought I'd forgotten the flask and sandwiches, given the fluster I'd been in earlier. Then I remembered I'd left them in the Land Rover.

I ran to the lane to get them and when I got back, Saul was sitting with Frank under the oak, listening to him describe how Daddy had made the land profitable after years of crop failures. I poured their tea and took mine back over to the beans. Mother had never got involved in men's farm talk and I'd followed suit. Although there was nothing I liked better than to work on the land, I would never presume to express an opinion on it, or very little else for that matter. It wasn't the done thing.

I rubbed my dirty hands on my cords and bit into a sandwich. Frank never bothered to try to clean his hands when he was in the field — 'That's good clean dirt,' Daddy would say. Ordinarily I couldn't stand corned beef sandwiches but after a while working in the field, they tasted divine, especially with the stewed tea.

'Hope you've left some for me, boys.'

I knew it was Ivy Best before I turned

around to look. Her squeaky girly voice was unmistakable.

She waved over at me, cheeky grin full on, and plonked herself down beside Frank. She'd brought cans of Coke from her father's shop. I nodded at her, with a watery smile, and grabbed my last sandwich in case she'd come over and help herself, as she usually did. A little too far away to join in their conversation, I turned away and ate like a lone wolf.

'Heard you'd a big order in and thought I'd give you a hand,' Ivy said.

'Much appreciated, Ivy.'

Frank was easily charmed by Ivy's pretty face. He'd been her childhood sweetheart and still would have been, had she not outgrown him and his safe, dependable ways.

'So aren't you going to introduce me?'

I could well imagine the cut of her lounging there on the grass, hips forwards. Saul, of course, would be intrigued by her.

'Oh, now. Thought you'd manage that yourself. This is Saul. Saul — Ivy.'

'Hi, nice to meet you, Ivy.'

I pictured her acting all ladylike and leaning over to shake his hand.

'The pleasure's all mine, Saul.'

God, I couldn't stick her.

'Here, have a sandwich. Made them myself.'

'Oooh, a man of many talents.'

What do you mean by that? I wanted to know. That his looks are a talent? I heard her twitter on about riding a donkey in Newcastle on her holidays, and could take no more. I threw out the dregs of my tea and set the mug aside. It was probably the only time that I was the first to start back at the beans after the lunch; I usually fell into a daydream after eating and would have to be dragged back out of it.

I had the bucket a third filled before they made a move.

'Ivy, you and Saul take over down there at the bottom. Go on ahead. I've to go and switch on the banger, Grace. Them crows will have the new seeds all ate.'

I had my mouth open to say it was going to be a scorcher but they passed me by without acknowledgement. Ivy broke into a run, as if the slope was too steep to hold her up. She whooped and giggled the whole way down, charging ahead, I supposed, to give Saul a clear view of her rounded rear end in her snug red jeans. He followed her with long swinging strides, pausing halfway to turn and call to me.

'Meet you in the middle, Grace. Look — the sun's coming out.'

The flat light lifted rapidly and gave way to

a continental glow, giving lustre to bean pods and turning the lough denim blue. I worked as fast as I could, only lifting my head to check what I was missing out on. The two dark heads were lit up by the sun like black gloss paint. They looked right together, and Ivy's laughter tinkled like bells.

They're in for a shock, I consoled myself. It didn't take long. I heard the click and braced myself.

BOOOOOM!

Ivy and the crows squawked in fright as the banger cracked through the air like a slap in the face. I squinted down at them with a silly big smile, but Saul's stricken face took me aback.

'It's only the banger going off to scare the crows away,' I shouted. 'Did you not hear Frank saying he was putting it on?'

Ivy reluctantly let go of Saul's sleeve. She'd leapt into the row beside him when the banger went off.

'No we did not!' she shouted back. 'Frig, Grace, you might have warned us.' She turned to Saul and let out a whinny of a laugh. 'Saul — you're as white as a sheet under that tan! Did you get a fright? Ah, you're not a wee cissy, are you?'

I gawped as he turned to her, hands on his hips, and slowly shook his head. Then quick as a fly bolts from a swat, he grabbed a discarded stalk and shoved it down the back of her T-shirt.

I looked on in consternation.

Oh God! He's only known her five minutes! How people could become so familiar in so short a time was beyond me.

She squealed and giggled, thrilled. He smiled up at me, pointing sideways and inclining his head at her. I forced a smile back as Ivy scooped a handful of soil and rubbed it into his hair.

God, he'll be getting her down to listen to the ground next.

I heard stalks snap in the row behind me and was glad to see Frank's big spoilsport expression. He hated Ivy flirting with anyone else.

'What's going on down there?'

'Hi, Frank — just teaching this one a lesson,' Saul shouted. 'We'll get right back to it.'

I worked quietly on for the rest of the day, ignoring the prodigals but wishing that horseplay wasn't so alien to me. I could hear Sister Joan's refrain — 'far far too serious, Grace Kane'.

I knew it was true of course. After all, I'd learned from masters.

★ ★ ★

Josie Moore wasn't expecting callers until the afternoon. The car that pulled up in front of her bungalow at midday was unfamiliar, but although her sight was failing, she immediately recognised the driver as a Kane.

A bit like Grace was, she thought as she drew herself up from her armchair to answer the door. A broken hip and crumbling kneecaps had left her a wispy old woman who rarely ventured out, but a steady stream of visitors kept her entertained and well informed of the local goings-on.

'Hello, Mrs Moore — do you remember me?'

'I do. Sean's girl, aren't you?'

'That's right. How are you keeping?'

'Not so bad, apart from the pains in the legs and a touch of asthma. I've a touch of the cold coming on too, it's going around.'

Georgina looked down into the faded green eyes and wondered when she was going to be invited in.

'I believe poor oul' Grace's not long for this world.'

'Well, she's not getting any better, it seems. Actually, that's why I'm here, Mrs Moore. Can I come in?'

'Oh, you see, I'm expecting young Father McCreanor any minute with the Holy Communion — '

'That's fine — I just wanted to borrow your key to check on Grace's house. Mr Moore said to ask you.'

'Oh. Right you be — hang on a minute.'

Georgina shivered on the doorstep, impatience beginning to niggle her. She rubbed her hands together to warm them up and peered in through the partially open door. Josie was rummaging in a sewing box on a hall table.

'Ah, there you are. Found them,' she said, hobbling back to the doorway.

Georgina reached out for the bunch of keys, thanked her, and hurried to her car.

'Drop them back now, won't you?' Josie called after her as she drove off.

Georgina tooted her car horn in reply.

A small grazing field and a silo separated the Moores' bungalow and Grace's farmhouse. Georgina pulled into the yard and left the car at the front door. Someone had pulled down the blinds on all the windows, as they did during wakes. It has the look of death already, thought Georgina, stepping into the darkened porch. She took the largest key and let herself in, automatically calling out 'hello'.

A whiff of damp mixed with lavender met her. The walls were painted cornflower blue and a grandfather clock stood in the low-ceilinged vestibule. The panelled mahogany doors to the living room and to the hall were shut but the kitchen door was slightly ajar. She pushed it open and walked in, subconsciously expecting a waft of welcoming heat from the stove, but the narrow room was chilly and dark. She set the keys on the table and tugged on the blinds. A flat cheerless light only slightly lifted the gloom, but the unveiled view beckoned like an old friend.

Georgina leaned up against the sink and stared out at the landscape her father had loved. The grass, energetically green as ever, had grown long from lack of grazing but the rugged shoreline and languid stretch of water remained unchanged. Georgina rubbed her ear lobe and pictured the view from the kitchen in her apartment — rows of cars and another block. Ignatius and Bobby's home wasn't much better, she thought, picturing their shabby back yard down in The Scrog, the unyielding patch of land her father had tried to farm.

And cousin dear has had this all to herself for years, she thought bitterly. She turned from the window and scowled at the higgeldy-piggeldy teak cupboards and fraying floral wallpaper, the drooping plants and the assortment of fragranced candles along the work surfaces. She circled the room with disdain, opening and shutting cupboard doors, until she came to a corner unit full of unopened bottles of spirits, their labels slightly discoloured. She ran her fingers along the bottles, lingering on the whiskey bottle, then quickly shut the cupboard door.

Suddenly thirsty, she went in search of a glass, and finding none in the kitchen, headed for the sitting room. It was musty and pitch dark when she walked into it, the heavy brocade curtains as well as the blinds having been drawn. Georgina flicked the light switch and made straight for the display cabinet in the corner, selecting a Waterford crystal hi-ball. Auntie Elva had better taste in her crystal than her furnishings, Georgina thought, eyeing the aged raspberry Draylon suite and the huge lacquered sideboard beside the door.

Only one framed photograph stood on the sideboard, along with a silver teapot and tray, and a Viennese red glass vase. Georgina immediately recognised the youthful, black and white images of her Uncle James and her Aunt Elva, both self-conscious, with smiles that didn't reach their eyes. The identity of the bewildered toddler on her aunt's knee was not immediately apparent to her, but on closer inspection of the tilt of the mouth, she saw it was Frank.

She wondered if there were more old photographs inside the sideboard and tried the top-drawer handle. It was locked, as were the two cupboards below it. Her curiosity raised, Georgina went back into the kitchen, put the glass on the table and went through the bunch of keys. In the middle of it was a smaller separate ring, with three tiny ornate keys attached. She went back into the living room, ignoring the mild qualms whispering in her mind. The drawer slid out easily, bringing with it the evocative smell of antique wood. A silver-backed hairbrush and mirror lay on a linen doily, a few pairs of leather ladies' gloves on one side; rain hats and scarves, one silk and one woollen, on the other. The left cupboard held neatly folded piles of linen tablecloths and bedsheets smelling of mothballs. Georgina shut the door quickly against the pong; it conjured up school nuns and enforced rosaries. The other cupboard door was stiffer. She knelt on the carpet and tugged on the key. After a few pulls it inched open with a slow squeak. Inside, three biscuit tins were piled on top of each other.

'Eureka,' whispered Georgina.

Her mother had kept photographs in biscuit tins. She lifted the tins out and opened one.

'Even *better*,' she said to herself, seeing

bundles of papers and brown envelopes inside. She rose nimbly to her feet and brought the tin boxes into the kitchen.

Outside soft rain was drizzling down. Georgina filled the hi-ball with water and sat down at the table to sift through the first of the biscuit tins. The bills and receipts it contained were of little interest to her and she pushed it aside.

The second box seemed to hold more of the same, but as she rifled through the layers of papers she came to a red hardback notebook in the middle, sitting on top of a black plastic bag. On the front of the notebook, someone had printed HOME-WORK. She spilled the contents of the box on to the table. The notebook was filled with single-spaced lines in an old-fashioned shorthand script she could not decipher. All that was clear to her was the random dates from the seventies, on the top of some of the pages.

Not even a damn doodle, she thought, examining the inside covers. She flipped the notebook aside and reached for the black bag, but before she could open it, a faint tapping sounded from the window. Holding her breath, she looked up. A twitching blue-cap looked back at her, hitting the pane with its miniature beak in little bursts of impatience. Georgina peeped in the breadbin, took out a blue-moulded soda farl and threw it through the window. The bird swooped down to investigate and she went back to the table and emptied out the bag. Tied loosely with a white ribbon was a small bundle of white linen handkerchiefs and delicate lingerie, faded by time yet folded as new. With it spilled out an old Swan matchbox and a long brown envelope.

Georgina pulled out a lacy bra from the bundle and examined the label.

'Playtex . . . 36C,' she read aloud, trying to picture Grace's bustline. She put down the bra and pulled out a document from the open envelope. Stamped 'Birth Certificate' on top, it gave Grace's details in longhand. Georgina drew her chair closer to the table, picked up the matchbox and shook it. Something rattled faintly inside it but Georgina was distracted by a now louder disturbance at the window. The blue-cap had been joined by a friend and both were tapping insistently and darting their thumb-shaped heads. On impulse Georgina flicked the matchbox at the window, scattering the agitated birds.

'Grace obviously has you spoiled rotten,' she muttered.

Then, from the vestibule, came two clear ringing chimes from the grandfather clock.

Georgina checked her watch and sighed. Better clear off before Moore comes noseying, she thought, dragging over the plastic bag. As she attempted to slide the birth certificate back into the envelope, she noticed inside it another piece of paper, creased and fragile. She unfolded it slowly and saw it was a rough hand-drawn map of an island, mostly covered in barely decipherable tree symbols. Georgina spread the map on the table and looked at it more closely. In the left-hand corner was a tiny pencil drawing of a round tower, and beside it, what looked like a cross. Georgina brought the map over to the window and scanned the length of Matt's Island in the distance.

Could be anywhere, she thought, dropping the map on the worktop and turning on the tap. The rain had eased off, leaving a bleary sun in its wake. As she dried the heavy crystal glass, Georgina noticed the matchbox lying on the windowsill. The impact had slightly dislodged its cover, revealing a wad of cotton wool inside it. She plucked out the cotton wool and found a round silver locket and chain in the middle of it. The locket popped open easily. Inside was a loop of dark hair, stiff and without shine. She prodded it, then lifted it out and sniffed it. It smelled of silver polish. Georgina raised an eyebrow. 'Either

Aunt Elva had a fancy man or Grace found some other oddball to be her boyfriend,' she said aloud, smirking at the thought. She bit her lip, suddenly feeling guilt over the snooping.

Abruptly she shoved the items on the table back into the bag and stuffed it into the tin. In the rush, she became disconcerted and convinced that Dalloway was about to appear on the doorstep. She half ran into the sitting room with the biscuit tins and hi-ball, and with clumsy clammy fingers, re-locked the cabinet doors as quickly as she could.

'Right. That's it. I'm out of here!' she said to herself with an exhalation of relief. Only when she was outside did she remember the matchbox and locket.

'Shit!'

She dithered at the car door, frantically debating on whether to leave the matchbox there or put it back.

'Put it back, stupid.'

She let herself back in and retrieved the matchbox, but before she could put it back in the cabinet, she heard a car turning into the yard. Stress drained her face of colour as she stood in the vestibule, grappling with the bunch of keys. Then, taking a deep breath, she shoved the box into her pocket and walked back out. Preparing to greet the occupants of the car, she raised a polite smile. But, seemingly lost, the driver had only used the yard to turn in, and was driving back out on to the road when Georgina appeared.

'Thank God for that,' she muttered, looking up at the restless sky. She took the matchbox from her pocket and threw it on to the passenger seat. It'll never be missed, she thought, starting the ignition.

Outside the wind heaved like a yawn and the rain returned gently.

4

I wonder if the snowdrops are still up. Such tender brave little things, sprouting up every year and shivering to death half the time. I miss my bit of gardening in the afternoon, and walking through the fields. I'm too high up here to see what's trying to grow, except the leaves on those cherry trees outside the window. Will I see them bloom in May, Georgina? It was a close shave, after all. They even moved Blue Rinse out, in case she'd get a fright.

God, I want to go home. I want to walk. Don't care if I can't speak. I was never was able to chatter like Ivy Best. Or dance like she could, or laugh like she did. But I'm damn sure I could work the fields better than she could, and her with the best land in the country.

Where did that get me, though? A girl was never admired for hard-toiling hands. Oh, she was so beautiful at the festival dance. Couldn't take my eyes off her myself. You should have seen her, Georgina — she was even prettier than you, ebony hair pinned up with a white carnation and her bare shoulders tanned and gleaming. She wore a little lilac dress with daisies on it, and frittery high heels, and hot pink nail polish. How could I blame him? They all wanted her.

I remember that the rims of my fingernails were still green from shelling beans. No matter how hard I scrubbed them, the stain would stick. Once I'd tried opening the pods with a knife, but that took too long, and there was always a rush on for the dinner. That day had been no different. We'd had another big order for beans, and peas as well. Ivy had dropped by the field — she'd come every day for a whole week after meeting Saul — and gave us tickets for the festival dance. She didn't stay long; had to go into town to get her hair done. How I envied her that. By the time the dinner was over and the dishes were cleared up, I'd barely the time to arrange my new slides. But then Mother gave me a new skirt, and I was so happy with it, I didn't care about my hair. It was a flouncy gypsy skirt, in three panels. It was a 'second' from the factory shop in town but it didn't matter; it made me feel exotic, like Ava Gardner.

Saul admired my outfit on the way to the parochial hall. He was shaved and shining for his first country dance. Frank didn't pass any remarks, but then he never did. It was only when I saw Ivy Best on the dance floor that I was relegated to Category Gauche, third division. How could I not have seen that the busy print blouse clashed with the skirt? Or forgotten that I was better off blending in with the magnolia walls?

Ivy was voted Miss Preacher's Bay that night. They lifted her up into the air and paraded her around the parochial hall. Saul stood with me and watched them, clapping and laughing. He even danced with me afterwards, but in my clumpy wedge sandals I was taller than him and awkward as a bag of coal. She butted in for the last dance. I bolted to the ladies' toilets and sat in a cubicle, eavesdropping on the talk at the mirror. I came out at the end and stood up with everyone else for 'The Soldier's Song', gloomy as Good Friday.

I had to squash into the back of Frank's Morris Minor with the two of them on the way home because Charlie Mulholland was roaring drunk in the front seat. In his open childish way he was as miffed as Frank at Ivy's flirting with Saul, having fallen for her, like the rest of Preacher's Bay, from a very tender age. I had my nose right up against the window to avoid her nearness. I feigned exhaustion. Saul was on the other side and in the dark I could hear the muffled whispers and low giggles, and the smack of a kiss or two when Charlie was howling 'The Lonely Banna Strand'. I felt like a child trying to ignore another taking his sweets. I had always existed in a state of subdued anxiety, and to tell you the truth I wasn't really surprised at what was happening. When you are constantly anticipating the worst, sometimes it's almost a relief when it comes.

You're not there, are you? Can't sense you near. You know, I've a picture of Ivy Best that night, cut out of the newspaper. And he was in it too, and Frank and Charlie. It can be so hard to forget the things in your life that hurt you; harder still to remember what made you happy. I'd have settled for a run-of-the-mill youth, but it passed by in a dialectic of extremes.

* * *

'You wouldn't know what that weather's going to do next,' said Ignatius. 'Best wait to see afore we split those blocks.'

The Sunday morning mizzle had gained momentum. Rain sluiced down, carried at an oblique angle by a sudden sharp wind. Ignatius hung up his coat and cap on the back door and stood scratching the sides of his narrow greying head with both hands, his brow furrowed by the rise of his thick dark hither-and-thither eyebrows. His thin bottom lip hung open slightly, revealing too many off-white teeth in too short a gum, and the thickening of his middle was exaggerated by an old Aran sweater gone bell-shaped.

'There's plenty of coal to do us the day,' said Bobby from behind his newspaper.

Ignatius took a Bramley apple from a cardboard box by the door and drew up a chair to the fire. Bobby had laid claim to their father's fireside armchair after he died, and there was an unspoken rule that no-one else sat in it. Ignatius sat opposite him and rubbed the thick-skinned apple on the leg of his trousers before settling it at the side of the fender. His father had taught him to coddle apples as a child when he'd refused point-blank to eat any other fruit or vegetables.

'At least we've an oul' orchard, if nothing else,' he would often remind his two sons when they came into the house with armfuls of fallers, which his wife Ginny would use to make apple tart and apple bread, and stewed apple for rice pudding. It had been a long time since the cottage had been filled with the calming smell of baking. A loveless fustiness pervaded the air, born of stale smoke and cooking fat and dried muck. The only feminine touch in the kitchen-cum-living room was an elaborate pelmet above the blue gingham curtains in the deep-set window by the door, a fussy affectation which limited the daylight coming in from the yard outside. Used envelopes, nails, elastic bands, matches, rolling tobacco and cigarette papers cluttered the large windowsill; sticky sauce bottles, a pan loaf, tea bags, sugar cubes and finger-marked stainless steel condiments remained on the table from meal to meal. The cupboard doors were painted baking-bowl beige, the plain wallpaper tainted with nicotine. Rough tweedy brown rugs at the fireside and the doorway took the hard look off the quarry floor tiles that their mother had blamed on giving her varicose veins, after long days standing by the gas stove making jam. Old newspapers were thrown in a pile in the far corner beside the grimy gas cooker, and opposite them sat a fifteen-year-old television set on a fake teak cabinet.

The dreariness of the brothers' living space was lifted only when the fire was lit in the traditional open fireplace where their great-aunt did all her cooking in the days before electricity and gas. Her old black kettle and frying pan still hung on the sides of the once-white overmantel as ornaments of sorts, and when the cottage was passed down to Ginny, she told the boys they'd be worth a fortune some day. Ignatius warmed his big blunt hands in front of the flames and watched the skin of the apple blacken and crack in the heat. The hiss and spit of the juice and the sweet scorching smell that went with it always reminded him of his father and the way he used to stare into the fire, speaking to no-one, in the long evenings of his last winter. For three months the old man said nothing, then one night he took everyone by surprise by asking for a priest. By the time Father O'Loan arrived, he had taken to his bed, and never left it again. Ignatius had strained to hear the murmurings behind his father's bedroom door but Bobby had pulled him away. Father O'Loan's rumpled face was paler when he emerged, accentuating his purplish open-pored nose. Ignatius would recall later that the clergyman looked neither brother in the eye as he made his swift exit, and though Bobby had joked he was probably rushing to make last orders in McRoberts's pub, Ignatius was perturbed by the shock in the priest's eye. The next morning his father slipped into a coma and a week later was buried beside his brother under the cypress tree in St Luke's graveyard.

Ignatius pierced the melted apple with a two-pronged fork. 'How long do you reckon that one is going to hang on? I'll bet you she's doing it for badness ... probably has her senses about her rightly. Christ, I can hardly bear the waiting.'

Bobby lowered his paper to his lap and yawned noisily. 'Aw, you wouldn't know a damn. She could have a good healthy ticker in her. Moore says she ate a raw onion sandwich for her supper every night and that would've kept the blood good.'

'And the breath bad.'

'Not as bad as Georgina's after a feed of that oul' garlic she's always at. God, she'd knock you down. Washes it down with plenty of that oul' wine too.'

Ignatius took a penknife from his pocket and began to peel the destroyed skin of the apple. 'You know, I'd be a bit edgy about her taking all to do with this here business.'

Bobby sniffed and wiped his gaping nostrils with the edge of his forefinger. 'Sure what harm's she doing? Isn't she sitting with her, plenty?'

'That's the whole point. You wouldn't want her going soft on the woman. You know what women's like.'

Bobby stretched back in his chair to dig for a handkerchief in his pocket. 'Now, I'm telling you ... she's just as hungry for the money if you ask me. Hasn't she got that big mortgage to pay off? And all that fancy living takes a bit of paying for.'

'Well that's another thing. What's she entitled to at the end of the day? It was us left to mind Da when she was gallivanting in England. Sure we never heard from her from one end of the year to the next. And now she's back all airs and graces, and taking over. It's far from a tin bath and an outside bog you'd think she was reared.'

The discarded apple skin sizzled on the red coals. Ignatius sliced the mushy white flesh and ate it from the knife, puckering his lips against the heat of the juice.

'Suppose you've a point there. Gone all polite, she has all right. Mind you, she always had notions — '

'I'm just saying we'd better look after number one here, Bobby,' Ignatius cut in. 'It wasn't her who had to struggle all these years with an oul' bit of bad land.'

Bobby nodded at the window. 'Speak of the devil,' he said, blowing his nose into his crumpled cotton handkerchief.

Georgina's car pulled up in the yard. She made a dash for the door, head bowed against the rain, and lifted the latch to let herself into the cottage.

'Rotten day,' she said, and hurried over to the fire.

'It is that,' said Bobby, winking at Ignatius.

'Were your ears burning?'

Georgina turned her back to the fire. 'Why, were you talking about me?'

'Just wondering how you got on last night,' said Ignatius, licking clean his penknife.

'Oh, just the same as usual. She's just the same. But I had a look around her house there now.'

'You did not,' said Bobby, looking up at her. 'How'd you get in?'

With an inner jolt she remembered that she'd forgotten to give back the keys.

'Oh, the Moores loaned me the keys.'

'Right enough. Would hardly hand them over to us boys, though. Well, anything interesting?'

Ignatius snatched a poker from the hearth and began to prod the coals behind where Georgina stood. She stepped away, frowning, and shrugged off her coat. The Moores' keys jingled in her pocket and for a second she considered giving the keys to Bobby, but thought better of it. She realised quickly it would be to her advantage to get back in, before her brothers could go through Grace's things. Ignatius' tightened lips made her uncomfortable. She took the matchbox from her handbag and handed it to Bobby.

'I didn't have that much time to poke around. The place is in pretty good shape — I found that in the sitting room. Unusual, isn't it?'

Bobby had opened the matchbox and was holding up the locket and chain to the light.

'Could you not have got your hands on something useful, like the books for God's sake? Sure she's bound to do her own VAT and stuff,' Ignatius snapped.

Georgina hung her coat over the back of a chair at the table and fiddled with the strap of her watch. She knew she should have gone through Grace's papers but a feminine curiosity had come over her when she'd uncovered the personal things, and she'd always been bored by figures.

'Eh, as I said, I hadn't much time. I had to get the keys back . . . but I think I know now where she keeps that kind of stuff — so I could get it the next time for you and bring it here, and we could make copies — '

'Be sure you do,' said Ignatius, reaching out for the chain Bobby was twirling in front of him. 'Let me see that oul' thing.'

Georgina busied herself brushing the floor, the way she vaguely recalled her grandmother doing. The sweet sharp aroma of the coddled apple had made her suddenly hungry, and she craved a heap of junk food.

'I'd better be on my way,' she said, stooping to brush up a small pile of dust and breadcrumbs on to a shovel.

'Sure you only got here,' said Bobby, back behind his newspaper.

Ignatius had snapped open the locket and was peering inside. 'Don't recall anybody about the place as dark as that.'

'I was thinking Grace must have had a boyfriend one time,' said Georgina, putting on her coat.

Both men grimaced.

'Wonder if it's worth anything? Good weight of silver in that,' Bobby said.

Ignatius ran the chain through his fingers. 'Maybe I'll hang on to this and ask around about it. Maybe get it valued.'

Georgina paused by the door. 'Yes — OK. Fine. It'll never be missed. It doesn't look like Grace's getting home soon anyway. Look, I'll see what I can do about getting the accounts. I'll let you know. Bye.'

'Right you be,' said Bobby, picking up his newspaper again.

Ignatius nodded and watched his sister hurry back to her car and drive off. Then he snapped shut the locket and shoved it in his pocket.

So much for her and her snooping, he thought to himself as he closed his eyes for his Sunday nap. I'll get to the bottom of Grace Kane's damn secrets before her or anybody else. And I'll get the home place if it kills me.

★ ★ ★

Mother wanted to know everything about the dance. We were in the two-deep queue at the cake shop and she was bored waiting, whereas I could have stood there quite contentedly, watching people. Frank had already told her about Ivy winning Miss Preacher's Bay, so I duly answered her list of questions about what everyone wore and which stewards had been on the door. I gave her more information than usual, for there was something about the cake shop that made me feel good. It was softly lit and smelled of warm scones and icing sugar, and the three small banty women behind the glass counter had gentle voices and peachy homely faces. They were sisters and they took over the shop after their father dropped dead on the street one twelfth of July. They wore frilly caps and clean white overalls, and smiled at all their customers. Josie said that they had the lightest touch with pastry in the world, and that Protestants always make the best pastry. Indeed, they made the most ladylike buns I'd ever seen, dainty little expressions of themselves. It was a pity, I thought, that the iced ones went

124

all sweaty in the heat.

When our turn came, Mother called out her order in the polite voice she put on in town: 'Give me half a dozen snow-tops and fresh cream meringues, and a couple each of those caramel squares and cherry tops, oh — and throw in an apple turnover and a chocolate éclair.'

As she spoke, I became uncomfortably aware of the scraggy woman on the other side of me craning to observe her.

'Elva Crangle! Goodness, it's a long time since I saw you last. You're looking very well.'

'Oh hello, Olive — how are you keeping?' Mother replied, ever polite, though she disliked being referred to by her maiden name.

They talked over me as I hunched my shoulders and inched back, uncomfortably close to the queue behind me. I flicked a glance at the woman, noting the long jowls and matching eye-bags on her narrow face, then fixed my gaze on the petite gloved hands behind the glass counter, deftly scooping Mother's pastry order.

'And who's this?' Olive enquired.

'Grace,' Mother said, handing a five-pound note over the counter.

'Oh.' Olive ran her tired eyes over me and inclined her head at Mother. 'Well, Grace,

125

you should have seen your Mammy when she was your age. Beautiful she was, beautiful. Always had lovely eyes, and never a hair out of place. Our Eddie always said he never saw a better-looking girl in the country, and he had quite an eye for them, tee-hee! And you know, Elva, you haven't changed that much at all — how do you do it?'

I cringed. I'd washed my hair that morning to get rid of the smell of smoke from the dance, and thought I was looking presentable. But one look at Mother's delighted face, with its fine bones and bright blue eyes, and it was clear that twenty-five years older or not, she was still prettier than I could ever be. Sometimes I forgot this. I was more familiar with the sour expressions that shielded her beauty.

I listened to Mother describe her skin-care routine to the fawning Olive as I stood, trapped between them.

'I must say, your husband was a fine-looking man too, Elva. And sure his brother Sean's the picture of him. Shame to see a good fella like that hit hard times, though.' Olive then raised her voice a pitch and averted her eyes to the pastries. 'Do you see much of Sean and the boys these days?'

The smile froze in Mother's eyes but her graceful lips remained upturned.

'Oh, the odd time,' she lied, taking the cake boxes from the counter and handing one to me. 'We're powerful busy in the fields and we'll be at the hay again any time now if the weather keeps up.'

Olive took in her breath to reply but Mother had turned to leave.

'Goodness, is that the time? Come on, I've to do the flowers for the chapel. Cheerio, Olive. Be seeing you.'

We were out the door before Olive could bid us goodbye. Mother held her tongue until we got to the car across the road, and I knew what was brewing from the rigid walk of her.

'Did you *ever* hear the like of that?' she rasped, pulling open the car door.

I got in.

'A good fella like that? Christ, and him that lazy he wouldn't walk out of your way! My God, when I think of your father killing himself working in those fields, and then the likes of her *daring* to cast aspersions! The *nerve* of her . . . '

The car ignition gave a squeal as Mother overdid it with the key.

'And him married to an oul' Paisleyite, that's the good fella he is. Bitch.'

'But she didn't really say anything that bad, did she?' I ventured.

'What? Look you, don't you dare contradict me!' It was her stock line of defence and it was always delivered with a totalitarian fury. 'As if I hadn't enough annoyance, without having to listen to you. And your hair isn't nice.'

I leaned further into the hot leather of my seat. The sun had beaten down through the windows while we'd been getting the groceries and the air inside the car was stifling. Sweat broke above my lip and the back of neck.

Great, now my hair's going to be even flatter.

Mother's predictability half amused me and half depressed me. We didn't speak for the rest of the way home but I could hear the shouting going on in her head as she raged and rehearsed how she would deliver the story to Frank, and anyone else who would listen.

Anyone else turned out to be Saul. Frank had already started the bailing, and Saul was polishing his boots on the back doorstep. Mother unfolded a deck chair beside him and sent me into the house to put on the potatoes. She'd taken a shine to the Belfast boy, as she called him, noting his good manners and willingness to help out in the house as well as the fields. Her welcome didn't surprise me; she'd preferred boys to girls, and often said she'd always wanted sons.

She let him stay in Daddy's room when he worked late and introduced him as a friend of the family, granting him immediate acceptance in Preacher's Bay. To them, he was just another wanderer looking for work because his religion meant he couldn't get a job in Belfast. Only Bear McNicholl and I, for very different reasons, thought differently.

Mother and Saul stayed outside until the dinner was ready, and when Frank came in, I heard the whole story of the cake-shop encounter again, dramatically embellished in the second telling. Frank tutted and rolled his eyes at all the right junctures, but said nothing. Saul had fallen completely silent and I could see Mother's frustration rising. She needed a partner in her outrage. When she finished her meal she left immediately for Molly Doherty's.

Frank pushed his empty plate in front of him. 'I could do with the two of you to help stook the bails this evening.'

Saul sprang to his feet. 'No problem. Let's get these dishes done and go, Grace.'

Frank looked over at me and raised his eyebrows. He'd never done the dishes in his life, and suspected any man with such a ready inclination. Yet he'd taken to Saul in his own quiet way.

'Just leave them. We've a fair bit to do before dark — come on, I'll give you a lift on the Massey.'

Saul wanted to drive the tractor but Frank wouldn't let him, so we wedged in on either side of the driver's seat, gripping the metal shanks in the tractor hood to stay upright. I kept my eyes on the road ahead, and although Saul appeared absorbed in Frank's driving, I became horribly conscious of the jiggling flesh under my shirt as we bumped and rocked along the dirt path to the meadows, ripping into the quiet balmy evening with a high-pitched mechanical din.

I crossed an arm over my chest to detract from the wobbling but lost my balance and fell into Frank, causing him to swerve along the hedge.

'Jesus, Grace!' he shouted as I struggled to pull myself back. 'Clumsy hussy, you.'

I caught Saul's glinting eye opposite me, and flashed an embarrassed grin back at him. I hadn't had a chance to talk to him since the dance, and the crunch and screech of the tractor engine made conversation impossible.

I hung my head and held on tight until the tractor braked and swayed to a halt at the edge of the meadow. I jumped out first and

130

breathed in the thick yeasty air, heavy with pollen and hay dust. Tightly packed rectangular bails formed broken lines along the narrow strip of dry yellow land, like hair tufts on a skinhead.

'You can get started along there,' said Frank, pointing to the nearest corner. 'I'm away back for Dalloway and Josie.'

Saul followed me over to the first bail. 'I take it 'stooking' is propping up the bails together, right?'

'Right,' I replied, lifting the bail by the twine and dragging it over to the next one. 'Three in each stook.'

'Heavy, aren't they?' he remarked, following suit. 'Hey, you'll wreck your hands on that string.'

'Oh, they're ruined already with pulling the peas and beans. It's the arms that get it, with the hay. You end up with welts and prickles up to your elbows. I spend most of the summer with red arms and green nails.'

He worked quickly, with the same easy rhythm he'd fallen into with the beans, a piece of straw between his lips. I suddenly wondered if Ivy had stuck her tongue in his mouth the night before. The thought of it gave me a pleasant quirk in my stomach that took me completely by surprise. I squeezed close my eyes to shake off the image,

131

disgusted with myself.

He stood back to admire the first three stooks.

'You work pretty hard on the farm, don't you? I mean, it's fairly tough work for a girl.'

'It would be all right if it was appreciated,' I blurted.

'Frank isn't grateful for your help?'

'Not him so much . . . ' I said, regretting my openness.

'Oh I get it. Your mother's the boss, isn't she?'

I involuntarily shrugged and pursed my lips, immediately aware of how sulky I must have looked.

'She sure has a temper,' he said, scratching behind his ear.

'Quite something to behold. The *energy* of it! You know, she probably could do anything she put her mind to if she put that feeling into something worthwhile. Could be a worldbeater, your ma.'

A fleeting image whizzed through my mind of Mother in her apron, crossing the finishing line of an Olympic sprint in first place. My tongue loosened again. 'When I was wee and she'd go on like that, I thought I would have a heart attack. I'd hold my breath in and quiver like mad on the inside. But her bark was always worse than her bite. Well, most times.'

'I would hope so! God's sake, she created so many bad vibes in that kitchen I couldn't wait to get out. She'd seriously need to relax — in fact, you all would. Loosen up a bit.'

I flinched. 'Like Ivy, you mean?' It was out before I knew it.

He wiped his brow with the back of his hand. 'I wouldn't say Ivy is all that cool . . . she's kinda forced, really. But she knows how to have a good time.'

I had sounded petty and I knew it. 'Oh yes, she's *always* been a good laugh,' I said in a rush. 'Even at school.' I floundered for an example but he threw me by propping his chin on an upright bail, and looking at me intently.

'By the way, Grace, you don't happen to know if anyone was messing with this, you know, when I was out of it?'

He leaned back from the bail and pulled out the locket and chain from under his T-shirt. By sheer force of will I kept my face from flaming, focusing hard on stabilising a bail. The fading light helped; in the cold light of day, I was defenceless against the cruel surge.

'No . . . don't think so,' I lied. 'Unless Dalloway or Josie . . . no, . . . um, there was only Mother and I, and Frank, I think. No, nobody would've.'

He flicked back a lock of hair from his face. 'OK.' He stretched his arms out behind him and walked towards another bail, his calm face unreadable.

'Why do you ask, anyway?' I asked, hearing the rise in my guilty voice.

'Oh, there was just a little keepsake in there. Nothing important. Must've dropped out somewhere.'

Yes, *right into the middle* of Crime and Punishment. *How could I have forgotten?*

My mind raced in search of a surreptitious way to get the piece of paper back to him, but the rattle of the returning tractor distracted me. Dalloway helped Josie out and Frank strode towards us.

'Good work, lads,' he shouted, grabbing a bail in the next row. 'The five of us'll have her done in an hour.'

Shame stabbed at me as Josie's delicate little face broke into a smile at the sight of us. I had implicated her and her big honest lump of a husband in the interference of Saul's locket. I was a right sneak. The backs of my knuckles burned from gripping the twine too tightly, and my eyes stung from the invisible army of irritants in the air. I decided to offer up the pain as penance, but no sooner had I made my silent pledge, than I had another bad thought.

Kind of forced. That's exactly what bloody Ivy Best is.

★ ★ ★

'You shouldn't let those two get to you, Gina. You don't owe them anything, after all.'

Elaine handed Georgina a mug of coffee and perched on the edge of her desk.

'Yes, I know, but they make me feel so guilty all the time.'

'About what exactly?'

'Well, about not being there, especially when Daddy was ill. It's not that they say anything directly about it, but it's always there, hanging in the air. And then when I do something minor they don't like, I feel doubly guilty about it.'

'Like leaving those accounts behind when you snuck into your cousin's house?'

'Exactly.'

Elaine ran her well-manicured fingers through her short blonde hair. 'All that damn guilt will make you ill. It's bad enough having priests make us feel like the whores of Babylon. You've got to shake off the past, Gina.'

'That's easier said than done,' said Georgina, taking a sip of her coffee. 'The thing is, Ignatius and Bobby don't realise I've still got the keys to Grace's. I'm going to slip out there this afternoon and get the stuff — would you ever come with me?'

Elaine glanced at the wall clock. 'Out to the sticks? Um, suppose I could. Might be a bit of a laugh.'

'Right — good. I'll say we're off to the library to do some research.'

'That's exactly what we should be doing. I haven't the first clue how to handle local tourism campaigns, and I've still stuff to do from last week.'

'Well, I'll go and look up the waterways on the Internet,' said Georgina, walking to the door. 'It might give us a starting point, at least.'

'OK — give me a shout when you want to split.'

Clear spring sunlight spilled through the tall leaded window of Georgina's office and on to her untidy desk. She left her door ajar and eased open the window to let the air in. She had become inured to the rush of traffic and people six levels below her, preferring to take in the view of Napoleon's Nose on Cavehill Mountain and the constantly shifting sky around it.

The gentle brightness ushered in by the afternoon lifted her spirits and she went straight to work on her computer, immersing herself in the geography of the six counties of Northern Ireland. Glowing travelogues on the Antrim coastline and the Fermanagh lakes and the Giant's Causeway brought back memories of school trips, and she warmed to her task. She scrolled down through the less relevant sections until she came to Lough Neagh.

All those years and I never saw a tourist near you, she thought to herself as the familiar facts and figures appeared on the screen.

. . . *The largest freshwater lake in the British Isles. 144 square miles. Fished for trout, pollan and eels. Windsurfing, pleasure cruises. Outstanding natural beauty.*

'God, they're making you sound like Lake Como,' she said aloud. 'What about all those awful sand holes people have drowned in?

She read on . . . *Dangerous in parts . . . unsuitable for swimming . . .*

'Bit of an understatement,' she muttered, scraping her bottom lip along her front teeth. As she read on, she came across illustrations of the small islands dotted along the lough's shoreline.

'Aha — now this looks interesting,' she said, picturing the rough map of an island in Grace's envelope. Seconds later she had located it on the screen and saw it was St Matt's.

'St Matt's,' she read aloud. 'So called after Blessed Matt Talbot, who suffered unselfishly as penance for his sins. *Idiot.*'

The brash beep of the telephone on her desk broke into her thoughts.

'Georgina, it's Peter Brady from Nelson Brady Walsh on line two,' said the receptionist.

'Did he say what sort of a company that is?' Georgina asked, still staring at the screen.

'No, but I think they're solicitors in town.'

Georgina pressed the flashing button on the telephone. 'Hello, Georgina Kane speaking.'

A clipped officious voice emanated from the receiver. 'Miss Kane, Peter Brady here, Grace's solicitor. Your brother Ignatius called in this morning when I was in court and I've been trying to get back to him, but his phone seems to be out of order.'

'Oh, I see. I can pass on a message.'

'It's in regard to Grace's will. All I can tell you is that she has indeed made a will, and that it is, of course, entirely confidential.'

'Oh, OK. It's just that she isn't too well, and we're the nearest of kin — '

'I understand that, Miss Kane, but I do not have my client's permission to reveal the terms of the will until after her death.'

'Can't any exception be made, under the

138

circumstances? She could linger on for ages and there's nothing being done on the land . . . '

'The only course of action you could possibly take would be to ask Grace herself about it, if she ever regains consciousness. She's the only one who can tell you anything.'

'Right. Well, thank you for calling.'

'Goodbye, Miss Kane.'

Georgina immediately dialled her brothers' home but found the line dead. I bet they haven't paid their bill, the losers, she thought. She looked down at her notepad where she had jotted 'confidential' and underlined it several times.

'Hey, what's with the big serious face?'

Elaine stood in the doorway, coat across one arm.

'Grace's made a will and the solicitor won't tell us what's in it. We'd hoped she'd die intestate. So the land would automatically come to us.'

'Uh-huh. You're just going to have to pray she wakes up and then worm your way into her affections, dearie! Come on, we'd better get a move on.'

Georgina followed her friend to the lift. 'Ignatius will go mad if they don't get the farm. I've got to find out who she might have left it to.'

'Well, let's start the detective work then! It will be a hoot.'

'It might be a hoot for you but it's serious shit for me,' said Georgina as they walked out of the office building. 'Just when I was having a nice stress-free day.'

'There's no such thing in this world, Georgina Kane. No such bloody thing.'

Georgina took her sunglasses out of her handbag and slipped them on as they approached her car.

Elaine's perky face lit up with a grin. 'Poser!'

'I am not!' Georgina objected, getting into the car. 'It's very bright and I don't want to be screwing up my eyes when I'm driving.'

'Afraid of a few crow's feet, are we?'

'Of course. You know you twenty-somethings sicken me, you're so ageist. You've it all ahead of you, you know. You'll know all about it soon enough, then you'll cringe about slagging the likes of me.'

'All right, keep your hair on. I was only joking.'

Georgina snapped shut her seat belt and sighed. 'Sorry — that solicitor guy has got to me. They can be so imperious, can't they?'

Elaine pulled down her eyeshade and peered into the mirror. 'Law students were always the most pompous at university, even worse than the medics. Always looking down on the Arts. And look at them now — most of them stuck in dreary desk jobs, bored to death. At least there's a bit of crack in marketing.'

'Sure when I'd tell people my degree was in archaeology they thought it was a complete joke, especially when I ended up in marketing. But you know, I'm beginning to see the attractions of the farming life. There's not one sign of stress on old Grace's face, you know. She hasn't got one line on her forehead, and mine looks like a ploughed field under this fringe.'

'Tee-hee-hee! There you go again. It's eternal youth *and* a big farm you're after.'

'Oh, I'll settle for a few quid. Right — I think I'll give the M1 a miss this time. Motorways are so boring.'

Georgina started up the car and drove quickly through the city and on towards the hills to the east. A fine damp mist hung in the air as the car climbed high above the urban sprawl and deeper into the joyless terrain that lay between the city and the lough's shoreline.

Elaine adjusted her seat and stretched out her legs. 'God, what a wilderness. I thought the world was supposed to be more beautiful the higher up you got.'

Georgina stepped down a gear and drove carefully, eyeing the steep ragged drop to her left.

Elaine yawned. 'Well, I'm off for a snooze — didn't get to bed until three last night. Wake me when we get there.'

A desolate light had descended and though she tried to appreciate the stark landscape, Georgina slipped into a wintry gloom, and wished she could lie back and sleep too. Further on she had to brake sharply to avoid a lone sheep wandering across the road but Elaine dozed on, oblivious.

'Stupid bloody animal,' Georgina muttered, growing impatient.

She cast a sharp glance at Elaine. She'd brought her along for the company, not as a sleeping passenger, and now the road had become long and lonely. She tutted as she manoeuvred a sharp bend but was relieved to see a gentle downward slope in the road ahead. The dull mist cleared and the pale sunlight returned, and the mousy barren land gave way to vibrant green fields and slews of bobbing wild daffodils along the hedges.

'Look, Elaine, it's springtime again.'

Elaine cocked open an eye and quickly shut it again. 'So it is. How weird.'

Georgina smiled to herself and pushed her

foot down harder on the accelerator. The road had levelled out and as she drove past the sign for Preacher's Bay village, Georgina felt a strong sensation she hadn't had since her childhood.

'This is strange — I've got this funny feeling of coming home, or something,' she said, relaxing her grip on the steering wheel. Then, letting her shoulders drop, she exhaled slowly and unclenched the muscles in the calf of her right leg.

Elaine straightened up her seat. 'Getting sentimental in your old age. Ooops! Didn't mean the age thing — sorry!'

Georgina laughed and turned left on to the road that led directly to the lough. The long dark outline of Matt's Island stretched beyond the fields and water to the right; fat Friesian cattle grazed on the farms to the left. Georgina slowed down to turn on to the sloping back road leading on to Grace's farm and the lough shore. Directly ahead now, an uninterrupted band of silvery water rippled under a vast chalky sky.

'Wow, now *that's* impressive,' said Elaine. 'I could have this all right, if the weather was good. A big hunk with a speedboat, that's all you'd need.'

Georgina wasn't listening. She was beginning to understand why her father so coveted his brother's land, and as the mild rush from the spectacular view subsided, a sense of urgency overtook her.

'Jesus, Elaine. I've just realised I'd really like to live out here,' she said, swinging the car into Grace's yard.

'What? Why?'

'I don't know — it just feels right.'

'Really? Well, by the look of that guy in the porch, you might not be all that welcome — '

'Shit! That's Ignatius, my brother. What's he doing here?'

'Well, whatever it is, he doesn't look too happy about it.'

Georgina parked the car along the side of the house. Virginia creeper clung to the gable like a wild russet rash and overhead a flurry of crows cawed its disapproval at the sudden disturbance. She stepped out of the car, subconsciously mirroring her brother's stern expression. Elaine split her glossy red lips in a sunny smile and followed Georgina to the doorway.

'Ignatius, this is my colleague Elaine,' said Georgina, looking at her friend. 'She came out with me for the run.'

'Pleased to meet you, Ignatius,' chirped Elaine, extending her flimsy hand. Ignatius shook it briefly, and though he appeared distracted, deep in his eyes Georgina could see a flicker of male appreciation for Elaine's impish face. The look was fleeting, and his eyes narrowed as he turned to his sister. 'Dalloway tells me you never left back the keys.'

'Oh — I know. I completely forgot all about them,' replied Georgina quickly, rummaging in her handbag. 'I only realised I still had them late last night. Here they are — shall we go on in?'

Ignatius jangled coins in his roomy pockets. 'Sure you can go on ahead now if you like. I'll have a look round and give them back to Dalloway later on.'

Elaine clasped her hands in front of her chest. 'Oh, you know, I would really like to see inside a real country farmhouse. Seeing as we're here?'

'Certainly you can,' said Georgina, stepping up to the door. 'Come on, Ignatius, I'll get you those papers I was talking about.'

Overruled, Ignatius quickly remembered his manners. 'Oh right enough, you might as well. You're from the big smoke, are you, Elaine?'

'Born and bred, Ignatius.'

Georgina unlocked the door and held it open for the others. Lit by the meek sunlight, the blue vestibule appeared more welcoming than before.

'Why don't you show Elaine the old scullery and pantry, Ignatius. Wee townies like her never saw one before. I'll go and get the papers.'

Ignatius rubbed the soles of his boots on the doormat and watched Georgina's elegant reflection in the hall mirror, as she gestured towards the kitchen.

'Oh yes, let's. It's all so quaint and old-fashioned, isn't it?' said Elaine, heading to the kitchen door.

Ignatius met his sister's eyes in the mirror.

'Don't be long,' he said, following Elaine into the kitchen. 'Have to get them keys back.'

Georgina went into the sitting room and opened up the cabinet. She had left the curtains open on her last visit and, like the vestibule, the unlived-in room seemed friendlier now. She crouched down and took out the biscuit tins, then, keeping her eyes fixed on the door, she emptied the plastic bag from the first tin into her handbag and zipped it closed.

Elaine's laughter rang out from the kitchen. Georgina began to sift through the documents in the second box, but before she could read anything of interest, Ignatius appeared at the door.

'What's keeping you?'

'Coming now — some of this stuff spilled out on to the floor,' she lied, getting to her feet.

Ignatius walked slowly to the cabinet and took the biscuit tin from Georgina's outstretched hand.

'Look, why don't you go and show your friend around the place and I'll go through this,' he said, setting the tin on top of the cabinet. 'Might as well take a wee look — '

'Fine by me,' replied Georgina, seeing the gleam of impatience in Ignatius' grey eyes. 'I'll leave you to it.'

In the kitchen, Elaine had found the drinks cupboard.

'Hey, Gina — what about a wee shot?' she stage-whispered, sloshing gin into two small glasses. The clear liquid caught the light from the kitchen window as Elaine held out a glass.

Georgina hesitated. 'There's no mixer,' she whispered.

'Who cares? It goes down better straight. Bottoms up!'

Georgina took the glass and watched Elaine knock back the drink. A distant instinct told her to throw hers in the sink but she blanked it and drank.

'Ooh, that was good,' giggled Elaine, screwing the top back on to the bottle. 'Have to have a few more back in town.'

Georgina put the glasses in the sink and ran cold water over them. 'Yeah. Let's celebrate.'

'Eh . . . Gina — '

'And what exactly would you be celebrating, miss?'

Dalloway Moore's ageing bulky frame filled the doorway. Impulsively, Georgina turned back to the sink and put the glasses on the drainer.

'Mr Moore — you're always turning up out of the blue,' she replied, pulling open a drawer to look for a drying cloth. 'We'll have to stop meeting like this.'

'The door was open. Didn't think you'd have much to celebrate with Grace lying near dead in the hospital,' said Dalloway, leaning against the doorframe and folding his arms.

'Oh, Grace's stable again, thankfully. Actually, we were just talking about work — we've just landed a great new project with the tourist board, you see. We're going to be doing a bit of promotion on the lough. This is Elaine, by the way. We work together.'

Elaine smiled sweetly at him. 'Do you live locally, Mr Moore?'

'I do.'

'Then maybe you could give us the benefit of your knowledge of the lough some time. It's so beautiful here, but we really don't know much about this part of the world, and I'm sure you're an expert.'

Dalloway raised an eyebrow but his lips pursed and twitched, threatening to smile. 'Well, I know a thing or two about the lough all right — it's a powerful interesting stretch of water.'

Elaine raised her chin and held out the palms of her hands. 'Well that's great. You can be our special lough consultant, Mr Moore.'

Georgina had rubbed her glass with the cloth until it squeaked. Dalloway glanced at her, then looked back at Elaine, his dark eyes widening and his lips slightly parted.

He unfolded his arms and held his knuckles on his sides, and was about to speak when Ignatius appeared in the vestibule behind him.

'There's no better man in the country to tell you about the lough,' said Ignatius, an ersatz bonhomie in his voice as he slapped a hand on Dalloway's broad shoulder. Dalloway stepped into the kitchen and stood by the range.

'Didn't know you were here,' he said, eyeing the biscuit tin under Ignatius' arm.

'Ach, just making sure the place is still in one piece. I told Georgina there you were looking for the keys back.'

Georgina took the keys from her pocket

and set them on the table.

'Sorry, Mr Moore. I forgot all about them yesterday, in the rush. God, is that the time? We'd better be making tracks, Elaine. It'll be getting dark soon.'

'I'm away on too,' said Ignatius, turning back into the vestibule. 'I'll leave you to lock up, Dalloway. All the best.'

Dalloway nodded and took the keys from the table. He turned them over in his work-hardened hands, then began to examine them one by one. Georgina buttoned up her coat, winked at Elaine and inclined her head at the door.

'Cheerio, Mr Moore. See you sometime,' Elaine said on her way out.

'Right you be,' Dalloway replied, still looking at the keys.

Outside a new bullying wind was whipping around the side of the house, blasting the tepid sun away. Elaine linked arms with Georgina on their way to the car. 'Wonder what bit him? I thought the charm offensive was working nicely.'

'Oh it was — you're an expert at it.'

'So could you be, if you weren't so aloof, Miss Kane.'

Georgina rolled her eyes and dug Elaine's ribs with her elbow. They were opening the car doors when Dalloway came out of the house and strolled towards them.

'I'll have a yarn with you sometime, if you like . . . if you're still interested in the oul' lough,' he said.

Both girls turned to him and beamed a smile as they thanked him and waved goodbye. Dalloway turned up his collar and watched them drive away. Along the fence beside him, the last of Grace's snowdrops were blown flat against the ground.

5

I have a disease of the blood. It sneaked up on me. Abnormal white cells are on the rampage, attacking my bones. It's a strange and unpleasant sensation, having a sore skeleton. Not the sort of thing you bring up in conversation. It started not so long ago, with a nosebleed. Then bruises from nowhere. Yes, I left it too late. I didn't want their bone marrow.

It's funny. I always wondered if I'd bad blood in me. They siphoned some out this morning. The titchy nurse said I was going to have to snap out of it and fight a bit harder. Maybe I will. You can only take so much sky-watching, especially through useless half-closed eyes. If only someone would read to me. What a treat it would be.

Those girls are so deft with the bedpans, but I'd be dying of the shame if I was myself. I'd rather be dead than incontinent. I'd have to get someone to bump me off, though. Couldn't get a hold of those pills, even if I wanted to.

What about you, Ignatius? Sitting there in the corner with a face like a slipper. Would you do me the honour? You know, you used to be a nice wee boy. A bit watery, with those sludge grey eyes and no chin, but pleasant enough all the same. Look at you now. You'd need a good strong jaw to hold up that sour mouth.

Of course, what's cute in childhood is weak in manhood. I remember you and Bobby so clearly as youngsters, standing with your father at Cemetery Sunday. Funny, I was just thinking about that time, because Saul was there. He'd been invaluable in the fields and Mother had insisted he came to the graveyard with us, as if he was one of the family. I remember him standing there quietly, facing the headstone, a dark slender stranger amongst a solid and ruddy country tribe. Yet he blended in. He'd cut off his long hair and he was the right religion, and the ability to work hard goes a long way in the country. And he had a stillness about him, like an old Red Indian. Maybe he had us hypnotised. We Kanes had a good big corner plot near the caretaker's hut. Mother positioned Frank and me to her right, along the side facing the rest of the graveyard, so she could see who came to pray for their dead and who didn't bother their heads.

Most of the parish made an effort, knowing full well they'd be talked about if they didn't.

153

Some even enjoyed themselves. A well-tended country graveyard isn't a bad place to be on a summer's afternoon. I stood watching the various sets of Mulhollands — there were squads of them in the parish — and all the village families make their way slowly along the narrow pathways between the graves and line up around their plots like small groups organising themselves for a square dance. The living and the dead, all together for a knees-up in the sunshine.

Mother and I had spent the whole afternoon on the previous day scrubbing the headstone and washing the marble stones. The white roses she'd planted behind the grave had flourished well in that nutritious soil. They'd crept up over the headstone and draped themselves in a leisurely fashion over the front of it, nature's little victory over death. Plants had the edge over us, I reckoned. We both burst into life, flourished, faded and died, but they came back every year. Maybe we did too, to some other mother, in some other place. And if that was true, what were we doing here praying over old bones?

We all got a shock when your mother appeared with you and Bobby and your father in tow. Auntie Ginny, she was to me. Frank and I had always liked her. So did

Mother, before Uncle Sean decided to marry her, that is. It was a huge affront to her that her brother-in-law brought a Presbyterian into the family circle. They were all right at arm's length, but it was a grave sin to marry one. Mother never spoke to either of them after that. Daddy did when he really had to, on the sly.

Anyway, Ginny walked around to the opposite side of the grave, her stomach swelled in her over-stretched orange dress like a space hopper, ankles waterlogged, marmalade hair frizzed, skin clammy, face puffy and unhappy. She'd brought the unborn into the mix, casual as you like.

It had turned hot as hell again that day. Maybe that's why you were wearing your school shorts. I felt embarrassed for Uncle Sean and Ginny, not being able to afford anything else for you. I was sweltering in a long-sleeved blouse and one of those long wallopy maxi skirts that were in at the time —

'Nurse! She seems to be moving her lips. Is she trying to talk?'

Goodness, I thought I was only talking into myself. The redhead nurse he's summoned speaks into my ear.

'Grace, Grace — can you hear me? Come on now, talk to me.'

155

She waits, in vain.

'Mmm. Maybe she's saying a little prayer to herself. You'd never know in these cases.'

She squeaks out. He draws his chair closer. I'm slipping back . . . now it's Frank's long-lost voice I can hear in my ear.

★ ★ ★

'Don't be gawking over at them, Grace. They're only looking for trouble.'

I had winked at you boys. You'd smirked back. Chubby, you were then. You were standing at the other side of the grave in front of Uncle Sean, hip level to him. I'd forgotten what a smasher he was, the picture of Robert Mitchum, everyone said. He was keeping a steely eye on the gravestone, most likely to avoid looking at us, I suppose. Nobody had expected to see Daddy's name up there so soon after his own father's. Now, here we all were, forced to contemplate the scene six foot under.

At breakfast, when I'd suggested that it would be a better idea to pray for Daddy in a place where he was alive and happy, like the top of the meadow, you'd have thought that I'd announced I'd taken up stripping for a living. Mother pulled a similar expression, as if she'd smelled something off, when she saw your mother in the graveyard.

'Bad enough Sean turning up without bringing her too,' she moaned to Frank.

But I felt sorry for the woman, standing there all puffed up in the heat, trying to follow the unfamiliar service.

Father O'Loan, dramatic in his soutane, droned on mournfully as if he was the bearer of the sorrows.

'May this place, prepared in the sure hope of resurrection, never cease to remind us of the life we are to share in Christ, who will transform our earthly bodies to be like his in glory, for he is Lord, for ever and ever.'

'Amen.'

Mother boomed the responses and enunciated her Hail Marys throughout the sorrowful mysteries like defiant poetry. I barely mouthed them. Frank had just warned me to stop gawking again when Ginny, her weary face perspiring, caught me staring right at her radically rounded bosom. I darted my eyes away from her as if they'd been scalded, only to meet the insolent countenance of Ivy Best a few plots away, inclining her glossy head and sticking her tongue out at me. I wrinkled up my nose at her but she had turned her attention to Saul, and was swishing her hair behind her bare brown back like a brush on a kettledrum.

But instead of watching Ivy, Saul was staring at Ginny. I'd been so transfixed by her bust that I hadn't noticed her wilting in the direct sunlight. She took two faltering steps back from the side of the grave. Uncle Sean prayed on obliviously, his hands resting on your shoulders, your eyes on Father O'Loan's wandering tabby cat. Suddenly Saul made a dash to the caretaker's hut. Rows of eyes followed him as he came out with a watering can and ran over to Ginny. He was just in time to catch her as she crumpled. He eased her down on to the grass, took out his handkerchief and soaked it with water and laid it across her brow. Uncle Sean jerked round and you and your brother looked on, round-eyed. Mother's hand flew to her mouth, her eyes flitting around to see who had noticed.

'Right there boy, she's all right, she's all right,' Uncle Sean urged, stepping over to his swooning wife. 'Go on now, it's all right.'

Saul shot an earnest look at him. 'Tell you what, if you hold her I'll go and see if I can get a drink of water for her. That water's dirty.'

Seeing his wife's distress, Uncle Sean had no option but to get down on his knees and do what Saul said.

'C'mon — you're making a holy show of

158

me,' he whispered to Ginny, taking hold of her freckly arm. 'C'mon, try and get up, would you.'

Ginny pulled the hankie down over her eyes and made no attempt to move, beyond inelegantly splaying out her feet on the grass. You and Bobby began to whimper, and I wasn't at all surprised when Ivy Best turned up and produced a can of cola from her bag. By the time Saul got back from the sacristy with a jug and a glass, Ginny was sitting up glugging from the can, cola flowing down the sides of her mouth, Ivy holding her hand like a ministering angel. Uncle Sean got to his feet and roughly moved you boys aside by the shoulders. The three of you stood by Auntie Ginny's side, as if hiding her.

I stared at the upturned soles of her cheap but neat white shoes, then looked down at my feet, with their over-long toes hanging over the edge of my flat sandals like globs of spilt wax. I curled them back, envious of Ginny's small feet, and watched sourly as Saul and Ivy helped her up and led her out, along the hedge.

'Grace, would you quit gawking, for Christ's sake,' Frank repeated, louder than he meant to. 'Get ready to go now, quick.'

Such was the distraction, only Frank had

noticed Father O'Loan bringing the ceremony to an end.

'May we who believe in Christ's resurrection from the dead live with him in glory for ever and ever.'

'Amen.'

'And may almighty God bless you all, the Father, and the Son, and the Holy Spirit.'

'Amen.'

A ripple of coughing broke out across the graveyard. Mother was itching to make a run for it but forcing herself to bow to decorum. She turned slowly to leave but Willy and Sadie were strolling towards us down the narrow pathway, Charlie bobbing along behind them.

'Well isn't it nice to see the whole family out together for poor oul' James, wee children an' all,' said Willy, fat face alight with goodwill.

Mother forced a small tight smile and shoved her rosary beads into her handbag.

'Aye, your brother's fairly missed, Sean,' said Sadie, nodding towards the headstone. 'Powerful decent fella he was.'

Uncle Sean took hold of your hands.

'Didn't show me much decency, did he?' he replied coolly, his face impassive.

I didn't dare look at Mother but I felt Frank bristle beside me.

'You did all right out of Daddy dying, Sean, and you know it,' he shot back, keeping his voice as low as he could.

Uncle Sean flashed Frank a slow, charming smile. 'You call half a dozen pigs and a couple a hundred pound doing all right? Ha! What about you, Willy — do you call that fair? And them sitting on a hundred acres and a full herd of prime cattle?'

'Aw now, Sean, sure that's the way your da before you had it all laid out,' said Willy, the light leaving his eyes. 'Sure James was only doing what he was bid.'

Uncle Sean raised his jaw, showing the jutting tendons in his thick-set neck. 'The place should've been mine and that's all about it. I'm the eldest, amn't I? But James, he sucked round my father till he got all. Put me out of my home, he did, and me with these wee children to rear.'

Mother turned and pulled Frank's sleeve. 'Frank, get me out of here. I'm not listening to any more of this.'

'Can't hack the truth, can you, Elva Crangle?' Uncle Sean shouted, a sneer curling his lip.

I thought he looked quite sexy. All eyes were on him now.

'Sure what does the likes of you need with all that good land? Naw, but you couldn't do the decent thing by me, could you?'

'Don't you dare talk to me like that — '

'Come on now, Sean, can't you just leave it,' Frank interrupted. 'The whole country will be talking about us — '

'All she has to do is give me my share. By rights it's all mine, but I'm not greedy.'

'Look, you,' Mother snapped, 'if your father and your brother didn't want you to have that land, I'm damn sure I'm not going to give it to you.'

'My father was cajoled into making that fool will — '

'He was not indeed!' Mother suddenly screeched, her head wobbling. 'You didn't get the place because you're no damn good, and into the bargain you went and married a Protestant, in the Protestant church, and now you're sending your sons to a Protestant school! And you expect me . . . Jesus, I've heard it all now! And bringing your Protestant wife here to insult us and make a show of herself, her that had to get married — '

A hush fell upon all within earshot. Frank took Mother sharply by the elbow and led her on to the path. I felt the shame of her words hang in the air like escaped gas. She had used her trump card to silence Uncle Sean, and he had paled in the face of her vitriol. You boys, your eyes were wide and glistening, and you were pulling at him and rhyming at him to bring you home.

Willy and Charlie cleared the path for Frank, Mother trembling slightly behind him. I followed them, my head hung low. I didn't look up until we reached the chapel gates. Ivy Best was sitting swinging her slender legs on the churchyard wall. In the hot air I could smell coconut sun oil off her from yards away.

Mother and Frank went straight to the car but I stopped to ask her where Saul was.

'Took your auntie over to Dr Mooney's,' she said, looking past me on to the road. 'Looks like she's ready to drop one any minute. I had to bail out.'

She flicked her hair over both shoulders and arched her back. The usual assortment of men had gathered around the newspaper stand opposite the chapel gates for a smoke, and naturally Ivy had to check them out.

I trudged on to the car, my head suddenly throbbing. Nobody spoke the whole way home. Frank drove at his usual unhurried Sunday pace, Mother beside him staring straight ahead, her mouth in a tight line. The Mulhollands followed us in their ramshackle van, and I imagined Charlie bumping up and down in the back as it went over ridges of sand on the road. They always came to our house for tea after Cemetery Sunday, and as we turned into the yard, Mother looked into her side-view mirror to check that they were following. When Frank pulled up she went straight into the house without acknowledging them. Sadie started to chatter inanely the minute she got out of the van and Willy said he was dying for a cup of tea.

In the kitchen Frank and Charlie went straight to the sports pages of the Sunday newspapers on the table. Willy and Sadie sat down on either side of the range and I put on the kettle. Mother had gone into the hall to take her hatpins out in front of the mirror and though she'd left the kitchen door open, she didn't join in the small talk Willy was making about the extremes in the weather. Frank gave the odd monosyllabic reply to Willy's remarks without lifting his head from the newspaper, and Sadie yawned and fanned her weather-beaten face with her hand. She had tawny brown eyes, the same shade as her short wiry hair, and the tiny distance between her button nose and full top lip gave her the look of a deer.

The kettle was boiled by the time Mother came back into the room. She took a seat at the table and for a second I thought she was going to start reading one of the papers, but she merely scanned the headlines and pushed it away from her. She folded her arms on the table and stared out at the lough, her back rigid, her silence palpable.

Willy busied himself with his pipe and for once Sadie seemed to be at loss for what to say. Then Charlie laughed and glanced up from his paper as if to relate something he'd read, but thought the better of it and read on. I made the tea and was glad of the breakfast dishes to keep me occupied. I was careful not to create too much noise but each squirt of the tap or clatter of cutlery jarred in the heavy silence.

'I'll dry those, love,' Sadie said, coming over to me and taking a cloth from over my shoulder. 'I must say that's lovely fine china, lovely. Blue willow pattern, isn't it? They don't make crockery like that any more, I'm telling you. No, you'd pay a fortune for the like of that craftsmanship nowadays. There's the Belleek, now, but it's a bit fancy for my taste, if you ask me. Not partial to all that frilly stuff, at all at all.'

It seemed to take an age for the tea to draw, and all the while Sadie twittered incessantly, addressing no-one in particular. I poured the tea and out of the corner of my eye I saw Mother unclasp her hands and begin to noiselessly drum her fingers on the table. I'd been taking too long with the tea, in my efforts to be quiet and unobtrusive. I turned swiftly to the fridge, grabbed the jug and sloshed milk into the cups, spilling some on the worktop. Mother sighed, and then Willy came over and got in my way when I was reaching into the cupboard for the cake boxes. He was looking for matches but Sadie began to fuss and shoo him back to his seat, and as he turned I knocked against him, sending one of the boxes crashing on to the floor.

The lid flew off and meringues skittered across the tiles. Two éclairs landed face down below the table, splattering fresh cream up Charlie's Sunday-best trousers, and a coconut puff disintegrated on impact with the table leg.

'Ooops-a-daisy!' Sadie exclaimed, swooping down to the floor. She scooped up the meringues and blew specks of dust off them. 'No harm done — good as new!'

I bent down and picked up the eclairs. A long strand of hair stuck to one of them and I turned to the sink and tried to discreetly remove it, knowing Mother wouldn't tolerate waste. I waited for the onslaught. It never came but her silence grew louder. Then Sadie launched into a verse of 'Nearer My God To Thee' in a key far beyond her range, and Charlie began to giggle inwardly, his shoulders going up and down. I haphazardly arranged the buns on a plate and put them on the table, gesturing for Willy to take a seat as I went and stood by the range. Sadie handed out the teacups and broke off her hymn before the high bit in the chorus.

'Beautiful service, wasn't it?' she said, sitting beside her husband. 'Those Aldergrove ones are great singers, must say. Great tug-o-war team they have too, haven't they, Frank?'

'Awhuh,' Frank replied, half a currant square in his mouth and his eyes still on his folded newspaper.

Mother clattered her cup down on her saucer. Sadie flinched.

'Is there anything the matter, Elva?' she asked in a small voice.

Mother's lips twitched downwards as she spoke.

'I didn't see anything beautiful about that bloody farce. In fact I've never been as affronted in my life.'

Willy and Sadie exchanged quick looks.

'Oh I didn't mean it that way, Elva. It . . . it must've been awkward for you, right enough.'

'And not one of you to stand up for me!' Mother intoned, her eyes glittering.

The tension in the room had finally

snapped. Frank calmly picked up his paper and walked out, throwing Willy a box of matches on the way. Charlie shuffled in his seat, then snatched a cherry top and followed Frank out.

Mother raised her cup to her lips, looking scornfully from Sadie to Willy. Once again, in the space of an hour, I found myself observing a drama with Mother in a starring role. Sadie began to blink like a Christmas tree light and wrinkled her high sloping forehead in confusion.

'What do you mean, Elva?' Willy piped up. 'Sure there was nothing we could do.'

'You could've backed me up, that's what you could've done,' she shot back, a tiny spray of icing sugar flying from the corner of her mouth.

'Now, Elva — I spoke up when I could but that other stuff you were saying, well that's none of our business.'

'It's every Catholic's business when one of them turns his back on the religion and then has the cheek to . . . Jesus! Do I have to spell it out again? You were supposed to be one of James's best friends, Willy Mulholland, never mind being his second cousin, and you stood there in front of his grave and let his name be insulted, and let me be insulted — '

'Elva, I'm powerful vexed that you'd think

that of us,' Sadie interrupted, slowly shaking her head.

'And have none of you a thing to say about that dirty clart Ginny Wilson standing up at our grave, and her big belly and that bust bulging out of that indecent dress, making a mockery out of the whole thing? Well?'

'Right enough, suppose Sean shouldn't have brought her,' Willy agreed quietly.

Mother's voice rose in a sarcastic sneer. 'And imagine that Saul one going and bloody attending her! And us saved the scitter's life! And those wee children being brought up as Presbyterians. Frigging Paisleyites! I'm telling you, James would've been wriggling in the ground below them, and nobody but me with a word to say. When I think of it!'

I shifted my weight from one foot to another, awaiting the well-worn diatribe.

'My father and your father and theirs before them working until it killed them in that oul' mill, humping hundredweight bags all their miserable lives till their backs were broke, for the sake of a few shillings. Worked like a dog, my father did. They could only get the dirty jobs, the Catholics. And our Sean and our Malachy, God love them, walking to the metal foundry to beg for a job, and the damn war on, and them a notice up on the door saying 'No Catholic need apply'. And our Malachy having to join the frigging air force to earn a shilling. Jesus, when I think of it. What we suffered, nobody knows.'

Mother's face was radiant with indignation. The years had failed to quell her bitterness, and it was the emotion with which she was most at home. Willy tapped his pipe against the side of his broad brown hand.

'Aye, that's the God's truth,' he said. 'But them civil rights crowd's not going to stand for the like of that now. Them ones with a bit of education behind them, like we never got. He's a good talker, that Hume, and your man Currie gave them some doing in Cookstown about giving the council house to the wee Prod secretary when there was a whean of families waiting on one. You know that's — '

'And do you really mean to tell me that I should be even thinking of giving our fields to the likes of them?' Mother interrupted, her voice shrill.

'Nobody said that, Elva,' Willy replied.

'Sure nobody wanted to make a scene, Elva,' Sadie added.

'A scene?' Mother snapped, mocking Sadie's small voice. 'It was them who were making a holy show of themselves, and her ready to drop, right there. An expecting woman with a stomach like that shouldn't be seen out. She's only a tramp. Sure she couldn't wait to get married before she lay with a man.'

Sadie reddened slightly and fidgeted with the teaspoon on her saucer. Mother took a sip from her cup and grimaced.

'That tea's stone cold.'

Sadie sprang up and flicked the switch on the kettle. Willy re-lit his pipe and turned sideways in his chair to watch an army helicopter fly over the lough.

'Getting ready for the twelfth, them boys. Suppose half the country'll be out painting and mowing this week.'

'Sure they'd near wash the blooming lawns for the twelfth,' Sadie said with a small nervous laugh. 'Mind you, they're fairly tidy, the Protestants. Keep lovely gardens.'

Mother's eyebrows flew up, wrinkling her carefully powdered forehead. 'Haven't they the best places in the country? Sure this land wasn't worth a damn until James got to work on it, weeding night and day, and he'd be up all hours keeping an eye on the pigging sows and the cows. He couldn't afford some lackey to do it for him, like they could.'

Sadie came over and insisted on refilling my cup. I wanted to run and escape the bile.

'And that frigger McIntosh down the road sitting on that lovely meadow beside ours, not a pick of interest in it, and wouldn't sell it to you if you gave him a million. Oh they'll let the land to you all right, but they'll never sell it to a Catholic.'

Willy frowned. From the set of his mouth I could see irritation creeping up on him.

'Now, Elva, that's just the Orangemen. Didn't Horace Pinkerton buy the slaughter-house on James's behalf when he was in the pigs, and him with the house coming down with pictures of the Queen.'

'It suited Pinkerton to keep in with James,' Mother scoffed. 'He made a killing at the markets out of the fresh pork. And he made sure he got a cut out of the bacon sent to England. Everybody knows he only went on the boat over with James to get himself inveigled into the deal.'

Willy opened his mouth and raised his hand as if to refute this but stopped when he caught Sadie shaking her head at him. Mother's eyes had grown wide and fierce again, like a hammy actor's. I knew she enjoyed these rants. I knew the rhythms of them, the shrill outrage, the high-pitched sarcasm, the ugly mocking tone and the constantly accusing stance, as if whomever she was addressing was in league with the subject of her wrath and derision. In that moment I saw that she was putting on an act of sorts, knowing she'd get more attention from giving off than from being nice. She was bullying Willy into silence, so she could continue her performance.

'When I think of the good hard pigs we kept, and the balls that Sean made of them, keeping them locked up in their own dirt, with no room to lie down. And us had them trained only to do their business in the dunging passage. You only had to show them once and they never went anywhere else. All you had to do was put a wee bit of dung on a piece of straw in the passage and they knew. I'm telling you, those pigs were far cleaner and smarter than bloody Sean.'

The truth, I reminded myself, was Mother didn't even like the pigs, and Frank couldn't bear the squeals of them when they were being killed. The minute they saw the stun gun they knew what they were in for. So Daddy gave the business over to Sean, as a sop after he was left out of the will.

'Sure at the end of the day they did the Catholics a favour not giving them jobs,' Sadie piped up. 'Forced them to make something out of themselves instead of slaving for them, wouldn't you say so, Willy?

'Aye, but Sean hasn't the contacts James had in the business. He couldn't get a good bit of land to rear them right. Mind you, they say Ginny's not bad at handling the pigs, no offence, Elva.'

Mother slammed the palms of her hands on the table. 'He was too lazy to get off his ass, you mean! Jesus, if I'm not sick of people making excuses for yon. You don't know what you're talking about — sure what do you know?'

I'd never heard Mother say 'ass' before and her vehemence spurred me into speaking up.

'But, Mother, Willy was only saying — '

'Don't you dare contradict me!' she shouted, springing to her feet.

Her fury brought out a hint of masculinity in the set of her well-sculpted jaw and in her upright posture. Her neck jutted out like a dog's barking at a stranger.

Sadie took a step towards her. 'Elva, for God's sake, calm down — we're all on your side,' she pleaded.

'That's it! I've had enough of the whole damn lot of you — get out of here this minute. Out! Out!'

I watched in disbelief as she pulled Willy up by his sleeve and pushed Sadie and him out the door. Then she grabbed me by my sleeve and shoved me into the hall behind them. Willy stumbled on the back doorstep and fell into the yard, his pipe flying out of his mouth. Sadie and I helped him up as Mother slammed the door behind us.

'Jesus, that's a madwoman,' Willy gasped, bending down to pick up the pipe. 'She needs a cooling in the lough, that's what she needs. I'd dunk her in headfirst if I could get the hold of her, twist her round by those skinny ankles. I'd soon put manners on her, so I would.'

I began to giggle. Willy looked at me in surprise, then Sadie threw her head back and cackled. Willy scratched the side of his head, making his cap move up and down.

'Jesus, you're all mad. I'm away home the hell or that.'

He took off, still muttering. Shaking with laughter, Sadie linked my arm and led me on to the verandah. We sat on the rocking seat and I felt high and disloyal at the same time. I envied Sadie her life away from here and the smile slipped from my face as I imagined going back into the house. Sadie squeezed my arm.

'Don't fret, love. It's the change, Grace. It's her time, you see. Don't you worry, it will pass. All things pass.'

6

Yes, Ignatius, my heart went out to you that day. You were such an appealing little boy. Don't see much of that child in you now, though. Just the same crabby look of your father — oh, there's no need to come any closer, I prefer you at a distance.

You're not supposed to sit on the bed, you know. You're invading my personal space bubble. I wish those nurses would tuck my arms under the sheet instead of leaving them out, all bare and vulnerable.

What are you looking at anyway with those biscuity-rimmed eyes of yours? And you've a big groove scorching down your brow, just like Frank's. Too much frowning. I can smell dried-in dung off your jeans. Very organic. Not as unpleasant as the human variety, I must admit, but not very hygienic in a hospital ... Something else too ... Brylcreem, I think, and fried bacon. You can tell a lot about a man by the smell of him ... all right, what are you fumbling in your pocket for? Are you going to knife me or something? You couldn't get away with that in here, sure that would be stupid ...

What is that? Oh! Oh, I don't believe it. How did you find it?

I haven't even touched it myself in thirty years. Damn you. You couldn't violate me more if you pulled down the blankets and peed on me. What's this? Trying to hypnotise me, are you? . . . It's pretty, the way it catches the light . . . but you can swing it there all you like — you're not going to put me under a spell —

'Ignatius! What on earth are you doing?'

Georgina comes in and stands at the end of the bed.

'Just testing her. I reckon she's fooling us all lying there. Knows damn well what's going on round her.'

'But Ignatius, look how frail she is! We don't want to upset her, no matter what, do we? We have to tread carefully . . . '

'What do you mean?'

'Oh . . . just — it's best to keep things friendly.'

Ignatius leans forward and brings the locket closer to Grace's face, until it is swinging past the end of her nose.

'Come on cousin dear — wakey-wakey. Wake up and tell us your secrets. Where did you get this, then? Rob it, did you? Oh now. Heard all about you and your light fingers. Robbed the town blind, I believe . . . '

'Ignatius! Really!'

'She did, you know. The butcher's wife told me all about it. Caught red-handed she was, regular. Pockets full of stuff from the chemist. God knows what else she's nicked in her time.' He leans closer, almost touching Grace's left hand with his knee. 'But she's not going to rob me the land off me. Yes, Gracie, I'm taking it back and I'm going to pull down the old house and build a new bungalow for myself, and then I'm going to sell off field after field for sites, and then I'll give the shore to the shooters. What do you think of that?'

Georgina moves around to the side of the bed and implores Ignatius to stop, but she is distracted by a tremor in Grace's right hand.

'Yip. Think I'll dig up that wilderness of a garden of yours and cut down those crags of trees. Stop those frigging birds squawking — '

Georgina steps back in surprise as Grace's arm suddenly shoots up and she snatches the locket, closing her hand around it in a thin tight fist. Her eyelids lift only slightly, but her gaze is direct.

'Get — your — ugly — face — out — of — here . . . '

Her voice is slightly slurred but distinct. Ignatius flinches, his eyes widening and shoulders jerking back. He releases the chain and stands up.

178

'I — I . . . didn't I tell you she was putting it on!' he shouts.

'Just get out, would you,' Georgina shouts back, aware of the ECG monitor beeping rapidly. A nurse, followed by a doctor, burst into the room.

'What's going on here?' the doctor snaps, rushing in to take Grace's pulse. The nurse elbows past Georgina and looks down into Grace's eyes. They are fixed.

'Pupils dilated — fibrillation increasing — muscular contraction in the left hand,' she says as she tries to guide Grace's arm back on to the bed.

As the voices around her merge into a slow deep echo in the distance, Grace tightens her grip on the locket and sees the boy who wore it, wading into the lough, the sun on his back, gold glints in his hair. His whole life in front of him.

PART TWO

PART TWO

7

It was the hottest day of the year. Even Mother was in the water, paddling along with her skirt hitched up below her slim knees, her lovely face in the shade of a huge floppy hat. The Mulhollands' tiny stretch of shore, being fairly sandy, was open house to all the neighbours on a hot Bank Holiday. Sadie held court from her deck chair in the middle of the small gathering, while Charlie bobbed along in the water with a tyre around his waist to keep him afloat. I would have preferred if they'd all chosen another patch further away, but as long as they kept out of our bit of shore and away from our shooting hut, I could live with it. I lay on my stomach on a rug on the other side of the low wooden fence which divided our patch from the Mulhollands' and tried to read my book, but I was distracted by the constant disturbance to my left. Tinny pop songs blared out from transistor radios, and the McNicholl children whooped and splashed in the water. I watched them from behind a pair of plastic Jackie-O sunglasses I'd taken from the market. Ivy Best was wearing a pair nearly the same, and they looked good on her. Earlier she'd made quite an entrance, sauntering along in a yellow bikini, her breasts like hard pears on a narrow slab of toffee, snake hips swaying. Her exotic beauty seemed out of place in this peasant place, and the light growth of dark downy hair in her armpits made her look wanton and free.

She and Saul had been as thick as thieves since they'd become the heroes of the hour on Cemetery Sunday. They huddled together among the bean plants and went for endless walks. From my bedroom I could hear them laughing on the verandah at night, and I was always relieved when I heard him come back after walking her home.

Frank had to persuade Mother to let Saul stay on to help him on the farm, pleading the shortage of hired help. It would have been a very different story if she'd known that he'd helped deliver Ginny's new baby two hours after Cemetery Sunday. He'd held her hand, Frank told me, and he'd said it was the first time in his life he'd been completely awestruck. He never confided the experience to me, and as Mother forbade any mention of Uncle Sean and Ginny in the house, I never got to hear the whole gory story.

And now as I watched him wade out waist-high in the water, I knew he'd never tell me what really brought him to Half Moon Lake, or what he was running away from.

Ivy slunk in after him. I tried not to look as she swam out to where he stood, looking out towards the island, but I couldn't stop myself. She glided along in an effortless breaststroke and flipped on to her back beside him. He slipped his hands under the arch of her back and guided her around in a circle. I couldn't make out his or her expression but I imagined, with a shudder, what was happening in his togs.

I put my book down and rested my chin on my folded arms, and closed my eyes against the languid sight of them. I resented the heat for making people lazy and sexy, and silly, and I was gratified to hear Josie yoo-hooing like a cuckoo to Ivy, and beckoning to her from the water's edge.

'You're wanted at home, love,' she called out as Ivy reluctantly waded towards her. 'Your mother needs you to make sandwiches for the whist.'

I smiled despite myself. I usually got that job, but Mother had fallen out with the whist co-ordinator and hadn't been going to the recent games. I waited until Ivy flounced off, then sat up to look out for Saul. He had swum out further, near to where Charlie had drifted, and seemed to be talking to him.

185

I picked up my book but the print was dazzling through the cheap lenses of my sunglasses, and my head was too cooked to take in a word. I shifted in discomfort as I felt a puddle of sweat spill over from bellybutton under my sensible navy swimsuit. I'd kept on my shorts to hide the hair that would not be held in, and which I despised as much as warts, but I was so uncomfortable I had an urge to strip off and plunge into the water. I felt the sun rushing me and forcing me up, and everything — the air, the noise, the water, the paddlers — seemed to quicken around me, as if there was far too much going on, far too fast.

I shot over the grass tufts and the assortment of flat and pointy stones to the water. The initial coolness of it took me by surprise and momentarily quelled my headiness. I hunched my shoulders and ploughed in, butting my toes on the larger stones for the first few yards before the water deepened and the bottom became smooth and sandy. Then the old fear of treading on an eel hit me and I cut through the water towards the shooting hut, dragging the water in slooshes behind my knees. I was aware that I could have been attracting attention from the Mulhollands' shore but I was too hot to care.

A stray cloud passed over the sun as I

climbed through the flap into the hut and in the lessened glare I suddenly felt exposed and conspicuous. It was easier to hide in the full blast of disorienting heat. I peeped back at the shore through the spyholes at the back of the hut and reassured myself that no eyes had followed me. Then, bam! The sun burst back, fiercer than ever, with a fast, urgent sort of heat.

I pushed my sunglasses on to my head and stretched out on a narrow bench along the wall, aware of my quickened breathing from the exertion and the thick hot air. The dense silvery green water, visible between the wooden slats beneath me, glimmered and lapped casually against the foundation legs of the hut, and earwigs and the odd fly zigzagged across the tin walls. In my new-found solitude, the jangly music from the shore and the children's shrieks became muffled and the world slowed down again. I pushed down my shorts and kicked them off, taking a halting sigh as some comfort returned.

Alone with the cobalt blue sky, I lay with one arm dangling at my side, the other draped across my middle. I relaxed my shoulders against the bench and closed my eyes, and followed the melody of a song wafting faintly in the air.

The mild lulling of the water all around me lent a sensation of movement and gradually the shore seemed to slip further into the distance, as I let the sun seduce me. I must have drifted off quickly because I didn't hear a thing until the flap squeaked open and a long tanned leg appeared through it. Saul grinned down at me.

'So this is where you're hiding.'

I automatically drew up my knees and pushed my sunglasses down over my eyes.

'I'm not hiding,' I replied, my voice an octave higher than usual. 'Just getting a bit of peace.'

'Oh — all right — I'll be off then — '

'No — stay!' I squeaked, arching my back awkwardly and sitting up on the bench. Without my shorts, I could only clasp my hands in my lap to cover the hated hair, and hope desperately that he wouldn't notice it. By the slow shake of his head and upturned corners of his mouth, I saw he'd been joking. He slouched down beside me and gently slapped my leg.

'Better watch you don't burn up there, baby.'

I looked down at my pinkening flesh and could think of nothing but our last sow. I cleared my throat in an attempt to keep my voice normal. 'You're lucky you're dark-skinned. Where do you get that from anyway?

'Oh I reckon there's a bit of Spanish sailor in me, from generations back. The Armada sunk off the coast near where the ancestors came from, you see.'

'Oh.'

He was slouching so close that my ample thigh was within a cat's whisker of his waist. 'But you never know. Could be just an old yarn. God, I wish I had a hat — oh these will do. Do you mind?'

He reached down and picked up my discarded shorts and put them on his head, arranging the legs over his eyes. I swallowed hard and silently prayed they weren't malodorous.

'Yeah — there's more than one way into a girl's pants,' he said, his nose poking out from the crotch of the shorts.

I giggled, more at the look of him than at his smutty joke, and leaned back against the hot tin wall. Overhead a helicopter hovered.

'Keeping an eye on us, are they?' Saul asked.

'They fly over here all the time. It gets worse coming up to the twelfth.'

With his eyes shielded by the shorts, I sneaked a look at him out of the side of my eye. His bruises had faded and tiny droplets of water wobbled on the fine dark hair on his lean forearms and legs. The top button of his cut-off jeans lay open, exposing a fuzz-encircled bellybutton, and his nipples were small and jutting, miniature like football studs. I looked away quickly when he started to yawn.

'Do you hear that carry-on?' he jabbered behind the yawn.

I listened but heard nothing but the whirring of the helicopter.

'There it is again — it's coming from over there,' he said, gesturing to his left with his thumb.

'Yes, I hear it now — sounds like Charlie messing around. He's usually very quiet but he gets a bit rowdy sometimes.'

'Yeah — he was swigging a beer earlier on. God, I'm tired.'

He yawned again and slunk down further on the bench, and we fell into an easy silence. But the heat began to make me fidgety and prickly, so I stepped over to the other side of the hut, pulling my swimsuit down on to my hips as far as it would go, resisting the urge to scratch an itch on the back of my legs. I knelt on the bench and squinted through a gunhole in the wall, smelling lead from it. Out on the water to my far left, I could just about make out Charlie in his tyre, waving and hollering at the circling helicopter. He slid out of view and I turned my eyes straight ahead to the island in the distance, imagining how its wild garlic, sodden for the previous week, would reek on a day like this.

For a moment I was lost in a memory of playing there as a child, and falling into the foundations of the round tower, and trying not to cry as I screamed for help. What seemed like hours later Charlie and Frank had got me out, Frank climbing down and hoisting me up on his shoulders, Charlie nearly pulling my arms out of their sockets as he hauled me up. Frank and I were sent to bed without dinner that night, for being late home.

A sudden awareness of being watched snapped me out of the reverie. I dropped to my hunkers and half turned on the bench, crossing my arms over my groin. At least I didn't have to worry about wobbling breasts, for the severity of my swimsuit flattened them down. Saul now had my shorts around his neck and I was compelled to fill the new silence.

'He seems to have quietened down again . . . that's some racket he was making, wasn't it?'

He nodded and I twittered on.

'Pity Ivy had to go. Imagine having to stand making sandwiches on a day like this.'

'Mmm.'

'Is she coming back later?'

'Where?'

'Here, or . . . our house — to meet you, I mean . . . '

I bit my lip in annoyance at myself. Saul slipped on to his knees, letting the shorts slide off his shoulders, and shuffled across the slats until he was facing me.

'She doesn't own me, you know.'

He looked me square in the face. I flinched as he reached out and stroked my flushed cheek.

'Oh Grace. There's something I've got to tell you.'

My arms went stiff with panicky excitement. I hunched my shoulders and stared down at my knees.

'God, you're such a funny girl,' he said. 'Don't you know how pretty you are?'

His fingers moved from my cheek to my chin, and tilted up my face. As I met his eyes he leaned forward and kissed me full on the mouth, a big honest clamp of a kiss that made my right haunch zing. I'd only been kissed once before, by a spotty schoolboy with a mouth still wet from slobbering over another girl on a bus trip home from the Knock shrine. Now I sat rigid as Saul's lips slid from my mouth to neck, one hand around my waist and the other behind my neck. I felt the flush in my cheeks darken and a tide of tickles threatening to spasm my shoulders. His hair smelled like olive oil. My hands fluttered uselessly in my lap as I strove single-mindedly against the ticklishness, but when his lips reached my ear, I burst out into gasping laughter, involuntarily turning and jerking up my shoulder, knocking him under his chin and making his teeth snap together.

I clamped my hand over my mouth in mortification, but before I could say sorry, he pushed me flat back against the bench and straddled me.

'Got the tickles, have we? Well how do you like this!'

His fingers dug into my sides, tickling them mercilessly. I grabbed at his wrists and tried to push him off but he was too quick and strong. I laughed so hard my face was sore and my legs kicked out wildly against the tin. Dizzy and mad for him to stop, I managed to get one hand under his armpit and tickle him back, but in an instant he had both my wrists pinned above my head. He put his mouth back on my neck, driving my nerve endings into a frenzy of tickles. I was in heaven and hell at the same time, and when I heard my name being called, I thought I was imagining it. The second time, I heard Saul's name too, and I knew it was for real.

Saul jumped up and stood on the other bench, peeping over the wall.

'Yeah — over here,' he yelled. 'Grace's here too.'

'Get out of there right now,' I heard my mother shout. 'Charlie's missing!'

I froze. Saul stepped down from the bench and looked at me in alarm. He lifted the shorts and thrust them at me before ducking through the flap.

I pulled them on in a daze and followed him out. The helicopter still hovered overhead and I had to shout.

'He was out that direction — that chopper might have seen where he went — he could just have drifted over to the other side of the pier . . . '

'You go and tell the others and I'll swim out,' he said quickly, lunging into the water.

I turned sheepishly towards the shore, where everyone was now standing, shielding their eyes against the wallop of the sun. Sadie stood with Josie linking her at the water's edge, her hands clasped in front of her mouth. The children had been called in from the water and the Mullen men were running across our shore towards the boats moored at the pier. Only Mother was left in the water, waiting for me. For half a moment I hesitated, considering following Saul, but I knew I would be useless, for I couldn't bear to swim under the water. Then as I waded in towards the shore, it hit me that Charlie had not been fooling around in the water. He'd been in trouble with the tyre, and as I met my mother's appalled eyes, I knew that it was too late. He'd been under too long.

'What the hell were you doing out there?' she hissed as I drew level with her.

'Nothing . . . I was just sitting in the hut. I — '

'Did you not hear or see anything, and you the nearest to him? Too busy enjoying yourself with that fella, were you? Jesus, we'll be the talk of the country . . . '

I hung my head. 'I wasn't doing anything wrong — I thought Charlie was only carrying on . . . maybe he's drifted on round the other side of the bay . . . maybe — '

'Get out of my sight. Go and put your clothes on and keep your mouth shut.'

I ran over to the fence and climbed over it, getting my ankles stung in a bunch of nettles on the other side. My mouth constricted absurdly as I battled tears and the rising nausea in my gut. I snatched my shirt and buttoned it up to my neck, squinting at the water through smarting eyes. The Mullens' boat was nearing Saul and the spot where I thought I'd last seen Charlie, but it was hard to tell exactly from the shore.

Saul dove under for unbearably long minutes at a time. I pictured Charlie in the murk, his curly hair floating out from his head like a Medusa, his mouth open in a silent scream. I imagined eels nosing past him and flicking his body with their slithering tails, and there I was, only yards away, laughing like a fiend with somebody else's boyfriend . . .

My stomach lurched and I tried to pray but couldn't think of the words. It had gone eerily quiet on the shore, the only sound coming from Father O'Loan shuffling down from the bank. I watched despairingly as Sadie suddenly broke away from Josie and walked dazedly into the water, her sandals still on. Mother turned and took hold of her arm, stopping her from wading out further. They had not spoken since Cemetery Sunday. They huddled together as if it was cold, even as the sun grew fiercer. I couldn't bear another minute on my own, so I climbed back over the fence and walked over to Josie. My lip quivered uncontrollably when she looked at me.

'Oh Grace, he's been under too long,' she whispered behind her spindly steepled hands. 'We thought he was only codding, splashing about out there. He'd been yo-ho'ing at the 'copter. Sure how were we to know . . . '

I felt a small desperate surge of selfish relief rush to my head. 'That's what I thought too, I . . . and then with the noise of the helicopter, I couldn't hear him and . . . I forgot all about him.'

'Aye, but Grace, you weren't that far away from him out there . . . could you not have . . . ?'

I closed my eyes against her child-like questioning face and swallowed hard.

'Oh Grace . . . you and that fella? Oh, never mind. Look — he's doing the best he can out there now. He's the only one can swim, for God's sake. Come on, pray. Oh most tender and loving Virgin Mother, that never was it known, that anyone who fled to thy protection was left unaided . . . '

Josie's prayer was drowned out by the sudden blare of a motorboat taking off from the pier. All eyes watched it bounce along the water, and then a strange thing happened. The sun disappeared behind a phalanx of solid white cloud that came out of nowhere, but instead of coming out the other side, the sun stayed hidden behind it. The air remained stifling but a light breeze rippled the water and the light went flat. Then, as the motorboat came to a halt beside the Mullens', Saul yelled out.

'Here — over here! Down here!'

Later he would tell me how he'd had Charlie by the hair but couldn't get one of his feet untangled from the weeds, and how, when they pulled his body out, his eyes were staring in that funny confused way of his.

All Josie and I could see from the shore was Charlie's wet curly head flung down on his chest as Saul and the motorboat driver hoisted him up, and then the white lifeless legs and feet splayed apart, as the Mullens hauled him in.

Sadie's awful scream curdled the air. Mother put both arms around her neck and led her out of the water and into Father O'Loan's waiting embrace, but she slid down on to her knees and started to pound his feet, wailing like a blackout siren, her mouth wide open like an infant's.

I watched her in horror until Mother pulled me aside.

'Well I hope you're proud of yourself,' she hissed. 'Get you back to the house and don't dare show your face out your bedroom door till I tell you. Tramp, you.'

'Oh Elva, don't be so hard on the girl — '

'Keep out of this Josie, please,' Mother snapped, shoving me backwards.

I turned and raced towards the bank, stumbling over sand buckets and almost

knocking over one of the youngest Mc-
Nicholls. At the top of the bank my stomach
buckled and I vomited until I could only
retch. I ran through a gap in the hedge to our
field, stopping only to catch my ragged breath
at the foot of the silo. From there I watched
the two boats slowly crossing back to the pier,
and then the sun came back, as if everything
was all right again. Once more the water
sparkled invitingly, a radiant seductress with a
dirty black heart. I lumbered to the house,
slowed down by an acute stitch in my side. I
got into bed and shivered uncontrollably.

Outside the sun began its slide to the west
and a helicopter flew eastwards, fast.

8

This dark aloneness is not unfamiliar. I am crouched on an ocean floor, I am far under the ground, yet uncrushed by the weight above me. Perhaps I am back in the womb, waiting to be reborn. But I am an old soul, and my head feels huge, the size of a television. I am deep within it, running through black halls, shutting doors behind me that will not open again. I take a turn and fall and spin into a void. The whirl subsides and I am still again, waiting in the dark.

'It will be far worse if you don't show your face, you know.'

My head on the pillow was as heavy as Frank's voice. It was his third attempt to persuade me to go to Charlie's wake.

'Even if you just went in and shook Willy's hand, that'd do. God help him, he's lying up on his couch half dead himself with the shock, trying to make conversation with the people. Get up and get your clothes on. I'll wait for you outside.'

I took the sheet off my face. It'll be all right if you don't have to see Charlie, I told myself over and over again.

I edged out of bed, my limbs leaden and a prickle of dizziness in the crown of my head. Mother hadn't called me to get up and I hadn't eaten in a day and a half. The oily odour of unwashed skin and hair was about me, but I had no energy to bathe. I had watched my body for hours under the sheets and dwelled upon the life force that moved the different parts, that made salty water run out of my eyes, that woke me when all I wanted to do was sleep for a year. Now as I stood up and dressed, I removed myself from my body and scurried back up into my head.

Frank had left the back door open and from the hall I could hear him talking to someone on the verandah.

'Haven't seen him since the drowning. Pity, he was fairly useful about the place, and now with no Charlie . . . '

'I'm telling you, he's brought nothing but bad luck, that stranger. First my Florrie, now young Charlie. Mark my words, there'll be another one. You'll rue the day you let him through your door.'

Bear. I loitered in the hall, loath to face him. I heard the crack of match striking in the still evening air and the creak of the rocking seat as someone got off it.

'Never liked the look of those black eyes of his neither. *Sleekid*-looking.'

'Aye, he's an odd-looking being. But to give him his dues, they say Sean's wife could've lost the child if it wasn't for him.'

'Well that was kinda queer too, if you ask me. What call had he being there in the first place? For all we know, that wee child mightn't have been meant for this world at all, Sean bringing them up Protestant and all. God might've been putting a stop to it, and the stranger interfered.'

Slow clumping footsteps crossed the verandah.

'That's a funny way to be thinking, Bear.'

'Now. That's just the way I see it, Frank. You be careful now. Be seeing you.'

'Right, Bear.'

I waited for a moment before going outside. Frank stood up and stubbed out his cigarette, and we walked in silence up the road. The light had turned tawny and the midges were out in force. Dogs had been locked up in sheds, where they whimpered and yelped, and a line of cars was parked as far up as the Mullens'.

I followed Frank through the Mulhollands' gate, as if someone else's legs were carrying me. The tiny trellised garden was full of mourners and Sadie's cheerful camellias, the air pungent with cigarette smoke and mowed grass. My heart started to jump as the clusters of people parted to let Frank and me through. I made work of buttoning up my jacket to avoid their eyes, acutely aware of the looks and the whispers behind hands, like the breeze zipping past shutters.

I stepped on to Frank's heel as he paused at the front door to let Molly past with a tray of buns. Dalloway stood imperiously inside the doorway, gesturing towards the boxroom opposite him. Through the open door I caught a fleeting glimpse of candlelight glinting off brass coffin-handles, and realised Dalloway was showing us directly into Charlie's bedroom. There was to be no reprieve, no cups of tea with Willy and time to prepare. I shuffled in behind Frank. Sadie sat wan-faced in the gloom to the right of the coffin, whispering prayers, her eyes shut tight like slits in an uncooked apple tart. She swayed slightly back and forth, her hands locked around her sunburned wrists.

Josie stood quietly near the foot of the coffin. It was white and meant for a child. She had her index finger to her mouth and was shaking her head to indicate that we should not disturb Sadie. Frank stepped up to the left side of the coffin and blessed himself. I stiffly copied his every move but I could not look at Charlie's face. My eyes would go no further than his waxy clasped hands. I had never seen his chunky fingers and bitten nails so clean and still, and I became gripped by the idea that those hands weren't his at all. I stared at them so hard I began to see double and triple, and when I brought my eyes back into focus, there was a dirty black fly crawling over the blue crystal rosary beads which someone, probably Mother, had entwined though Charlie's fingers. I became mesmerised by the fly but had to close my eyes when it began to crawl up the silken shroud towards Charlie's throat. I tried to think of a prayer but my mind drew a blank. Then all of a sudden Mother was beside me, with a rubber fly swat in her hand.

'Take this and go and stand up there with it,' she whispered into my ear. 'Don't let anything light on him.'

She handed me the swat and left the room. For a second I thought she was joking, but Josie was nodding at me, and Frank had stepped back to let me past him. The swat shook in my sweating palm as I inched along the side of the coffin, keeping my eyes on the floor. Sadie prayed on, oblivious, and behind the shaded window someone went into a fit of chesty coughing and spat out the gathered phlegm. At the top of the coffin I turned to face the open door and caught Dalloway looking at me from under his wiry eyebrows.

He looked away quickly and nodded solemnly at new callers at the door.

My hair shook around my face as I looked down into the coffin from my new position, keeping my eyes away from Charlie's face. I stood dumbly with the swat by my side until Frank cleared his throat to draw my attention to the fly, which was impudently fixed on the lace around Charlie's throat. I hesitantly raised the swat and without looking, shook it in the direction of the fly. It shot off immediately and Josie winked at me, but I could see nervousness in her eyes, just like Dalloway's.

The new arrivals were Mrs O'Mahoney and her niece. They came into the room and I became even more painfully awkward, my shoulders raised and stiff, my neck rigid. At least I had something to do with my hands, I thought, absurd though it was.

Mrs O'Mahoney went straight over to Sadie and kissed her on the cheek. Her niece hovered behind her, staring wide-eyed into the coffin. I could see that she felt as out of place as I did. Then she turned and caught sight of me with the swat, and our momentary connection died. She arched a sleek eyebrow and smirked.

'Ach, isn't he just like an angel,' Mrs O'Mahoney gushed.

She'd had no response from Sadie and now she was leaning over the coffin, holding on to the side of it.

'Never seen a lovelier shroud nor lovelier curls on a young fella, God rest him.'

She blessed herself to pray, and I was relieved she'd taken no notice of me. Frank turned to leave and I made a start to follow him but he shook his head, and I took an ungainly step back. A huge bluebottle was now crawling along the far edge of the coffin, and the niece was eagerly watching me. I pretended I hadn't noticed anything and my inner ears began to pop, as if I was at high altitude.

All at once the strain of not looking at Charlie's face, and my screeching self-consciousness gathered in a fist in my throat and a faint sob escaped from it. The top of my head prickled and a film of hot tears blurred my eyes as I struggled to keep in the sounds from my throat and keep track of the fly and the bluebottle. Suddenly they both darted on to Charlie's hands and in a split second of impulse, I brought the swat down on top of them, flattening them on to the rosary beads.

The bluebottle's ruby red guts splayed out on to Charlie's fingers and splattered on to his shroud, and despite myself, I turned and looked at his face, half expecting a reaction. All that registered before I looked away was the strange beige pallor and the firmly shut mouth, as if his lips had been sewn together from the inside.

I stood rooted to the spot, with the swat still raised. Mrs O'Mahoney gasped, staring at me in disbelief. The niece had her hand clamped over her mouth. I glanced fearfully at Sadie but her eyes were still shut, her face unperturbed. Then Josie was beside me, taking me by the arm and leading me out, past a stony-faced Dalloway and the men in the garden, and around to the side of the house. She took the swat off me and leaned me up against the whitewashed gable wall.

'Look, Grace, don't worry,' she said in earnest, rubbing my arm. 'You just need a bit of air — you haven't one bit of colour in those cheeks. Wait there and I'll get you a cup of good sweet tea.'

She hurried off and I slid down the whitewashed wall, the ridges of the rough surface digging into my back. I settled on my hunkers and held my head in my hands for what seemed an age. Then, to my horror, I began to laugh. I imagined Charlie lying giggling in his coffin and that made me worse. I began to shudder, overtaken by images of Mrs O'Mahoney and me dancing around the coffin, swordfighting with fly-swats, and of Josie and Sadie clapping and singing along. I bent over and crossed my arms over my stomach, heaving with the hysteria and giving myself up to it. My ears popped continuously and water poured from my eyes, down my flaming cheeks and into my open mouth. The last thing I saw before the kicking was red painted toenails in a pair of black platform sandals.

'You fucking witch!'

Blood streamed out of my nose and down the back of my throat. The shock of the impact of Ivy Best's foot on my face made me gag for breath and I began to choke. She fell to her knees and pulled my head back by the hair. Her eyes were wild and excited, and I smelled beer on her breath.

'You ugly piece of shit, fucking stupid spastic! What the fuck are you laughing at, you mad cunt? Think it's funny about Charlie, do you?'

As I tried to splutter a denial, she abruptly let me go. Sadie appeared and some of the men who'd been in the garden were watching from the corner.

'Ivy! What on earth's going on?' Sadie cried.

'I found her here laughing her head off! Then she saw me and started thumping herself in the face! She's mad! Bonkers! She's dangerous!'

'Be quiet, Ivy!'

'Grace — is that the truth?'

I looked up at Sadie and saw Mother appear beside her. I began to twitch.

'Oh God, she's taking a fit! Ivy, run and get a spoon!'

Sadie swooped down and eased me on to my side. The twitching turned to trembling.

'My God, that's it,' Mother exclaimed. 'It's come back! That explains . . . oh! . . . go on now everybody, mind your business. She can't help herself, no more than we can. Go on now, back to your business.'

Mother got down on to her knees beside Sadie and felt my pulse, then took off her cardigan and put it behind my head.

'At least it doesn't seem as bad as the ones she used to get, Elva. Ah God love her, all the same. I was sure she was over them.'

'We'll say nothing about it. She won't remember anyway.'

Sadie put her lips close to my ear. 'Don't forget your guardian angel, Grace. He's there minding you.'

I said a silent thank you to a man with the face of Jesus and a pair of luxurious white ostrich wings. In that misread moment, I had been let off the hook and excused of all wrongs. I lay back with glazed eyes and kept up the shaking and the shuddering, and bit down on the tablespoon when it was pushed into my mouth. If there had been anything in my bladder, I might even have wet myself.

After a while I sat up and asked for some water, then Dalloway took me home in his car. I missed the funeral, and the wake was never mentioned again.

★   ★   ★

Mother's diamonds glittered in the sunshine coming through the windscreen. She kept flexing out her finger on the steering wheel to admire them and to show off to Josie. Josie always came to Belfast any time we were going, for the run, she said.

The drive was taking longer than usual. Dalloway had warned us about the IRA man's funeral and we'd taken a circuitous route to the Royal Victoria Hospital.

I walked close in behind Mother and Josie after we parked the car on the Falls Road, afraid of losing them in the crowd, yet wanting to run in the opposite direction to the hospital. The doctor's verdict could put an end to the softest treatment I'd had in ten years and re-open the file of my misde-meanours. I couldn't sleep at all the night beforehand. I was still fixated on Charlie, three weeks after the drowning. I knew this would happen if I saw his dead face, and that I would continue to obsess until his spirit had gone deeper into the ether. It even happened with people I didn't know, like film stars. I dragged my feet along, grateful at least for the illusion of malady brought on by my deep fatigue.

We were approaching the ornate hospital gates when a man in a too-tight denim jacket came up to us with a leaflet.

'You're all invited to Mossie Quinn's funeral. Will you show your support for the cause, missus?'

Mother took the leaflet from the man and without looking at it, handed it to Josie.

'Excuse me, my daughter has an urgent doctor's appointment and we've no time,' she said in her town voice, marching on ahead.

Josie smiled nervously at the man as we followed Mother.

'You can always come afterwards,' the man called after us.

We caught up with Mother at the swinging doors.

'That's all we need, going to the funeral of some bloody back-streeter,' she said out of the corner of her mouth. 'Sure they're only making themselves as bad as the other side.

Right, we've to go to the fifth floor in the old wing — I'm taking the stairs. You go in the lift if you want.'

We watched her march off to the entrance to the stairs before getting into the lift. The range of her prejudice never failed to surprise me.

'Don't know where she gets the energy from, your mother,' Josie said, pressing the button marked five.

'She's claustrophobic,' I said, leaning against the mirrored wall inside the lift.

Josie looked at me sharply, making her small face even more beaky. 'You know, you've a lot to thank your mother for, Grace. She's a good woman, and she done well getting you educated till eighteen at all.'

I wanted to retort that I didn't need reminded but the respectful look in Josie's marble green eyes stopped me. 'I know. It's . . . it's just a pity I couldn't have gone on to college.'

'Well, it's not my place to say. Sure you're needed at home.'

The lift doors opened with a jolly ping. Mother was already in the ugly windowless waiting area, casing the joint like a cat. Josie and I sat on uncomfortable orange plastic chairs while she announced our arrival to the receptionist. We were ten minutes early and I watched every stroke on the clock on the custard yellow wall until eleven. Josie flicked through a dog-eared magazine and Mother drummed her fingers on her handbag, watching tentative-faced patients arrive and young nurses push trolleys down the corridor. At ten past eleven, the receptionist called out my name. Mother was on her feet immediately.

'Come on, over here,' she ordered, heading over to the reception area.

'OK,' said the receptionist. 'It's Dr Kennedy — room 3A. No need for you to accompany your daughter if she's over sixteen, Mrs Kane.'

'Oh, but I really would prefer to. I was a nurse, you see.'

I dug my nails into my palms. The receptionist looked over the top of her over-sized spectacles at me, then back at Mother.

'Eh . . . oh, I see. Well, I suppose it's all right.'

Mother led the way to the room and knocked on the door. The doctor was writing notes on a loose page and with a wave of his arm absently invited us to take a seat by the door. The room was the shape of a small batch loaf, with cracks on the curved ceiling above the sash window. An examination bed stood along one wall, opposite the doctor's desk and chair.

We waited in silence for two or three minutes. Mother patted the sides of her hair and ran her tongue along the teeth under her top lip. Eventually the doctor tucked his pen into the thin white tuft of hair above his right ear and surveyed us through glasses as thick as ice cubes. The pate of his head was bald and candy pink, his accent anglicised.

'Right — which one of you two ladies is Grace, then?'

Mother gave an unnecessary little tiff-tiff of a laugh. 'Oh this is Grace, doctor. I'm Elva Kane.'

'Right. Well I see from your records, Grace, that it's quite some time since your last convulsion. Now, tell me your sins.'

I gaped at him in confusion. Mother tiff-tiffed again.

'Only joking, dearie! Don't look so frightened — I won't eat you.'

I blushed puce and tried to smile.

'She's a nervous type, doctor — always has been. She hasn't had a fit since she was twelve, until a fortnight ago, that is.'

'Hmmm. What exactly happened, pray tell.'

I listened to Mother relate the incident in careful, long-winded detail.

'And what do you recall, Grace?' the doctor asked.

'I don't remember anything,' I said in a small voice that took me back to myself at five or six, in another doctor's surgery, in another hospital far from here.

'Okey-doke. Well, roll up that sleeve and we'll take your blood pressure.'

My sunburned skin flaked as I pushed up the tight sleeve of the new white blouse Mother had bought me for the appointment. The doctor strapped on a black belt contraption and began to slowly pump it up, and I had to bite my lip against the sensation of my arm exploding.

'Mmmm. No problem there. Jump up on the bed, would you, dear?'

I took off my shoes and he pulled a curtain across the bed. It was my cue to switch off. For the next five minutes, while he probed and prodded, I took myself off to the Yorkshire moors to meet Heathcliff. When I'd done with him, I ran off to Manderley and became the new Mrs de Winter. I was having such a good time, I was reluctant to leave when the examination was over.

The doctor gave Mother a prescription and bade us good day. I sensed the shift in her immediately. The doctor couldn't give her a diagnosis, therefore there mustn't be too much wrong with me. And although she despised the state to which I was reduced by the fits of my childhood, this wasn't what she wanted to hear.

Back in the waiting room, Josie was deep in conversation with an obese woman in a purple dress. She had a hard flat Belfast accent and was giving Josie directions.

'If I was you I'd get a move on before the stones start flying,' she said as Josie stood up to leave. 'You culchies don't know the half of it.'

Mother gave the woman one of her derisory looks and put her arm behind Josie's back to direct her out.

'Come on, Josie,' she said brightly. 'We'll go and have a bite to eat downtown.'

The fat woman harrumphed and shook her head.

There was a queue for the lift, so we followed Mother downstairs, our six heels clattering like maracas all the way down. Outside Mother told Josie to keep the third of October free for the next appointment, as if she was organising a day out. I dawdled along behind them, filled with relief. At least the doctor hadn't exposed me as a fake.

'If we hurry now we'll get in to The Viking before the lunchtime rush,' Mother said, fishing in her handbag for her keys. 'Come on now, smarten up.'

In the car Mother grinned into the driver's mirror to check for lipstick on her teeth and fluffed up her glossy silvery blonde waves with a comb. She drove assuredly out on to the busy road, nosing out into the traffic until a bus driver flashed his lights to let her across to the other side.

'I don't know how you can drive through a big place like this, Elva,' said Josie, in awe. 'Them big buses and lorries would put the fear of God into you.'

'Oh, it's all right as long as you know where you're going,' Mother replied blithely, turning right towards the city centre.

I slouched in the back seat, counting the armed soldiers we passed on the footpaths. They sauntered along in berets and fatigues, ignored by the passers-by. Up close I was surprised to see they were mostly short, and not much older than I was. Josie tutted at the sight of them as Mother parked the car in a side street.

'There's an awful lot of Brits about the day, isn't there, Elva?'

'Bastards,' said Mother. 'Didn't take them long to turn on the Catholics, and them supposed to be here to protect us. Bundle of dirt, the whole lot of them.'

She pulled into a narrow side street close by the City Hall and parked the car. A light sprinkle of rain had begun to fall, freshening the muggy city air. Josie put a see-through plastic hat on her little dark head and tied it under her chin as we crossed Howard Street and made a dash for the smoked-glass-fronted restaurant. Mother pushed the door open with the side of her forearm.

'Easiest way to pick up the cold, touching public door handles,' she said, leading the way through a small foyer and an archway.

Inside, the formally attired maître d' stood by the ornate cash register, slipping freshly typed menus into red leather-bound folders. His clipped black sideburns ran down almost to his well-padded jaw and when he turned to extend a greeting, his lozenge-shaped eyes slid quickly over the three of us before settling back on Mother's carefully made-up face.

'Table for three please,' she said, smiling up at him.

He smiled back, baring plentiful gleaming white teeth, and showed us to a booth upholstered in camel velour, in the middle of the large windowless dining area. From experience, I knew to slip in beside Josie to give Mother a seat to herself. It was not yet lunchtime and there was only a handful of people scattered around us. In one corner, a gaunt elderly man in an evening suit sat at a baby-grand piano, tinkling elevator music on the keys without a trace of passion. But the sound was delicate and lulling, and light from the chandeliers soft and flattering, and the thick pile carpet was soft underfoot.

The maître d' handed out menus and in a BBC voice offered us drinks from the bar.

'No thank you,' Mother replied cheerfully. 'We'll wait.'

I would have died for a cola.

'I'll send your waitress over shortly,' said the maître d', an appraising look in his exotic eyes.

Josie eyed him up and down as he strode away.

'Isn't he just the spit of Engelbert Humperdinck? Isn't he Elva?' she whispered, peeping over her menu like an awestruck teenager with premature wrinkles.

'That's just what I was thinking,' Mother replied, slipping off her jacket. 'A bit on the greasy side, though. Would you take off that hat, Josie — what are you like!'

Josie pulled off the hat and went back to her menu. From one swift glance at my own, I had already chosen what I would have liked, then what I would end up ordering.

An indifferent middle-aged waitress in a

fusspot Danish milkmaid outfit came along with large jugs of iced water and left one on our table. I picked it up and poured for the three of us, my wrist wobbling against the weight of it. Josie thanked me and I gulped back the water, knocking the ice against my teeth. I winced and a trickle of water escaped out of the corner of my mouth and down the side of my chin. I discreetly dabbed it with the side of my index finger and looked around to see if anyone had noticed, but Mother and Josie were still studying their menus as if they were crossword puzzles, and the girl seated nearest to us was reading a magazine.

She wore a cream silk blouse and seemed to be on her own. Her dark hair was scooped up in a bun and I was thinking how elegant she was when she opened her mouth wide and licked her thumb to turn a page. I looked away from her and turned my attention to the piano. The old man had just played a half-hearted flourish at the end of a low-tempo 'Rhapsody in Blue', and was shuffling through the sheet music on the stand. His spindly fingers had the slight tremor of the aged and when there was no applause, I felt a sudden flare of pity for him. No-one was paying any attention to him and I couldn't bring myself to clap. I lifted my glass with the intention of surreptitiously raising it to him while Mother and Josie weren't looking, but he started to play something I didn't recognise and I couldn't catch his eye.

'Where did that waitress go?' Mother said, fanning herself with the menu. I noticed a faint flush on her neck and realised she was feeling hot from the inside. She lifted her glass and pressed it against her neck and cheek.

'Ah, here we are now,' she said, nodding at the maître d', who was sending a waitress down to us. It was the same woman who had brought the water and her expression was as detached as before. She was too flabby and too mature for the fancy low-necked costume and by the look on her bland square face, she knew it.

'Ready to order?' she enquired, politely enough, taking a pen and notepad from her frilly apron pocket. Mother set her menu aside.

'Yes — I'll have a prawn cocktail to start with, then the chicken and bacon with baby potatoes and mixed vegetables.'

'Em, the same for me, thanks very much,' Josie said, smiling at the waitress.

I cleared my throat.

'Soup of the day and salad, please,' I said

quickly, wishing Josie wouldn't look into my face.

The waitress wrote down the order. 'Anything else?

'Not for the moment,' Mother said, taking the menus and handing them over. The waitress took them and walked away, her bare soles slapping against her wooden clogs. Josie was still looking at me.

'Is that all you're having, Grace?' she said, her fine eyebrows raised. 'That'll never fill you. You'll fade away'

'I'm not very hungry. I had — '

'Picky eater, always was,' Mother interrupted. 'Always turned her nose up at our good sprouts, imagine. You'd think you were poisoning her. Yet she'll stuff herself with sweets.'

'Oh well, all the more room for a nice bit of dessert, eh Grace?'

Mother arched an expertly pencilled eyebrow. She took her purse out of her handbag and opened it.

'If I've enough left,' she said primly.

'Oh — I didn't mean that, Elva — I'll pay my share of course,' Josie spluttered.

'No you won't, Josie. My treat.'

'No, Elva, really. I wouldn't dream of it, and that's all about it.'

Mother leaned back in her seat and began

222

to hum along to the music. I excused myself and headed to the ladies at the back of the room, passing the piano on my way. The old man glanced at me with pink-rimmed eyes. I raised my lips at the corners in acknowledgement, but he blanked me.

I hurried on into the olive green cloakroom and ran cold water over my hands. I looked into the mirror and ran my wet hands through my hair and tapped my putty-coloured cheeks. I swallowed hard against the tightness in my throat brought on by the old man's snub, straightened my blouse and walked back out.

The waitress was delivering the starters to the table when I returned.

I spooned the soup into my mouth, vaguely aware of a faint hint of mushroom. Mother and Josie squeezed lemon wedges on to the pink sauce covering the prawns and lettuce in their champagne glasses, and picked up the dainty silver forks from their side plates.

'The frozen variety,' Mother remarked after her first mouthful.

'Oh but it's lovely and tasty all the same,' Josie enthused. 'Would you like to try some, Grace?'

My mouth watered at the thought. 'No thanks.'

The tables had begun to fill up with

lunchtime clientele, their chatter almost drowning out the old man's tepid playing. A bunch of burly grey-haired men in suits was sitting on one side of the girl with the bun hairdo, a couple with a bald baby in a high-chair were on the other side. The girl was reading and eating at the same time, putting chip after chip into her mouth without lifting her head from the page.

Mother scraped her glass clean, despite her objections, and bit into a slice of wheaten bread.

'Not bad, but you can tell it's not home-baked,' she remarked. 'Needs a bit of sugar to make the crust crunchy.'

'Sure you make the best wheaten in the country, Elva,' Josie said. She had a sliver of marie-rose sauce on her bottom lip.

'So I'm told, Josie, so I'm told.'

The waitress appeared with the main courses before the starters' plates had been cleared away. Josie nimbly stacked them up for her and she took them away wordlessly. For some reason I felt sorry for her too.

'Dour one, that,' Mother said, cutting into her chicken.

Garlic butter spurted out on to the plate and I wished Josie would ask if I could try some of hers. She didn't offer and I didn't ask. I played with the limp pre-prepared salad as they ate enthusiastically, mmmm'ing and mopping up their plates with the bread. I forked half a slice of beetroot on to a lump of raw onion, the only items that looked fresh in the salad, and popped them into my mouth. The onion made my nose fizz inside and the beetroot was soggy. I ate on and when I looked up from my plate, the baby in the highchair was grinning at me as if I'd just handed it a packet of sweets.

I smiled back at it in surprise and it shouted 'ba-ba!' and flung its tiny dimpled arm out over the tray of the highchair. The mother put a spoon in its mouth but it continued to stare and grin, with gloopy white food over its gums and lips. It had locked eyes with me and I couldn't look away. I thought it resembled an alien but I was strangely disarmed by the way it kept on looking at me as if it knew me, like there was an old soul behind its eyes, who'd met me in another life.

Mother broke the spell.

'Ssstttt, sssttt! Grace — you've gone and stained your good blouse, for goodness' sake.'

I looked down at my chest. The beetroot had made a vivid red splodge on the white cotton-jersey. I was hit with the memory of the squashed bluebottle on Charlie's dead body, and I broke out in a sudden sweat.

'Bloody beetroot the hardest thing to get out, too,' Mother complained.

I snatched my napkin, stuck it into my glass and started to dab roughly at the stain. Josie passed over another one and told me not to worry.

'Don't drag the material like that!' Mother admonished, louder than she meant to. 'Just leave it alone — I'll wash it when we get home. God, can I bring you nowhere?'

The baby shouted again. It had stopped smiling. I felt the tears welling up and couldn't stop them. I looked at the baby and for a split second saw Charlie looking back.

'I . . . can I go and wait in the car? I don't feel well.'

'Oh dear, Grace, it's not the other thing, it it?' Josie whispered anxiously.

'No . . . no, I just feel sick, that's all.'

Mother opened her handbag and handed me the car keys. 'Don't be throwing up in the car, will you? We won't be long.'

I took the keys and got up, still holding a napkin on to the stain. The baby called out as I walked away and the maître d' asked me if I was all right when I passed him in the archway. I bobbed my head at him and rushed out on to the sunlit pavement and across the street towards the car, ignoring the curious looks of the passers-by.

The side street was shaded and quiet as I unlocked the car. I lay down on the backseat and cried hard, without really knowing why. The hot fat tears ran into my hair and the side of my face stuck on to the pocked leather upholstery as I tried to make sense of the whirlwind of emotions passing through me. What was that waitress or that old man or that baby to me, anyway?

My wet cheek began to itch on top of the sticky upholstery but as I began to peel it off, a huge cracking sound ripped into the air outside, and I was flung violently on to my side, between the back and front seats. I lay there stunned and winded, aware only of faraway sounds of hissing and shouting and glass smashing, and thick bitty brown dust whirling past the side windows.

After what must have been a minute, I moved my elbow on to the back seat and slowly raised myself on to it. The windscreen was shattered and thin shards of glass were lying everywhere. I brushed what I could off the seat, slid slowly over to the door and got out. The air was thick with acrid smoke and people were running up Howard Street towards the City Hall. Water was gushing across the side street and shop windows were spilling out on to the pavements. The shouting and screaming seemed to be further away. I leaned against the car, covering my mouth and nose with the napkin I'd been clutching, against the sharp stench of burning.

Suddenly out of the cloud of dust a soldier was at my side, dragging me along by the arm. 'You've got to get out of here, miss — come on, hurry!'

I stumbled along behind him, cold fear beginning to surge through the waves of shock. I tugged on the soldier's arm and tried to shout at him but my voice caught in my throat with the smoke and dust, and he kept running. I went into a fit of coughing and couldn't stop until we were at the City Hall, where the air had cleared. The soldier let go of my arm and jumped into the back of a passing military Jeep.

I stood alone in the middle of the milling crowd and looked back down on Howard Street. I saw a cauliflower-shaped plume of pink and yellow flames and billowing black smoke shooting up into the sky at the other end.

I didn't need to ask where it was coming from.

9

I can just about reach the table. The fading sunlight is catching the silvery traces on the pinky-brown fish in the plate of milk. There are bones in my mouth. The salty taste is repellent. Please may I leave the table. Not until you've cleaned your plate. I sit at the table until bedtime. My bottom is numb. The dog wouldn't eat any either. Dopey dog. We never gave him a name. The breeders had christened him Satan and he wouldn't answer to anything else.

There's something inevitable about this silence. It's what I've always wanted, the bliss of solitude. A neglected place, where no words are required. Perhaps it is Purgatory. How long, I wonder. The silence is not absolute. The sibilance is still in my head. Sometimes it is high and sharp, sometimes it's a whooosh, like the wind rushing through leaves. My ears were never the same after the bomb.

★   ★   ★

I stood in the hospital corridor with a dozen or so dirty people, some moaning and some struck dumb, some half mad with the waiting. Nobody knew anything, doctors and nurses included. I'd phoned home but there was no reply.

A man with a grime-streaked face, who had been in the army Jeep that had brought me to the hospital, handed me a plastic beaker of watery tea and set another down on the linoleum floor. Then he took a hip flask from the inside of his jacket and poured a dash of whiskey into both cups. I thanked him and began to drink the hot sweet mixture in quick successive sips.

'Had you somebody in there?' the man said, his voice choked.

When I found my voice, it was like listening to someone else speaking. 'My mother and our next-door neighbour.'

'My girl was there too. I was on my way to collect her when it went off.'

The girl who was eating the chips flashed into my mind. 'Does she have black hair up in a bun?'

'Well, it's dark, but I don't know if it's in a bun. Why do you ask?'

'I noticed a girl on her own in there. She was sitting near us.'

The man looked at me closely. Under the dirt he was square-set and handsome, like George Peppard. 'You mean, you were in there and got out? Did Tricia get out, do you think? The dark girl?'

'I don't know. I'd left before it happened. I'd gone to wait in the car.'

'You're a very lucky girl,' he said, shaking his head.

I finished the drink and put the cup on the floor. His words spun around in my head, clamouring to be heard over the hiss. Lucky? *Lucky?*

I asked him for some more whiskey. He quarter filled my beaker, then drank straight from the flask. I took a swig and felt the alcohol burn along my raw throat.

'I'm not a lucky person at all. I bring bad luck, terrible luck.'

'What?'

'Bad things keep happening when I'm around.'

The man screwed the silver top back on to the flask. There was an engraving on it, but I couldn't make out what it said.

'That sounds mad, if you ask me,' he said.

'I was in this hospital earlier today.'

'What's that got to do with anything?'

'I think I have something bad in me.'

'What, like a disease?'

'Just badness.'

He drew back his face a fraction, doubling his chin. 'Don't be stupid. This is the

231

nineteen seventies, not the Middle Ages. You didn't plant the bomb, did you?'

'I just wish I'd stayed in that restaurant.'

His voice cracked. 'Look, just shut up, would you? I can't believe you're saying that. Jesus, Tricia could be blown to . . .'

'You see? That's what I mean. I'm only thinking about myself, in the middle of all this. I think about myself all the time, far too much. I can't help it.'

'For Christ's sake, don't we all think about ourselves all the time? Why are you telling me this anyway?'

I recoiled, the rush in my head that had loosened my tongue abruptly subsiding. The voice I knew as my own came back in a whisper. 'I . . . I don't know. I'm sorry. The whiskey's making me feel funny.'

'Don't drink any more of it then. Look, I'm sorry. You're probably still in shock. Take it easy. I'm going to try to find out something.'

I swirled the whiskey in the cup, hesitated, then drank it back. Within seconds a searing headache took hold and I had to sit down on the floor. Names were being called out from somewhere but I couldn't take them in. I pictured Mother on a mortuary slab with her face blown off, Josie beside her with no arms.

I stood up, too quickly, to get away from

the thought, and blacked out for an instant. When my vision returned, a nurse with a rushed red face was in front of me.

'Are you Grace Kane? Are you all right?'

'Yes — what's — '

'Your mother has been quite severely injured but she has come round. Dr Stanaway is examining her.'

'What . . . what about Josie?'

'The lady with your mother escaped with lesser injuries. I'm afraid that's all I can tell you for now — if you can wait here I'll keep you updated.'

The nurse disappeared through the swinging doors. On the other side of the corridor a woman in a ripped blouse began to snivel. A policewoman put her arm around her and she cried louder.

I wondered why I didn't feel relief. I pictured Mother on the slab again, with her body broken, but her face back on, and talking. I felt nothing, other than an urgent thirst. I walked to the end of the corridor and bent over a water dispenser. The water tasted stale but I drank a lot of it, then joined the short queue for the payphone. I was about to pick up the phone when Frank and Dalloway arrived, Frank pale and agitated; Dalloway out of breath and sweating.

'Grace — you're all right!' Dalloway

wheezed, pulling off his cap. 'Where are they?'

'I was just about to ring you — they were hurt, Josie not too bad. They're still examining Mother.'

Frank put the side of his fist to his nose. 'How bad is it?'

'I don't know. They're awful busy, can't tell much yet.'

'Thank the Lord they're not killed,' Dalloway puffed. 'Do you think I could get to see Josie?'

'I don't know — go and ask a policeman or somebody.'

Dalloway made his way up the corridor to the policewoman.

'Better stay in the queue — I'll have to ring Sadie,' Frank said, his eyes still fraught. 'It was her who rang me — she was expecting Ma to call in with her on the way back. How come you're not injured?'

'I . . . I was lucky.'

The Belfast Telegraph   26 June 1974

VIKING BLOODBATH: 13 DEAD

A ten-month baby was among the victims of a huge no-warning explosion which completely destroyed The Viking restaurant

234

on Belfast's Howard Street at approximately 1.15 p.m. today. So far the RUC has announced 13 casualties but a spokesman said the toll could increase. According to a spokeswoman for the Royal Victoria Hospital, many survivors have suffered massive injuries, including severe burns and loss of limbs.

No group has yet claimed responsibility but the RUC spokesman said the explosion bore all the hallmarks of a Republican attack. Many of those in The Viking at lunchtime, including staff, are thought to be among the dead. According to a window-cleaner who witnessed events from scaffolding at offices on the corner of Great Victoria Street, the blast appeared to be the biggest ever perpetrated on a civilian target.

'I heard this sort of ripping sound then a big bang,' said the man, who did not wish to be named. 'I saw two women blown right out the door and on to the street like rag dolls. I was nearly blown off my ladder. The building caught fire awful quick and I was nearly choked with the smoke. I went and tried to help but the army wouldn't let anybody near it.'

The attack has so far been condemned by the Official Unionist Party.

Mother's face was unmarked but her forehead was creased in pain. She lay flat on the bed, looking tiny and vulnerable, and terrifying. Frank had told her that Josie and I were all right and she had nodded, but did not speak. Her arms were bandaged and the surgeon said her legs were badly damaged. Frank had almost cried when he heard that. Mother had always prided herself on her well-turned ankles.

In the evening Mother fell asleep and Frank went home to do the milking, telling me to get a lift with Dalloway when he was going. I sat by Mother's bed and watched her sleeping, a slight snicker of a snore escaping at the peak of each inhaled breath.

After a little while, the nurse with the flushed face drew back the curtain around the bed and beckoned to me.

'Mr Stanaway would like a word with you, Grace.'

My head thumped dully as I followed her out of the intensive care ward and into the casualty area. The surgeon was looking at X-rays mounted on to light-boxes on the wall.

'Grace, as we feared, your mother's lower vertebrae have been injured and we're going to have to operate.'

The thumping mounted in my head. 'Will

. . . is it a big operation?'

'We have a good success rate with this procedure. We'll have to assess her fitness for surgery in the next half-hour. I'll see you later, Miss Kane.'

The nurse held open the swinging door for me.

'Look, why don't you go back in and I'll get you a nice cup of coffee. Don't worry, we will notify your brother.'

I walked back through the quiet ward like a crumbling old woman. Mother was awake when I reached her bed and I had no idea what to say to her. I sat down slowly, newly aware of the beetroot stain on my blouse, which the dust had turned to purple. She watched me for what seemed like an age, then inclined her head towards the glass of water on her bedside table.

I hesitated, realising I would have to raise her head to help her drink. I could not remember the last time I'd had any physical contact with her. She closed her eyes and I picked up the glass with one hand and slipped the other behind her head, gently directing it towards the glass. She took a small sip and moved her head back. Her hair felt coarse and mealy in my hand. I quickly slipped it out from under her and went back to my seat.

A minute or two passed by before she spoke.

'I know it's bad.'

She was looking at me with half closed eyes and speaking through barely parted lips. I wanted to run.

'I heard them talking about those people burning. In the ambulance . . . I didn't get burned, Josie neither, I don't think.'

I cleared my throat. 'No, no you didn't.'

'Do you know why?'

'Why what?

'We were on our way out . . . because you were . . . acting funny . . . '

She closed her eyes again and seemed to drift off. I bit my lip as a faint wisp of hope fluttered through my mind.

'Had to go to see . . . if you . . . were all right.'

Could it be true? Could that have saved her? Had I made up for Daddy, at last? I cupped my hands over my mouth and nose and said a silent prayer to Padre Pio. Then the nurse came back with a man in blue overalls, and they wheeled Mother away. I sat in the empty cubicle, drinking tasteless coffee, until Dalloway came and brought me out to his car.

'They're keeping Josie in a while just to make sure,' he said, opening the passenger door for me. 'She said to tell you to mind yourself, Grace.'

We said the rosary for Mother in the darkness of the car, breaking off when we had to stop at a police checkpoint on the outskirts of the city. As we neared the top of the hill that would lead us back down to the lough shore, I looked over the strings of lights across the city beneath us and wondered where, in that contained sprawl, was the man who planted the bomb. Was he walking, or driving, or sleeping, or eating, or drinking, or laughing, or having sex?

For a fleeting couple of seconds I considered the daring that would have earlier been required of this individual. I drove the guilty thought from my mind just as Dalloway said that we should be praying for the bomber too.

'We'll dedicate the next decade to the reform of his poor misguided soul,' he said, throwing the car gears into neutral for the downward stretch ahead.

I lowered the car window as we drove past the village and exhaled the city out of my lungs. A Lambeg drum thudded in the distance like a call to arms, struck all the harder, I imagined, in the aftermath of the atrocity. I breathed in the mild night air and let it swathe my face. My headache had gone.

Frank was alone on the verandah when we pulled into the yard.

'They rang and said they're waiting till tomorrow to do the operating,' he said, flatly.

Dalloway joined him on the seat.

'I'll make tea,' I said, longing to go to bed.

'It's already being made,' Frank said.

I opened the back door, expecting to see Sadie or Molly in the kitchen, but it was empty. I walked in and saw mugs and a plate of sandwiches on the table, and heard the toilet flush. Then the kitchen door opened and Saul walked in, as if he'd never been away.

'Grace — God, are you all right?'

I lowered my startled eyes and brushed the front of my blouse with my fingers.

'I'm all right — this is just a beetroot stain,' I said, wishing, for dramatic effect, that it had been real blood.

'Beetroot? Sit down there and I'll get you out some tea.'

I watched him take the lid off the pot and stir the tea leaves, as Mother had shown him.

'Em, no thanks. I'm too tired,' I said, rubbing the back of my neck, seized by the need to get clean again.

'OK then — I'll see you in the morning,' he said, pouring tea into the mugs. 'Sleep well.'

I lay on my back in bed, the scent of Mother's lavender bath salts on my skin and my hair slightly damp against the pillow. I felt calm spread within me like the evening sun crawling over fields and hedges. Sleep crept up quickly; a long, deep, dreamless escape. When I awoke it was midday, and my blankets were undisturbed.

★　★　★

A note was wedged in between the butter dish and the milk jug.

Big order in for scallions. No word yet from hospital. Come and give us a hand if you're able. F.

Outside the window the sky was chalky blue and in the distance a faint sheen hung over the glassy water like a length of organza. Beyond the fence a lame cow stood stock-still in the breezeless air, and further down the slope towards the back of the field, I could just about make out a lean figure in the scallion patch.

Saul. He'd been the first thing in my head when I'd awakened, even before I'd remembered about Mother. I suddenly felt ravenous. After two bowls of Sugar Puffs I was still hungry. I boiled two brown eggs and toasted a farl of soda bread, and ate with my feet up on a chair.

I poured a second cup of tea and watched the starlings and a lone blue-cap congregate in the birdbath, flicking up the water with their frisky wings.

They're washing under their arms . . .

Charlie's words came back to me so clearly, I felt an assurance from deep inside that he was alive, someplace else. I put down the cup and tried to catch hold of the thought but it was swept away as swiftly as it had hit me, and replaced by a niggling urge to rush. I stood up and cleared the dishes into the sink, then realised there was no need to hurry. There was no-one there to make me. I washed the dishes in a leisurely fashion, enjoying the feel of the bubbles on my hands from the extra large squirt of detergent I'd added to the warm water. Then I poured the last of the tea over the breakfast scraps on a plate and brought it outside.

The birds shot off at the sight of me but returned within seconds to claim the morsels. I shooed away the crows that had gathered along the fence to investigate, and marvelled anew at the cheek of the rogue magpies as they dived down and snatched the smaller birds' meals from their beaks.

I became lost in their world until I felt a sharp twinge in my back. I'd been shocked by the bruise I'd seen in the bathroom mirror and now the flesh felt tender to the touch. I went into the scullery and pulled on an old cardigan and a peaked cap of Frank's to shade my eyes against the clear bright light, and set off across the field, avoiding the cowpats and the bluebells.

Frank knelt between the furrows at the top of the scallion patch, pulling out the scallions by the roots and piling them up behind him. Saul stood at the flat trailer at the bottom of the field, taking handfuls of scallions from the mound at his side and putting elastic bands around them. The long stringy roots rasped as they were pulled from the soil; other than that the field was silent.

Frank turned his head when he heard me approach behind him. He had dark pouches under his eyes and a five-o'clock shadow.

'Nobody phone?'

I shook my head.

'I'd say we won't hear much till this afternoon. No point in going in till evening, anyhow. You're looking better the day.'

'I don't feel too bad,' I said, glancing down towards Saul. He waved.

'Grab a pile of them and you can do a bit of pre-packing. Mind and don't make them too big. Twenty-four in a bunch.'

I bent over and scooped up an armful of scallions, relishing their clean zippy aroma and the sheen of their pearly white bulbs. The smell shot my mind back to an afternoon of sandwich-making for the whist, when I'd chopped off all the heads and used only the green bits in the hard-boiled-egg mixture. Mother had come back from getting her hair done and freaked. I had to get the heads out of the bin, wash them, slice them and put them into every one of the thirty-five egg sandwiches already made. Josie ate a load of them at the whist and complained that they repeated on her for two full days afterwards.

I made my way down to the trailer.

'Hey — how are you feeling today?' Saul asked as I drew level.

I spread my pile of scallions on the other end of the trailer.

'All right,' I shrugged. 'How do you like this job then?'

He frowned slightly. 'It's tricky enough. I think I was trying to shove too many of these things into the bunches, but I'm getting the hang of it now. Any word of your moth — '

'People always go for the big ones but the small ones are the tastiest. A wee fine bunch is far nicer than a big bruiser. Could you pass over some elastics please?'

He slid over a box of bands and I spilled some out beside me. We both began to speak at the same time.

'You first,' he prompted. I doubled a band around the first bunch of scallions.

'I was going to ask you where you'd disappeared to all this time,' I said quickly, selecting another bunch.

'Oh, I had some people to see in town. And, you know, I didn't want to outstay my welcome here, after the funeral and all.'

'You went to Charlie's funeral?'

'Yes.'

'Oh. I couldn't go.'

'Yeah, I heard about you and the fly.'

My nonchalance dissolved. 'Oh . . . who told you?'

'Oh it doesn't matter. I wouldn't worry about it. You know, flies are drunk half the time on fruit.'

I pulled a dry end off a scallion.

'What's that got to do with anything?' I said, unnerved.

'Nothing. I'm just telling you. Flies have oral sex too.'

I shook my hair over my reddening face, my mind boggling at the turn of his conversation.

'I'm not kidding. I read about it. The male comes up behind the female and gives her a lick but the female isn't too keen on returning the favour.'

'That's disgusting,' I said, refusing to look at him.

He laughed. 'You mean the fact she won't do it back?'

'No — no, the whole thing, I mean,' I squeaked.

'But it's only nature. Natural instinct.'

I felt him watching me but I kept my eyes down.

'Anyway, have you any news of your mother?' he asked after a moment.

'No. We'll know this afternoon. How did you hear about it?' I heard the curtness in my voice and cleared my throat to kill it.

'I was here when Frank got the call. Decided I'd better stick around.'

The heat in my cheeks had receded sufficiently for me to look up at him. 'That was good of you.'

'No bother. Do you want to talk about what happened?'

'No.'

'That's all right.'

We worked on in silence. I struggled to regain the calm I'd woken up with, but Mother's operation began to weigh heavily on my mind. I began to drop scallions on the ground and the pre-packing became monotonous. Then, out of the blue, a spot of rain landed on my cheek, and Frank was coming down the field.

'Make a run for the trees — that's going to be a big one,' he called out to us, a huge sheaf of scallions under his arm.

I had barely noticed the momentary change in the light. By the time we'd all reached the trees, the rain was falling straight down in long pellets.

'That's a real godsend,' Frank said. 'The ground fairly needed that.'

I stood between the two men, watching the rain make puddles on the trailer. Saul had gone quiet. I followed his gaze across the lough. It had missed out on the shower and the water was glistening under a sunburst behind a cloud.

The rain stopped as abruptly as it started.

'I'll give you a hand now — I've enough pulled,' Frank said, heading for the trailer. As I made to follow him, Saul touched my arm.

'Grace, how long would it take somebody to come up if they went missing in the water?'

I had to think for a few seconds.

'Well, it was eleven days the time Molly's husband drowned,' I said, relieved his attention had turned elsewhere. 'I think it's usually about that before the body fills up with water. Sometimes they fall into sand-holes and never come up, though. Why do you ask?'

'I was just wondering what would have happened if we hadn't found Charlie,' he said, with a slight shake of his head.

'That's very morbid. You shouldn't think like that . . . ' I hesitated, hearing myself sounding like Mother. 'Anyway, I know Charlie's all right now, wherever he is.'

I walked on. He caught up with me at the trailer and slapped me on the back.

'Nice one,' he said, the carefree look back on his face.

My muscles winced against the inoffensive slap and there was pain in my smile. Frank had already begun to pre-pack at speed and I endeavoured to keep up with him, but the rain had given the scallions the zeal of a heap of freshly cut onions, and my eyes began to sting excruciatingly. I tried to blink away the searing water but my eyes filled relentlessly.

Then through the haze, I spotted a figure at the top of the field.

'I don't believe it,' Frank said under his breath.

'What's wrong, Frank?' Saul asked, looking up at the man, who hadn't moved.

Frank said nothing. I pressed against the sting in my eyes with the flats of my fingernails and peered at the man. He started to walk forward. My heart missed a beat.

'Jesus! It's Daddy!'

'For fuck's sake, Grace! It's bloody Sean!' Frank said, rolling his eyes at me. 'Have you lost the run of yourself all together?'

It took a few seconds for the image I'd envisioned to take on the features of my uncle, and for the first time that day I became aware of the continuing hiss in my ears. Saul was looking at me with raised eyebrows and a twitching mouth, and I had to bite my lip to hold back a nervous giggle.

'Never let on you know,' Frank said. 'Work away.'

The sky brightened, the sun dazzling the rows of wet scallions and making the field cheerful again. Saul took a pair of sunglasses out of his pocket and handed them to me.

'Got them the other day. They'll help your eyes.'

The frames were round and the lenses deep blue.

'But you need them yourself.'

'No I don't. You do. Put them on.'

I glanced up the hill at Uncle Sean. He was halfway down and stooping over, pulling out a weed on the edge of a furrow. I opened out the fragile wire legs of the sunglasses and slipped them on.

'Would you quit messing around and get on with it — I don't want him to see we've even taken him under our notice,' Frank said, slapping a bundle on top of another. The scallions were slippery now, and squeaked when the elastic bands were put around them. The coloured lenses of the sunglasses snatched away their green vigour and greyed the grass, the sky and the hedges, but they eased my smarting eyes and I was grateful for them to hide behind when Uncle Sean sauntered up to the trailer.

'You've a few chokers coming up there,' he said, addressing no-one in particular. 'Ground could do with a drop of weedkiller.' He dug into the ground with the heel of his boot and gently kicked over the soil. 'My father used to put a spray on, this time of year.'

'Too many chemicals in that stuff,' Frank said.

He didn't look at Sean, who was intent on the soil. A few seconds passed before Saul spoke up.

'How's Ginny and the baby doing, Sean?'

'Doing the best,' he said quickly, sliding his eyes over to Frank. 'The Royal was ringing our house there a while ago — couldn't get a reply here. You've to go in.'

Frank pulled out a length of twine from his

trouser pocket and slid it under the bundle of pre-packed scallions in front of him.

'Right,' he replied, tying up the bundle.

'I think it was sorta urgent.'

'Why didn't you say so in the first place then?'

'You go on, Frank — I'll finish these and bring them into the market,' Saul interjected.

'I told you before, you couldn't handle the tractor and you're not insured anyway. I don't want any — '

'I could take them,' Sean offered mildly. 'Going up there anyway.'

'We'll manage,' Frank said, his voice tight.

'Whatever you like,' Sean said, turning to leave. 'But you'd need to get a move on, by the looks of your man up there.'

I blinked away the remaining moisture in my eyes and saw Dalloway standing at the top of the field, waving and calling.

Frank dropped the bunch he was pre-packing.

'Come on, Frank! I've the car running,' Dalloway shouted.

Frank took out a checked handkerchief from his pocket and rubbed his hands on it. 'You come with me, Grace. You stay here, Saul, and finish out.'

I handed the sunglasses back to Saul and hurried after Frank. Another spot of rain splashed on my face as we made our way past Sean, who stood with his arms folded, watching us.

'Them scallions is going to get ruined, boy,' he said. 'Sure I'll take them for you, this once. I've the truck parked on the road.'

Frank looked up at the rolling clouds and pushed his bottom lip to the side. 'Well there's only a couple more bunches to do . . . ah, to hell — all right then. I'll see you later.'

Sean nodded. Neither he nor Frank looked at each other. From the top of the field Dalloway urged us to hurry. Frank broke into a run then abruptly turned to me with distracted eyes.

'Tell you what, you better stay, Grace, and make a drop of tea,' he said. 'I'll phone and let you know if there's anything to know. Keep an eye on your man, won't you? Ma need never know.'

He ran on without waiting for an answer. By the time I reached the top of the field, he and Dalloway were pulling out of the yard in Dalloway's car.

The relief I felt at not having to go was tinged with apprehension. I had never been left in charge before, not with Uncle Sean there. I walked to the house to put on the kettle, wondering how I was going to feed the men. The cupboards were virtually bare and I'd eaten all the fresh bread for breakfast. I toyed with the idea of going into the supermarket in town but the chiming of the clock in the hall told me it was already lunchtime, and that it was too late to make a dash for it.

I washed my hands at the sink, peering down the field at the two distant figures standing side by side at the trailer, and imagining Mother's face at the sight of them. I shook my hands to dry them and walked outside. My hip throbbed on the side on which I'd fallen into the car well, and I felt a crack of bones as I stepped stiffly down into the yard. The damp had got me and I knew the walk to the village would be too much.

I turned to go back, then on impulse walked around to the front of the house, to Frank's car. He'd left the keys in it. I opened the door on the driver's side and slid in, a flutter of excitement rising in my chest. I ran the tips of my fingers around the narrow-ridged steering wheel, breathing in the familiar male aroma of old leather and strong tobacco. I adjusted the windscreen mirror and the seat, and quickly switched on the ignition. The engine coughed and quit. I started it again, pressing more firmly on the squeaky accelerator. The engine revved alarmingly. I checked the side mirror to see if the yard was still empty, then pushed the gear stick into first and drove slowly out of the yard and on to the road.

The sun had splintered through the foaming clouds and the newly cut hedges opened up views of the fields and the water previously obscured by unruly foliage. I slipped through the gears easily, relishing my control over the ton of metal and glass around me. The road was free of traffic and within minutes I'd pulled into the village.

I got out of the car and walked up to Best's Store. Mr Best's dark head was bent over a ledger on his elevated Formica counter. He ignored the jangle of the door chimes as I came in, but I was immediately aware of eyes peeping over the two cluttered aisles. I made a beeline for the bread and no sooner had I grabbed a loaf than Mary Mullen was in front of me, clutching my forearm and frowning into my face. The vertical crease in her powdered forehead met her flat nose in one long swoop, and with anticipation making an 'O' out of her mouth, she looked like she had an exclamation mark on her yellow face. She briefly lowered her eyes and nodded slightly when I flinched at her touch, showing empathy with what she assumed was my fragile state.

'It's an awful thing you're going through, dear,' she half whispered. 'Any word of your mother yet? The whole country's praying for her, you know.'

I wanted to move my arm but she held on to it.

'Frank's away in to see her now. She wasn't too bad when I left her last night.'

'And tell us, is she badly hurt at all?'

'We don't really know yet. She was going to have an operation — '

'An operation! My God. What for exactly?'

The mawkish concern in the woman's eyes had given way to a glittering curiosity. I knew Mother wouldn't want her to know but I felt somehow obliged to satisfy the blatant nosiness.

'Her legs were damaged.'

'Ah, God love her, the woman. Badly burned, were they?'

'No, I don't think so. I think they were a bit crushed.'

'Crushed. My God. Will she be able to walk at all?

'We don't know yet.'

'My God. I say, there's somebody looking after you, isn't there? Getting out of yon. And I believe Josie Moore's not too bad, is that right?'

'I think she's getting out today.'

She let go of my arm and squeezed a loaf

on the shelf with her yellow fingers.

'Well dear, if you need anything at all don't be a bit afraid to ask, now,' she said, pursing her lips and inclining her head sideways.

'Thanks very much. I'd better go.'

'All the best, now.'

I walked over to the fridge against the wall and lifted a block of cheese, aware of Mary whispering to another woman who'd been hovering in the background. I hurried to the counter and handed the bread and cheese to Mr Best. He put them in a bag and refused the money for them.

'Don't mind that, this once,' he said, sliding a pen behind his small round right ear. 'You've enough to be worrying about, Grace.'

I thanked him and bolted, narrowly avoiding a pyramid display of cat food on the way out. Outside, fat white clouds had swallowed the sun. I walked quickly to the car and rolled down the driver's window to let in some air. It had become stifling and I began to worry about the time. I turned the key and the car lurched forward, then cut out.

'Try putting it in neutral, stupid.'

Ivy Best's pert face loomed outside the open window. I caught my breath at the sight of her, recalling the whack of her foot on my cheek. I began to roll up the window, but in the next instant she was sitting beside me in the passenger seat, sun-baked knees resting against the walnut dashboard.

'Joyriding, are we?' she said. 'Give us a lift, would you.'

'I only took the car because I was in a hurry to get things for the lunch,' I blustered, carefully restarting the engine.

'Oh, who's for lunch then?'

I hesitated to tell her, concentrating on getting the car moving.

'Saul there?' she asked casually.

'Yes. And Uncle Sean.'

'Sean too? He's a bit of all right as well. Think I'll come with you and help you with the lunch.'

My throat tightened. 'It's all right. I can manage.'

'Sure you were near blew up. Heard all about it. Drive on — I'm coming whether you like it or not.'

She took a comb out of her skirt pocket and ran it through her black hair. The car chugged, and she chuckled as I wrestled with the gears.

'I see you've actually got a wireless in this old jalopy,' she said, switching it on and turning up the volume. The blaring of it threw my concentration and I felt a trickle of sweat roll down my cleavage.

'I just love the Stones,' she said, slapping

out the beat of the song on her raised legs. I reached out and turned down the volume slightly but she turned it up again and began to sing along. My ears started to pop and my fingers felt slithery on the steering wheel. I listened to my tormentor's honeyed singing voice and knew the apology I was awaiting would never come. And when we pulled into the yard, I saw my peace end.

Ginny was standing on the doorstep, a strange look in her eyes and a small suitcase at her feet.

* * *

Under my skin I'm slowly rolling and ascending, as if I'm on a slow-motion fairground ride, or submerged in a gentle whirlpool. It's quite lulling. Maybe it's my soul beginning to detach itself from my body, this mass I've lugged around all these years. There was always too much of it and no grace in its movement. I'd much rather be invisible. I don't mind about my blocked-up lymph glands. I just hope my mouth isn't hanging open. In this swirling cocoon I have no concept of where my lips are, or where my arms are, or the rest of me, for that matter. For the first time in my life I'm comfortable in my own skin, for I cannot see or feel it.

10

'Hullo there. I'm only just here.'

Ginny's right shoulder drooped with the weight of a packed wicker basket she was carrying. A spare tyre bulged under her poppy print dress and her marmalade hair was cut close to her head.

I hadn't spoken to her since Daddy's funeral but she was acting as if her visit was a regular occurrence.

'Are you looking for Uncle Sean?'

'No, not really. I thought I'd come and give you a hand, with your mother in the hospital and all. Glad to get out of the house, to tell you the truth. Children are staying with my mother up in Ballymena for a few days.'

Ivy followed me out of the car.

'Hi there — remember me?' she said, winking at Ginny. She loved new people.

'Eh . . . have we met somewhere?'

'Yip, at Cemetery Sunday. Don't you remember? Oh, doesn't matter — come on in. We're making lunch.'

Ivy opened the door and went into the kitchen. Ginny shook her head.

'You ones are awful carefree, not locking

your doors,' she said. 'You wouldn't get away with that where I come from.'

'I was only away ten minutes and there are men down the field,' I explained, gesturing for her to go in.

She picked up her case and left it in the hall.

'Are you going anywhere nice?' I asked her tentatively.

'Oh, thought I might stay over, if you needed me.' She sighed. 'Do you know, I'm dying for a cup of tea.'

She put the basket on the kitchen table and sat on the edge of the armchair nearest the door. Ivy bounced around the kitchen taking crockery from cupboards and making tea.

'There's a pile of good honey-roast ham sandwiches and two apple tarts there, girl,' Ginny said, a hint of the Scots in her northwest accent. 'Might as well get them used up.'

I thanked her and lifted out a parcel of square-cut sandwiches from the bag. Ivy handed me a plate and I arranged them on it. The loaf bread was fresh and the ham smothered in English mustard.

'Right — the tea's wet,' Ivy trilled. 'I'll go and give the men a shout.'

Ginny's clear round eyes followed Ivy out.

'Hhmmpf,' she said under her breath.

'Who's she anyway?'

'Just a girl from the village,' I shrugged, looking at the clock. 'You know Best's store? That's theirs, and they own the old mill now too.'

'Very nice. Two sugars in the tea, by the way.'

She looked around the kitchen, rolling her eyes at the Sacred Heart. Up close, she was the most colourfully marked person I'd ever seen, with that vivid hair and the splotches of freckles, eyes the colour of the Atlantic in the winter sun, and plenty of blood in her wide lips.

'Who has Frank got working the day?' she asked.

'Just Saul.'

She crossed her legs and clasped her flat mannish hands on her lap. 'He's got good hands, that boy.'

I poured out the tea, watching her out of the corner of my eye.

'Them curtains are far too fancy for a kitchen. Your mother always was one for fuss and muss.'

Outside a gate's hinges squealed.

'That's them now, by the sounds of it.'

Ivy's tinkling laughter preceded her. Uncle Sean walked in behind her and stood in the kitchen doorway, leaning his shoulder against the frame. From the window I could see Saul splashing his face with water from the pump at the top of the field.

'What's going on?' Uncle Sean asked Ginny.

'Don't worry — the children's with my mother,' Ginny replied quickly, shifting on to her left haunch and angling her body away from Uncle Sean. He stepped over to the table and pulled out a chair.

'It's well seen Elva's not about,' he said under his breath.

I took a china cup and saucer out of the cupboard for Ginny and poured her tea. Uncle Sean began to eat, demolishing the sandwiches in two bites. Ivy sat down beside him.

'You've quite an appetite, Sean,' she said cheerily. 'Does Ginny not feed you?'

Uncle Sean smirked and chewed on. Ginny sipped her tea.

'I'd say you've your hands full with those wee ones,' Ivy continued, turning towards the door. 'Now *there's* a boy could do with a bit of feeding too.'

Saul closed the door behind him and flopped down in the armchair on the other side of the range. Ginny turned sharply to look at him and he smiled at her. I caught the look that passed between them and the penny dropped. He'd been staying down at The Scrog. It occurred to me then that he'd engineered this whole encounter, like some kind of bridge-maker. Whatever he was at, he made no move towards the table, sitting in a preoccupied silence that infiltrated the room, making Ivy giggle.

I stood by the window, studying the cobwebs that were beginning to form under the guttering. After an uncomfortable moment, the silence was broken by the clatter of a low-flying helicopter.

'Ssst, ssst, that thing'd nearly take the roof off,' Ginny said, setting her cup and saucer on the range.

'There's an awful lot of them flying over these days,' Uncle Sean said, lighting up a cigarette.

'Huh. They soon made themselves scarce when Charlie drowned,' Ivy snapped.

Saul quietly excused himself and went to the bathroom. Ginny glanced at me, then turned her attention to Ivy, whose fresh young features had hardened. I was relieved she'd found something else to blame for Charlie.

'I heard about that wee fella, all right. And there was a helicopter, was there?'

'Yes, and it flew off and did nothing to help, and it's bound to have seen Charlie getting into trouble.'

'Imagine that.'

Uncle Sean rose from the table and pulled a folded cap from his back pocket. 'Sure, what would you expect from them ones?' He put on his cap and pushed his chair back under the table. 'I'll have to get them scallions shifted. Be seeing you.'

Ginny nodded but didn't look at him.

Saul came back into the kitchen as Uncle Sean was leaving and followed him out, wordlessly. Ivy stood up and put her cup in the sink.

'I'm away on, too. Hope your ma will be all right, Grace,' she said, her kohl-lined eyes sheepish. 'Cheerio, Mrs . . . Ginny.'

I saw her to the back door and thanked her for her help, glad she was leaving. She bent down to tighten her shoe buckle.

'That's a good one, isn't it? Her leaving her wee baby like that. You'd need to watch her, you know. Looks like she's trying to get in with you . . . bet you they're hoping Elva'll kick the bucket so they can get hold of a bit of this oul' land. Frank'd be a far softer touch than your ma, after all.'

She sauntered off, leaving me even more perplexed. Could it be true? I shook my head and went back in. I longed to have the house to myself again but Ginny had installed herself at the sink, with one of Mother's pinny aprons on.

'Dry those dishes and we'll get the jam on,' Ginny said brusquely.

'Jam?'

'What do you think's weighing down that basket? Got at least a fiver's worth of good strawberries for the price of a jar of that oul' shop-bought stuff. Hope you've plenty of jam jars.'

'Auntie Ginny, I don't think anybody would expect you to be making jam in the middle of all this.'

'Look, you're going to need a bit of jam no matter what happens. Make yourself useful girl, and go and get the jars.'

I went reluctantly into the scullery and took out an armful of empty jars from the bottom shelf. Mother always kept far too many stashed away for the annual jam-making, claiming they'd come in useful for something. I looked at the clock. Frank had been away for two hours without any word, and suddenly I had a picture in my head of serving soda bread dripping with runny red jam to a houseful of people in mourning for Mother. In the daydream I had the stolen slides in my hair and mascara on my lashes. I was wearing a black cocktail dress and short white gloves, and everyone was admiring my poise in the face of the tragedy … I shuddered, aghast at my imagination.

'You couldn't possibly be cold,' Ginny said, looking over her shoulder at me. I lowered the jars carefully on to the table.

'No. Somebody just walked over my grave, that's all.'

She looked at me absently. 'Your mother always used to say that.'

I fetched another armful of jars, then began to dry the dishes. Ginny stood staring out at the water, her lips slightly parted. When she eventually spoke, there was a faint catch in her voice.

'I remember me and your mother running around with the butter dripping down our arms, down at Granny's after the churning,' she said quietly. 'We were chums you know, when we were young. Never thought she'd turn so bitter … I can't understand that sort of bitterness.'

I hesitated, then felt compelled to apologise to her. 'I'm sorry, you know, about what happened at Cemetery Sunday … I think Mother's going through the change, and it's making her crabbid.'

'I was all right by her until I married into the family — that's what got her. Anyway, pass me over those jars to steep.'

The faraway look in her sea green eyes had

gone. I did as she asked, then joined her at the table to prepare the strawberries.

'They said they couldn't sell them to the shops but there's not a thing wrong with them,' Ginny said, sliding half the punnets towards me. 'They're washed and all.'

The sweet tangy aroma of the fruit belied its grotesque appearance. The larger strawberries had malformed into lumpy puckered blobs of patchy colour, like cancerous moles on some feudal face. I reached for one and plucked off its hull.

'How come they look like that?' I asked Ginny.

'They just grow like that.'

'Do you think it's the artificial stuff they put on them when they're planted?'

'It's just the way they grow. They taste the same as the good ones.'

I picked up another and it mushed between my fingers. The sensation made my skin crawl, and made me think of dead bodies.

'There's quite a few bad bits in these,' I remarked as I sorted through a punnet.

'What do you want for nothing? Use that.'

I picked up a steak knife Ginny had left on the table and began to slice the mushy bits off the strawberries. After a while a squadron of flies appeared and began to hover above the table. Ginny rose slowly to her feet and took a folded sheet of newspaper from the bottom of her basket. She rolled it tightly, never taking her eyes off the flies, then with the swiftness of a guillotine, she brought down her paper stick and flattened the lot of them on to the table.

'Bastards,' she muttered, sweeping the victims on to her open palm and depositing them on the hotplate of the range, beside the pot she had warming for the jam.

'That's to teach their friends a lesson,' she said calmly. 'I don't know how you stick those damn lough flies every summer. Dirty so-and-so's.'

She paused, then laughed suddenly, a deep-throated haw-haw that revealed her lower teeth. 'Your face is a picture! They can't feel it, you know.'

I laughed with her. 'I know — I just never saw anyone roasting them before.'

'Far better than that useless honey-strip in the corner. Now where do you keep the weighing scales?'

I took the scales down from a shelf and Ginny began to weigh the strawberries. She threw the most of them into the pot and added five packets of sugar from her bag.

'It's a bit thinny, that,' she said as she stirred.

'Maybe it hasn't boiled long enough.'

'I think it needs a drop more sugar. Keep

going with them until they're done.'

My fingers were sticky from the dark pink juice, and the heat from the range made my shirt cling to my back. Unlike the sun, this heat slowed my movements to a dull languor, and my neck and shoulders began to feel the full weight of my head. I grew sloppy with the trimming of the strawberries, letting past the odd imperfection.

When I'd finished, Ginny asked me to rinse out the jars and set them on the range to warm them. I lacked the energy to speak to her, or respond to her quiet scrutiny. I shuffled listlessly back and forth from the sink to the range with the clean jars, my feet and eyelids leaden.

Outside, the sky rumbled like a giant belly, but underneath it the lough lay still. When there was no more room on the range for jars, I slumped into one of the armchairs, ignoring the pile of lids that needed washing. Ginny tasted the jam on the wooden spoon and added more sugar.

'No more bastard flies anyway,' she said, glancing at me.

I smiled lazily in reply, dying to close my eyes and sleep. Ginny shifted her weight from one dainty foot to the other.

'I heard about the fits coming back, Grace,' she said casually.

I lowered my eyes to my lap.

'It's nothing to be ashamed of, no matter what anybody says. It's just a wee imbalance in the brain causing a mini explosion, like that lightning we're going to get any minute.' Her voice was softer than usual.

'It's . . . it's just — '

'Now don't be torturing yourself. I reckon it was Elva brought those fits on, putting the blame on you for your father. Wasn't fair, that. Sure it wasn't your fault the bloody bullock fell into the glar. He shouldn't have tried to pull it out.'

I flinched inwardly. Hearing it stated so bluntly took me aback and I wanted to explain it away.

'But Frank and I shouldn't have taken it down to the reed bank.'

'But you didn't force your father in after the thing.'

I watched her stir the jam.

'I think, I think Mother was so grief-stricken that she had to blame it on someone, the heart attack, I mean. I think she nearly went mad with the grief.'

'Huh!' Ginny shook her head and gave a wry smile.

I looked at her in confusion. 'Don't you think so?'

'No I do not.'

'But don't you remember the state she was in?'

'Yes, and a brilliant performance it was too.'

'But . . . but she loved him.'

Ginny turned to look me full in the eye.

'Loved him?' she said, screwing up her eyes. 'She hated him. Hated the sight of him.'

My grip tightened on the arms of the chair. I gaped at her.

'What do you think made her so crooked all these years? I'll tell you. She despised having to give up her work and her money. Mad for money, you know, and God help you, she took her grudges out on your wee head. Sure not a bit of wonder you're a bit . . . oh, here. I'm speaking out of turn.'

'No, no. Go on.'

She licked the wooden spoon. 'The thing is, those men are hard to love. There's no love in them. It's the way they were dragged up, nobody to say a soft word to them. You know, it's hard to stick sometimes. I was always used to a bit of affection.'

'Uncle Sean is very handsome.'

'Huh. Men change after they get married, Grace. They'll promise you the moon and the stars to woo you, but that's all forgotten when they've got you cleaning out the pigs. I don't care what anybody says, farming men thinks

271

women are inferior to them, that's the truth. Sure my father thought the same, and I always swore I'd never end up ignored, like my poor mother, going about the house like a ghost. I want a better life for myself. Sure if I hadn't been expecting . . . ssst, now I am talking too much.'

She scooped some jam on to a saucer and tilted it. The jam quickly formed a skin and wrinkled.

'Good, it's ready. Now get up there like a good girl and do those lids for me.'

I dragged myself off the chair, lifting my hair off the back of my clammy neck. In my eyes, Sean and Ginny had always been a rather sexy couple, a perception encouraged by Mother's repeated excoriation of their shotgun marriage. Now I knew where that jaded look in Ginny's eye came from. And the source, perhaps, of Mother's discontent. But to imagine one's parents locked in the loveless embrace of a dead marriage is a dispiriting thought, so I pushed Ginny's talk to the back of my head and we laboured on in the muggy air until every pot was filled with the aromatic hot preserve.

Afterwards we spread a drop of it on two slices of the fresh loaf and ate them, lounging back on the armchairs, and as the afternoon waned, I fell into a half doze, a deeper sleep fended off by the anticipation of the phone ringing. When it came, my skin seemed to leap from my bones.

On the other end of the line, Frank's voice was business-like. 'Well, she's through the operation but she hasn't come round yet.'

'So you don't know . . . '

'Don't know a thing yet. They think it went all right. Did they get the scallions away?'

'Uncle Sean's just away with them.'

'Right. I'll have to wait around for a bit.'

'Ginny's here.'

'Some good that is, unless she can do the milking. Can get you get Dalloway to show Saul what to do? Don't be involving Sean, do you hear. I mightn't be back in time and I don't want the cows bursting. Oh, there's the pips — '

The line went dead.

'No news yet?' Ginny called.

'She hasn't woken up out of the operation yet,' I replied, dialling Dalloway's number. There was no reply. I opened the front door for a breath of air, wondering if I could work the milking machine. Out in the field the cows were slowly munching their way towards the hedges, instinctively seeking shelter from the accumulating summer storm. I watched the unhurried progress of their bulks across the grass, their tails lifting and swishing against their dung-encrusted haunches. In the middle of the herd, a frisky heifer casually mounted a Friesian. She broke into a clumsy trot, her belly swinging from side to side. The bull's got there first, I thought to myself as the Friesian bent her legs underneath her and collapsed on to the grass.

I was about to call Dalloway for the second time when I heard Uncle Sean's truck pull up at the gate. Saul jumped out and Uncle Sean sped off, the truck wheels lifting small stones off the road as he went.

I met Saul at the front door and told him about the milking, feigning indifference to him.

'Come on and we'll give it a go — I've watched Frank doing it,' he said without hesitation, taking off towards the byre.

I pulled on a pair of Wellington boots Frank had discarded in the porch and followed Saul across the yard, admiring the way his hair had begun to curl around the sides of his neck, and imagining Ivy running her fingers through it. He must have felt my eyes boring into him for he turned around and began to walk backwards.

'Your Uncle Sean's all right, you know,' he said. 'Oh, and he said he'd be back for Ginny sometime later.'

'Did he?'

'He could have left you well in the lurch today, you know.'

'But he has ulterior motives.'

'Don't be so suspicious. You sound like your mother.'

He smiled at the look on my face and turned around again. I followed him into the long narrow byre and pointed to the suction clusters hanging on a bar along the opposite wall.

'You've to attach those things to the cows' elders, then switch on the machine at the side,' I explained.

'Elders?'

'Udders. That's just what we call them.'

'Oh. Well that sounds easy. I'll go and get them — you shoo them into the waiting pen.'

I hung back in the byre, struck by the stillness of it. It must have been almost a hundred years old, and the new milking machines looked incongruous against the stained stone walls. Shafts of light spilled in from four roughly hewn windows along the wall opposite the milking stalls, but the corners were dark and forbidding, as if there was something lurking in them. I stood staring until I was spooked, and seized by an acute sense of trespassing.

I ran outside and down the short passage

between the calf sheds to the pen, and opened the gate. The cows lumbered across the road and into the lower end of the yard, silent but for the shwoot of their collective heavy breaths through their noses and the clop of their hooves on the concrete.

They made their way lethargically into the pen, each one seemingly self-contained in its own mysterious consciousness, making no eye contact with each other or with me. Saul eventually emerged from behind the last of the herd, swinging a hawthorn stick.

'They fairly take their time, don't they?' he said. 'They've held up three cars on the road and made a right mess of it, too.'

'You've seen nothing yet,' I said. 'We take five of them at a time — turn them up this way.'

I closed the gate and Saul drove the first lot of cows into the byre. He nudged them gently with the stick into the stalls, impressed at how they seemed to know automatically where to position themselves. When they were lined up, I stood back to watch him attempt to attach the clusters to the cows' teats. The first cow shifted nervously at his stranger's touch and kicked out her knobbly back legs.

'Warm your hands first,' I suggested.

'They're sweating like mad. Jesus, what a wriggler.'

'Just you relax, then she'll stay still for you.'

He persevered until he got the hang of it and within twenty minutes had all five cows linked up to the machines. I flicked the on switch and explained to him how the milk was carried through the overhead pipes into the cooling tank in the neighbouring shed, which we called the milk house.

'Well oh well. I have a new-found respect for these creatures,' he said, patrolling up and down the byre.

I thought I saw something approaching pride in his eyes, and it dawned on me why my father had been so attached to these big unhappy-looking animals, beasts I'd always thought of as dumb, with their dense eyes and long ugly faces. They produced the miracle of milk. They had been his girls, much more to him than the real women around him. And while the presence of a pregnant woman in his midst made him uncomfortable to the point of embarrassment, calving a cow was as natural to him as putting water in his whiskey.

After the first five, Saul managed the rest of the cows easily, with only the odd kick delivered in defiance. It was only when the last of the cows was back in the field that he noticed the amount of manure they'd left in their wake. The passage swam in its hot stink, great steaming sludges of it inches thick on the ground.

We cleared it with brushes into a shallow pit in the corner of the yard, where it would stay until it was sucked up into the dung spreader and flung over the fields.

'My father spent most of his time in this,' I said as we washed out the brushes with the hose. 'Wouldn't you wonder what he thought life was all about?'

Saul narrowed his eyes at me. 'The smell isn't that bad — at least it's natural.'

'That's not what I meant.'

'I know, I know. God, you take everything so seriously.'

I set the brush against the wall and began to wash the dung off my boots. To my surprise, I felt the smarting of a tear in my eye. I finished hosing down my boots and handed Saul the hose without looking at him.

'I'm sorry, Grace. I shouldn't have said that. What was your father like?'

I shrugged. 'I'm supposed to look like him.'

'He must have been a good farmer to build up a place like this.'

I nodded, still stung. 'He used to like walking around the fields in the evening to check on how everything was growing. That's when he looked the happiest.'

Saul turned off the hose and hung it up on a hook on the wall of the calf shed.

'What happened to him?'

'He . . . there was a shadow on his lung. They said it was because he didn't wear a mask when he was spreading the artificial. But he had a heart attack in the end. He . . . he over-exerted himself one day.'

'Artificial what?'

'Fertiliser. You can't throw manure on everything.'

Saul stood against the wall with his arms folded. 'So how did he overdo it?'

'A big Charlois bullock fell into the reed bank and he tried to pull it out, but he couldn't. It drowned in the glar.'

I walked over the byre and slid the door shut.

'Grace, you have a real strange look in your eye. Were you very close to your father?'

'No. We'd better go in — the dinner will be ready.'

I turned to go but he pulled me back and put his arms around my waist.

'Not so fast, miss. I think we have some unfinished business, don't we?'

I pushed his arms away and stepped back from him.

'Get lost,' I snapped.

'Jesus, Grace — what's the matter with you?

I was only messing. Why can't you just relax?'

I felt a rush in my veins. 'I . . . it's just something Ginny said . . . oh, you wouldn't understand.'

'No, go on. Try me.'

The rush quickened.

'It was my fault Daddy died,' I whispered.

He stared at me, his indigo eyes searching mine. 'What do you mean?'

'I — I was there . . . at the time. Frank and I were hiding the Charlois because we didn't want it to get slaughtered, and it was our fault — my fault — it fell in and Daddy had to try and pull it out.'

'But weren't you just youngsters? It wasn't your fault your father was ill.'

The rush subsided. 'I don't want to talk about it — I shouldn't have said anything. Promise me you won't say anything . . . please?'

'But maybe you should . . . oh, all right. I won't say anything.'

I took in a long breath and walked away. The air had become stifling and I longed for cold water on my face. I went into the house and straight to my room, ignoring Ginny in the hall.

She has put my head astray with all that talk, I told myself. And if Ivy's right, how can I trust her?

'I've the dinner ready,' she called after me. 'On the table in five minutes.'

I opened my book and took out the piece of paper from Saul's locket. I picked it up and sniffed it, then dropped it in the wastepaper basket. It had no smell. Then I sat at the dressing table and looked into the mirror. My father's eyes looked back at me, distant and empty. I quickly glanced over to the window and back to make the pupil change. It narrowed to the size of a poppy seed and the yellow flecks stood out in the mousy irises. I watched the pupil grow again like a dot of ink spreading on a blotting page, and did the same thing again and again.

As a child, Frank had told me that if you stared hard enough into your own eyes in the mirror on Hallowe'en night, you could see the devil looking back. Now as I stared, all I could see was emptiness and a physical reaction to light. I moved my face closer to the mirror and kept staring, the memory of a school trip to a Dublin museum flooding into my mind. I'd had the same disturbing feeling when I looked into the glass eyes of a model of a prehistoric Homo sapiens in the anthropological section, the same immutable loneliness. I pulled my face away and flinched at Ginny's reflection behind me.

'Oh sorry, Grace — I was worried about you,' she said, a flutter in her voice.

'I had something in my eye.'

'Come on and get your dinner.'

I stood up, mortified, and followed her to the kitchen.

Saul was seated at the table, peeling a potato. I sat to his left and spooned some peas and beans on to my plate. Ginny passed me a bowl of potatoes and we ate in silence, the atmosphere as heavy as the air outside. Mottled clouds obscured the setting sun and the leaves lay motionless on the hedges and trees. I finished before the others and cleared my plate into the sink.

'Did you get enough?' Ginny asked.

'I'm not hungry,' I replied.

She looked confused, as if lack of hunger was an alien concept to her. Her expression irked me. I washed my plate and cutlery, full of loathing that startled me with its intensity. I hated the sight of both of them, hated their gorbing and the way they held their knives and forks. I hated Ginny's firm chin and Saul's hooked nose. I hated their small talk and I despised their composure. My mind began to reel.

As I struggled to steady my thoughts, a door slammed outside.

Frank came in and stood at the range, his

face drained with exhaustion. 'Are the cows milked?'

I nodded, my voice seeming miles away from my throat.

'Any news?' Ginny asked, her palms flat on table.

Frank nodded absently. 'The good news is they think the operation went well.'

Ginny looked at me, then back at Saul. 'So what's the bad news?'

'She can't feel her legs.'

★ ★ ★

I floated up near the surface. The heaviness lifted for a while and squiggly patterns rushed past. It's too busy up there, too bright. Then the blackness shrunk. The space around me became narrow and tight. Once more I am encaged by bones, by a skull with solid sides and a hard top. I'm stuck. I want to swim back into the soft liquid place, where I am weightless, where I don't have a face. Would He leave me like this? I used to think that when an evil person died, his soul is left in him so he has to suffer the process of his own decay, then lie there with his bones for ever.

The good go into the air, and remain in light.

11

Ginny ended up staying for a fortnight. I thought it strange she didn't miss her children, especially the baby, but she never mentioned them. Nor did she ever talk about Mother again.

We rarely spoke, but we were at ease with one another. Together we painted Mother's bedroom a pale shade of blue, and mowed the lawn and cut the hedges. She showed me how to whiten net curtains by soaking them in cream of tartar and putting turpentine in the rinse. Then she had me rubbing sour milk on to the old oilskin coats and leaving them to dry in the sun, to get rid of the mildew on them.

She filled every day with chores, anything to keep her mind occupied, and she wasn't amused when Frank laughed at the sight of his socks hanging on the line with her cardboard sock-shaped cut-outs inside them. It was the first time I'd seen his spirits lift since Mother's operation.

'It'll stop them shrinking and save you a fortune,' Ginny maintained.

She was warmer with Saul. He appeared

every morning to help Frank with the silage, never mentioning where he'd slept. I avoided him as much as I could, trying to rub out the impact he'd had on me.

On the eleventh of July, Ginny decided she would have to get home before the marching on the twelfth. I walked her to the bus stop that evening. While we waited under her claret coloured umbrella in the delicate rain, she took a five-pound note out of her pouch purse and shoved it under my armpit.

'Don't be letting those damn daisies come back on the lawn — they're only weeds, you know,' she said, speaking out of one side of her mouth.

'Thanks, Auntie Ginny. Will you be coming back?'

'Depends on what happens with your mother. I'll come if I'm needed.'

The rain glanced lightly off the umbrella and danced around our feet, a warm swirling breeze blowing droplets off the ends of the spokes. I stood quite contentedly watching the quiet interplay of the elements in the clear sun-tinged light, but Ginny grew impatient, looking past me at regular intervals to check for the bus.

'It's always late,' I said.

She sniffed and looked at her watch.

I fished around in my head for conversation. 'Your umbrella is a nice colour.'

'It was dear, you know.'

'Mother says you should always have a warm-coloured umbrella to put a glow on your face on a grey day.'

She sniffed louder. I could think of nothing more to say to her. She turned slightly towards me, then away again. 'You have a face like a flower, you know.'

'A what?' I thought I'd misheard her.

'You've nice rosebud lips and baby kind of skin. Make sure you look after it, do you hear?'

I shrugged. 'Yes. All right.'

We heard the bus coming before it appeared.

'There it is at last.'

She handed me her bags while she closed her umbrella and stepped on to the bus. I smiled uncertainly up at her but she was rooting in her purse for change. I stepped back and the door clanged shut. Ginny took a seat in the middle and raised the back of her hand in a stiff wave as she passed by. She didn't smile. I'd offered her a book but she said reading in motion made her ill.

I watched the bus until it disappeared out of view. Fragile raindrops settled on my eyelashes and formed a fine wet net over my hair. Now and again the breeze carried with it the rumble of a Lambeg drum and the faint disjointed whistle of flutes, sweet and clipped. A feeling came over me I slowly recognised as happiness. This feeling only ever came outdoors when the light was good, and it made moving and talking and doing and *being* so much easier. Suddenly I understood exactly what Mother's doctors meant when they coolly referred to the power of the human will. Each time Frank returned from the hospital, he brought the same story from them.

'Mind over matter, that's all there is about it,' he'd duly report. 'At least her physical injuries are healed. We'll just have to wait for the rest.'

I set off for home, half expecting to see Nelly and Mary Mullen out in their garden, but the dampness had kept them inside. A child yelled behind the walls of the McNicholls' house. With all the heartbreak over Charlie, I'd almost forgotten about Florrie dying. I walked on quickly, reluctant to bump into Bear. He'd been very cool with me since Florrie died. I knew it was to do with his strange resentment of Saul.

I kicked a stone in front of me with the edge of my foot, trying to make it go in a straight line as Charlie had once shown me, but it veered off into the hedge outside the Moores' house. I was trying to chip it out with my foot when Dalloway appeared at the door with a newspaper in his hand.

'Grace, Josie's asking for you — come on in and say hello to her.'

I hadn't seen Josie since the day she'd got out of hospital. She'd been dopey with medication and cried when she saw me.

I opened the garden gate and walked up to the door of the cottage.

'I can only stay for a minute,' I said to Dalloway.

Josie was propped up on a high-backed Jacobean chair in the cosy front room, her short swollen legs resting on a stool in front of her. Her cheeks had lost some of their roundness and her skin had thickened into deep lines around her mouth, but I could see the real Josie back behind her twinkling eyes.

'Do you know, I'd know that loose-limbed walk of yours a mile away, Grace dear,' she said, pushing her reading spectacles down on to her tiny beak of a nose. 'Was that Ginny with you?'

'Yes, she's away back home on the bus.'

'What did you say, love?'

'She said Ginny's away home on the bus,' Dalloway half shouted. 'Her hearing's a wee bit affected, Grace.'

'Fine horse of a girl, Ginny,' Josie said, looking into the middle distance. 'Pity she didn't turn. And what about your poor mother? I hear she'll only take visits from your Frank.'

'He was saying that she's getting the odd tingling in her legs now, and she's getting stronger every day,' I said in a raised voice that felt alien.

'Thanks be to God for that. Maybe she'll be all right. Do you know, Grace, if it wasn't for you we would have been killed stone dead, I'm telling you. If you hadn't taken sick, we would've of been in no rush out of yonder.'

'That's the God's truth,' Dalloway said.

I pushed my hair behind my ear and gave Josie a faltering smile. I'd no idea how to respond to a statement of that magnitude.

'It said on the news that the Provos have admitted it,' Josie said. 'It'd make you ashamed, wouldn't it. God help whoever they'll take in revenge.'

'Some young innocent off the street, no doubt,' Dalloway said, folding his newspaper. 'Them tartan gangs are desperate cruel. Sure they gave that wee fella from Lurgan an awful doing the other week there, and him no connection to anything. Took him from the chip shop and dragged him to one of their oul' romper rooms. Found him in the Bann the next day, butcher's hook through his neck.'

I blanched.

'And what about you, love. Any wee bad turns?' Josie enquired

'No, none.'

'What's that?'

'No — no, I haven't had one since. I'm all right again.'

'Just you mind yourself anyway.'

I nodded and looked away, wondering what to say next.

'I see you've been getting the place ready for the twelfth,' Dalloway said dryly.

'Yes, it's a bit more Protestant-looking since Ginny came.'

Josie whooped. 'Oh that's a good one! A bit more Protestant, indeed!'

I felt very grown up, joking with the neighbours on my own, yet oddly out of place. I glanced at the gold carriage clock on the tan-tiled mantel and took a step back towards the door.

'Right, well . . . better get home and polish up my bowler hat,' I said, edging towards the door.

'What's that you say, Grace?' Josie beamed.

'She's away to do up her bowler. All the best now, Grace,' Dalloway said, opening the door for me.

I bade them goodbye and darted out, feeling light. The rain had waned and left the air fresh and new, and smelling green and clean. I walked home with renewed vigour and turned the kitchen wireless to the jazz station. I mopped the floor to some erratic beat and threw out an extra handful of nuts to the starlings and the blackbirds, then made myself a cup of coffee with a dollop of whipping cream and two heaped spoonfuls of brown sugar.

I lounged back in the armchair and drank, pulling in my stomach after each sip. Mother had a habit of surreptitiously looking at my body, then running her hands around her waist, and it had made me even more aware of my chunky middle.

I could keep my sweet tooth in check when she was around but I savoured a rare treat. I licked the cream off my top lip and sat with one ankle up on the opposite knee, like Frank, so relaxed that I had no compulsion to move when I heard the back door opening.

Even when I saw it was Ivy, I sat my ground.

'Well look at King Farouk,' she said, parking herself on the kitchen table.

'Who's that?'

'A big fat lazy Egyptian shite.'

I drained my mug and bopped it on my leg,

for once unfazed by Ivy's cheeky face. 'You've brought the dark with you.'

'Sure it's near ten o'clock. Where's Frank?'

'He went to buy a tractor in Dundalk. He should be — '

'Good — come on, we'll go to the bonfire,' she interrupted, getting off the table.

'The bonfire. Are you mad?'

'Why not? Nobody's going to bother with us. Aw come on.'

'It's all right for you.'

Ivy took me by the arms and pulled me up off the chair. 'Don't be such a ninny. It will be a laugh.'

I looked into her fizzing eyes and made a snap decision. 'Wait and I'll get my coat.'

★   ★   ★

A clay pigeon spirals down through the chalk white sky and falls into a cowpat on the other side of the hedge. Gunfire cracks and echoes. I can feel the hot breath of the Charlois on my back as we lead him quickly down towards the meadow. I am tall for my age and can see over the hedge, to where the shooters are. Frank tells me to keep my head down. We go faster. I hear a snap in the grass and peep over my shoulder. No-one is there. I can feel every pump of my heart. I am excited. The Charlois stumbles on a mound and tugs us back on the rope we're clutching. I feel the burn on my palms. Frank calls the blond bullock his good big boy and promises to keep him safe. I tell him we're going to get killed. We cross the meadow, keeping in along the hedge. When we get to the edge of the reed bank, Frank becomes afraid. I tell him it's all right, that the glar doesn't start for a good few yards in. He points to a pole on a small clearing ahead and says we'll tie the Charlois to it. The ground begins to soften and we tread carefully, close to the thickest clumps of reeds. Near the pole, the Charlois halts and refuses to move on. We tug on the rope, to no avail. Frank waves me aside and goes and whispers into the animal's ear, and holds out a stick of liquorice. He leads him slowly ahead; I hang back and wait, peering through the reeds behind and straining my eardrums. Silence. Then a sudden human gasp and an animal roar that sounds surprised . . .

I spin around. I can't see Frank. I see only the craning neck and head of the Charlois above the muddy surface. Its eyes are wild and it's mwaaahing like a baby calf. I can't speak. I step forward and start to slide. I try to shout Frank's name but it comes out in a squeak. The Charlois sinks up to its chin, its head thrashing pathetically. I am light-headed with the quickening of the blood in my eardrums. I catch a glimpse of a movement under the surface. I get down on my knees and stretch towards it, plunging my right hand into the mossy green and purple slime. Nothing. I open my mouth and scream Frank's name over and over again. I feel something brush against my hand and I grab it and pull. It slips away. I stretch further towards it and begin to slide into the goo. I grab on to some fallen reeds with one hand and grope with the other. A forearm bursts out and a flailing hand, fingers webbed with slime, like a horror movie prop, clutches at the ear of the frantic Charlois. I edge myself forward until I almost lose my grip on the reeds. I grab Frank's arm. I pull but there is resistance. I let go of the reeds and lie down flat and haul the arm with both hands. The Charlois sinks further. Its eyes roll up in its head. Beside it a lump emerges. I grab it, I grip on to sludge-covered hair and with a sudden burst of livid defiance my strength bolsters and I'm on my hunkers with one half of Frank beside me. He looks like a newborn monster. I push him on to his side and stick my fingers into his mouth and dig out the muck. I clear out his nostrils and pound him on his back. He coughs and gags and spews. I *slide my wrists under his armpits and heave backwards until his legs are out. I shout into his ear and clean his eyes. He rocks his head and clutches at my chest. When I look back, the Charlois is gone.*

★ ★ ★

'We'll have a gawk from The Leap first.'

I was infected by Ivy's energy, even though the cataract scared me. The morning's heavy downpour had swelled the water and the cascade rushed violently down the jagged basalt fall, transforming into a cloud of silver spray at the bottom before rejoining the river on its course to the lough.

We stood under a silver birch and watched the crowd below us mill around the burning stack of pallets and planks of wood and tyres on the tiny village common.

'Do you know how what height The Leap is?' Ivy asked, throwing a stick into the fretted water.

'Forty-five feet exactly. And the slope is a hundred and five feet.'

'All right, swotty face. Damn bit of good your studying did you anyway. I can see frig all from here — let's get a bit closer.'

I opened my mouth to object but shut it again. We crossed the footbridge over the river and slipped into the village through a laneway between the pub and the post office. We hesitated when we got to the pavement.

'What about watching from the clock?' I whispered.

'I was just gonna say that — come on, and don't run.'

We made our leisurely way to the clock tower facing the common. The night air was full of the acrid reek of burning rubber and the crackle and hiss of the howling fire. An effigy of the Pope blazed on top of the conflagration, its stuffed arms akimbo and a trajectory of sparkles flying out of its spherical head. The small crowd stood in clusters, some drinking from bottles, some carrying flags emblazoned with the Red Hand of Ulster.

I leaned against the slated side of the tower and watched the flames change colour from pinky orange to blue green to purple and back. Ivy stood out front, her arms folded and her feet shuffling.

'God, would you look at the state of oul' Billy Gascoigne's son with the collar on him already. Blert.'

'Mr Gascoigne's all right.'

'He's as black as your boot.'

'Auntie Ginny says the Black Perceptory are fairly respectable.'

'Yeah, right.'

'You're fairly bitter for a half Prod.'

'I'm more of a Romanist — sure my da's an atheist and my ma's a half nun, for God's sake. She'd sicken you, running to her novenas all the time.'

She took a cigarette from the breast pocket of her denim jacket and struck a match, momentarily illuminating the graceful curve of her profile.

'Ivy, get back — somebody will see you.'

'Sure what odds? I'm bored.'

She sucked hard on her cigarette and circled it in front of her. In the dark it looked like miniature spinning fireworks. An unexpected breeze whipped around the common and flared up the bonfire, sending sparks shooting into the blackness. An arm burnt off the Pope and careened on to the ground, evoking a cheer from younger sections of the gathering. A boy with a band stick ran up to it and jumped on it, until a laughing woman pulled him away. They narrowly missed a burning tyre that had dislodged itself from the megalith and rolled free — to my horror, towards us.

'Ivy, watch out for that thing!' She stood with her hands at her side, directly in line with the tyre, then stuck out her platform shoe and stopped it in its tracks. 'This'll keep us warm.'

I could have hit her.

'Ivy, somebody's coming — would you come over here!'

She threw her cigarette butt on to the smouldering tyre at her feet and ignored me. I slunk back further along the clock tower wall into the shadows. The footsteps I'd heard came closer and a rangy figure emerged from behind the bonfire. He stopped a few yards away from Ivy, a long black silhouette against the flames.

'You'd need to watch you don't get burned, miss.'

He spoke with a Geordie accent.

'I can look after myself, mister.'

He stepped closer, twirling a beer bottle in his hand. 'In Africa they put those around the necks of the enemy. Burning necklaces, they call them.'

'Really? In our house we boil Brits' balls for breakfast.'

He laughed. 'I like the cut of your jib, missy. Take a drink?' He held out the bottle.

'Bring it over to me.'

He hesitated. 'Now, you wouldn't be laying a trap for me, would you darlin'?'

'Don't be daft.'

He stepped closer and handed the bottle to

298

Ivy. I held back, waiting for a signal from her but she seemed to have forgotten I was there. She took the bottle and swigged from it. I could see the man's face more clearly now. He looked about thirty, with sandy hair and fair eyebrows, and a smiley mouth.

'Fancy taking a stroll?'

'If I can keep the beer.'

He laughed again. 'Of course. I know where there's some more. Let's go.'

'All right then. Just a wee walk.'

I watched with rising consternation as Ivy followed the man in the direction of the river. Then just as they were about to go out of my line of vision, Ivy turned and dashed back. I straightened up in relief but she stopped short and bent down to pick up her box of matches on the ground.

'Wait there for me, Grace — I won't be long,' she whispered, a grin spreading across her face. I started to protest but she turned and ran back to the man.

I kicked the back of my heel against the wall. I felt my mother's brand of wrath within me and the innate force of it took me unawares. I bit down on hard on my lip as Ivy and the man disappeared from view. I'd guessed he was a soldier and knew she had too. Above me the clock struck eleven and minutes later drinkers began to spill out of the pub. My palms broke out in a sweat.

O clement, o loving, so sweet Virgin Mary, Pray for us o holy Mother of God, That we be made worthy of the promises of Christ . . .

I had known the prayer by heart since my schooldays but I couldn't remember the rest. The drinkers' singing drowned it out.

I edged along to the corner of the tower and slipped around to the back of it. The singers grew louder as they approached the bonfire.

'And the colours they were fine, 'Twas worn at Derry, Augh-rim, Enniskillen and the Boyne . . . '

I waited for them to pass, then peeped out to see if the road was clear. A trio of stragglers followed the main group, one of them stumbling along the edge of the pavement. As they approached the common, he broke away from his companions.

'Going for a slash,' he shouted, his voice thick with beer.

I jerked back as I realised he was heading for the clock tower. Would he go to the front or the back or the side? I dithered for a few seconds, than moved back to the far corner as quietly as I could. The drunk staggered over, mumbling to himself. I held my breath and tried to make out the direction of his footsteps. When he came to a halt, I guessed he was at the front of the tower, as I could see no shadows at the side.

I heard a glass fall without breaking on the ground, and a zip go down. I waited for the splash of urine but none came. Instead there was a shout and running footsteps.

'Hey you can't do it there, boy — there are people watching — get around the back.'

I froze.

The voice was Saul's. Indubitably. I took a step sideways in confusion, the option of coming out into the open flashing through my head, but an overriding instinct propelled me back to the side of the tower.

My ears popped, making the sound of my own breathing uppermost in my head. Inches away, there was shuffling and the swishing of wavering urination.

'Are you ready?'

It was definitely his voice.

'Fuck away off. I'm staying here.'

'All right. See you later.'

The clock chimed for the quarter hour. Up ahead, another two men loitered outside the pub, putting paid to my plans to make a run for the shortcut.

Keep calm. Ivy will be back soon.

No sound came from the drunk and the singing had stopped.

All at once I felt cold and tired from standing. I lowered on to my hunkers, my thoughts zigzagging in confusion. The two men outside the pub walked away in the opposite direction but the fear of meeting others in the lane kept me from running. I leaned my head against my knees and shivered, imagining the heat from the bonfire, and Saul standing beside it. Saul?

Prickling with curiosity, I dropped on to my knees and turned to peep around the corner again. I saw him immediately, talking to youngish men I didn't recognise at the side of the still billowing bonfire.

I thought back to his arrival on our doorstep, to the sense of otherness that hung around him, to the strange connection I'd felt with him, and I began to feel very naive, and very stupid.

The awareness of someone watching me came too late. I turned my head slowly, fear clogging my throat.

'Who th'fuck are you?'

I looked up into the beer-bloated face and began to shake my head.

'I . . . I'm just waiting for my friend. She went for a — '

'What in fuck you doin' down there?'

'Nothing . . . nothing, just waiting . . . '

'Looks to me like you're spying, Fenian.'

I tried to clear my throat. 'She'll be back in a minute — maybe I'll go and look for her.' I made a move to get up but he swung his foot out, skimming my chest. I sat back on my hunkers.

'You're a wee Fenian, aren't you?'

I grappled for an answer in my head. In the back of my mind a nun's voice whispered never deny your faith.

'My friend Ivy's a half . . . she's a Protestant.'

'That right? And what are you?'

'I . . . I don't really know what I believe . . . '

'Fuckin' answer my question, wee girl.'

He swayed slightly.

'Look, another friend of mine's with your crowd — Saul.'

'Sole? Never heard of him. Stop fuckin' — '

As he swayed again I got to my feet but he lurched forward and pinned me to the clock tower by the arms. Sticky white secretions clung to the inside corners of his half open mouth and wobbled with each exhalation of his foul breath.

I stiffened from head to toe as he leaned into my face. I tried to move my head to the side but my neck was rigid.

'Pl . . . please don't — '

He lunged his stinking furred tongue into

303

my mouth and pushing it in as far as it would stretch. I gagged on it and he withdrew his head and spat to the side.

'Dirty Fenian mouth,' he said, smirking. 'Go on t'fuck.'

He pushed me aside, then rubbed his crotch.

I stood gawping at him in stupefaction.

'What're you waitin for? Get t'fuck!'

I didn't stop running until I reached the shore path.

I clung to a tree, heaving great gulps of air into my bursting chest, and watched stringy wisps of cloud float over the big friendly new moon. Then I rubbed my mouth along the arm of my blouse and walked home, my nerves shrieking.

I needed my mother.

12

Frank drank straight from the jug of milk, same as Daddy used to when he was thirsty.

'You're terrible pale,' Frank said, putting the jug back in the fridge.

I pulled my dressing gown tighter around me. 'I'm all right. Didn't hear you come in last night.'

'Called in with Willy and couldn't get out. He hardly ever goes out of the house, but he said he'd drop in the day for an oul' game of poker.'

'Poker in the middle of the day?'

'Sure there's nothing else to do on the twelfth.'

'I forgot it was the twelfth.'

'Dalloway and Bear's coming too. Speaking of which, you couldn't do us a favour and get Saul out of here for the afternoon?'

'Saul?'

'He's out there reading the paper on the verandah. Thought he was needed down the meadows. You could take him up the road to see the marching. You know Bear can't abide him. Thinks he's a bad omen.'

'Do I have to? I'm sure there are others he could go with.'

'Like who? Sure he doesn't know anybody.'

'I wouldn't be so sure about that.'

'About what?' Saul stood stretching in the kitchen doorway.

'The marching — Grace's going to take you to see some Orange action.'

'Great. It's a good day for it.'

He walked over to the range and lifted the teapot from it. I declined his offer of a warm-up and got up to go to my room.

'They've taken Hugh Best's big field at the front of the mill for the speech-making — you'll catch the last of the bands going in if you head up soon,' Frank called after me.

I closed the bedroom door and lay down on the side of my unmade bed, silently cursing Frank. How could I spend the day with Saul after what I'd seen last night? For all I knew, he could be some sort of Loyalist spy. Once again, I could trust no-one.

The hiss in my ears had grown louder. I shifted on to my side and pulled the eiderdown around me and rolled in it to the other side of the bed. I lay in the padded tube, my arms by my sides, my face against the ruby red velour, and listened to the relentless high tone in my ears. I became a newborn infant, with no language in my brain, wrapped up tight to keep the world out a little while longer, helpless without the freedom of my arms. Sunlight from the window glowed through the fabric, casting me in a warm red light.

A piglet under an infra-red lamp. That would be all right. Easier than being human.

The light turned to shade and the fabric darkened. The glow dimmed. The sleep I'd missed the night before began to tug on my eyelids and pull me deeper into my cocoon, the red glow still visible through my eyelids.

A baby in the womb. That would be nice, to start again . . .

'Grace! Grace! Are you all right? I heard an awful thud . . . '

My nose throbbed. I tried to wriggle free.

'What are you doing down there like a sausage roll?'

Saul leaned down and pulled the edge of the eiderdown from underneath me. I scrambled to my feet, clutching my nose.

Saul laughed but beside him, Frank's face was strained. I sat on the bed, too startled to be embarrassed.

'Give yourself a shake now and get on out,' Frank said gruffly. 'I'm away to do a bit of weeding. No point in trying to get to see Ma t'day.'

He walked down the hall, tutting to himself.

Saul stood at the side of the bed. 'Did you hurt yourself?'

'No.'

'Yes you did — look, your nose is bleeding. Wait there . . . I'll go and get something . . . '

I drew my hand away from my nose and stared at the dark red blood. I felt it run down and wobble on the top of my lip before spilling on to my dressing gown. I took a tissue from the box on my bedside table and held it to my nose.

Saul ran back into the room with a cream towel.

'Better not use that — it's one of Mother's good ones,' I objected.

'Don't be silly — lie back and tilt your head back for a few minutes,' he said, replacing the tissue with the towel.

I leaned back and felt the blood trickle down my throat. Saul looked around the room and took the bloodstained tissue to the wastepaper bin.

I hadn't emptied it in ages and I remembered immediately what was inside it.

'I see you found my nirvana.'

My heart skipped a beat and I was glad of the towel to hide behind. 'Oh . . . oh, that. I thought it was some old rubbish. Sorry — '

'It's all right. I was just wondering where it had got to.'

'Sorry, I forgot to — what is it anyway?'

'Ssssh. Put your head back again and get that blood stopped. We don't want to miss the Orangemen, now do we? I'll leave you to it. See you outside when you get cleaned up.'

He went up the hall, whistling.

I swallowed hard and shook my head. Lunatic. Ape.

I caught sight of my cringing reflection in the mirror and propelled myself off the bed. In the bathroom I washed the blood off my face and teeth. The nosebleed had stopped abruptly, leaving me as pale as milk. One of Mother's lipsticks lay in the unit under the sink. I snatched it and rubbed the greasy colour into my cheeks. I put a dash under my eyebrows, like I'd seen in a magazine article on how to achieve a healthy glow, and a tiny dab on my mouth.

Dirty Fenian mouth. What? No. Shut up.

Outside, Saul sat in the driver's seat of Frank's car. He tooted the horn and waved me over. I slipped into the passenger seat.

'You look much better. Frank says I can take his car. Trusts me at last.'

'Good.'

He drove out on to the road and towards the village without needing directions.

'You're very quiet, Grace.'

'I'm just a bit tired. You seem to know your way about now.'

'Yeah, it's not a hard place to get to know.'

The intersection leading to the Bests' field was lined with cars on all sides. Saul pulled up and rolled down his window, drilled his fingers on the car roof.

'Can anyone go in and watch?' he asked, leaning out of the window.

The distrust I'd begun to feel for him suddenly intensified and I almost told him I'd seen him at the bonfire. But I held back, bowing to an instinct.

'Well you'd get tourists going to have a look and you'd get a handful of Catholics from the village at it, knocking about with the hangers-on.'

He took his sunglasses from the dashboard and slipped them on.

'Do you ever drink, Grace?'

'I don't really like the taste of it . . . but I like the thought of being drunk.'

He laughed. 'What do you think you'd like about it?'

'Just . . . just being in another world, I suppose. Forgetting all your troubles.'

'Are you troubled?'

'I . . . no, not really. Just sometimes I have this chattering in my head I wish I could stop

. . . oh, ignore me. I'm talking rubbish.' I stopped before my mouth ran away with me and turned away from his gaze.

'Well, it just so happens I — oh! Look who it is. Hey, Ivy!'

He beeped the horn and Ivy spun around, her long black hair whipping back from her face. She had plucked her eyebrows into thin astonished arches and stuck an orange lily above her ear. Her expression darkened when she caught sight of me. She walked over to the car, swinging a yellow patchwork bag that matched her mini dress.

'Jump in,' Saul said, leaning back to open the door for her.

'Where the frig did you go last night?' she demanded as she stepped in, ignoring Saul.

I turned round and widened my eyes at her, with a slight shake of my head. Saul caught my hesitation as he turned in his seat and looked at me in puzzlement.

'I was out for a walk. Must have just missed you.'

Ivy raised a ravaged eyebrow. 'Right, Kane. Just keep taking the tablets.'

I blushed and forced a laugh.

Ivy leaned forward in the seat and gleefully pretended to burn her finger on my cheek. 'Take a reddener!'

'Leave her alone, Ivy.'

His words made the blush deepen to puce. Ivy pointed and giggled as I suffered the familiar undignified agony, made all the worse by the irrational nature of it. I turned away from her and rolled down my window, feeling a streak of sweat breaking behind my knees.

A lone tinny drumbeat sounded in swift regular strikes in the near distance. Saul reached out and adjusted the driver's mirror.

'Here they come.'

'It's the Crumlin lodge — that's the last of them. Cooled down, Grace?'

I hadn't.

'Ivy!'

'Look would you both keep quiet,' I snapped, my face flaring again. 'I've got high blood pressure, that's all. My ears pop — '

'And your head spins around! Ach sorry, Grace, I'm only joking, frig's sake.'

She ruffled my hair. I felt as if I'd been turned inside out for all to see. The drumbeat grew louder, accompanied by the rhythmic clatter of hard soles on the ground as the band came into view, flutes by their sides, their gold rope regalia on their neat royal blue uniforms glinting in the sunshine, their beret feathers fluttering in the mild breeze.

'We'll wait until these ones pass then scoot

up to the mill. I know a spot where we'll have a perfect view.'

She stretched out along the back seat and lit a cigarette. Saul reclined his seat halfway and clasped his hands behind his head.

'I've only ever seen this sort of thing on the television,' he said with a yawn. 'Fairly harmless, isn't it?'

I nodded.

'The majority of them's all right. You get a few bad bastards, though,' Ivy said.

'I'm sure there are bad bastards on both sides.'

I stole a sidelong glance at him. His face was as impassive as always.

Ivy straightened up. 'Jesus, there's the postman!'

I tried to pick out the postman in the orderly rows of hard-hatted heads following the band into the field. Older than the flute players, their faces were stern and they all looked the same.

'I must train the dog to bite him,' Ivy said, leaning forward to pat her hair in the windscreen mirror.

Saul looked up at her. 'You wouldn't do that, Ivy.'

'Why not?'

'Sure the man's not doing any harm.'

'I don't like him anyway. Right! This is

boring — let's go.'

She slid over to the door and stepped out. I followed her, leaving Saul to lock the car. She skipped on ahead like a child. I caught up with her and lightly touched her arm. She shook it off.

'Away and boil your head.'

'I was only going to ask you if you got home all right,' I whispered.

'Fat lot you care.'

'You don't understand — something happened.'

'Something happened, my ass. You cleared off. And what's all the secrecy about anyways?'

'Ssssh. I'll tell you later.'

'Weirdo.'

Saul ran up between us and put his arms around both our waists. I pulled in my stomach; Ivy wiggled.

'Up this way,' she instructed.

We fell in behind her, past the field and on to the lane leading to the mill. In the field people gathered in front of a sheltered makeshift stage with a podium in the centre. Women and children from the village sat in folding chairs, some waving mini Union Jacks. They passed around sandwiches and flasks, smiling and bantering in the mellow sunshine.

The lane sloped gently upwards to the mill, a tall narrow grey stone building, long defunct. Beyond it the river rolled quietly, gently staggered in its course by the remains of an old-fashioned wheel-generator once used, Ivy said, to motor-power the mill in the days it used to produce flour.

Ivy paused at the mill to light another cigarette. Saul stood on his tiptoes to look through one of the high tall windows flanking the huge decaying double doors. He tried the tarnished brass knob but the door held fast.

I watched him with the eerie feeling that something was watching us from inside. I turned away and followed Ivy to a small cluster of trees on a natural ridge overlooking the now swarming field.

'Come on, Saul, the balcony seats go the quickest,' she yelled.

We sat down on the grass and she patted the ground beside her. Saul gave the mill door another rattle before he joined us, lowering himself on to his stomach and elbows. Below us an Orangeman self-consciously tested the microphone on the stage, clearing his dry throat between every 'one, two'.

Ivy pointed and laughed at him. 'Twit! Isn't this the perfect view? You can see far more side-on, though it's a bit hard to make out their faces. I love spotting the ones I know, don't you, Grace?'

I felt the clench behind my temples subside, relieved that she'd dropped her snappy attitude. Suddenly she clapped her hands.

'Right — who's for tequila and orange?' She produced the bottles and a packet of paper cups from her bag. 'Dee-daa! Always come prepared, that's what I say. Da brought this stuff back from holidays.'

'Now you're talking,' Saul said, taking the tequila bottle from Ivy and opening it.

Ivy sloshed a little orange into three cups and then filled them up with tequila.

'Down in one! You first, Grace.'

I raised the cup to my mouth and gulped it.

'Yo! You're a right gull, Kane.'

I grimaced. 'It tastes like a dirty dishcloth.'

The fleetingly guarded expression I'd seen on Saul's face slipped and he laughed. He lifted his cup to Ivy.

'Sláinte!'

'Cheers, big ears!'

Ivy refilled the cups and proposed a toast.

'To the Orangemen, God bless them!'

I held my nose and drained my cup, choking on the last mouthful. Ivy fell on to her back and hooted with laughter. Saul watched me as I spluttered, with a smile on his mouth but concern in his eyes.

'I'm fine,' I told him before he could ask. I was already experiencing the first spangly effects of the alcohol in my brain and I liked it.

On the stage, the first speaker had begun to read from the Bible, his words floating precariously in and out of earshot on the eddying breeze. Then a short sharp buzz emitted from his microphone and his voice rang out with a squeal from the speakers.

'There are also many rebellious people, idle talkers and deceivers ... rebuke them sharply, so that they may become sound in the faith, not paying attention to Jewish myths or to the commandments of those who reject the truth. To the pure all things are pure, but to the corrupt and unbelieving, nothing is pure. Their very minds and consciences are corrupted. They profess to know God, but they deny him by their actions. They are detestable, disobedient, unfit for any good work ... '

A click and a thump sounded, and the scorning voice was carried away on the breeze.

Ivy scoffed and poured out more drink. 'No prizes for guessing who he's talking about.'

I leaned one arm behind me and sipped the

drink, beginning to feel a sense of ease spread within me. The speaker's voice drifted back. He held the Bible shut and aloft in his hand.

'Yes, my brethren. The seditious residing in their whited sepulchres, holy and respectable on the outside, but on the inside — dead, rotten and stinking!'

A ripple of applause broke out among the crowd. Ivy giggled but Saul hushed her by putting a finger up to his mouth.

'Heads of gossip peeping from their doors, slaves to superstition. Wasting the powers of their souls on barren ecstasies. Damning their young in heretic rituals . . . '

I strained to catch the words but a stronger breeze tossed them in the air and flung them away like confetti.

Saul shook his head. 'That's a pity. It was just getting interesting.'

'It's a bundle of nonsense,' Ivy said with a snort.

Saul jumped to his feet, his arm thrust out in imitation of the speaker.

'So you're not worried about your poor lost soul then, Ivy Best?'

'Damn sure I'm not.'

'And what about you, Grace Kane?'

'Sometimes I wonder — '

'Well fear not!' he boomed. 'For He will transfigure your wretched bodies into copies of His glorious body. He will do that by the same power with which He can subdue the whole of the universe!'

He thrust out his other arm, spilling his drink.

'Big galoot,' Ivy said, kneeling up and taking his cup. 'And there's nothing wretched about my body. I'm quite proud of it in fact.'

He reddened under his tan and sat down. I opened my mouth to speak but immediately lost what I was going to say. All thoughts fled and my mind went blank. I covered my cup to prevent Ivy giving me more tequila but she pushed my hand away and poured.

'One last one down the hatch, then we'll start on the wine.'

She gave me her most charming smile, seducing me into drinking with her. The taste had become less objectionable and the drink slid easily down my throat. Saul sipped slowly, refusing Ivy's urgings to knock it back.

'Ponce,' she said, rooting in her clinking bag.

More applause sounded below us. The sun was cutting in and out of the filtering veils of cloud, heightening the light in short bursts. I narrowed my eyes against the renewed brightness and the scene below became a blurred melange of golden strokes and black spots, like a painting by a Dutchman whose name would not come to my muzzy mind.

' . . . for the soul is dyed the colour of its thoughts . . . '

The breeze shifted again and chased away the words with the sun. Goosepimples rose on my upper arms yet I didn't feel cold.

Ivy began to tut. 'Oh God, I've forgotten the corkscrew — wait there and I'll go and get one.' She got to her feet a little unsteadily and narrowed her eyes at me. 'You won't clear off, will you, Kane?'

I shook my head and gave her a quick smile. She strolled off towards the lane, flicking her gleaming hair off her shoulders. I leaned back on my elbows and drew up my knees, watching the speaker step down from the stage.

Saul rolled over on his side towards me and rested his head on his hand. 'What was all that about?'

'What?'

'Doesn't matter. Grace, are you sure you should be drinking when you're on medication?'

The wooziness in my head began to recede. 'I . . . how did you know . . . I was — '

'Frank asked me to watch out for you, that's all.'

'Well, he shouldn't have bothered.'

'But what if you had a fit?'

I felt my hips jerk in irritation. 'I won't.'

'But you could have a reaction to the drink.'

I sat up and straightened out my legs. My calf muscles were clenching. 'I won't.'

'Jesus, you can be exasperating. Epileptics shouldn't drink like that.'

I stiffened. Then a cold, flat anger pressed down on me and I felt myself looking at my interrogator with contempt.

'Who do you think you are? I am not an . . . epileptic and I'm not taking any tablets and it's absolutely none of your business anyway.'

I stood up and began to walk away but got pins and needles in my head which blinded me for an instant. I swayed and he caught me by my outstretched arms, and led me over to the trees. I sat down and leaned against a knobbly trunk, holding my head in my hands. Saul grabbed the bottle of orange and poured a cup full. He handed it to me and knelt beside me.

'Look, Grace, maybe I should bring you home. You've already whacked your nose today, and I wouldn't know what to do if you went into a f — '

'Don't say that,' I snapped at him.

He flinched, confusion in his eyes.

'I don't take any bloody fits. I was only

pretending at Charlie's wake, so stop fussing!'

'I don't understand . . . '

'Tough.'

'Jesus, Grace. What's wrong with you?'

The sun had fought its way back but the goosepimples on my arms jittered. I saw myself reflected in Saul's blue-black eyes and became afraid. He glanced down at my hands and I realised I was clutching at my fingers, two at a time.

'Grace, tell me what's wrong.'

'Nothing. It's just the drink.'

'No, look . . . I've noticed you being a bit . . . nervy, before.'

I swallowed back the orange. 'You're torturing me,' I wailed.

He held my face. I saw myself in his eyes again and pushed his hands away.

'I keep feeling as if . . . as if . . . there's something evil inside me. Like there now. But I . . . it's scary, Saul. I don't want to be like her, I . . . '

'Who?'

A sound shot up my throat and out of my mouth like a shout of laughter, but it came with rushing tears and heaving ragged breaths. Saul put his hand behind my neck and drew my face to his. I clung on to his sides, unable to stem the sobbing.

When it eased, his shirt was sodden. He

passed me a tissue from Ivy's bag.

'Grace, there's no-one inside you but yourself. And you are a good person,' he whispered.

'I . . . I don't . . . '

'You are your own person. No-one controls you.'

'But you don't understand . . . the feeling that comes is so strong. It's cold and empty, and when it comes, I know there is no God.' I dried my eyes, suddenly feeling calmer. 'I did have . . . fits when I was wee. I'm afraid of them coming back.'

'But, but they can be controlled. There's nothing to be afraid of.'

I sighed. 'They are disgusting. All this stuff comes out . . . '

He rubbed the side of his jaw. 'But you can't help that. That's no big deal.'

I stood up slowly and stepped from under the tree into the fervent sunshine. I felt a tinge of loneliness seep into my new calm, and knew I'd said enough.

'You're right. I'm just being dramatic.'

He stood beside me and took my hand in his.

'You know you can talk to me any time. If there's anything bothering you,' he said, turning towards the lane.

High-pitched laughter rang out from it. I

extracted my hand from his, just as Ivy appeared with a man. As they approached, I recognised him as the one she'd gone off with the night before.

'Grace, Saul — say hello to Andy. I found him wandering around on his own like a lost pup.'

He stood squinting at us, his fleshy top lip pushed up almost to his nose. Sweat stood in his neat, straw-coloured hair and glistened in his pale eyebrows, and his fair skin was a painful shade of rhubarb pink.

Saul and I said hello at the same time.

'Don't I know you from somewhere?' he said, looking at Saul.

'Don't think so,' Saul said evenly.

'It's just . . . you look familiar — look, if you don't mind, I'm just going to take the shade under those trees,' he said, tugging on the neck of his T-shirt.

'The little lamb chop's got a bit of sunstroke,' Ivy cooed. 'Plonk yourself down there and I'll get the wine — oh, I see you left it in the shade. Good thinking folks.'

I walked back to the ridge, still slightly unsteady on my feet.

Saul followed and sat down beside me. 'Do you know that English guy?'

'No. But Ivy was with him last night, in the village.'

'She was in the village last night?'

'Yes.'

I waited for him to tell me he was there too, but he lay back and said nothing. In the field the crowd were standing and singing. The breeze had gone and their voices rang out clearly, proclaiming themselves Christian soldiers, marching out to war.

Saul banged the sides of his boots together, then sat up abruptly.

'I'm going to get some of that wine. Do you want some?'

'Better not.'

He sprang to his feet and walked over to the tree. I lay back on the ground and covered my eyes with my arm. The singing stopped and it became quiet, apart from the odd squeak from Ivy under the tree, and the swish of the river. The heat made my body heavy, and I no longer cared if Saul came back and saw me sprawled out. Slowly the swirl in my head slowed down and the effort of lifting my arm and opening my eyes became too great. I remembered what Saul had said about listening to the earth, and felt like I was lying on the edge of it. I listened, imagining that I was rolling in tune with some rhythm far beneath me, then my leg shot out with a jolt and my heart leapt in protest at the sensation of falling. Then I was back on terra firma, sinking into the soil . . .

★ ★ ★

Great bony fingers of red and pink streaked the sky in the west. I blinked in the glare, immediately feeling ravenous. I sat up stiffly, my hunger overtaken by a deep thirst. Only a few weeded-out groups remained in the field below and there was no-one under the tree. I stood up, swallowing against the dryness in my mouth, and stretched my arms over my head. The lowered sun was hitting the windows of the mill, making them look alight and expelling the gloomy resonance of the old granite walls. I shaded my eyes against the glow as I walked past the mill to the river behind it, resisting the urge to run into it.

I knelt by the side and splashed my face and neck with the fresh cool water. I wet my mouth and stood up, jittery from heat and dehydration, and walked slowly towards the lane. Mild shakes hit me and I paused in the shade at the back of the mill, the power draining out of my legs. I leaned against the mill wall, thankful for the returning breeze whipping around the corner. Then I heard a muffled groan.

I stepped forward and looked around,

wondering if it was the wind, but when it came again, I realised it was from inside the mill. I edged along the wall and peeped in through a window, but it was obscured by criss-crossed planks of wood. The breeze gained momentum and I was seized by a sense of déjà vu.

No, it couldn't possibly be. He'll be away home ages ago.

I moved away from the window and gently slapped my face, trying to quell the shakiness, and the groan came again, followed closely by a whimper. Panic shot through me. I walked to the next window and found it wedged open with a rusty oil-can. Inside was a dark galley-shaped room with two blackened and cracked Belfast sinks against one wall and an archway opposite them. I stepped in through the window and scanned the four corners of the musty room. The whimpering had stopped but as I tiptoed across the layers of sawdust on the floor, I heard the groan again, coming from the archway. The panic surged and propelled me towards it. I shouted Ivy's name and in the same instant saw her face, flung back in ecstasy like St Teresa. She sat astride the Englishman, her unbuttoned dress hitched up around her hips. I gasped. Ivy's head jerked up, her eyes widening as they met mine. The man began to laugh and she joined in.

'Seen enough, Kane? Look at this,' she said, beginning to writhe.

I stumbled backwards, then bolted to the window, tripping over the sill on the way out and falling on to the grass. I scrambled on to my feet and ran to the lane, a pain piercing one of my ankles. Halfway down, I stopped to rub the ankle and Frank's car pulled up on the road.

'Hi, Grace.'

Saul got out of the car and walked up the lane to meet me. I limped towards him.

'You look like you've seen a ghost.'

I was hit with a surge of revulsion for Ivy, and a sudden bitchy need to punish her.

'Ivy is doing it with that English guy up in the mill.'

'What?'

'I saw them. Could you please take me home?'

The surprise on his face ebbed into a cold blankness.

Bingo.

I trembled quietly the whole way home and he said nothing. In the yard he handed me the car keys before getting out of the car.

'I'm going for a walk. I'll see you soon.'

I stood in the doorway and watched him walk away. Then I went into the house and stood under the shower until the water ran cold.

★　★　★

Was that lurking evil I felt inside me innate or learned? It took me many years to see it for what it was. My mother's contempt had oozed into my soul from the moment I was born and lay festering until I unleashed it under the guise of my own anger. I didn't stand a chance. When the word came that she'd made a full recovery and was walking again, I felt only relief for myself.

13

The dancing shoes are pinching me. I bunch up my toes to ease the squeeze, same as I do when the woman in the shoe shop puts my foot in the measuring contraption. I am ashamed at the length of them. I climb up the steps on to the back of the trailer and wait. It's too early. The lorry hood is still attached to the trailer. Later it will become a float for the carnival procession, with dressed-up grown-ups riding along on it. I look down at the people gathered in front. Mother points at my leg. I pull up my socks. I am queasy, and too warm in the hand-me-down costume with the Celtic swirls. Music cranks up from the trailer behind. Some move towards it. I slide my foot up the back of my leg to scratch an itch, and wobble. Ivy Best takes her place beside me, her chunky ringlets bouncing on her golden epaulettes. She lifts up her chin and points out her tidy toe. The small smile I have for her goes unseen.

Ready, girls? And a one, two, three, four ... Ivy takes off like a whirlwind to the music, her skirt flouncing up and ringlets flying. She's going too fast, too many steps all at once. I falter and lose the rhythm. Am I going too slow? I'm lost. The music doesn't make sense with this flurry beside me. Ivy is a hand-held whisk at full throttle, arms tight by her upright sides, legs on fast-forward. My feet drag along the boards of the trailer, one, two steps behind the beat. My shoulders rise up to meet my ears. I try to ignore her. By the time I get back in time, the music stops and a smattering of clapping breaks out. Ivy steps forward and takes a deep bow, her hands clasped behind her back. I bop my head forward and stand where I am. She strides past me with her shoulders way back. I follow her down the steps and make my way over to Mother and Sadie. Sadie says I did all right. Mother walks away.

★   ★   ★

Saul didn't come back until the last week in July. He sauntered into the kitchen with a block of raspberry ripple ice cream. His skin had darkened in the sun.

'I dropped into the hospital to enquire about your mother, but they said she didn't want any visitors.'

'She said only Frank can visit. He's away to see her now,' I said, putting the ice-cream in the freezer.

'Good. Have you got a spare bike?'

'Well, there's Frank's old racer, out in the shed with mine.'

'Right — let's go for a spin.'

I had stuck to the house since the twelfth, my nose in a book, and I was loath to break my hibernation. He grabbed my wrist and led me outside.

'No excuses. You need some colour in those cheeks.'

'But I have to be back to put on the dinner.'

'Forget the dinner, Grace. Live for the moment for a change.'

He went into the shed and came out with the bikes. I took mine and pumped up the back tyre.

'This one's as good as new,' he said, bending over the bar. 'Ready? Follow me.'

He rode out of the yard and into the middle of the road. I zigzagged from side to side until I got my balance, then drew up level with him. A heat shimmer rippled the air ahead and the ground glistened from a light shower. Saul did a U-turn and rode to the other side of me.

'Where are we going?' I asked him.

'It's a surprise.'

He raced up the road ahead of me, trying out the racer's jarring bell. The McNicholls' dogs' ears shot up at the pprrrrring of it and ran out in front of me as I tried to catch up. My front wheel slammed into the belly of the Alsatian and it sprang to the side with a yelp. I threw my foot on the ground to steady the toppling bike, then rode on with the Jack Russell snapping at the pedal. All the gardens' cottages were deserted except the Mullens', where Nelly and Mary were running nets. They eyed me askance as I whizzed by, perturbed, I supposed, by the missed opportunity to ask questions.

Saul turned right at the bus stop and sped in the direction of town. I cycled furiously behind him and began to enjoy the thrill of the speed and the air zooming past my ears and through my hair. I caught up with him as he braked at the last turn for Half Moon Bay.

'You look like a child,' he said as I pulled up beside him.

I smiled back at him, breathing hard.

'Uncle Sean lives up there, at The Scrog. There's their laneway up on the left — oh, but you've been there, haven't you?'

'That's where we're going. He wants to ask you something.'

Before I had a chance to reply he'd taken off on to the bay road, keeping in by the hedge to let a tractor past. I followed close behind, returning the raised-hand greeting of the boy behind the wheel.

'That child couldn't be more than eight,' Saul said as the tractor trundled by.

'Never mind him — I can't go up to Uncle Sean's.'

'Sure where's the harm?'

'Why can't he ask me whatever it is over the phone?'

'I don't know. Come on, would you? You can see your new baby cousin. Sean says she's the picture of you.'

'Did he?' I felt absurdly pleased.

'He did. Will you come on.'

We cycled up to the narrow lane in tandem, the sun dazzling the round metal bell covers and handlebars on the bikes. I followed Saul on to the lane, swerving to avoid the potholes and brambles spilling out from both sides. The lane was short and led straight into a small clean yard with a stone-wall pig house running the length of it. Behind it, the roof of Uncle Sean's cottage was visible. Saul rode up to a gate at the top of the yard and went through a narrow dark passage at the side of the pig house.

I followed him, blanking out pangs of claustrophobia. The smell of pigs was strongest there, and made me think of a black sow at home that went mad and chased her piglets into the lough, a memory so old and fragile, I wondered whether I'd dreamt it.

The passage opened out on to another small yard facing Uncle Sean's tiny low-slung cottage. It had a dark red tin roof, with loose grey stones on the ground around it, and looked on to a dense orchard of squat gnarled apple trees. Saul dismounted his bike and leaned it up against the side of the cottage. I left mine behind his and followed him around to the back. Opposite the cottage, nappies dripped on a clothesline tied between two trees on a patch of grass bound by a wooden fence. A little home-made cart lay on its side under one of the trees and a bunch of sweet peas spilled out of a clay pot at the side of the back door.

Saul turned and winked at me, sliding his eyes towards the window. Two blond heads, side by side, peered out, eyes round with curiosity. I waved at them and they disappeared. Saul went to the door but it opened before he rapped the knocker. Ginny stood with a long black bucket in her hand, her hair an even fiercer shade of orange than I recalled, her face drawn and sallow.

'Sean's not here,' she said, stepping out and setting the bucket down on the step.

'Right. How are you keeping, Ginny?'

She stepped back into the doorway and lifted out another, smaller bucket. 'Oh, not too bad, thanks, except for my back. Could you do me a favour and carry that big bucket for me? The pigs need fed.'

'Certainly.'

I glanced around awkwardly. Ginny had not looked at me.

'Now you two keep an eye on the wee one,' she called through the door as she drew it closed.

Saul shifted the large bucket from his left to his right hand. It was filled with gloopy meal.

'I brought Grace,' he said.

She flicked a glance at me and nodded. I wondered what I'd done.

'Come on this way,' she said, heading to the fence. 'The both of you.'

Cold water from a nappy splattered on the back of my neck as I ducked under the clothesline, and rolled down my back as I straightened. The grass was overgrown and still damp, wetting my feet through the thin canvas of my plimsolls. Ginny wore white sandals and a shapeless sleeveless overall, and the flab swung on her dimply upper arms as she leaned over to open the fence-gate.

'They'll be down in the water,' she said, holding the gate open.

The stream glinted between the sparse trees at the foot of the narrow lumpy field.

Thick whin bushes and lurid yellow ragweeds erupted all over the grass, bluebells sprang from the overgrown hedges.

Saul wiped the side of his face on the sleeve of his shirt.

'Bring that bucket over here,' Ginny said, walking over to a long tin feeding trough at the top of the field.

'Give it a rattle, and wait till you see,' she said.

Saul put the bucket on the grass and rattled the lid. Within seconds a line of smiley-faced pigs emerged from behind the trees, one behind the other, running and farting up the field.

Ginny chuckled and threw the water from her pail into the trough. 'You see, they only have to hear the rattle. Throw that meal in now.'

She picked up a stick and with both hands mixed the meal and the water. Her hands were reddened but slender, like her feet, and adorned only by a thin wedding band.

'Where's my lovely sweethearts?' she called out in a startling high screech. 'Come and get your din-dins, my darlings.'

The pigs dispersed and lined up along the trough, and began to wolf the sloppy mixture. As I watched them, a straggler emerged from behind a whin bush and trotted straight up to me. I let it butt and sniff at my feet, its snout burrowing into my shoelaces.

'Ach look — he's playing with you,' Ginny said fondly. 'They're very loving animals, you know.'

'Daddy always said pigs were smart,' I said, immediately regretting mentioning him. But the ice was broken.

'Oh they are, and very clean too. I'm telling you, once they're trained where to do their business, you won't catch them dirtying anywhere else.'

I nodded, relieved. The straggler pig lost interest in my feet and nosed his way over to the trough.

'Good lean pigs, aren't they?' Saul said, catching the gleam of pride in Ginny's eyes.

'The man from Lovell and Christmas in England said they were the loveliest firm pigs he's ever seen in his life. Not too much of that oul' hard hair on them. Sure we've had them since they were wee handfuls.'

She lowered her eyes and sighed.

'You know, your head's astray for the whole week when they've to go to get killed,' she said quietly, turning to look at me. 'Your father used to do them in himself. But you're hardly old enough to remember.'

'Oh, I do. I remember them squealing. But Frank would never tell me what was happening, or how they were done in.'

I felt Saul staring at me.

Ginny ran her stick over a cluster of dead dandelions, scattering their seeds into the air. 'They're done with the stunner first. The squeals of them's desperate. Then they're hung up and their throats are cut. Then they're plunged into a tank of boiling water ... you know our boys can't stick the squealing at all. I don't know what's going to be done unless they grow out of it.'

She pulled her wide lips over to one side and shook her head.

'I believe there's not the same money in them now,' Saul said, as if he knew what he was talking about.

'Only in the smuggling,' Ginny replied, under her breath.

She and Saul exchanged quick looks. It suddenly dawned on me what he'd been doing to earn money during his disappearing acts, and I felt a jag of irritation. I turned away and watched the pigs scour the walls of the trough for the last of the slop, as if they'd never see another bite. When they'd finished, they snuffled in the dried-up muck around the trough and poked their heads in the empty buckets, grunting cheerfully.

Ginny walked up to the fence and opened the gate. At the clink of it, the pigs were off again in a line, at a slower pace this time, Saul and I walking behind them. They followed Ginny to the pig house and trotted in past her.

'Ach, they're dead tired in the evening, God help them. They'd make your heart sore. And look — you see? Straight over to the dunging passage before they lie down.'

I stood beside her and watched the pigs arrange the scattered straw along the wall with their snouts, then lie down and cuddle up beside each other, their thick white lashes slowly fanning their wide pale eyes, like a row of fat and contented albino women without any make-up. They were snoring within seconds.

'You have them well trained, Auntie Ginny,' I said.

She cast her eyes upwards briefly and allowed herself a small smile. Saul had walked across the yard to wash out the large bucket under a pump in the corner.

'You and him an item now?' she asked unexpectedly.

'No! No we're not,' I replied quickly, feeling heat in my cheeks.

'Hmmm.'

I looked away and scratched the side of my nose.

'Come in for a drink of tea,' she said,

sliding the door closed.

'Oh no thanks, we'd better — '

'The kettle will be boiled,' she interrupted, walking to the house. 'Hey, boy! Tea.'

Saul put down the buckets and crossed the yard.

'I can't stay long,' I whispered to him on the doorstep.

He nodded absently and stepped into the room, side-stepping a basin and a Wellington boot. A shoal of sunlight barrelled in from the small window, showing up dust on every surface and small greasy fingerprints on the sage green wall linoleum.

'Leave that door open — the heat's powerful,' Ginny said as she poured hot water into a stainless steel teapot. 'Sit down there at the table, would you. I'll go and see what these ones are doing.'

She set the teapot on the blue formica table and opened the door of the connecting room. The two boys were standing on the other side of the door, giggling.

'Get in there and say hello to the visitors. Have you been minding the baby?'

The boys walked in and began to play with a jigsaw on a butcher's block in the corner. Saul joined them, playing dumb and making them laugh. I brushed crumbs from the table into my cupped hand and eyed a wasp crawling along the top of an open jar of jam, wondering how someone who took so much pride in the housekeeping of another's home could keep her own like this. Then the baby cried, answering the question. Ginny came back in with her.

'They have the child's face all crayon, whatever they were at,' she said, handing her to me. 'Hold her there and I'll get a face cloth.'

The baby's eyes widened in alarm as I took her but the crying tailed off. She stared at me accusingly with her sapphire blue eyes as I rocked her, then began to wriggle like a pup. She smelled of sour pee and talc, and she stretched her miniature mouth open at the sight of my crooked finger when I hesitantly went to touch her yellow and green striped cheek.

'Here — rub her face with that and I'll get you a bottle,' Ginny said, handing me the wet corner of a towel. It smelled of feet. I reluctantly began to wipe off the crayon from the baby's face and she squirmed and yelled in protest. I felt a damp patch spreading on my trouser leg underneath her and felt an urge to go and put her into the sink. I rubbed off the last of the crayon and almost laughed at her outraged red face and dramatically downturned gummy mouth, yet everyone but me seemed oblivious to the noise.

I rubbed her tiny back and rocked her but she screamed harder, stiffening and stretching out her legs like someone being tortured. I began to panic, then felt a sudden surge of impatience and near hatred for the hysterical living thing in my arms.

'Now, now, now! That's enough of that yapping,' Ginny shouted.

She stood beside me and spilled a few drops of milk on to her wrist from the bottle before handing it to me.

Still wailing, the baby initially turned her face away from the bottle, then did a double take and clamped her quivering mouth on the teat. Her eyelids drooped, tears glistening on her long curling eyelashes and sliding into her delicate ears and wispy hair. The transformation was sudden and complete, and after a few minutes of frantic sucking, she appeared to fall asleep. I tried to ease the bottle from her but she latched back on to it and looked up at me with tears standing in her eyes. I fell for her then, in the most total and fixed way, and when she gave me a fleeting toothless smile, I was a goner.

'She'd need to bring up a bit of wind now,' Ginny said as she sliced a ring of wheaten bread.

I slipped the bottle out of the baby's

puckered-up mouth and leaned her against my shoulder, patting her back. She burped gently and fell asleep, the back of her warm head pressed into my neck. Ginny came over and wiped milk off the baby's chin.

'I . . . eh, think she needs her nappy changed,' I said to Ginny, reluctantly handing the baby over to her.

'Ah she'll be all right till she wakes up,' Ginny said, taking her out of the room.

I touched the wet patch on my trousers, then got up to wash my hands at the sink. The teapot was boiling on the cooker, the pungent waft of stewed tea in the hot air swallowing up the baby smells. I shook my hands in the air to dry them, and felt a tiny sharp prick on the inside of my ankle. I lifted my foot and a midge flew up and buzzed in my hair. I shook it out, watching Saul and the boys doing the jigsaw. I walked towards the back door.

'Saul, I have to get home and get the dinner on.' Ginny came back into the room and pointed to the table. 'Sit down there and take a cup of tea, for God's sake.'

The heat began to agitate me. 'No, I'm sorry — I really have to go.' I opened the back door.

'Wait and I'll come with you — sorry about this, Ginny.'

'No skin off my nose, boy.'

She wiped her hands on the smelly towel and followed Saul to the door. The boys stood and watched, their faces long. I stepped out on to the yard, just as Uncle Sean drove up in his rattling truck. He got out and took a draw on his cigarette, holding it inverted between his thumb and forefinger.

'These ones wouldn't stay for their tea,' Ginny said as she went back inside.

'Grace has to put the dinner on,' Saul said.

Uncle Sean walked over to the cottage wall and scratched his back against it.

'Right, well. I won't keep you,' he said.

I took my bicycle and walked across the yard. Saul hung back and checked his tyres. I waited impatiently, weary and sticky from the heat. Eventually Saul got on to the racer and rode slowly across the yard, Uncle Sean strolling behind him.

I got on my bike and prepared to take off.

'Hang on a second, Grace,' Saul said, frowning slightly as he pulled up beside me.

Uncle Sean threw his cigarette on the ground and stubbed it out with the heel of his steel-capped boots. He glanced at me, rubbing the side of his angular chin.

'Ah say, girl. We're getting the child christened in the chapel and she needs a godmother. This fella's doing godfather on account of him being there, you know. Are you up for it?'

I looked from Uncle Sean's awkward face to Saul, who was giving me a half-smile.

'You mean, me?'

'Seeing as you're related.'

My ears began to pop. 'Well . . . I suppose I could, but . . . why . . . '

Uncle Sean nodded and began to walk back to the cottage. 'See you at the chapel on Sunday, then.'

'This Sunday coming?'

'After Mass,' he said, opening the back door.

Saul laughed at the expression on my face and sped off down the passage. I followed him and shouted for him to wait for me. He braked abruptly at the end of the lane and leapt over the handlebars like an acrobat, then whisked around and caught the bike as it fell.

'Your turn, Grace — come on, rev it up a bit!'

I pulled up beside him, shaking my head.

'Chicken! Race you home instead.'

He took off again, bent low over the bar, his dark lank hair whipping out behind him. I kept in close behind but could never quite catch him, and by the time we reached the uphill turn for home, he was able to spurt on effortlessly while I slowed to a crawl. I looked down at my labouring thighs and cursed them, and forced myself to struggle on. Saul had ridden out of sight but as I neared the bus stop I spotted him up ahead, talking to someone in a car at the T-junction.

The car drove off and he waited for me at the corner.

'Frank says he'll get a chip in town — he's away out for the night,' he said as I approached.

'I thought that was him,' I panted.

He pushed up his T-shirt and scratched his stomach. His skin had darkened to the colour of treacle in the horizontal creases above his waist, and the sight of the crinkled wisps around his bellybutton made me look away.

'You know, you're doing the right thing, agreeing to be the child's godmother.'

I stalled beside him and wiped my forehead with my wrist. 'I think they're up to something. Why would they baptise the child a Catholic when the other two are Presbyterian. It doesn't make sense.'

'It was Ginny's idea. Maybe she wants to make a gesture. Maybe she thinks it's the right thing for the wee girl.'

'Ivy thinks they're trying to get round us, because of the land and — '

'Ivy's a baloon.'

'But I shouldn't have said yes, I know that. My problem is that I can't say no to anybody.'

'You would have offended them if you'd refused.'

'I'm going to be killed. God, if Mother — '

'Anyway, what do you mean you can't say no to anybody,' he interrupted, his hands on his hips.

I shifted uncomfortably on the hard seat and began to fiddle with the bell.

'It's like, my first thought is to com . . . comply with everything, so I don't, you know, rock the boat. Even though sometimes inside I'm screaming out against whatever it is.'

'Appeasement.'

'Yes. Like what they did with Hitler before the war.'

'Who's your Hitler?'

'Don't be daft. There is none. It's just a form of cowardice, I think. I can't help it.'

'You're no coward, Grace. You just need to set yourself free.'

'Free from what?'

'What do you think?'

'I don't know . . . from this place?'

'No.'

'From home?'

'Not necessarily.'

I put my feet on the pedals and began to

move slowly past him. 'I . . . I don't know what you're on about.'

I was halfway down the road before he turned to follow me. The McNicholl children were playing hopscotch on their garden path and Bear was weeding his flowerbed. I waved to him but he turned away when he saw Saul ride up.

'Tell you what, Grace, why don't I make you dinner?' he said cheerfully.

I glanced at the Mulhollands' window. Someone stood motionless behind the lace curtains. At the Moores', a newsreader's clipped voice resounded from the cranked-up television just beyond their open door. I could see Sadie's slippered feet on her footstool.

'Well? What do you say?'

'No, thanks anyway.'

'Hah! What do you mean you don't think so? I thought you couldn't say 'no' to anybody?'

'Oh!'

He swerved in and out towards me, shaking his head and tutting.

I blushed and laughed. 'All right, then. Point taken. But there's not much in the house to make.'

'Just you leave it to me.'

★ ★ ★

I stepped out of the shower and wedged open the window to let the steam out, and caught a movement out of the corner of my eye. I peeped out and jerked back again in surprise. Saul was hosing himself down beside the shed, in full view of the yard and the road. I stood and looked at my heart beating under my wet skin, then peeped out again. He was holding the hose over his head, water flattening his hair over his face, the slanting evening sun behind him. Something buried deep inside my abdomen jumped. I stepped away and wrapped a towel tight around myself, and when I rubbed a circle in the steamed-up mirror, there was trepidation in the eyes that looked back.

It's not my fault. I didn't know he was there.

Naked, within feet of each other. Imagine.

It's just a coincidence.

You enjoyed it.

I didn't!

Look at your diddies. Dirty thing, you.

I grabbed the plain white bra and pants I'd laid out on top of the washbasket and threw them on, and instantly felt safer.

Good. All tidied up.

Then I wrapped my hair in a towel, pulled on a dressing gown and darted out into Mother's room. Her good blue dress hung in its clear wrapping at the back of the cherrywood wardrobe. I took it out and laid it on the bed. The little flounces at the hem swished under the plastic and a sweet scent, like vanilla essence, wafted into the air, bringing back the last time I saw Mother wearing it. Frank's graduation from agricultural college had warranted a big spend.

Pots clanged in the kitchen. I shook my hair out of the towel and sat down at Mother's dressing table with its triptych mirror, angled for profile-checking. I ran her elaborate silver-edged comb through the tangles in my hair and pulled out her make-up drawer. Fancy silver and gold tubes of lipstick and little pots and palettes rolled forward, and a faint cloud of face powder puffed out, sweet as the perfume on the dress.

I plunged my fingers into a jar of Pond's Cold Cream and slathered it over my face and neck, then put a layer of foundation on top. It went bready under my fingers, so I rubbed it off and started again with a smaller drop, blending it carefully around my nose, as Ivy had once showed me.

'Hey, Grace — five minutes!' Saul shouted from the kitchen.

I gave a start.

'Right,' I called back, scrabbling in the drawer for an eye pencil. I stroked it finely over my eyebrows and eyelids, and sat back to admire them, but the drawn lines, though faint, looked incongruous beside my despised fair-tipped eyelashes.

Oh, to hell with it.

I snatched a tube of mascara and flicked the wand over the lashes, transforming my eyes from insipid nothings to movie-star peepers. I marvelled at the effect, turning my head from side to side and checking the side mirrors.

Pity about the nose.

I sighed. It was too late to try any of the disguising tricks I'd read about. I swivelled around in the stool and reached across the bed for the dress. I slipped off the dressing gown and unwrapped the dress, holding it out in front of me. The silky fabric shimmered in the peachy haze of sunlight coming through the window and I saw the skirt swish around mother's slender knees as she crossed the college lawn, her spiky beige heels piercing the turf.

I put it back in its wrapping and returned it to the wardrobe.

'Ready, Grace!'

I ran into Frank's room and grabbed a white shirt from his wardrobe and ran with it into my room.

'Give me a minute!' I yelled.

I pulled on the shirt and tucked it into a pair of jeans.

Your backside's far too square in those, like a farmer too long sitting in a tractor.

I pulled the shirt out over the jeans, then flew back into Mother's bedroom and dabbed a rosy-coloured lipstick on my mouth. My hair hung around me in wet straggles, making the top of my back damp. I lifted it and pinned it up with a ferocious-looking toothed clasp Mother used for waving her hair, pulling roots from my scalp. I yelped and loosened it, ran to leave the dressing gown in my room, rushed up the hall, then walked calmly across the vestibule into the kitchen.

The table was covered in the damask linen tablecloth we used at Christmas, and Mother's good crystal glasses glinted in the warm evening glow.

Saul gestured to the chair facing the window and poured out some beer from a can.

'Sorry, no wine this evening.'

He looked radiantly clean, as if he'd washed the whites of his eyes and in between each eyelash. I wanted to go and blot my coloured-in face.

'That's all right. That stuff Ivy had nearly put me off drink for life.'

He went to the range and took two plates from the dish rack.

'Pork chops, apple sauce, peas and fine dry floury potatoes for the lady,' he announced, placing the food in front of me. I wasn't one bit interested in it.

'It looks lovely. Where did you learn to cook?'

'Oh, here and there, travelling around the place. You look nice. Different.' He sat down and forked a knob of butter into the potatoes. 'Isn't it funny the way they call them 'good eating potatoes' on the signs on the road? I mean, what else are you going to do with them?'

I smiled, still wallowing in his compliment.

He raised his glass. 'Anyway, here's to you. Cheers.'

We clinked glasses and drank, then he tore into his dinner, eating all the vegetables before starting on the meat.

'That's a strange way to eat,' I remarked.

He chuckled and ate on. I took a few forkfuls and pushed the rest around on the plate. When he'd finished, he cleared the plates away and served up ice cream and wafers. The beer tasted revolting with the ice cream.

'Thank you very much, that was all lovely,' I said, pushing the half-full bowl away.

'You didn't eat much,' he said, scraping his bowl.

'But I liked it, really. I'm just not awful hungry, that's all.'

He set the bowl down and stood up. 'Right, that's far too nice an evening to waste — let's bring these out to the verandah.'

He picked up the glasses and cans and I followed him out, mildly buzzed from the beer. The light had taken on an amber hue and the zapping heat had lost its energy and filtered into soft warm balmy air. Saul sat down and tied up his bootlace. I perched on the other end of the seat and watched a spider dangle from the awning, trying not to screw up my face in the setting sun.

'So you and me's going to be godparents, Miss Kane,' he said, leaning back in the seat and swaying it gently.

I shook my head, fixing my eyes on the spider. 'I can't believe I'm doing it.'

'Yes you can. You've got to trust your instincts. I know you trust them when it comes to me.'

I pulled my eyes away from the spider and swung my knees up on the seat, resting my back on the wooden arm.

'Do I? I envy you your confidence,' I said quietly.

'There's no reason why you shouldn't be

confident too. You know, Grace, you're far too timid sometimes, and it's annoying.'

I gawped at him.

He looked straight ahead at the water. 'It's annoying because it's not the real you.'

'You mean, you're saying I'm putting on an act?' I asked, my voice wavering.

'If you like. And speaking of which, what was all that about pretending to have a fit?'

'I — that's none of your business.' I swung my knees off the seat and crossed my legs tight.

'You told me you were pretending,'

'Only because you were hassling me. Why can't you just leave me alone?'

'Because I don't want to. And you don't want me to either.'

I looked at his placid face and snapped.

'I saw you on the eleventh night.'

His dark eyes widened a fraction. 'Where?'

'At the bloody bonfire.'

He picked up his glass and drained it. 'So?'

'So what were you doing there with those people? I thought you didn't know anyone around here?'

'Well, Grace, that's my business.'

I dazedly studied my glass and the greasy lipstick mark on it, and roughly wiped the remaining colour off my lips with the back of my hand.

'Well, for your information, one of your lovely friends attacked me and scared me half to death that night,' I snapped.

'What? Who?'

'I don't know his name . . . the drunk disgusting one.'

I gave a small shudder and hung my head. In a second he had his arms around me. I tried to shrug him off but he held on.

'Oh God, Grace, I'm so sorry. Jesus, what happened?'

I steadied my sullen voice.

'I was waiting for Ivy, behind the clock tower, and he grabbed me . . . it's all right, I got away.'

He relaxed his arms and pulled his head back to look at me. 'Did he hurt you?'

'Not really. Just scared me.'

'Why didn't you tell me?'

'I didn't tell anyone. I'm stronger than you think.'

He gave a vague smile. 'Sure, I know you are. That's exactly what I meant. I can see your strength. Trust me.'

'Should I?'

He stood up abruptly. 'There's something missing. Wait there, I'll be back in a minute.'

He disappeared into the house. I took a gulp of beer and choked on it, splattering Frank's white shirt. I coughed and drank the rest, wondering if I was angry or not. A discordant screech ripped from the radio in the kitchen, then a plaintive Irish tenor was singing about a girl at a fair.

Saul came back and sat down close to me.

'Grace, I'm sorry I can't talk about some things. But you know, you can tell me anything, if it helps. Remember, I owe you and your mother for helping me, and Frank, too.'

I closed my eyes.

> — *My young love said to me, my mother won't mind*
> *And my father won't slight you for your lack of kind . . .*

'I just wish people weren't so unpredictable. I never know whether I'm coming or going with people. You know, I wish I wasn't a person. I'd rather be a tree.'

'A tree? Why?'

'I'd rather not have . . . a body. I want to be alive, but not in a *body*. I don't want to walk around in this thing, take up space in rooms with it. I was appalled when it started to, you know, change. Daddy couldn't look at me. Frank was embarrassed. I used to go around with my hands sort of clasped in front of my chest, like some bloody nun. And I think

Mother's . . . oh, I'm sorry. I'm talking a bundle of nonsense. It's the beer.'

He touched my arm. 'No, tell me. You think she's what?'

'I think she's . . . I think I disgust her.'

— As she stepped away from me
And she moved through the fair . . .

My throat tightened, as if it was trying to stop the words coming out.

'I . . . the shape of me.' I leaned forward and held my head in my hands. 'I can't believe I'm saying all this in front of you.'

I felt him lean in towards me. I felt his lips brush lightly over my cheek, and his fingers barely stroking my hand.

— And then she turned homeward with
   one star awake
Like the swan in the evening moves over
   the lake . . .

He put his arm around my shoulders and eased me back against the seat.

'Sure I know you're only fishing for another compliment. Sitting there, thinking you're lovely.'

He sounded exactly like Mother, pulling up his top lip and flaring his nostrils as if he'd smelled something off, the way she put her face when she disapproved of something. We laughed and he sang and we sat and looked at the water changing from gilded blue to silver grey. Then the sun slid away and we fell quiet, and he took his arm away.

'I have to go, Grace. I'm getting a lift at the top of the road.'

He stood up and stretched out his elbows.

'Where . . . I mean, when will you be back?'

'Soon. Maybe tomorrow.'

He put his hands on the side of the verandah and sprang over it.

'Thank you for making me dinner.'

'Any time.'

He disappeared into the yard. I sat alone and re-winded the conversation in my head until the midges drove me back into the house. In bed, I prayed he wouldn't get caught with the pigs at the border, and fell asleep imagining I was with him, with no notion of coming back.

14

The phone woke me out of a sound sleep. I slapped one foot on the floor, half hoping Frank would answer it but the shrill ring continued, far louder than it seemed in the daytime.

Oh God. Mother.

I threw the blankets off and ran up the hall, my eyes not yet adjusted to the dark, and collided with the half-open door. Pain surged into my big toe and I hobbled to the phone.

'Grace, is that you?'

'Who's this?'

'It's me, Nelly Mullen — oh Grace, God save us, there's been some sort of commotion up at the top of the road — think one of your cows has got out and think maybe the bull. Me and Mary's afraid to go and see — would you ever get your Frank to go and see?'

I heard her slurp on a drink.

'Is it the Semental?'

'Sure we couldn't see in the pitch dark but there was an awful scuffling match going on and you don't want yon beast roaming the roads, and I didn't want to annoy poor Willy or Bear in the middle of the night, or

Dalloway neither, seeing as wee Josie's not well — ach, would you put your brother on, Grace?'

'It's all right, I'll tell him myself.'

'Tell him to watch himself, mind.'

I hung up and yawned. In the gloom of the hall I could see that Frank's bedroom door was slightly ajar. His bed hadn't been slept in. I stood in the darkness and wondered what to do, then padded back to bed. I curled up, telling myself Nelly had been imagining things.

But something kept nagging at me to get up. I flung back the blankets in a fit of pique and pulled off my nightdress. I dressed quickly in the dark, stuffing my bare feet into my plimsolls and gouging blears out of my eyes. In the scullery I took a torch from the shelf and switched it on, casting a small stark halo of light ahead of me as I made my way out.

The first orange strip of dawn stretched above the water but the birds were still sleeping and the air was still dewy. I breathed it in deeply and began to imagine what I could make for breakfast, and by the time I was halfway up the road, the thought of a cheese and bacon omelette with onions and mustard was tormenting me.

The cottages were in darkness but I could

see a glow behind the Mullens' curtains. I switched off the torch as I passed by and crossed to the other side of the road. The fiery streak over the water was bleeding into blotches of violet and cerise, gradually diluting the darkness. I stood and watched, tempted to take a run down to the shore and watch the show, but the Mullens' curtains twitched and I walked on, peering ahead into the dark. All I could decipher were the silhouettes of the hedges and trees, and the surreal gleam of dew on the black ground. I stopped at the top of the road and sat on the sign for Preacher's Bay, enveloped by the calm and the silence.

No cow, no bull.

My thoughts turned from breakfast to Saul, and his mouth. My stomach stirred and once again I was taken aback by the strange physical response to my thoughts. I gave a small quiver and held the torch up to the side of my neck, feeling quietly alive and somehow connected to the body I'd always disparaged. The emptiness had gone.

I stood up and stretched my arms above my head. An arc of light hovered in the near distance on the other side of the road, and I took a few seconds to realise it was the last vestige of moonlight falling on the top of the bus stop sign.

I bent over to touch my toes, suddenly energised, but felt a short sharp twinge in my back. As I arose carefully, something fluttered around my feet. At first I thought it was a butterfly but when I took a closer look, I saw it was a small white feather, almost incandescent in the pre-dawn darkness. A light breeze flipped another over my feet and suddenly I realised they were all over the road.

I began to follow their trail. Some seemed to be stuck to spots of something dark and shiny. I steeled myself for the sight of a destroyed bird. I stooped carefully and picked up a couple of feathers, and held them up to my face.

Pillow feathers?

I switched on the torch and swung it up and down along the hedge, but it flickered and dimmed to a weak yellow glow. It was enough to show me that the feathers were swirling from the direction of the bus stop and I walked towards it, training the dying light on the road. It was only when I was a few feet away that I saw something on the lower half of the pole.

I stopped in my tracks, straining to make out the shape. It didn't move or make any sound, and for a couple of fleeting seconds I thought it was a rolled-up rug someone had dumped. Then the moonlight glimmered on the outline of what looked like a head slumped forwards.

My breath caught in my throat. I stood completely still and stared at the thing. A feather skimmed my face, tickling underneath my nose.

Jesus, it's some sort of animal . . .

I tiptoed to the middle of the road, scared that the thing would waken up and run at me. A couple of yards behind it I turned and tried the torch again. I inched forward, the dim halo on the ground in front of me, the ringing in my ears suddenly deafening. Then I became aware of a smell. A thick, eye-watering reek.

Daddy's toolshed . . . burning sun on a new road . . .

I raised the torch. The scrap of light fell on a dangling rope. I swallowed back a wave of anxiety. I saw hands, blackened and bunched together, the rope tied around them. Small hands. I couldn't move.

The darkness began to thin, clearing the way for the muzzy dawn light. I switched off the useless torch and as I edged closer, the thin soles of my plimsolls stuck on to the ground and the smell grew more pungent. I didn't hear the car coming until it turned on to the road and its headlights lit up the abomination before me.

A car door slammed. Frank's voice shouted. My mouth hung open like a simpleton's.

'Jesus . . . what the? Who is that?'

The head, festooned with white feathers, hung forward on to a ripped and stained white T-shirt. The bare legs were bent at the knees. Beneath the feathers, long black stiffened strands of hair.

'Ivy . . . I think it's Ivy.'

Frank walked straight up to her and began to untie the rope.

'You catch her.'

I stepped forward and she slumped forward into my arms like a giant seagull caught in an oil slick, black eyes and mouth stuck shut. I staggered back and let the bizarre head fall on my chest, then Frank pulled her off and lowered her to the ground.

'You're all right Ivy, all right. We're here now.'

He leaned close to her face and felt for a pulse on her neck.

I couldn't find my voice. I knelt down and held her sticky hand.

'She's breathing, thank fuck. You stay with her and I'll go and ring the doctor. That oul' tar would destroy the car seats.'

He hurried to the car and drove away.

I tried to pull the feathers off the front of

Ivy's head. She lay inert but as I spoke her name into the side of her head, a croak sounded from her throat. I leaned closer. There was only a tiny parting in the centre of her clamped lips.

'Ivy, can you hear me? What is it, Ivy?'

'Bbbb . . . '

I waited.

'Yes, Ivy, I can hear you.'

She gave a faint sigh. 'Grace . . . '

'Yes, Ivy, yes — '

Her head fell to the side.

'Ivy, who did this? Who did you see?'

She made no sound.

I grabbed her wrist. 'Jesus! Jesus! Oh no!'

I felt a weak pulse. I clung on to it, praying out loud, then into myself in case it would scare Ivy. Frank came back and threw a blanket around her, and we held her as the sun came up. I couldn't look at the horror of her, the degradation.

'Grace, don't be saying anything about this,' Frank said. 'It'll be even worse for her if this gets about.'

He smelled of rum and cigarettes.

'But wouldn't we need to tell the police?'

'Christ, no. She shouldn't have been hanging around with soldiers — look, don't say anything — there's Oul' Yella and Mary coming.'

The sisters arrived just as the doctor pulled up. For once, Nelly was speechless. Mary cried and clung on to my arm as Frank wrapped the blanket around Ivy and carried her to the doctor's car. He followed them in his car and Nelly took me by the other arm and led me to the cottage.

She gave me brandy and thanked God over and over again in her reedy scared voice, that she'd had the wit to phone me.

'That wee girl might have been found stone dead this morning if it wasn't for me and you Grace,' she whispered. 'She could have been the third.'

Suddenly exhausted, I looked at her in confusion

'The third to die. You mark my words, there will be another. I can feel it in my waters.'

★   ★   ★

Now I know for sure. It's all a big lie.

And I always half believed that guff about the mind being just a receptacle — no — a medium, for the soul. I liked the thought of the body being a big coat you could cast off when you no longer need it. And yet here I lie, permanently buttoned into the thing I've always loathed. They're taking their revenge, these bones and flesh so long neglected.

. . . *Pity I can't hear you any more. It was mildly entertaining listening to all that theorising about the will. And the face on Ignatius. What a sight for dying eyes. It's so dark in here, and so very, very dull.*

Same, same, same, same, same. I can hear that old clock in the hall so clearly, those insistent tttrrrlocks telling you nothing ever really changes, whatever you do. Like the way the incoming tide makes you feel. No matter who you are and what you do, you don't really matter. The world will go on without you and you will be forgotten about, quickly, easily. Isn't that what they mean by time healing? More honest to shake hands and tell the bereaved that they will forget.

So, I get it all worked out, then that lovely nonsense poem butts in —

In the night of death . . . oh, how does it go? . . . night of death, hope sees a star — yes, that's it. Hope sees a star and a listening love can hear the rustle of a wing.

Come on, switch the damn thing off.

★   ★   ★

I braved the flies and walked the shore path every evening in the vague hope of seeing Ivy. I couldn't bring myself to go into the village

369

and when I'd phoned her house, her mother told me not to call back. Frank said they'd had to cut all her hair off, and that one of her eyes had gone wonky, and that she wouldn't speak to anyone.

When the shock had worn off, I'd cried bitterly for Ivy, the pain made worse by Saul's latest absence. All I'd had was one terse phone call from him, saying he'd meet me at the chapel for the christening. So I walked and pulled blackberries from the hedges, and counted them to hush my chattering mind. I made jam with them, the way Ginny had shown me, until I ran out of jars, and when I found myself with another full basket on Saturday evening, I took them to the end of the pier and threw them one by one into the still water. I sat on my hunkers and watched them bob on the glittering surface like clusters of abnormal cells, occasionally snatched from underneath by the peevish bucket mouth of a trout or an eel. Then the glossy green head of a male mallard appeared from the shooting hut to my left, where he'd been squatting. He swam over to the floating berries and darted his neck down and gobbled all around him. I was so absorbed in his robotic movements and horrible eyes, I didn't notice Dalloway's small fishing boat approaching from my right until I heard the sloosh of the oars through the water.

'Hey, Grace — catch the rope for us, would you?' Dalloway shouted as the boat neared the pier.

Even in the August heat, he wore his stripy tie. Bear McNicholl sat opposite him, the day's catch between them. I stood up and walked down to the post at the bottom of the pier and tried to catch the rope Dalloway threw, but missed it. The memory of constantly failing to catch the ball at school rounders flew back into my head and I cringed. Dalloway raised his eyes skywards and hauled in the rope. I caught it the second time and quickly secured it around the post. The fishermen climbed out of the boat and pulled it up on to the shore. It struck me as peculiar that they'd pull up at the pier instead of their own landing further up the shore, but Bear's sour face stopped me from asking questions. I walked back to the end of the pier and picked up my basket. The two men huddled over their catch, sifting through the slippy pile of gleaming eels. I stepped down from the pier and headed for the road, bidding them goodbye as I went, but Dalloway called me back.

'Grace, do you need that yoke?' he asked, eyeing the basket hanging over my arm.

I walked over and handed it to him.

'Not really, I was only using it for blackberries.'

I turned to go.

'Oh, Grace?'

I turned back. Bear was muttering something to Dalloway.

'Yes?'

'Would you lend us your cardigan?'

'My cardigan? What for?'

Dalloway scratched the side of his neck and screwed up his mouth.

'Ach, you might as well show her,' Bear said, pulling a wet weed from the side of the net.

Dalloway began to scratch the side of his head above his ear.

'Well . . . Grace, you're not to say a word about this. Come here till you see.'

I walked over to the boat.

'What am I supposed to be looking at?'

The fishy smell mingled with the whiff of dried sweat as the fishermen folded their arms.

'Do you see anything funny about that pile of fish?'

Under the direct evening sun the catch looked like a huge bejewelled silver shawl and I had to shade my eyes and squint at it.

'No. What's wrong with it?'

'In the middle, girl,' Dalloway sighed.

I stepped forward and stared. A black gun handle protruded between the curved backs of two eels.

'Oh, I see it! How did it get there?'

'It came in on the net. Who knows how it got there,' Bear said.

'Well, are you going to lift it out or not?' Dalloway said gruffly.

'What if the damn thing's loaded? Judge Turley shot the hand clean off himself when he grabbed the hold of an oul' gun he found down the fields.'

'Ach sure it'll be all right, it being in the water and all.'

'Aye but it looks brave an' new, no rust nor nothing by the looks of it. Now I wouldn't be in a rush to be handling it.'

'Sure, if you just take it by the handle and point it at the ground it will be all right — '

'You do it then.'

Dalloway went at his head with his nails again.

On impulse I stepped into the water. 'I'll do it.'

I reached over the side of the boat and stretched over the sparkling shoal, and gently prised out the gun. It had a stumpy black barrel, and it was heavy and slippery. I held it shaft down in front of me and stepped out of the water. Bear backed away.

'Lay it down on the ground there — don't point it this way!' Dalloway instructed.

Water trickled out of the opening. I put it down gently, pointing it towards the lough.

'You know somebody could have fired that thing out on the lough and we wouldn't have heard a thing if the wind was going in the wrong direction to us,' Bear said. 'They could of heard it in Cookstown, but.'

Dalloway lowered himself on to his hunkers beside the gun. 'What would anybody be doing with a gun out on the water?'

'Maybe they just wanted to get rid of it,' I said.

'Now, it's a funny business altogether,' Bear said, jutting his chin.

'It's not a good thing, that's for sure.'

'What are you going to do with it?' I asked.

'Well that's what we were looking your basket for, and your cardigan if you don't — '

'We've only the trouser pockets to put it in and I'm damn sure I don't want my balls shot off,' Bear interrupted. 'Begging your pardon, like.'

I took off my cardigan and handed it to Bear. 'I never liked it anyway. It's itchy.'

Dalloway gingerly picked up the gun and set it in the basket. Bear passed him the cardigan and he laid it on top.

'I'll hide it for the time being, till we think

what to do,' Dalloway said, walking back to the boat. Bear followed him.

I stepped back on to the pier and loosened the rope.

'Good girl — now not a word, mind you,' Dalloway called as I threw him the rope.

I watched the oars cut cleanly through the heavy water, past the shooting hut and on towards the curve of the bay that led home. The mallard had fled out towards the dark mass of the island and the flies had come out in force from the hedges and trees and wherever else they hid during the day. I swatted my way through a cloud of them at the gate and walked home, thinking of the christening the next morning. By the time I'd got home, I'd forgotten about the gun. There were more important things to think about, like my hair.

★   ★   ★

I sat under the dryer and tried to read the *Woman's Realm*, but my scalp was as hot as a baked potato and the hair-pins were stabbing me. Molly had insisted that she would do my hair on the morning of the christening, in between doing Sadie's monthly perm.

'Sure it will be nice and fresh and bouncy

for you,' she'd twittered down the phone. 'Oh, but now are you sure, Grace, you'd be all right to go under the dryer? You wouldn't take a wee turn on us, would you love?'

I assured her I'd be all right. I was relieved only Sadie was there. I knew the talk among Saturday's crowd would have been about Ivy, and I would have been interrogated. But Nelly had told everyone about it, and embellished it as she went along, as I soon found out.

'And I believe she'd no pants on,' Molly shouted above the dryer's din as she squirted acrid chemical gloop, the colour of dried blood, into Sadie's hair. I stared vacantly at Sadie in the mirror, picturing the terror on Ivy's beautiful face when they tipped the hot tar over her head.

'Grace? Are you all right there?'

'Oh, yes. Just a bit hot.'

Molly wiped her huge plump hands on a towel and turned the dryer off. I could smell hot skin.

'You're done now, anyway. Come on over here and we'll comb you out.'

I took the seat beside Sadie and grimaced at my flushed face in the mirror. My head looked like a baked ham with little rolled-up party snacks on cocktail sticks stuck all over it.

'Would that be right, Grace, about her not having her pants on?' Sadie said, feigning an interest in the magazine she was flicking through.

'No, as far as I know she had. She was wearing her mini skirt.'

Molly tutted as she unwound my cooked hair from the rollers, her chunky fingers surprisingly deft.

'She's an awful one for those short skirts,' Sadie said. 'And she was always tormenting my wee Charlie, God rest him, flirting like hell with him, and him that innocent.'

A maudlin look settled on her face, and a few uncomfortable seconds passed before Molly started off again.

'I'm telling you, she won't be parading around showing off her legs again in a hurry. Best has her grounded for life. Have you been to see her at all, Grace?'

'No. I phoned and Mrs Best said not to come.'

'Imagine. After you finding her. You didn't hear who done it?'

'No.'

'I'm telling you, they'll never find the ones that done it. They're a law unto themselves, anyway.'

Freshly out of the rollers, my hair sat in tight ridges of sausage-shaped curls. I squirmed my back in the chair, itching to pick up a comb and drag down the kinks. Molly let out a hoot of laughter.

'Your face, Grace! You look just like you did the time you were a wee girl getting your hair cut short when they had the nits at school — do you remember? I asked you did you like it and you closed your eyes tight at me and said 'it's rotten', cross as you like. Oh, what a giggle we had at that!'

She threw back her head and laughed, then started to cough and wheeze.

'God, I'll have to give up the fags. Oh, but do you remember, Grace? We all fell about laughing and Elva was raging! Gave you a right clip across the legs. Hee-hee-hee-hee.'

I smiled back at the two amused faces and told them I could still feel the sting of the slap, which they seemed to find hilarious. Then Sadie bit her bottom lip and turned to look at me with owl-like eyes.

'What about your mother, Grace?'

'She's getting out in a couple of weeks, Frank says. Her legs are getting better all the time. I . . . I haven't really been talking to her — she didn't want too many people in.'

'Just right and all,' Molly said, returning to Sadie's hair. 'Give the woman time to mend. But isn't it powerful when you think about it, all these calamities. First wee Florrie, then young Charlie, then your mother and Josie near blew up, then that Ivy tarred and feathered. You know there's some maintains that stranger fella brought bad luck with him.'

I caught Molly's narrowed eyes in the mirror and looked away quickly.

'Bear McNicholl says there's something sleekid about him. Oh, but you're right and friendly with him, aren't you, Grace?'

'It's just that he was helping Frank. I don't really know him that well.'

Molly and Sadie exchanged a quick look.

'Well, times hasn't been good anyhow,' Sadie said, sighing.

I pretended to read an article about Elizabeth Taylor in the magazine, which made me feel even worse about my hair, and Molly moved on to a rant about the UDA march in Armagh. When she eventually got round to combing out my hair, it sprang back into tight curls as if the rollers were still in it. I stretched my legs in annoyance and forced a smile when she held a round mirror behind my head and asked me if I was pleased.

'You know you've a lovely head of hair, Grace. You should do more with it.'

I stood up and took the towel off my shoulders. 'Well, I thought I'd make a bit of an effort, you know, for the christening.'

'Your mother's not going to be too pleased

about that,' Sadie said with a slight smirk.

'I know. We're not letting on for the time being, until she's a bit better anyway, so could you — '

'There won't be a word out of us,' Molly interrupted. 'And you're doing the right thing. Your mother will see that in the long run. Sure blood's thicker than water.'

'Aye, and sure her and Ginny used to be the best of friends when they were wee,' Sadie said. 'It's that oul' fighting over the ground that kills your ma. Desperate business altogether.'

I took a pound note out of my pocket and gave it to Molly.

'Thanks, love. Now you have a good day.'

'So long, Grace. Good luck.'

The minute I got out I was tugging at my hair, trying to relax the stubborn fat curls. I was as outraged as I had been on the day of the nits, full of venom for Molly. By the time I'd got home, I'd calmed down, but Frank's startled face got me going again.

'Holy God! It's Fanny Craddock.'

He turned the page in his newspaper and continued to read, the remains of his breakfast on the table in front of him. I went into the hall and attacked my hair with a brush, creating a helmet of fuzz. The clock chimed eleven — no time to wash it and fix it. I ran to the bathroom and ran the brush under the cold tap, then dampened my hair through with it.

'Hey Fanny — there's a bit of bacon here for you,' Frank called from the kitchen.

I grimaced at myself in the mirror.

'You'd better eat something before going to the chapel — you don't want to be collapsing on them.'

He'd never let me forget fainting at Mass when I was twelve. He had to drag me out, his face flaming and mine pure white.

The smell of the fried bacon got my mouth watering.

'You're in a good mood,' I said begrudgingly to him as I took the plate from the shelf on the range. He put down his paper.

'One good thing about Ma being laid up in the hospital is not having to go to the chapel,' he said, clasping his hands loosely behind his head. 'Mind you, I'd say she'll be out in a couple of weeks.'

I sat down opposite him and poured a cup of tea. 'I'd say there's something more to your happiness than that.'

He pursed his lips and looked past me, out the window. He looked solid and healthy in the warm late morning light, his hair glinting like a new penny. 'I saw Ivy last night.'

I quickly swallowed a mouthful of bacon

sandwich. 'Where?'

'Out the back of Best's. I was leaving a bag of lime for her Da and she snuck out. Just for a second.'

'Well?'

'Well what?'

'How was she? Is she all right?'

He pushed the back of his hair up and down with his clasped hands, his face preoccupied. 'I'd say that fright she got could be the making of her.'

My impatience rose.

'What? How do you make that out?'

'She's a damn sight more polite than she used to be.'

'Polite? Ivy?'

'You know, quieter like. She's an awful-looking baldy head on her but she's dressed decent for a change. Don't know about that eye, though. One's going to the shop and the other one's coming back with the change.'

I watched him over the rim of my cup. He looked strangely content.

'She asked about you. Told her you were going to be a godmother, then she had to run back in. Heard the car coming round the front.' He picked up his paper again. 'Say, you'd better hurry yourself up.'

I shoved the dishes in the sink and ran to mother's bedroom. I undressed and pulled her blue dress out of the wardrobe, stepping into it and pulling up the zip at the back, this time without hesitation. If Mother was coming home soon, I was going to get the good out of her dress if it killed me.

I *knew* it was too big on her, I said to myself as I smoothed out the silky fabric around my hips. It was cut and lined to hang gracefully on the figure, barely glancing off the curve of the waist and hips, and disguising the excess flesh there. I pulled out the delicate chiffon flounces from the hem of the sleeves, which ended below the elbows, and patted down the little ruffle around the V-neckline that revealed the merest hint of cleavage.

'Grace, hurry up there and I'll give you a lift.'

'Right — give me a minute.'

I gave my hair another brusque tugging and rubbed make-up on to my face, already glowing from my exertions. Then it hit me that I had no suitable shoes. I pulled up the bedspread and scanned the row of dainty slingbacks and high-heeled court shoes under Mother's bed. I pulled out the flattest pair of sandals and squashed my feet into them, ignoring the crush on my big toes.

'Come on, Grace.'

I grabbed a patent blue handbag from the

shelf at the top of the wardrobe and threw in a tube of mascara and lipstick, and a white lace-edged handkerchief that smelled of violets. One last pull of the brush through my damp hair finally tamed the springy curls into soft waves but as I checked my reflection on the way out of the room, I felt something was missing.

Yes, a little gleam of silver and diamonds works wonders with powder blue . . .

I felt a prickle on the back of my neck. It was as if she was sending me a hint. I opened the pink shell lid of the jewellery box and took out the rarely worn diamante necklace handed down by Granny Crangle. I snapped the box shut and opened it again — yes, her engagement ring was there. I plucked out the three-diamond gold band from the velvet slit and pushed it on to the middle finger of my right hand, then put on the necklace.

Oh wow.

I swished around in the dress my mother loved and told myself I deserved it, just this once.

Sure, didn't you save my life?

Frank was waiting in the car.

'Roll that window down. You've enough perfume on to choke a bull.'

I rolled it down an inch. 'I don't want to wreck my hair, after all that.'

'Ssshhh. They're going to nail President Nixon over that break-in carry-on in America.'

He turned the radio up.

'The trial, watched by millions on live TV, will be presided over by the US Chief Justice,' read the newscaster. 'The US senators will set up a jury in their own Chamber, where Nixon has often presided. The question remains, will he jump, or will he be pushed?'

Frank tutted. 'They're going to hang his guts for garters over an oul' bit of chicanery and look what Heath's getting away with here. Sicken you.'

He switched off the news and drove quickly to the village, pulling up behind the short row of cars outside the chapel. The fishermen who'd escaped at communion time stood under the trees opposite the chapel gates, smoking and talking quietly, and by the look of the red watery eyes of the Mullens, sharing a communal hangover.

'I suppose you needn't rush in yet,' Frank said, settling back in his seat.

I raised myself slightly and straightened out the dress underneath me.

'You've a bit of brown stuff down your cheek.'

I yanked down the passenger mirror and blended the make-up with my fingertips.

'There they're coming out now,' Frank said, straightening up in his seat.

I slicked on some lipstick and waved a wand of mascara over my eyelashes. The Mass-goers were spilling out, pulling their faces into frowns against the bright midday light. Mrs O'Mahoney's niece was among the last to emerge from the archway, fresh and young in a crocheted suit the same shade as her long poker-straight hair.

As she strolled by, one of the Mullens said something out of the side of his mouth, raising smiles either side of him. Mrs O'Mahoney scowled at them but her niece walked on with her head high, flicking her hair behind her. The men's shoulders went up and down. My ears began to pop and my breath went shallow.

'On you go now,' Frank said, reaching for the ignition.

'Could you just wait a minute longer? I'm not ready yet.'

'Not ready? Sure what do you have to do?'

I rooted in the stiff, satin-lined handbag.

'I have to powder my nose.'

'You've enough of that oul' muck on.'

I patted the powder puff on my nose and chin. 'I have to take the shine away.'

He began to drum his fingers on the steering wheel. Only two cars were left in the row in front of us. I bent over and fidgeted with the straps of mother's sandals. There was a small bruise on my lower left leg and I wished I'd put on a pair of tights.

'Are you done now?'

I looked up. A few of the men had broken away from the group and were walking into the village but the Mullens still stood under the trees.

'It's nearly twelve anyway,' he said, turning on the ignition. 'Don't be worrying about that shower of eejits.'

I cleared my throat. 'I'm not.'

'Oh here, would you ever ask Sean has he a taker for the oul' apples? I know somebody looking a few dozen.'

I opened the car door and stepped out, forgetting to put both feet first. 'All right. See you later.'

'Right.'

I walked in front of the car and on to the pavement leading up to the chapel. Frank did a neat U-turn on the road and headed for home. I put the handbag over my shoulder but the straps were too short. I slipped it down to my elbow and walked with my head down, my toes pinching with each step. I willed the sun to burst out fully and dazzle the eyes I felt on me as I neared the chapel gates, but it stayed obscured behind layers of flimsy cloud in the quiet sky, gathering its momentum for the afternoon ahead.

I tried to relax my raised stiff shoulders and lift my chin but I heard someone snigger as I approached the gates. I made a pretence of looking for a hankie in the handbag.

'Looking well there, young Kane,' one of the Mullens called out.

I ignored him and walked quickly through the chapel gates.

'But I'd say you'd have got a truer reading about two and a half hours ago.'

His lowered words weren't intended for me to hear but they scorched through my head and eyes, and danced in front of my face all the way to the chapel doors.

I dipped my shaking fingers into the holy water receptacle on the wall and dabbed it on my hot forehead. A drip fell on to the front of the dress and made a small dark splodge on the fine fabric. I blew on it and shook the neckline to dry it out, and suddenly felt ludicrous.

Dolled up in chiffon and jewels, indeed. Why didn't Frank say something?

I pushed open the heavy panelled door into the back of the empty nave and slipped into the back pew to wait for the christening party. Generous though my padding was, the hard wood of the long narrow seat was immediately uncomfortable under my backside, and the air was thick with the smell of quenched candles and the lingering whiff of men's hair oil. The essence of the congregation was heavy all around me, as if they'd never left. I felt crowded and unable to pray. Instead I gazed at the Stations of the Cross, etched into the bone white marble between the rows of arched stain-glass windows on the pinkish walls. The chapel had always reminded me of an oyster, with its black stone exterior and pearly interior, and there wasn't an occasion when I didn't feel slightly nauseous within it. The time I fainted, Frank said, matter-of-factly, that it was because I was the spawn of the devil.

I was studying 'Jesus Consoles The Women' when Father O'Loan poked his head out from the vestry door at the side of the altar. His chasuble was bunched up around his pudgy neck.

'Those people are running late, Grace.'

His voice echoed in the parapets. He ducked back in before I could reply.

I reached around behind my neck and unclasped the diamante necklace. It caught the steep shafts of light from the window and twinkled seductively in my open hands. I put it back on.

A truer reading . . .

Surely I didn't look that different? A tear tickled the corner of my eye. I jerked back my head to kill it and took in a deep breath, and crossed my eyes to look down the side of my nose. Too long. That's it. I'd be all right if my nose was smaller. I ran through all the female noses of my close acquaintance. Mrs O'Mahoney's niece's, Ivy's, Ginny's, Mother's, Josie's. All small. Mary and Nelly's, Molly's, Mrs O'Mahoney's, mine. All big. Brutal.

Even the Virgin Mary in the corner had a slip of a nose. Even Joseph, in the other corner, had an unobtrusive one. I supposed they had to make Jesus and all his saints pleasant-looking to help you warm to them, right?

I listened for the small voice that had come to me in the bedroom. Silence. Then it hit me. She'd been tricking me.

Oh God.

I bit my lip, a cold prickle spreading down the back of my neck and spine. As I clutched at the necklace, the door creaked open and Uncle Sean appeared, even more handsome than Robert Mitchum, in a steel grey suit and navy blue shirt and tie. He held the door open for Ginny, blousy as usual in an ill-fitting floral two-piece, with the baby wrapped in a lace shawl in her chunky arms. The two boys shuffled in behind her, prayer books held in both hands in front of their chests, round eyes taking everything in. There was no sign of Saul.

I stepped out of the pew into the aisle.

'I suppose we may proceed on,' Uncle Sean said, nodding in my direction but not looking at me. He pulled the two boys towards him.

'Father O'Loan was there a minute ago,' I said, inclining my head towards the altar.

'Grace, take that child a minute till I hitch up this petticoat. It's digging into me desperate.'

Ginny handed the warm bundle to me and leaned sideways, twanging at her at her waistband.

'Go on ahead. I'll follow you up,' she said to Uncle Sean.

He put his hand on the end of the opposite pew and genuflected. The boys stared at him in puzzlement.

'Come on then,' he said. I saw the unease in his eyes and realised he was waiting for me to lead the way. I drew the bundle closer and walked ahead, conscious of the now heavier weight of the baby.

Her eyes were shut tight in her little creamy face, her softly grooved lips puckered slightly in forgotten anticipation of milk, and when I studied the sweep of the fragile bones in her face, I guessed she'd have her mother's nose when she grew up, and felt relieved for her. I wanted to kiss her plump downy cheek and look at her all day, and not to have to promise to bring her up in a faith which made you feel so bad.

Father O'Loan's large head appeared once again at the vestry door.

'Oh there you are — take a seat at the front and I'll be with you momentarily,' he said, his index finger up in front of him.

The baby gave a little start in my arms and her eyelids flickered as I handed her back to her mother.

'Do you have no singing at these things of yours?' she said.

'Ginny — not so loud,' Uncle Sean whispered, shunting the boys into the front pew.

Ginny sat down beside him and I slipped in beside her.

'You would've needed to organise that with Kitty, the organist,' I whispered.

'Huh.'

The door creaked behind us and the boys swung around in their seats. Hard soles clattered on the floor's stone surface and the boys giggled. Saul got to the seat just in time for the arrival of Father O'Loan in his purple and white alb.

'Good morning and welcome everyone,' said the priest, with a solemn nod of his veiny forehead. 'We're a little late starting, so we'll begin at once. Now, what name do you give your child?'

No-one spoke. Ginny turned to Uncle Sean. Father O'Loan cocked an eyebrow and gestured to the pile of folded sheets of paper in front of me bearing the order of the rite of baptism.

'Eh, the name's Georgina.'

Georgina?

I couldn't think of a name less suited to that tiny round face. Saul nudged my foot with his. He smelled of good soap and was wearing a white shirt and black trousers, flared out at the knee. He held a long thick candle with a decorative band around it. I gave him a baptism rite and passed the rest along.

'And what do you ask of God's church for . . . Georgina?'

'Baptism, Father,' Uncle Sean said, reading from the leaflet.

Father O'Loan looked squarely at Ginny.

'You have asked to have your child baptised. In doing so, you are accepting the responsibility of training her in the practice of the faith. It will be your duty to bring her up to keep God's commandments as Christ taught us, by loving God and our neighbour. Do you clearly understand what you are undertaking?'

'I do,' Ginny piped up.

'We do,' Uncle Sean said at the same time.

Father O'Loan turned his purple-lidded eyes to Saul, then to me. 'Are you ready to help the parents of this child in their duty as Christian parents?'

'We are,' Saul said.

'We are,' I said, a beat behind.

Father O'Loan stepped forward and traced the sign of the cross on the sleeping baby's forehead, then walked over to the carved mahogany baptismal font and beckoned us to join him. Mother's dress slid coolly over my knees as I stood up and for a moment I felt elegant again. I followed Saul to the far side of the font, where Father O'Loan directed us, and stood bathed in the dusty flume of light from the opposite window. The sun had banished the weak clouds and I felt its heat through the jewel-coloured glass, and momentarily I was back in the shooting hut in my swimsuit, with the water lapping under the boards beneath me and Saul's lips clamped on my neck.

'Lord hear us,' Father O'Loan intoned.

I hadn't heard a thing.

'Lord graciously hear us.'

Then I remembered what I saw through the bathroom window.

'Make the lives of her parents and godparents examples of faith to inspire this child. Lord hear us.'

I felt my face redden.

'Lord graciously hear us.'

I listened hard to the litany of saints called upon to pray for us, Saint John the Baptist. Saint Joseph. Saint Peter. Saint Paul.

I began to imagine them in the nude.

I gulped and cleared my throat, trying to force the erotic images out of my mind as Father O'Loan launched into the prayer of exorcism and anointing.

' . . . pray for this child. Set her free from original sin, make her a temple of your glory, and send your Holy Spirit to dwell with her. We ask this through Christ our Lord.'

'Amen.'

One of the boys, Ignatius, was staring at me. I grinned crookedly at him but he looked away coldly, as children do. The fantasies rushed back, perverse and persistent.

Thou shalt not have impure thoughts . . .

All the saints in heaven were enjoying an energetic orgy and there was nothing I could do to stop them. Bobby was staring blankly into my stricken eyes and nudging his brother.

Seed of the devil . . .

'And if your faith makes you ready to accept this responsibility, renew now the vows of your own baptism. Reject sin; profess your faith in Jesus Christ. This is the faith of the Church. This is the faith in which this child is to be baptised.'

I closed my eyes in shame. My dirty mind had now inflicted on me an image of a naked and excited Father O'Loan.

'Do you reject Satan?'

I mouthed the words 'I do' with the others, but only a faint sound came out.

'And all his works?

'I do.'

'And all his empty promises?'

'I do.'

I wondered what Satan had ever promised me. Then it hit me — it was him putting this stuff into my head, right under the nose of the shining tabernacle. Right. Once I had him to blame, the panic began to recede, and I was able to say yes, I believed in God and the Virgin Mary and the communion of saints and life everlasting.

Father O'Loan took the baby from Ginny's arms and held her over the font.

'I baptise you in the name of the Father,' he said, cupping his free hand into the water and pouring it over the faintly beating head before him.

The baby's neck shot into her shoulders and her fingers splayed open. Then she opened her mouth wide and yelled in protest. Ginny laughed and took her from Father O'Loan, stroking her face. The boys scowled and Uncle Sean scratched his thick black eyebrow, and all the while Saul stood beside me, still, silent and self-contained.

'Receive the light of Christ,' said Father O'Loan, presenting a lit Easter candle to Saul. The baby yelled on when Father O'Loan put his thumb on her mouth and her ears. 'You have put on Christ. In Him you have been baptised. May He soon touch your ears to receive His word, and your mouth to proclaim His faith.'

It was over. Georgina Kane stopped crying. She had put on Christ.

She waved her little pink pin-cushion of a hand and blew bubbles through her mouth with a succession of rude noises, and this time everyone, bar the retreating Father O'Loan, laughed out loud. I looked around at the various sets of bared teeth and felt a flare of happiness. I was a link in a circle, at last.

15

Ginny had set up a table in front of the two oak trees that held up the washing line. In the middle was a huge butter-cream sandwich cake from the bakery in town, and on either side, bowls of Smarties and crisps, and plates of sausage rolls and mushroom vol-au-vents.

'Now you're not to touch one thing until you get out of those good clothes,' she instructed the boys, shooing them into the house. 'I'll have to get this child down for a sleep.'

Uncle Sean took his coat from behind the car seat and draped it over his shoulder. 'I'll bring out a drop of drink. The two of you rest yourselves.'

After the jiggling and crush in the truck on the journey from the chapel, I wanted to stretch out on the grass in a field on my own. Saul had put his arm across the seat behind my head and I'd been flung against his ribcage every time Uncle Sean swerved around a corner. I'd accidentally dug my elbow into his groin at one stage and he'd winced in pain, so by the time we'd arrived at the house, I wanted to get myself away from him as far as politely possible.

I walked past the party table and over to the fence at the top of The Scrog. A lone pig was snuffling along the hedge further down the field, oblivious to our presence, his fellow swine lounging by the trees in the near distance. I shaded my eyes with my hand against the bright sunshine and leaned forward on the fence.

Saul came up behind me and gently tugged my hair.

'Very glamorous,' he said, pulling himself up to sit on the fence beside me.

'Molly did it. You should have seen the state of it earlier on. It was a fuzz ball.'

'Well, it looks good now.'

'Thank you.'

I wanted to believe him.

He stretched his neck to see ahead, towards the house. 'Grace, do you fancy having a bit of fun?'

I took my hand down from my forehead and looked at him. 'What sort of fun?'

He reached into his back pocket and took out a box of matches. Inside was the folded piece of lilac paper I'd taken from his locket.

'Oh, that's that thing I threw away, isn't it?'

'It sure is. Want some?'

'What?'

He unfolded the paper and tore off a piece. 'Try some.'

'You mean, eat it? What is it?'

'It's harmless. It'll just make you feel good.'

I took it from him. The letters ANA were on it. 'Is it drugs?'

'It won't do you any harm. It's far better for you than a feed of drink.'

'But will it make me feel funny?'

'No. It will just relax you. You'll feel good. At ease.' He carefully tore off a bigger piece and put it in his mouth. 'Hurry up, Grace — here comes Ginny.'

I glanced at the curling square in my palm, then popped it in my mouth.

'What do I do now?' I whispered.

'Just swallow.'

It tasted of nothing. He slid down off the fence.

'Come and get it,' Ginny called.

I followed Saul over to the table and sat opposite Uncle Sean. He sat with his elbows on the table, resting his cleft chin on his overlapping hands. The children grabbed handfuls of crisps and sweets and put them in the backs of toy dumper-trucks under one of the trees. They came back for glasses of brown lemonade, then settled themselves down beside their trucks, pushing them along and making engine noises.

Ginny passed around the savouries and poured fizzy wine into four tumblers.

'Here's to the young un,' she said, raising her glass.

We clinked glasses and sipped the wine.

Uncle Sean stuck out his bottom lip. 'Desperate oul' stuff, that.'

'It's French. Isn't it a special occasion?'

'Aye.'

An awkward silence ensued, with Uncle Sean turning sideways in his seat and looking straight ahead of him. Saul fled to play with the boys and Ginny busied herself cutting the cake. I racked my brains for something to say.

'Oh, Uncle Sean, Frank told me to ask you if you've anyone for the apples this year.'

'I see. Right.'

'He knows somebody interested in them.'

He inclined his head towards the table but kept looking down. For the first time it struck me he was a shy man, rather than just plain boorish.

'How many?'

'A few dozen, he said.'

'Bramleys or eating?'

'Oh I don't know about that. You'll have to ask Frank.'

I took a drink of the wine, delighted with myself. I'd contributed something of interest. Uncle Sean took another sip of his, then threw it out on to the grass.

'Sean! That's pure waste,' Ginny scolded.

'I'm away to look a beer. Hi, boy! Are you coming?'

Saul was on all fours under the tree, acting as a bridge for the boys' trucks.

'Coming now,' he said.

Ginny passed me a slice of cake.

'Don't be too long,' she called after Uncle Sean.

He climbed into the truck and drove it around it to the gate. Saul ran over and jumped in, and they took off down the road.

'Don't mind him. He's awkward in women's company,' Ginny sighed. 'Odd as be damned. Your father was a bit like that too.'

I swivelled the wine in my glass. 'Ginny, did Daddy hate Mother back?'

She squinted at me. 'No. He was indifferent to her, which is nearly worse. Oh he was dazzled by her good looks and charm at the start, but she was a malcontent of a being underneath it all.' She took a long drink from her glass. 'Mind you, I think I know how she feels. I don't know how much longer I can stick this. I'm treated like a farmhand, not a woman.'

She went to refill my glass but I held up my hand.

'No thanks, Ginny.'

'Huh. You fussy too?' Her freckled lips turned down at the corners.

'Eh, no. It's just I have to watch, with the tablets,' I lied.

'Ah. That's right,' she said, her face relaxing again. 'Now, miss, when are you going to get yourself out of that house and get an education?'

I looked away from her and cut the corner of the cake slice with my fork. 'Well, it's just that I'm needed around the house. Especially now — '

'Especially nothing. You've a brain in that head and you should use it. Didn't you do all right under them nunners? I hear they're powerful good teachers.' She refilled her own glass and gulped it.

'But Mother will need me when she comes out of hospital.'

'Ssstt.'

I ate a piece of the cake and felt my stomach squirm slightly.

Ginny leaned back in her chair and held her glass up to the side of her cheek.

'No offence, love. But that woman expects too much. And going and eating the altar rails and then coming out and saying the worst thing in her stomach about you. Sure what sort of a Christian is that?'

'I don't think she really means to be nasty.

Sadie says it's the change.'

'The change my arse. She's just a crabbid oul' carn.'

I swallowed another piece of cake.

'No offence, like.'

A giggle burst out of me, sending cake crumbs flying. Ginny chortled and insisted on refilling my glass. I took a drink.

'Ah sure, it's not right to be talking about the woman, and her with the legs blew round her head,' she said, eyeing me furtively to see my reaction. I couldn't keep my face straight. She lowered her voice and nodded. 'I'd say those boys had their target right for once.'

I looked at her in surprise.

'Only kiddin'! Would you look at your face, and it all nicely done up too.'

I dabbed my lips with a piece of kitchen roll Ginny was using for napkins.

'Now look, being serious, like. I want you to promise me something, Grace.' She paused, looking at her nails.

'What?'

'Two things. The first is that you'll go and get yourself more education and a good job one day. Don't be like me.'

'There's nothing wrong with you.'

'Now! Don't be at it. Sure what sort of life have I? I've an ugly life, that's what I have.'

'But you've got — '

'Wheest. This isn't about me. Do you promise to do that?'

'I . . . all right. I'll try.'

'Huh. You know when somebody says they'll *try*, that means the thing won't be done at all. But I'll take your word for it just this once. Right. Now. You've to promise me something else, then we're done.' She drained her glass and thumped it down on the table. I thought I saw a faint quiver in her bottom lip but her voice was steady. 'I want you to promise that you'll always look out for the wee one.'

'The baby?'

'That's right.'

'Sure, aren't I the godmother. And thank you for asking me by the way, it was very nice of — '

'No! More than that oul' baloney about religion. Sure half the country doesn't know who the hell their godparents are and those oul' holy candles of yours get used when the electric goes off. No, I mean, really watch out for her. You know, in case something happens . . . to me.'

'What like?'

'Don't ask stupid questions,' she snapped.

A rising warm feeling inside kept me from being offended.

Ginny's voice softened. 'You know the way

people thinks a girl will be all right because she'll end up married with some man to look after her? You know the way men would be more worried about their sons because they have to make their own way?'

'Yes.'

'Well, then you'll look out for the child. You never know what's round the corner, you know. Or when you could be called upon.'

'Certainly, I'll help you. I don't know how I would get round it at home, but.'

She glared at me.

'But I will.' I raised my glass to her and smiled with genuine ease.

'That's the spirit,' she said, nodding emphatically. She raised her glass and saw it was empty. 'Oh, here. We need another bottle. Hang on a minute.'

She clambered out of her chair and strolled towards the house, calling to the boys to mind themselves. They had climbed up into the tree and were shaking early acorns off the branches.

I watched Ginny cross the yard. The sun on the back of her red head made it look like molten gold and as she moved, her shoulders loose and well back, I caught a fleeting glimpse of the past charms that must have attracted Uncle Sean. Then she bent over with her feet wide apart to pick up a clothes peg and scratched her back with it. I blinked. The flowers on her dress seemed to stand out for a second and jiggle in the sunlight. I blinked again and her dress was back to normal. She opened the back door and disappeared into the house. I pushed back my chair from the table and turned it towards The Scrog. The acorns had stopped falling from the tree and the boys were quiet, but I had a vague and unconcerned notion that they were watching me.

'Plenty more sweets and lemonade,' I called out, aware of calm spreading within me. I stretched out my legs and turned my face up to the soft sun. It stroked my skin with the gentlest touch and I began to imagine a warm, kind hand resting on my head, making all my thoughts ordered and peaceful. I lifted my right hand and put it where I felt the sensation and it intensified, and when I closed my eyes, the feeling moved down into my chest, down through my body and legs, and tingled in my toes. The sandals were no longer tight.

I stayed in this bliss until I felt a shadow cross me. When I opened my eyes, Bobby was standing with the bowl of Smarties, popping them into his mouth one by one. I said hello to him.

' 'Natius says not to talk to you.'

'Oh — why?'

'Because you're a witch.'

I shaded my eyes to look at him properly. He was like a mini Frank, only with straight blond hair.

'Are you not afraid of me then?'

'Nope.'

'You don't think I'm a witch?'

'I do. But I don't think you could do spells or nothin'.'

'Why not?'

'Just.' He lifted the bowl to his mouth and let the sweets slide in. 'Natius says you foam at the mouth like an oul' divil and wet yourself and wriggle about the place like somebody not wise.'

His words floated past me without impact.

'What do you be doing that for?'

'I don't any more. It was just a sort of sickness when I was wee.'

''Natius says you hit a dead fella with a mop in his coffin.'

'Oh, did he indeed?'

'Yes. And then you started thumping yourself to get a shower of divils out of you.'

I put my hand on my head again. 'Well, you might not believe this, but I've got God in me. Not the devil.'

'How d'you know?'

'I can feel Him, right here. You can feel

Him in you if you put your hand on your head. Go on, try.'

He looked at my hand for a few seconds, then put his bowl down and plonked both hands down on his head. 'Can't feel nothin'.'

'Not so hard. Don't push down. Just touch lightly.'

He continued to press down. I closed my eyes. When I opened them again, his were shut tight. I held in a laugh at his fervent face, then the leaves of the tree rustled and Ignatius jumped down from a branch.

'You! What are you doin' to my brother?'

Bobby spun around and ran towards the house.

'Mammy! Mammy! She's doing things to our Bobby!' Ignatius cried, running after him.

I straightened up in the chair and watched them disappear into the house. When Ginny didn't emerge to investigate, I relaxed again and poured out some lemonade. It was warm and sweet, and when I looked into the glass, it had gold sparkles in it. I stood up and lifted the bowl from the ground, just as Uncle Sean drove back into the yard.

Ginny appeared at the door. 'That was my mother on the phone. She wants us to bring the child over. She's a wee savings book for her.'

Uncle Sean shut the truck door. A white

plastic bag dangled from his hand. Saul jumped out from the other side and walked towards the table.

'Would you bring us, Sean.'

'Ah Jesus, Ginny,' he complained.

'Ach come on. Only for an hour. She'll take it thick if we don't and not give the child a shilling.'

Uncle Sean scratched the side of his head and headed to the house. 'Well, come on if you're coming. I'll throw this in the fridge.'

I put the bowl on the table and sat down again.

Saul was standing looking at me intently. 'Well, how are you?'

'All right. Good. I had a talk with Ginny.'

I started to tell him about the conversation. I told him every line, every description of Mother, every nuance.

He shook his head and gave a deep chuckle from his stomach. He turned around at the sound of the back door slamming.

'You two are very welcome to stay — we won't be long,' Ginny called out. 'You can help me feed the pigs again.'

'No problem,' Saul shouted above the sound of the truck engine starting up. Ginny loaded the newly excited boys and the cot into the back and they drove off.

Saul lay down on the grass near my feet

and took off my sandals.

'You're getting red marks across your feet,' he said, rubbing them.

I closed my eyes in relief that they weren't hot and sweaty. His touch was soothing when I'd expected it to be ticklish, but when he leaned over and kissed my toes, I dragged my feet away and tucked them under my chair. The warmth evaporated and I suddenly felt a strange churning in my stomach.

'You can be a real nervous nelly sometimes, Grace,' he said, rolling on to his back.

'I don't like people touching my toes, that's all.' I bent them into the grass.

'Hold it now. Just relax. Come on, stretch out. I hope you didn't drink too much of that plonk.'

'No, just a drop.'

'That's right. Stretch those legs out. Now breathe through your belly, as if you want to fill out your waistband. Then breathe out through your mouth.'

I did what he said and the warm feeling flowed back. I found myself smiling for no reason.

'Saul, I think that stuff is working.'

'Already?'

I nodded.

'Great.' He sprang to his feet and held out

his hand. 'Come on for a paddle down in the stream.'

'Along with the pigs?'

'Sure won't they be glad to see us?'

I stood up and took his hand. We strolled to the fence and he held open the gate for me. I seemed to glide through it, my bare feet touching only the soft places in the grass. He squeezed my hand and led me down over the uneven ground to the young silver birch trees by the stream, watching out for stones and brambles on the ground.

Most of the pigs were in the water, flicking it up with their snouts or lying along the shallow edges. One came over to us and butted Saul playfully on the leg. He lifted a stick and threw it into the water for the pig to chase.

'They think they're dogs half the time,' he said, laughing at the pig keeping its head above the water as it swam. I broke free of his hand and dipped my toes in the water's edge.

'They say if you throw a stick into the lough, it will petrify and turn into a stone,' I said.

He took off his shoes and laid them on the narrow bank. 'Well this stream runs into the lough, so that stick will be a boulder before you know it.'

'Lough Neagh stones, Lough Neagh

Stones. Put in sticks and brought out stones. That what they used to sing. The water was supposed to heal — but there's not a word of it. Nobody was ever cured in it. Why has your face gone all serious?'

It was the same look I'd seen cross his face when he first came to Preacher's Bay.

'You're imagining things.'

The water rippled over my feet like silk. The pigs lost interest in us and no longer looked, apart from a black and white one who occasionally grunted in our direction. I watched it sniff along the water's edge and thought I saw a streak of faint light behind it as it moved. I shook my head and trained my eyes on it. I saw it again.

'Saul, there's something weird about that pig. It has lines of light coming out behind it when it moves.'

He turned from where he stood on the bank to look at it. 'It's a magic pig.'

'I'm serious. I can see it. In fact . . . everything looks a little strange, like the television's not tuned in properly.'

'It's a trick of the light down here. Just enjoy it.'

I watched the dappled water ripple and flow in front of me and saw a faint blue glow off it. I looked at the birches and the silver sides of their leaves were lit up like stars. I

looked at Saul's face and his eyes were huge
and black, and his lips rose pink like a girl's. I
turned away from him and walked further
into the stream, hitching up the dress. It was
already wet around the edges. My feet sank
into the soft mud and it squelched through
my toes, and the water felt so cool and silky
on my legs, I wanted to feel it all over. I
looked over my shoulder. Saul had waded
into the middle of the stream, up to his hips.
He scooped up the water and splashed it over
his chest, sending out a radiance of droplets
on either side of him. I stared at the sparkling
jets of water and watched transfixed as one of
them, as if in slow motion, arced high in the
air between us and landed on my head.

'Oh! Oh God! Mother's good dress!' I
squealed.

The black and white pig squealed back at
me.

Saul laughed. 'Why don't you take it off?'

I wiped the water off my cheeks.

'You can put on my shirt if you like. It
doesn't matter about it.'

I looked down at the damp dress and the
little puckers in the chiffon where the water
had splattered, and paddled back to the bank
where Saul had left his clothes. I picked up
his shirt and turned to see if he was looking,
but he had his back to me, his hands resting

on the sides of his waist. The colours had gone flat again, as the sun splintered between the leaves and branches.

I stepped out of the dress, turned it inside out, folded it and set it on top of Saul's trousers, then pulled on his shirt and buttoned it up to the chest, getting a whiff of the soap I'd smelled earlier.

Saul turned around. 'Come here till you see, quick.'

I walked at a leisurely pace out into the water.

'Look, over here,' he said, pointing in front of him.

A squall of sprickley-backs swirled around just below the surface, seemingly with no place to go rather than around in a circle.

'I've seen more exciting things than that in the water, or that has come out of the water, I should say.'

He bent over and peered at the tiny darting fish. 'Like what?'

'I can't say.'

'Why not?'

'I was told not to. I promised Dalloway and Bear.'

He spread out his hands over the water. 'Aw come on. You've got me all curious now.'

A smile tugged on my mouth. 'I can't tell you.'

'You'll have to if I make you.'

'Oh, really? How are you going to make me?'

'Like this!'

He lunged towards me and poured the contents of his cupped hands down the inside of the shirt. I screamed and stumbled backwards but managed to steady myself before I fell. I pulled out the front of my shirt. Several sprickley-backs were squirming down the front of my bra. I screamed again and tried to pluck them out but they were too slippery and I was too panicky. Saul stood laughing behind his hands. In desperation I pulled up the shirt and yanked up my bra and the fish fell out.

'That wasn't funny!' I shouted, pulling down the shirt.

He stepped towards me, a mock serious look on his face. 'I think you'll find you haven't quite got rid of all your little catch . . . '

He reached forward and snapped out the waistband of my pants under the shirt. I felt something slither down my navel. I flinched and pounded my feet up and down.

'Oh my God!'

He hollered with laughter, throwing his head forward and holding his stomach. I ran headlong to the bank and pulled down my pants. Two sprickley-backs wriggled on the white cotton. I shook my fists in front of my neck in distress, then bent and picked up the pants between the thumb and forefinger of each hand and attempted to throw the fish back into the water, but they clung on. Saul's guffaws rang in my ears and I felt a sudden rush of energy. Impulsively I rolled the pants into a ball and flung them into the water, and watched them float downstream, Lough Neagh-bound.

Saul waded out of the water, clapping his hands above his head.

'All praise to the girl who would lay down her knickers for the lives of two fish,' he lauded in the voice of a deep south American preacher.

I tugged down at the bottom of the shirt to cover myself. The bra was still hitched above my breasts and making strange lumps in the shirt. I felt ridiculous but the welling feel-good sensation inside me was getting stronger, and with a deep exhalation of the breath I'd been holding in, I gave into it and let my body rock with laughter, from my heels to my knees to my hip to my shoulders. I staggered backwards with the force of it and leaned against a tree, at one distant level listening in amazement to the uncontrolled sounds I was making.

Water scooted out of the far corners of my eyes and my stomach muscles clenched in deep spasms. I bent forward and half-heartedly tried to stop. There was no wind but the tufts of grass waved in all directions and the soft ground between the clumps seemed to teem and jiggle. I pointed to the ground and tried to steady myself. Saul put his hands on my shoulders and guided me up against the tree. I looked into his face and stopped laughing. His skin was luminous and his teeth and the whites of his eyes seemed to be made of the same stuff.

Behind him the trees danced jerkily, leaves flopping like fops' wrists. I swayed my head from side to side and they jolted along, leaving a trajectory of zigzags in their wake. I became mesmerised by this effect and heard myself sigh, and the sound was exactly that of an incoming tide on a still, summer morning. Saul came closer and as his breath rose and fell with mine, I closed my over-stimulated eyes and we were on a seashore, Deborah and Burt, with the water racing up to see what was going on, and pulling back to let them at it.

But that pose of theirs was too awkward-looking, his neck straining and her bent inelegantly over him. No, we are Cary Grant and Grace Kelly. No. Too clean. Yes!

We're Johnny Weissmuller and Maureen O'Sullivan. Perfect, for I can smell the zing of the leaves and the dark treacley aroma of the soil, and he is dark and bare, and this is earthy and natural. Under my eyelids I see the African sunset . . . Tarzan and Jane are suddenly in Technicolor and their ribs are touching. Adam and Eve. The sigh of the tide falls into their slow rhythm. The breeze is whispering. It wants to know if I am unhurt. The grass is shifting under my back. It's peeling outwards from the middle and Jane's spine is pressing into the soil. Comfortably. Her hips rise and fall and sway. She's a very good dancer. Johnny leads her in the dance. Yes, he is dark and bare, and this is earthy and natural. And very, very sore.

★ ★ ★

When it was over, I got up and walked over to the water, and splashed my face with it. The churning in my stomach had become a cramp.

Saul stood behind me with the dress. 'I'm afraid one of the pigs trotted over it.'

I took it from him and held it out. Hoofprints covered the front of it, from top to bottom, and the hem was snagged. The pig was at the dress when he was at me, like the repulsive husband of the girl in that other French novel I read at school.

'At least it's inside out.'

I walked around behind a tree, took Saul's shirt off and put the dress on. The marks could be seen through the fine chiffon. I stretched out my arms and leaned my hands against the bark, willing the electrics in my head to switch off. But they'd only quieten down for a minute, then flash back on again.

'Are you all right, Grace?'

He slipped his arms around my waist. I nodded and walked with him back into the light of the field. Someone was walking up to the fence at the top.

'Hey! Just in time. Drive those pigs up for me till I get their feed ready.'

We didn't need to drive them, for they sprang into action at the sound of Ginny's voice. They careered past us and up the field, filling the air with their yeasty wind.

What have I done?

My foot slid into a shallow hole in the ground and I went over on my ankle. The shock of it brought me hurtling back to reality for a few seconds and I had to lean on Saul's arm the rest of the way up the field. The sun burned through the delicate material on my back, drying the damp patches and itching my skin.

'Saul, how can I turn this thing off?'

'What thing?'

'The thing in my head.'

'Don't worry about it. Just go with it. Don't fight it. Don't be afraid.'

Ginny appeared at the fence and held open the gate for us. 'Jesus, Grace, you're the colour of buttermilk. And what's that on your good dress?'

'She fell, down by the stream,' Saul cut in.

'Go on in and sponge it down. I'll be in in a minute.'

I walked over to the party table and sat down to put on my shoes. My soles felt like clay against the leather.

'You go on in. I don't feel like talking to Uncle Sean.'

He hesitated. 'You never told me your secret.'

'You're the one with all the secrets.'

He looked at me sadly. 'Come on, I'd better get you home.'

I thought of my bed and there was nowhere I wanted to be more than wrapped up in my red eiderdown. I got up and followed Saul to the open back door. Uncle Sean sat alone at the table, drinking from a bottle of beer.

'Sean, we have to go. Grace isn't feeling too good.'

'Ah, you'll have a beer first,' Uncle Sean

said. 'Go on ahead.'

Saul glanced around at me and I nodded.

'There's some more of that oul' wine if you want some,' Uncle Sean said, nodding at the bottle on the drainer.

'I'll take some water instead,' I said, my voice thin.

I filled a glass and leaned back against the sink. Saul sat down on the pine rocker in the corner, took a swig of the beer and put the bottle between his thighs. Then something happened that made me drop my glass on the floor. I screamed and held my hands over my eyes.

Saul jumped up and ran over to me.

'Your hands were melting into the chair! I saw them!'

'Grace! Don't be daft — you're seeing things.'

I lowered my fingers from my eyes. He was holding his hands up in front of me. Uncle Sean gave a snort and I slid my eyes over to him. One of his hands was melting into the wood of the arm of his chair, the other into his bottle of beer.

I pushed Saul out of my way and ran out the door.

Ginny met me in the yard. 'What the — ?'

'Could you please take me home, please, Ginny? I need to go to bed, please. Now, please.'

'Hang on a minute. What the hell's wrong with you?'

'I just feel funny, that's all. Too much sun. Can we go, Ginny?'

Her forehead creased in a vertical frown. 'You haven't been at those oul' mushrooms down The Scrog, have you?'

I gaped at her vacantly.

Her face lit up. 'I knew it! I knew by those dopey big eyes of yours. Standing there all stupid-looking.'

She set down her buckets and rubbed her hands on her apron.

'Well, are you coming or aren't you?' she said, heading to the truck.

I followed her over to it and climbed into the front seat.

As she turned the ignition, Saul jumped into the back.

'Oh, aye, John Lennon,' Ginny scoffed. 'You feeling a bit strange too?'

'What?'

'Now don't come the all innocent with me. I know what you've been at. You know it takes very little of those wee buggers to do you. I thought the pigs had ate the whole lot of them, mind you. How many did you take?'

'Just a handful,' Saul said quietly.

'Huh.'

Ginny turned the truck on to the road and

sped along, perilously close to the hedge. I watched it whizz by in a daze, grateful for something to keep up with my racing mind. Saul reached forward and put his hand on my shoulder, next to the window. I clung on to it, suddenly in desperate need for human contact. Ginny switched on the radio and Van Morrison's voice never sounded as high and searing, and every pluck of strings pinged in my ears as if he was in the truck with us, every thump of the bass hitting me in the chest. The high subsided again.

'I'm all right now.'

'Well that's a good job because I see Frank's car in your yard and I don't think he'd approve of that caper,' Ginny said, pulling up.

Saul jumped out and opened the passenger door.

I turned to Ginny. 'Thanks, Ginny. I — '

'You won't forget what you promised me, will you?'

'No. I promise.'

'You better stay away from that oul' stuff. I need to be able to depend on you.' She leaned over and kissed my cheek. 'One day you'll understand. Be seeing you.'

I climbed out and waved her off, reaching out for Saul's arm with my free hand.

'Got the jitters?' he asked.

'Sort of. But I'm all right now. I think.'

He put his arm around my shoulders and walked me to the back door. I walked in ahead of him, then on impulse turned and hugged him in the darkening hall. He pulled me closer and began to kiss me, little soft safe pecks that made me feel like a cherished child.

I pulled away from him reluctantly. 'Come on — let's get a cup of tea.'

I turned and opened the door to the kitchen, Saul's hands on my shoulders. When I saw Frank's face, I knew immediately that she was there. She stepped out from the other side of the room, thinner and older but still starkly beautiful.

I automatically pushed Saul's hands off my shoulders. All I could think about were the dirty marks on her dress, and my missing pants. Her eyes took me in from head to foot, pausing at my open mouth and my chest.

'Grace — '

'Shut up and sit down, Frank. You, close that door and get in here. Don't move, either of you.' Her voice was low and even but her eyes glittered. She leaned on a walking stick. 'I know what you did.'

I stared into the fierce blue eyes and saw tangled flesh by the stream. I couldn't speak.

'Mrs Kane, it's all my fault. I talked her into it.'

'Shut your mouth.'

She didn't even look at him. My jaw began to grind.

'Why did you do it? Answer me.'

'I . . . I don't know . . . '

'You don't know? You stupid, half-baked scut. You ape.' She stepped forward and thumped me hard on the top of my arm.

'I'm sorry! I'm sorry! I love . . . I — '

'What? You love who? You don't mean to tell me you love a thing that came out of that whore and that good-for-nothing blaggard?' She spoke in a falsetto sneer.

I gawked at her in amazement. She thumped me again on the same spot. I raised my hand to rub my arm and she shrieked.

'My ring! She's got my ring! Frank! And my necklace! Frank!'

She grabbed my hand and began to haul at the ring with her fingernails.

Saul put his hand out to stop her. 'Mrs Kane, don't, please, you're hurting her.'

She twisted me around and slammed my hand on the worktop.

'I'll get that ring off your fat finger if it's the last thing I do!' she screeched, grabbing the chopping knife from its holder.

I tried to wrest my wrist from her grip but

she held it down and raised the knife above her head. The scream stopped halfway up my throat as she brought the knife down. Saul pulled me away and Frank grabbed the knife.

She stood quivering by the sink. I frantically twisted the ring off my finger and set it on the table.

'You rotten dirty *clart*. You get my jewellery and my dress off and you get every mote off it. Get out of my sight.'

My legs barely carried me to the door.

'And you. You get out of this house and you never show your tinker face around her again, you piece of shit.'

'Mrs Kane, don't blame Grace. It was my fault.'

'Get him out, Frank!'

I opened the hall door and paused on the other side of it.

'Come on, boy, you'd better go,' Frank was saying.

I heard the back door slam shut and Saul's voice calling me.

I went to my room and locked the door behind me. For a long time I lay clutching my cramping stomach, way beyond lonely, and when I closed my eyes, I saw the side of a fist, that became a prawn, that became a foetus.

I opened my eyes and the image had burned itself into the grain of the wood on the wardrobe door. It was on the wall and on the curtains. It would not disappear.

Where are you, God?

* * *

So. Here we are again. The four links left in the chain. Only one with a vestige of youth. It's as if I came up for air after a long spell at the bottom of the pond, and you were still waiting at the edge, after all that time. It was close, wasn't it? You could've switched me off, you know, when the nurses weren't looking. Oh, but you haven't sussed it yet, have you? No, of course you haven't. I can't believe I'm still in this terrible room. Is that relief I see in your exquisite face, Georgina? I knew you'd grow up to be lovely. And you Ignatius, cold as ever. And you, Bobby, blank as ever. What's to become of us all? Obviously I wasn't meant to go yet. A little unfinished business perhaps? Oh. Come again? You're going to take me home? And look after me? Holy God, Georgina dear. Well, perhaps I can arrange a little surprise for you back at Preacher's Bay. When I get back my tongue.

PART THREE

16

'We brought Grace home today. They can't do much more when the liver starts to go. I thought you might like to see her.'

There was a pause on the other end of the line.

'I think we'll wait until she gets settled in. Tell her me and Josie were asking for her.'

'I will. Bye.'

Georgina hung up the receiver and went back into the kitchen. The light outside was fading rapidly and her laptop screen glowed out from the table. She looked at her watch. Teatime.

She tapped on the bedroom door. When there was no reply, she walked in and set the tray on the bedside table.

'I thought you might like a nice bit of scrambled egg, Grace. Easy to digest.' She reached over and plumped up the pillows and straightened the eiderdown. 'It's getting dark fast, isn't it? I think I'll pull those curtains.'

A faint sound came from the bed. When she turned around, Grace had her hand held out towards the window.

'Oh, no problem. I'll leave them.'

They brought me home in the middle of Lent. I brought some strange weather with me, they said. One minute there was a little dry snow like ashes swirling in the air, the next a crack and rumble of thunder and hailstones the size of gobstoppers bouncing off the windowsills. It got dark at half three.

She insisted on staying. Can't see how a girl like that could stick the life out here. I know she likes a drop of drink. I hear her stumbling around the place late at night. But then her mother had a weakness for the wine too.

I know rightly she's been talking to the neighbours. Molly and the Mullens will have told her about Saul, for sure. I can tell by the way she looks at me, with a renewed curiosity in her big soft eyes. And she'll have heard long ago all about Frank, and what happened to Ivy, no doubt. How flippant a bystander can be on these life and death contingencies. She brings me tea and toast every morning, and Horlicks at night. The home help, does the rest, thank goodness. She's married to a UDA man but not a bit bigoted herself. Gave me a hand mirror and a pair of tweezers the other day and told me to pluck my eyebrows. They've always been a bit untidy.

I have aged. My face is smaller, eyebrows lower, eyelids heavier. The top lip has shrunk a bit but the bottom one is as fleshy as ever. Funny to think I lay here all that time ago, thinking I better not cry too much, because crying uglifies, if there's such a word, and if you constantly screw your face up with weeping, you'll get a load of lines around your eyes when you're older. Of course, I wouldn't have been aware of this if Mother hadn't pointed it out to me, the very morning after the christening. She had calmed down overnight, but remained resolute.

★ ★ ★

'It's too late for tears now, anyway,' she said, on the other side of my bedroom door. 'You've made your bed and you can lie in it.'

I did. For two days. I began to re-read *Crime and Punishment* to stop me thinking. I think it made me feel worse. On the morning of the third day, Frank peeped in and told me to come up to the kitchen for breakfast.

'Just be normal, Grace. It's all forgotten now.'

He left the door ajar. I dragged a comb through my hair and pinched my pasty cheeks. Hope flared.

Of course. She's remembered I sort of saved her life.

I padded up the hall in my slippers and tentatively pushed open the kitchen door. Mother and Frank had begun to eat.

'Yours is on the range,' she said briskly.

I lifted the plate from the rack and set it on the table. The rashers were dried up and crispy, the way Frank liked them. I poured tea and quietly offered warm-ups before I sat down. Frank pushed his mug out for more.

We ate in silence. I kept my eyes on the plate or on the window, where the blue-caps fluttered in the muted sunshine, waiting for scraps.

When she'd finished eating, Mother spoke agreeably with Frank about his holiday plans, the annual break in Ballybunion at the end of August.

Then she clasped her hands under her chin and looked at me, a bland, polite look on her pale face, like a stranger making small talk at the table of a B&B.

'I've arranged some things for you to do today, Grace,' she said pleasantly. 'We'll go when you've done the dishes.'

I looked at her expectantly.

'We'll go to confession first.'

Frank raked his chair back noisily and stood up.

'You'll be wanting the car then?' he said on the way out.

'Yes, dear.'

I stood up and began to clear the table, acutely aware of every move I made. It occurred to me that I hadn't broken anything in ages.

Mother got up slowly and rubbed the base of her back. Bandages were visible under her tights.

I cleared my throat. 'Will you be able for driving?'

She lifted her walking stick from the side of the range. 'I hear you have been behind the wheel.'

The wet plate slipped in my hand and clattered to the bottom of the sink. 'I . . . there was nothing for lunch one day . . . when we were doing the scallions.'

'Nelly Mullen said you gave the gears an awful scraping. But never mind. Just don't try it again.'

She limped to her room and I dried the dishes, cursing Nelly. A blue-cap jumped along the windowsill impatiently. I grabbed a handful of nuts out of the drawer and threw them out. I watched the birds dive and clutch the nuts with their beaks and fly off to the hedge. These creatures and their feeding were the only consistent things in my life. Saul had not come back for me.

I swallowed back the self-pitying lump in my throat and hung the drying cloth over the bar of the range. Mother came back into the kitchen with her camel jacket on. It was a size too big for her now, and hung badly on her slight shoulders.

'You'll be glad to hear that the dry-cleaners made a good job of my dress — I decided to get it done properly,' she said dryly, pulling on her leather driving gloves.

'Oh. That's good.'

I followed her out and got into the car. She tapped the driver's window with her stick. I lurched over the seats and opened the door for her, kicking myself that I hadn't thought to do it first. She threw the stick into the back seat and lowered herself in, checking her teeth for lipstick in the side mirror. I watched the creases in her gloves smooth out as she gripped the steering wheel and drove the car on to the road, without looking left or right. She'd always claimed she could hear if there was a car coming or not.

She hummed 'This Is My Beloved' all the way to the chapel. I got out and opened her door, and held it open. She eased herself up, both feet first, and a phoney-sounding cough on the pavement. I lifted her stick from the back seat and walked a fraction behind her into the chapel. Bear McNicholl knelt in one of the back pews, despite his vow never to darken the chapel door again. Sadie sat with Mary Mullen near the front. Mother walked up to the pew right beside the confessional box in the middle of the chapel, and stood back to let me in past her. I butted my toe on the kneeler and made it bang against the hard floor. Mary's big moon face turned to us and she nudged Sadie, who did a double take and waved. Mother smiled regally and turned and raised her hand to Bear McNicholl. I inched along the seat and knelt down, clasping my hands over my nose. After a moment, Mrs O'Mahoney emerged from the confessional and spotted Mother. She slipped into the seat behind us and Mother prodded me to go next. She moved her knees sideways and nodded coolly to Mrs O'Mahoney, who immediately began to whisper to her.

I went into the pitch-dark box and got a whiff of fried food and whiskey, the lingering residue of the O'Mahoneys' kitchen and Father O'Loan's nightcaps. I knelt down and waited. The slot on the dividing grille remained in place. I breathed in the blackness and strained to make out something, but I could see and hear nothing.

Maybe this is what Purgatory's like. It's not too bad.

I practised what I was going to say to Father O'Loan. It was straightforward, for I had decided my biggest sin had not happened. I had banished the memory of it.

Still no sign of him. I shifted my knees and sat back on my hunkers, then straightened up again and ran my fingers over the grille. After a few moments I felt the darkness begin to close in on me. I grew increasingly anxious and hot, with a compelling sense of déjà vu. I couldn't remember being locked up in the dark before, but the feeling of familiarity, tinged with fear, was overwhelming and I couldn't stay in the box a second longer. I stood up, grappled for the door knob and stepped out.

Father O'Loan was rushing down the side aisle towards me.

'Sorry, sorry. Nature called,' he muttered, waving me back in.

Out of the side my eye I saw Mother glaring and Mrs O'Mahoney leaving. I closed the door tight behind me.

'Bless me, Father, for I have sinned. It's been three months since my last confession.'

Father O'Loan panted on the other side of the open grille, making the air even more pungent. 'Tell God your sins.'

'I lied and swore, and I stole two hairslides.'

'I see. From where did you take these items?

'From the market.'

'I see. Do you have anything else to tell me?'

'I . . . I think Mother thinks standing for Sean and Ginny's child is some sort of sin, Father, but I don't.'

'Mmmm. Anything else?'

'No.'

'Are you sure? Examine your conscience, my dear.'

How could I tell him?

'There is nothing else, Father.'

'Are you certain? You do not want to be going around with a mortal sin on your soul.'

A trickle of sweat ran into the well of my bra. How could he possibly know?

'Grace, have you been having any impure thoughts?'

'No.'

He sighed his disappointment. 'Grace, your . . . there are people very worried about you. Now, is there anything you want to tell me?'

My throat constricted. 'No. I don't know what you are talking about.'

'Have you acted upon impure thoughts, Grace?'

I heard a creak from outside and my breath shortened. What if Mother could hear? Isn't

439

that why she sat there? What had she told Father O'Loan?

'No. I mean, I haven't had impure thoughts. Just silly stuff. About saints.'

I could make out his hand going up to the side of his head. White dots juggled before my eyes and I began to breathe heavily.

'Well then, I suppose you may make your act of contrition.'

'Oh my God, I am truly sorry for all my sins and for having offended thee. With your help I will not sin again.'

'For your penance, say six Hail Marys and six Our Fathers. By the power invested in me by Our Lord, I absolve you of your sins. Go in peace.'

He slid over the slot.

I stood up slowly and wavered in the newly absolute dark. Someone went into the other side of the confessional but I couldn't find the handle to get out before they started confessing. A man's voice mumbled. I ran my hands up and down the door in a panic, eventually locating the handle, and burst out on to the side aisle, unintentionally slamming the door behind me.

Mother's eyes held a mixture of smugness and contempt. My exit had also attracted the curiosity of Sadie and Mary, and the newcomers at the back, and the postmistress, who was lighting a candle under the feet of St Anthony. Mother slid along to the edge of the seat, stood up slowly and stepped into the aisle, flicking her wrist at me in a gesture to follow her. My face turned from grey white to screaming crimson, and the white dots fled from the heat.

'You can say your penance in the car,' Mother said breezily at the chapel gates. 'Oh, there's Mrs Best — you go on ahead.'

I got into the car and sank down in the seat. Mrs Best greeted Mother pleasantly enough, but her smile didn't reach her eyes. I tried to lip-read their conversation, wondering if Mrs Best would mention Ivy, but they broke up abruptly, exchanging cold polite smiles. Once more I forgot to open the door for Mother. She stood on the pavement, jerking her elbow in annoyance. I leaned over to open it for her but she got to it first. She lowered herself in and gave out a long sigh.

'Have you finished your penance?

'Yes.'

'What were you given?'

I couldn't think. 'Eh, four Hail Marys and five Our Fathers.'

She started up the car and drove off, sliding her eyes over to me and back to the road again. 'That's very unusual.'

I looked down at my hands.

441

She switched on the radio and turned the dial to the country and western station. Tammy Wynette's voice went through me.

'I've to go back to the hospital for a check-up next week, in case you're interested,' Mother said, taking the turn for home.

'Oh. That's . . . good.'

'I could make an appointment for you to see your doctor before October, if you need to.'

'No, that's all right. I don't need to see him.'

She drove past home and pulled up at Molly's. 'Really? Those pills must be working, then.'

I nodded and got out to open her door.

'Are you getting your hair done?' I asked as she got out.

'No, you are. I thought I'd treat you.'

I looked at her in surprise. She pushed open the unlatched gate with her stick and headed up the path.

'Ooh, isn't Molly's sweet pea just gorgeous?' she said, walking up to the open front door.

Molly shouted hello from inside the house. 'Come on in — door's open!'

Mother ran her finger along the telephone table in the hall and held it up to show the dust. She pulled off her gloves and put them in her handbag before going into Molly's makeshift salon.

'Well saints preserve us! Doesn't she look well?' Molly exclaimed, her chubby hands splayed across her chest. Her nails were polished with glittery peach varnish.

Sadie's tawny head peeped around from the seat behind her. 'She does indeed. How are you, Elva?'

'Oh, as well as can be expected, girls,' Mother said, slipping off her coat.

Molly took it from her and hung it up behind the door. 'Sit down there in the good seat, Elva. Grace, away and pour your mother and yourself a cup of tea. The pot's on the cooker. God, Elva, you got some knock, didn't you?'

'Do you know, I can hardly remember a thing about it,' Mother began.

The door swung closed behind me. I went into Molly's grubby kitchen and washed out a cup before pouring milk and tea into it. I found a mismatched saucer and carried the cup carefully into the hall. Mother liked her tea full to the brim. Halfway down the hall, I heard her mention my name, and I paused.

'I don't know what the matter was with her but if I hadn't insisted to Josie that we go and see if she was all right, we'd have been blown to bits with the rest of them.'

'God the night. Sure we saw them taking away plastic bags with bits of the people in them. And there's an awful poster plastered up all over the place in town with some poor critter burned to a crisp,' Sadie said.

'They had no call to do that, those boys,' Molly said, tutting.

I walked up to the door and pushed it open. Mother held out her hand gracefully for the tea.

'Are you not having a cup yourself, Grace?' Molly said, brushing hairs from Sadie's rounded shoulders. 'I'm just tidying Sadie's perm.'

'No thanks. I'm all right.' I took a magazine from the floor and perched on the edge of the hair-dryer seat.

'And how's poor Willy, Sadie?' Mother enquired.

Sadie stood up and brushed tiny hairs off the side of her button nose. 'That man hasn't been the same since. Won't go out of the house at all. Sits there and listens to the wireless day and night. Sure the business is away to hell. He won't take the lorry out.'

I felt Mother look at me.

'Isn't that desperate? Oh, I'm vexed for you, Sadie,' she said, shaking her head.

'Elva, don't you be worrying about me. You've suffered enough.'

Mother took her tea in small, consecutive sips, eyeing Molly as she swept the fallen hair into the corner.

'Now, Grace, over here please,' Molly said, pulling out the chair Sadie had vacated.

I took the *People's Friend* with me.

'She's having it cut short,' Mother said. 'It's all tails.'

I looked in alarm at her partial reflection behind me in the mirror. She continued to drink her tea in tiny sips, her little finger crooked out.

'Grand. Well, we'll not bother with the bowl now — you're a bit big for that,' Molly cackled. 'Oh Elva, do you remember the face on Grace when she was a wee girl and the bowl came out? You'd have thought I was going to kill her stone dead with it! Tee-hee-hee!'

'It was the same with fish. You would have thought you were poisoning her,' Mother said, oblivious to Molly and Sadie's laughter.

'But do you know, I do think you got a far neater job with the children's hair with the oul' bowl,' Sadie said, pursing her lips and holding her head to the side, her fingers resting on the side of her jaw.

'Aye, but that's far too oul' fashioned for them nowadays. You daren't hardly open your beak to them, sure.'

'That's right, Molly. I never saw worse than those Belfast ones for answering you back. Should have heard them in the ward at visiting time. There was one brat giving back cheek to the woman in the bed beside me, imagine. If I was her, I'd have put my toe in his ass, I'm telling you.

'And you'd have been right,' Molly said, nodding at Mother in the mirror. 'Now, Grace, are you keeping the side shade or are you putting it in the middle?'

'The side. I — '

'Her head's not the right shape for a middle parting and she's a cow's lick you can do nothing with,' Mother interrupted. 'The Saturday nights I stood trying to get a curl into it. Of course she's a good head of hair but she won't do anything with it.'

Molly parted my hair with a wet comb and stooped to cut the back of it, the hard curve of her overfed stomach pressing against my upper back.

My shoulders stiffened and rose up to my ears.

Molly stopped after a few snips and straightened up with a moan. 'Frig but my back's sore. Oh here, Elva, did you hear about the police finding a gun in Dalloway's boat shed?'

'What?'

'A bloody big pistol it was, Bear said. They found it in the water and poor oul' Dalloway was hiding it and some oul' bastard must've give the Crumlin police a tip-off, for they raided the whole place and didn't they find it wrapped up in an oul' cardigan down the back of his toolbox.'

'Goodness, I saw Josie the other day and she didn't mention a thing.'

'Gave him an awful questioning in Castlereagh, they did,' Sadie piped up. 'Had him standing by his fingertips against the wall and some machine playing a sound into his ear, driving the man mad. God knows what else they did to him.'

'Apparently now they're looking to see where the cardigan came from. Dalloway said it was Josie's but didn't they go to see her, and didn't she say she'd never seen it before in her life. She's not right yet, that woman.'

'When was this?' I blurted.

Molly turned back to the mirror. 'Well, he only got out the other day. They held him for three days.'

She stooped to continue cutting my hair and I saw Mother crane to see my reflection. She frowned at the sight of my pale face and spooked eyes, but said nothing.

'Wee Josie must've got rightly shook,' Sadie said, holding her head to the other side now to watch Molly cutting my hair. 'I'd say she's half doting.'

'It's the shock of that oul' bomb, sure. I'm surprised you're not worse shook up, Elva.'

Mother set her cup down by her feet. 'Well I try my best to keep in control.'

'You're a great woman, Elva. A great woman,' Molly said.

She moved around to my left side and pulled my hair down over my face with the comb.

'About here, Grace?' she said, pointing the side of the scissors just below my ear.

'Shorter,' Mother said.

I gulped and put my hand up to my throat. 'I don't think I'd suit it that short. It's — '

'Nonsense. You suited it the best when you were small,' Mother said, looking at Sadie as if it was her she was addressing.

'It's just . . . I don't think I've the face for it.'

Molly hooted and pushed my head to the side. 'Grace, you've a nice face, the picture of your Granny Kane, and you shouldn't be having your hair hanging round it anyways.'

I felt on the verge of tears. I looked down and bit my lip.

'That's exactly right, Molly. Now cut away.'

'Don't worry, Grace, it'll be lovely. Oh Elva, did you hear that wee niece of Teasie

O'Mahoney's expecting? And no man on the scene of course.'

At any other time I would have listened with interest to the gossip about the pretty shop girl, but the howls of protest inside my head drowned everything else out. Sadie lowered her voice to a near whisper to fill Mother in with the juicy details. I had to keep swallowing back the lump in my throat, and I wound one leg so tight against the other, it went numb below the knee.

'Of course you know her mother had to get married,' Molly added, turning to incline her head at Mother.

'Have they no self-control, for God's sake?' Mother said sourly, flicking through her magazine.

I forced my eyes up from my fidgeting hands and peered through the curtain of hair in front of my eyes. It was cut straight across from ear to ear, just as if Molly had put the bowl on my head. I exhaled a jagged breath and made an involuntary squeaking sound.

Molly glanced at me. 'Oh, I think we'll give you a nice flick.'

I was beyond comment.

'Nothing too fancy, now,' Mother said. 'She'll want to be able to fix it herself for again.'

'Oh, there's nothing to it. She'll just have

to curl it round in the brush and blowdry it into shape.'

'I suppose we'll have to see about getting one of those hair dryers, then,' Mother said, reaching on to the floor for another magazine.

I had read the same two paragraphs in an article about UFOs for the last twenty minutes and not one word had gone into my head.

Molly lifted my new fringe up with the scissors and chopped into it. The muscles in my lower legs constricted and my throat began to ache.

I began to long for the fuzz helmet I'd had the last time I'd sat in this chair. Then the talk quickly moved to Ivy, and I braced myself for Mother's reaction.

'Apparently they'd balaclavas on, three of them, and they spoke with Armagh accents,' Molly said. 'Told her if she didn't keep away from the Brits and keep her mouth shut, they'd come back and kill her.'

'Nobody told me,' Mother said coldly.

'Ach, I'm sure they didn't want to go upsetting you, Elva, and you in the hospital and all,' Sadie said.

'I wasn't braindead. How come *you* were involved?' she said, looking into the mirror.

I kept my eyes on Molly's scissors. Fine ends of hair dropped into my eyeballs and itched them. 'I was just out for a walk and I found her.'

'What were you doing out walking at that time of the morning?'

'Mary and Nelly thought they heard one of our cows out and phoned — oh Molly, I think that'll do . . . '

'I'm just about finished . . . just a wee uneven bit here.'

'Let the woman do her job, Grace,' Mother snapped.

I blinked repeatedly to get the hair out of my eyes. Molly kept snipping around the sides until my ears were completely exposed.

'There, all . . . done . . . now,' she said, with a flourish of her comb.

I stared at myself. Two wispy strands stuck out from behind each ear, and a layered clump sat on my forehead like a duck's wing.

'Very nice, Grace — isn't it, Elva?' Sadie said timidly.

'At least those rat's tails are off,' Mother replied.

'And what do you think, missy?' Molly said, squeezing my shoulders.

I forced up the corners of my mouth. 'It's nice. Thank you.'

Their scrutiny made me redden. I leaned forward and brushed the cut hairs off the back of my neck to distract from the

451

embarrassment. I had no hair left to hide behind.

Mother paid Molly and they walked up the hall together.

'It is nice, Grace, really,' Sadie said, as I stood up, appalled.

I nodded at her.

'By the way,' she whispered, leaning in towards me. 'Did you have a good day at the christening? Didn't like to mention it in front of your mother.'

'It was nice . . . she's the loveliest child I've ever seen,' I said, a quiver in my voice. I wanted to lie down on the floor and beat my fists off it.

'Aaaah. And what — '

'Grace! Hurry up!' Mother shouted from the front door.

Sadie flinched at the sharpness of her voice.

'It'll take her a wee while to get over things, love,' she said, following me up the hall. 'We'll have a yarn some other time, you and I.'

Hesitant rain was pecking the tin roof but the sky remained baby blue. Molly handed Mother a small bunch of the sweet pea she was admiring and wished her luck.

'I'll see you in a couple of days for my shampoo and set,' Mother said on her way to the car.

'Cheery-bye,' Molly called.

'Cheery-bye,' Sadie echoed.

Mother opened the car door. 'You needn't get in, Grace — I'm just turning round and going into Dalloway's.'

I dithered at the end of Molly's path, not knowing whether she meant that I was to go too. I felt around the back of my head and recoiled at the lack of hair. I felt scalped and ugly. I pulled the side bits down on to my neck and headed for home. Mother turned the car and pulled up behind me as I was passing Dalloway's.

'Where are you going?' she shouted, one leg in and one leg out of the car. 'Come here immediately and open that gate for me.'

For all her beauty, sometimes Mother's classical face could turn milk sour. She marched ahead of me, hunching up one shoulder in irritation, and rang the doorbell. When there was no reply, she sent me around the back to investigate. The rain had become heavier and it splashed off the guttering on to my shorn head as I turned the corner of the cottage. I saw Josie through the kitchen window, kneading a lump of dough. I knocked on the back door and walked through.

'Holy Mother of God! Is that you, young

Grace? What've you done with your good hair?'

I flattened down the damp flick. Josie looked confused.

'I've just got it cut — Josie, Mother's round the front and she'll be getting wet. We came to see if Dalloway's all right.'

'Oh, run and let her in like a good girl. God, I never seen such a change on a young head . . . '

I left her muttering and ran to open the door for Mother. She stepped in and went straight to Dalloway's bedroom. I hung back in the hall, then went back into the kitchen.

'Ach Grace, isn't it good of you to call,' Josie said, smiling.

'Josie, is Dalloway all right?'

'Dalloway? He's a bit tired, now, after his wee holiday. Imagine going away to Spain on his own. Sure he's not wise.'

I smiled at her. She cut the dough into four rough squares and set two of them on the griddle on her range.

'He loves a wee bit of soda bread. Can't get none of that in Spain.'

Her tiny fine-boned face creased into her charming grin. It dawned on me that she wasn't joking.

'A wee drop of lemonade for you?'

'No thanks,' I said, feeling a new thickening in my throat.

'Well, you'll sit a while and mind that bread for me, will you? I've to go and lift the eggs.'

I watched her walk slowly outside to the henhouse, holding her flimsy hands out to feel for the rain. I wondered gloomily what was going on in her bomb-damaged brain. She disappeared into the henhouse and when she didn't reappear after five minutes, I got up and turned over the soda farls.

Mother's heels clicked against the floorboards of the adjoining living room.

'Dalloway wants to see you, for some reason,' she said from the doorway, half turning back.

'Oh, but I have to mind the bread.'

She began to walk away, then turned back and came into the kitchen, tutting. 'I suppose *I* could, for a minute. Where's Josie anyway?'

'Out getting eggs.'

I wiped the flour off my hands and made my way to Dalloway's room.

He lay on top of the bed with a hairy purple rug around him, looking out of the small window overlooking the lough. I loitered in the doorway until he saw me and beckoned me in.

'You're powerful scaldy, Grace.'

'I know. I hate it.'

'Don't be hating, now. Worse things could happen to you.' He steepled his hands in front of his nose and lowered his voice. 'No doubt you heard about the gun business?'

'Yes — Dalloway, why didn't you say the cardigan was mine? I could have backed up your story about how you found the gun.'

'No, Grace. I didn't want you getting involved. You wouldn't be able for those boys' questioning.'

'But I've nothing to hide.'

'Wheeest — is there somebody there?'

I looked around. 'No.'

The only thing I could hear was the whirr from the carriage clock in the living room.

'Thought I heard the boards creaking. Thing is, they were asking me up and down did I see these two fellas they'd these drawings of, and I'm telling you, one of them was the born spit of that one you've been hanging around with, before he tidied himself up. The other one was older.'

'Saul? What would they be doing with a picture of him?'

He leaned forward and I noticed deep grooved pouches under his eyes and a slackness around his broad jaw. 'That's what I'd like to know. I didn't want them getting to you on account of it anyhow, so you keep your mouth closed about the oul' cardigan.'

He lay back against the pillows and put his forefinger against his lips. This time I heard the creak.

'So if you could dig in during the break for the tea, it'd be a great help. They haven't too many helpers these days.'

I looked at him questioningly.

'Plenty of whist players but not too many volunteering to do the feeding.'

'Right. I'll be there.'

He closed his eyes. 'You wouldn't go and get me a drop of milk, Grace. I've an awful bad taste in my mouth.'

I met Mother in the living room.

'Oh — I was just coming to get you — Frank will be waiting for his soup,' she said quickly.

'Dalloway wants some milk.'

'I'll get it. You run on down to the house,' she said, glancing out of the window. The rain was hurtling down.

I dashed out through the front garden and ran home, ducking my head down as I passed Frank in the yard. In the kitchen I grabbed a folded towel off the plate rack and stuck my face in its heat. Dalloway's kindness made the tears that had been threatening all day suddenly run out of my eyes. I slumped down in the armchair and wrapped my whole head in the towel, listening to the rain battering the window, unaware that Frank had followed me in.

'Grace, Grace. What would you think if I got married?'

I slowly slid the towel down my face, patting the edge of it under my eyes. 'Who to?'

'It doesn't matter who to. What would you think?'

'You're a bit young.'

'I know. I know. But I mightn't get another chance — oh Jesus, here's Ma. Don't say a thing.'

I ran to put the kettle on, and stared out at the lough through the rain and my tears. My summer was over.

17

'You've changed, Georgina. You've gone all soft and hick.' Elaine pulled the cork out of the wine bottle. 'Well, I'm going to have some anyway,' she said, sniffing.

Georgina closed the lid of her laptop. 'It's funny, I haven't really felt like drinking these past few days. I've sort of fallen into the quiet rhythm of this place.'

'I don't know how you stick it. I'd be bored to death. And as for looking after a sick relative — yuk.'

'The home help does most of it,' Georgina said, putting loose pages into a file.

Elaine poured the ruby-coloured wine into a glass. 'What about those brothers of yours? Do they do anything to help?'

'They've only been here once, calling me a lick. They're convinced I'm trying to get in with Grace, so she'll leave me everything.'

'Aren't you?'

'It's not like that any more. Of course I could do with a few bob, but I like it here. There's something soothing about the land here — and I'm getting loads done on the project, into the bargain. Did you know the lough is supposed to have healing qualities?'

'Right, and I'm a banana.'

A tap sounded on the hall door and Dalloway shuffled in.

'She's rightly failed,' he said, his eyes vexed.

'Failed?' repeated Elaine, thin eyebrows arched.

'Lost weight,' Georgina said. 'Did she talk to you, Dalloway?'

'A little.'

'She'll only give me monosyllabic answers. It's very frustrating. I only want to help her.'

Dalloway folded his arms and leaned against the range. 'The woman's tired fighting, that all's about it. There's nothing much you can do, except be kind to her. She never had a soft word spoke to her for a long, long time.'

Georgina went over to the window.

'It's a pity we couldn't get her out on to the verandah, into that good fresh air,' she said, leaning over the sink.

'As long as she can see the water from her window, she'd be all right. Well, I better be going.'

Georgina saw him to the door. 'Oh Dalloway, do you think you could bring me over to the island one of these days? I'd really like to explore it, for work, you know.'

Dalloway stepped down stiffly on to the yard. 'Aye. Well, I'll give you a shout then.'

'Good. See you soon.'

Elaine refilled her glass and lit up a cigarette. The smoke made Georgina queasy. She wedged open the window, letting in a stiff breeze from the lough.

'What's taking you over there?' Elaine scoffed. 'Don't you know it's full of rats and trees and damn all else.'

Georgina reached down into her briefcase and took out an envelope softened and crinkled with age. She pulled out a folded sheet of yellowed paper and spread it on the table.

'What's that?'

'I found it in Grace's things. I want to go and investigate. You never know, all that stuff I half learned at university could come in handy after all.'

'Rather you than me. What else did you find when you were noseying?'

'Oh nothing much. But I think there was more to Grace than meets the eye. And I've a funny feeling she knows more about my mother than she ever let on.'

Elaine put down her glass and leaned across to touch Georgina's hand. 'Don't get your hopes up, friend. She seems to be a right stubborn one. What has you so attached to

461

her anyway? You don't even know her.'

'I . . . I don't really know. It's just a feeling I get when I look at her. It's like looking at an older version of myself.'

Georgina put the map back into the envelope and locked it into her briefcase, with the fine lace handkerchief and lingerie that smelled of violets.

★   ★   ★

Daddy's in the slime. The shooter tries to pull him back and Daddy swipes him off. Mother's running through the reeds. I am pointing. I know it's too late. There! There! Daddy plunges his arms in. He roars. The shooter pushes me back. I can't see what Daddy's doing. Mother is shouting his name. Frank is hiding. I step out from behind the shooter. Daddy's head's flung back and his lips are pulled back, and his teeth are shut together in a wide, straight line. His eyes are closed tight and he's pulling so hard all the veins in his forehead and in his arms have popped out. Mother stands beside me and shouts his name. He keeps on pulling but nothing comes up. The shooter tries to get him again. He is rigid. He makes another big scary sound, then he grunts and falls back. The shooter catches him and lays him down.

*His face is the colour of Cavehill. Mother
stands completely still and watches the
shooter kiss Daddy. Then she turns her head,
real slow, and hits me so hard on the side of
the neck that I fall down. I crawl away.*

★ ★ ★

I stood under the shower, rubbing linseed oil
into my scalp. Josie swore it would make my
hair grow an inch a week. After a fortnight,
there was no difference, other than it had
gone floppy at the front, like a boy's. I rinsed
out the oil and stepped out on to the new
fluffy pink bathmat Nelly Mullen sent down
for Mother.

I picked up my clothes and shoes, peeped
out into the hall and made a dash for my
room. A pack of Dr White's sanitary towels
and something in a long plastic covering lay
on the bed. I dropped my things on the floor
and pulled away the plastic. I caught my
breath. It was a white broderie-anglaise dress,
with short lacy sleeves and little pearly
buttons from the scooped neckline to the
nipped-in waist. I rummaged in my drawer
for underwear and flung on my whitest bra
and best pants, then put the dress over my
head and shimmied into it. It fell just above
my knees and fitted like a glove, but when I

463

looked in the mirror, I saw an overgrown
First Communion girl looking back at me
with a silly smile on her face.

I shook off the thought and rubbed my hair
almost dry, letting it sit flat against my head
instead of trying to make duck's wings out of
it. I sat on the bed to put my shoes on and
picked up the packet of sanitary towels. They
were covered in netting and had loops on
either end to hang on a belt. I looked up at
the calendar on the wall and counted on my
fingers.

'Grace! Come on — Bear's giving us a lift,'
Mother called from the kitchen.

I put the Dr White's in the underwear
drawer and fastened my shoes. Bear had
already started the car when I got outside. I
slid into the back seat behind Mother,
pushing a bucket and spade to the other side.
Bear drove fast. He and mother talked about
the weather and Bear predicted an Indian
summer.

'Soon be time for the second crop of beans,
Elva,' he said, looking out at the fields.

'Yes, and we've very little help to pull
them,' Mother complained.

Bear gave his teeth a suck. 'What about
that one that helped you the last time. That
stranger.'

'Don't talk to me about him.'

464

Bear changed gears to go up a hill. 'I hear he's hanging round The Scrog.'

'I don't want to hear about them ones either,' Mother said under her breath.

Bear adjusted the windscreen mirror. 'Always thought he was a suspicious-looking client. They're saying he's the one that got the O'Mahoney girl into trouble. Been seen hanging round around the time they reckon she was getting it, excuse my French.'

It was as if someone had nipped me in the face. I met Bear's guarded eyes in the front-screen mirror and looked away again.

'Oh, nothing would surprise me now,' Mother sniffed, looking into the side-view mirror to scrape a surplus of lipstick from the corner of her mouth.

Bear swung the car into the parochial hall car park and left us off at the door. Mother took an age getting out of the car, glancing around her at the steady flow of people going into the hall.

'You'll be at the Blessing of the Boats tomorrow, I take it,' Bear said as Mother thanked him.

'Wouldn't miss it, Bear — oh, and by the way — hope I'll see you at the chapel on Sunday. Father O'Loan has asked me to do the reading, to celebrate my recovery.'

Bear promised he'd be there and drove off.

'Don't be slouching,' Mother said as we walked in.

'Oh, thanks very much for the dress, by the way. It's lovely.'

'It's out of the factory shop but it was dear. Don't dirty it.'

Mother paid the postmistress at the back of the hall and got into a conversation with her. I stood aside, scanning the crowd for familiar faces around the long teachers' desks from the primary school, which were lined up in four rows from the stage down to the toilets. Bottles of brandy and whiskey, tins of biscuits, a large honey-coloured teddy bear and duty-free boxes of cigarettes were propped up on a basket on the side of the stage. The whole place smelled musty and unused.

I spotted Dalloway the very second he saw me. He was standing by the wide serving hatch to the left of the stage, and beckoned me over.

'I've got the wee dummy from Crumlin to give you a hand, Grace. She minds children and they've been letting her help out in the school canteen, so she'll know her way around. There's the kettles over there and the tea drums beside them, and the milk's in the window.'

'Are you better again, Dalloway?'

'There's not a thing wrong with me. It'll take more than that crowd to break me. But you watch yourself, and stay away from that Saul fella. He could be all right, the same boy, but just you keep to yourself.' The shaved skin on his throat rasped against his white shirt as he moved his head to loosen his tie. 'Ah, here's wee Maisie now.'

A short thin girl with thick spectacles and straggly chestnut hair to her shoulders walked up to the counter. I recognised her from Mass.

'Now, Maisie,' Dalloway shouted needlessly. 'This is Grace. She'll be helping you.'

Maisie held her hand out stiffly to me. I shook it and smiled at her. She smiled back.

'There are you now,' Dalloway said loudly, sliding his hands together. 'Oh, here comes your mother. How you doing, Elva? You're hobbling a bit.'

I watched her lean on her stick as she made her way over. She'd had her hair done and it framed her heart-shaped face in soft shiny waves.

'Oh I'm not too bad, Dalloway. Not too bad.'

Maisie stuck out her hand to Mother.

'Who's this?' she said.

'That's wee Maisie from Crumlin,' Dalloway boomed.

Mother put her stick into her left hand and briefly shook Maisie's hand without looking at her. Maisie glanced at me, then lifted up the flap on the counter and walked through it.

'Dalloway, would you find me a good table on the outside to start. I need to take the weight off my feet.'

'Certainly. Come on over here.'

He led Mother away by the arm and I followed. Faces turned to greet her and I knew from the way she held her head that she was giving her Queen Mother smile. It froze on her face when she turned to see me behind her at the chosen table.

'I thought you were making the tea?'

'Oh, she's time enough until the first half. The wee dummy knows what to do,' Dalloway said, pulling out a seat. 'And as far as I recall, young Grace is a fair good card player.'

Mother sat down carefully, her eyes cold. 'I wouldn't leave that young girl on her own back there, but whatever you like yourselves. It's nothing to do with me.'

She put up her hand to Father O'Loan at the top of the hall. Dalloway tugged his earlobe and looked apprehensively at me.

'I'll go and help her,' I said, unable to keep the disappointment out of my voice.

468

I walked away, feeling conspicuous and awkward in the white dress and the short hair, and joined Maisie behind the counter. She'd pulled up two stools for us and put on the kettles for the first boil. I sat up beside her and watched the crowd slowly take their seats, chattering and laughing heartily. Then Father O'Loan called for quiet and welcomed the ones who'd travelled far, and thanked Mr Best for donating the prizes. A muted ripple broke out at the mention of his name; no-one had expected him to bother with the other side again, after what happened to Ivy.

The game got under way. I counted the tables and peeped under cotton cloths covering the trays of sandwiches and buns on the counter. I counted the cups on the counter and the number of people wearing hats, anything to keep Saul and Mrs O'Mahoney's niece out of my head. Maisie sat beside me, staring straight ahead. We sat in silence for an hour, watching the players move from table to table after each game, listening to the burble of jumbled conversations between bouts, and the odd triumphant exclamation.

At nine o'clock Father O'Loan came to the corner and said we had ten minutes to go. He grabbed a handful of ham sandwiches and disappeared behind the stage. Maisie jumped down from her stool and began to make tea. She knew where everything was, so I followed her around, then poured milk and tea into the ninety-six cups.

They came to the counter all at once, hands grabbing from all directions as if the food was rationed. Nelly and Mary were among the first, oohing and aahing at my dress with their mouths full, and telling me I'd be getting myself admirers. Sadie and Molly said the same thing, and were surprised when I didn't flare up with embarrassment. I was too dead inside for that. I handed out cup after cup, while Maisie looked after the plates, nodding politely at anyone who said hello.

Mother didn't move from her table, but I saw that she'd been attended to.

Dalloway came up at the end of the serving for a second cup for her.

'You could always fall in with the second half, Grace,' he said, holding the cup out. 'Jimmy Burns has taken a funny notion and gone home. Said he saw the devil on the back of one of his cards.'

'I'll not bother now, Dalloway. Thanks anyway.'

He nodded and headed back to Mother. The game began again, and very deftly and quietly, Maisie began to load the dishes into the giant-size sink. I held up the drying cloth and she nodded, going about her business very seriously.

I watched her with increasing lethargy and let her do most of the work. I ate four buns in a row without tasting them, then felt sick. She handed me a cup of water and pointed to the stool. I perched up on it and after a while she came and stood beside me, pointing to my face, then my dress. I gave her a wan smile. She reached over and gently pulled down the lower lid of my right eye, then pointed to the dress again. I put my hands together and leaned them against my left cheek. She nodded solemnly and hitched her small body up on to the stool.

It was then the feeling crept up on me. My vision became blurred and the chatter from the tables out front slowed down and distorted, like a 45 record playing at 78. The laughter bounced off the walls and echoed in a swirl of sound, merging with the chatter and the shuffling feet into the cacophonic melee a warming-up orchestra makes.

I shook my head and the noise gathered speed, and the scraping of the chair legs on the floor became shrill violins screeching to a crescendo of white noise.

Sitting in an English garden waiting for the sun . . .

I felt Maisie's eyes on me and realised I'd been singing out loud.

Father O'Loan was peering around from the side of the table and heads were turned toward me from the top tables.

I slid off the stool, walked over to the sink at the far end of the room and threw up. Maisie came and handed me another cup of water and a tissue, and after a minute led me back to the stools.

I knew then that I might as well be as deaf and mute as the girl beside me. I was never heard. I was a shadow, only half alive. And if I stayed in Preacher's Bay, I would become invisible. I looked at Maisie and the people flicking their cards down on to the tables and saw my life unfold in front of me. I might never even make it as far as the tables. I saw summers in the bean fields and winters behind windows. I saw Masses and silent mealtimes, and solitary walks, and Easters and Halloweens and Christmases, all at the same table with two settings. One for me, one for Mother. I saw the bitterness already hovering on her face lodge in it and destroy her features. I saw her beauty fade and her body wither. I saw years of bedpans and insults. I saw a lifetime in my single bed.

I looked at Maisie and I saw myself.

She frowned at me. I'd been staring at her.

I pointed at my eye and tapped on my chest, where my heart was. She nodded. I made a T with my fingers, then tapped a beat on my hand, bent my fingers and ran them up and down my arm in jiggly movements, in imitation of a beetle.

She frowned again and shrugged. I didn't mind that she hadn't got it. She'd helped me make up my mind. I was out of there.

18

Georgina knelt on the carpet in the sitting room, scrunching up the newspaper into tight twists. She covered the grate with them and laid the sticks and twigs on top, struck a red-headed match and lit the paper at the edges, the way her grandmother had shown her when she went to live with her.

The fire whooshed and clucked. She took a brass-handled brush from the companion set and swept the coal in the narrow black scuttle so there would be no dust, then shook a sprinkling over the lit wood. The flames withdrew. She picked up the jam jar half full with diesel from the tank outside and poured a trace over the coals. The flames reappeared and licked the oil with relish. Gradually the fire took hold in the centre and a fragile heat began to build.

Georgina pushed the armchair closer to the fireplace and curled up in it. Gloomy people need a fire on a dark day for the light, her grandmother had said. The squally afternoon had been made worse for her by a niggling compulsion to drink the remainder of Elaine's wine. She had resisted but the battle had weakened her. She snuggled into the dusky-pink velvet cushions and watched the flames flirting, and tried to push away the anxieties that made her want to drink.

'Hullo? Are you there?'

Damn, she thought.

'In here,' she called.

The door handle turned and her brother stood in the doorway, dripping.

'Oh Bobby, take your boots off if you're coming in, and your coat.'

'Right you be.'

He reappeared seconds later in his sock soles. They had hay sticking out of them.

'Is Ignatius with you?'

'He's outside looking at that oul' bailer.'

'Does he think he could fix it up?

'Sell it, more like.' Bobby glanced around the room, then sat down on the side of the hearth. 'Soon dry off here. Well, how's your woman?'

'She doesn't say much. Molly Doherty and those Mullen women up the road have been filling me in, though I get the impression they're not telling the whole story. They say she built the farm from very little on her own. Even helped to put up the new gates and fencing around the place. Oh, and when she was young, apparently, she was involved with a guy who came out from Belfast to work here. He let her down, got somebody from the village pregnant. And she used to run around with a real tearaway called Ivy. They say she led her astray completely.'

'Aye. I remember talk of that. Powerful scandal at the time. That wee girl was tarred and feathered for going with a soldier.'

Georgina's eyes widened. 'God, that's horrific.'

Bobby gave an impatient shrug. 'Anyway, what way is she shaping up?'

'She seems weak. Reads all the time. I don't think the doctors have a bloody clue how long she's got. They don't tell you much, anyway.'

Bobby reached into the back pocket of his trousers and pulled out an open envelope with his name and address on it.

'Look, don't be letting on to 'Natius. I came across these in the back of the car. Must've fell out of one of those boxes of your woman's. Thought it was powerful curious, like.'

He pulled out a bunch of folded blue writing paper from the envelope and handed it to Georgina. The pages were thick and embossed. Georgina began to sift through them.

'They're letters, from them nuns at your old school,' Bobby said, rubbing the steaming leg of his jeans. The pong of silage wafted off it.

'I can see that,' Georgina said, frowning. 'They're all about me . . . like reports . . . ' She read on. 'Why on earth would Sister Perpetual be sending Grace letters about me?'

Bobby leaned forward and plucked out the sheet from the back of the pile and held it up.

Georgina read from it: 'Gratefully received, five hundred pounds in fees for Year One, January 1985. The Sisters of the Little Shepherd Convent Boarding Grammar School, Edenderry.'

She dropped the receipt on the floor and spread out the rest of the pages beside it.

'Jesus, Bobby. There's a load of them, right from when I started . . . look! Right up to my last year there? What's going on? Sure I didn't need fees paid . . . '

'Maybe it was that oul' eleven-plus test you'd to do to get into the good schools. You didn't get yours either, sure you didn't?'

'But I passed the review exam in my first year and that should've meant no fee . . . I don't understand. I'm going to ask her.'

She sprang to her feet and went to the door.

'Easy now, girl. Don't be getting excited — and don't be letting on to' Natius I give you those, will you? He's acting awful strange.'

Georgina paused in the doorway, shuffling the letters into order.

'No, I won't. Thanks, Bobby.'

★　★　★

I hear her coming. Why won't she leave me alone? I'm not ready for her yet.

The bed subsides gently under her weight as she perches on the side. She's got the letters and she wants to know everything. I'm not in the mood for disclosure. Dum dee dum . . . you know, that time I had the déjà vu in the confessional box, I think that might have been a premonition instead. A glimpse into my future comatose state. Sometimes I wish I was back there, for a bit of peace. I saw that Ignatius out snooping, through the window. Eejit.

Thank God for my books. She has pouches under her eyes. They used to say you got them after you lost your virginity. I think you get cynical too. I mean, it's got to be the first major disappointment of adulthood . . . oh, I tried so hard to pretend it wasn't true. But you couldn't keep secrets from her. Those brittle blue eyes missed nothing. Especially stains on a dress.

478

★ ★ ★

After the upset over Dalloway's arrest, Father O'Loan had asked for a full turn-out for the Blessing of the Boats. I'd left the house early to walk to the pier on my own, but Frank caught up with me halfway down the road.

'You look wrecked,' he said, leaning over to catch his breath.

'You smoke too much. I got no sleep last night.' I walked on.

'Grace, you're acting different. You're kinda changed, whatever's bit you.'

I pulled a blackberry as I passed a cluster of them on the hedge, rubbed the sand dust off it and put it in my mouth. 'Are you getting married or not?'

'I'm working on it. Ma's not going to like it.'

'What do you expect?'

He fell quiet.

'Who is it anyway?'

He kicked a stone in front of him. 'You'll find out soon enough.'

'Bit of a dark horse, aren't you?'

He gave the stone another swift kick and it scuttled off into the hedge and sent a rabbit darting out. It twitched its nose at us and bounced away.

'There's some crowd down there the day,'

Frank said. 'Come on and we'll get a good spot.'

He ran ahead and climbed over the fence at the side of the main gate in front of the pier. I followed him though the overgrown grass to the whin bushes to the left of the pier. Newly painted fishing boats bobbed from their moorings on the posts, which someone had garlanded with roses and carnations.

'Take a pew,' Frank said, holding his arm to two upturned barrels by the water's edge.

I sat down on one of them and watched people gather in front of the pier, carrying rosary beads.

'They'll get foundered standing there,' Frank said, straddling his barrel. 'We're far better tucked in here.'

I glanced at him and felt a wave of regret. I was going to miss him when I went away.

'Frank, I've something to tell you.'

'Oh?'

I heard the ground crunch behind us. I turned around and Willy was there.

'I see you've found the best seats,' he said, tipping his cap at me. Under the peak, his eyes were dead, the dancing lights in them switched off for good.

'Well, William,' Frank said, shifting over on his barrel. 'Haven't see you since . . . this ages.'

Willy lowered himself on to the other end of Frank's barrel. The padding in his cheeks had slid down and given him jowls.

'Thought I'd better make an effort.'

He took out a pipe from his pocket and tapped it on his knee.

'That was a bad business about Dalloway,' Frank said.

'Aye. Dalloway was well betrayed. Don't know how that one sleeps in his bed.'

I glanced at Frank. He shrugged.

'Who, Willy?'

'Ah, now.'

Willy flicked on his lighter but a sudden breeze swooped in and snatched the flame. Goosepimples rose under the sleeves of my brushed cotton blouse.

'He wouldn't have needed to look too far.'

He crooked his hand around the lighter and sucked on the pipe. I met Frank's openly curious eyes.

'Jesus. He wouldn't.'

'He would. The man suffers from his imagination. Thought somebody was going to come and shoot him. Ach, he hasn't been the same since Florrie was took. I can understand the man's head going but at the same time, it got Dalloway into a powerful bother for having the oul' gun hid. Sure, they wouldn't believe he got it out of the water then, no

481

matter what anybody said.'

Frank shook his head. 'Jesus. I thought Bear had a bit more sense.'

'We'll not get a minute's peace from them boys now. Sure look, that's more than likely a couple of them there.'

I followed Willy's gaze to the other side of the pier, where two unfamiliar men in suits with open-neck shirts were standing looking at the crowd, Mother, Josie and Dalloway among them.

I pushed my foot off the ground and rolled the barrel back, so that I was partially obscured by the bushes. The breeze grew colder and made a woo-woo sound.

'Here's O'Loan. Hope he doesn't keep us too long,' Willy said, his side teeth clicking off his pipe.

Father O'Loan's surplice swelled and flapped in the stiff breeze. He carried a brass ball of incense and a sprinkler. An altar boy beside him held a large black cross.

Father O'Loan began to warble the rosary. Frank and I mumbled along in response. Willy just smoked. All three of us watched the two strangers while they watched everyone else. One of them turned in our direction only once. I thought he saw Willy's smoke rising. I saw Mother scan the crowd, and look behind both of her shoulders. She linked arms with Dalloway and leaned heavily on her stick. Pain had tarnished her even more than the long disappointment of her marital years.

At the end of the rosary, Father O'Loan climbed awkwardly on to the pier and began to sprinkle the boats with holy water. The crowd watched in silence as he made his way up and down, silhouetted against the white sky and grey water. When he reached the end he said a prayer to St Peter, then Mary Mullen cleared her throat and started up 'How Great Thou Art'.

I closed my eyes and listened to the lulling melody of the hymn and the varying pitches of the voices carrying it. The sun blinked out just in time for the end, and the coughing and talking began. Willy stood up and turned away to surreptitiously wipe away a tear.

'I'll be leaving you,' he said, heading to the pathway.

'Right, well I'm away into town — be seeing you,' Frank said, walking towards the milling crowd.

I slipped up the road with Willy, listening to stories about Charlie I'd heard over and over again. I smiled and hmm'ed in all the right places, and let him lean on me when he got tired, and when we got to his cottage, he turned and put a big warm hand on my shoulder.

'Now, you listen to me, Grace. I've heard your Mother took an ugly agin you, blaming you for not spotting Charlie in his trouble, but I don't blame you, Grace. Me nor nobody else, no matter what oul' McNicholl says.'

'I . . . thank you Willy.'

'You're not to blame, Grace. No-one is. These things happen.'

I wanted to put my head on his shoulder. He took his hand away and reached into his pocket for his key. I waved to him and strolled down the road, my resolve bolstered. Up ahead I saw Dalloway's car pull up outside our house. Mother and Sadie got out and walked into the yard, and Dalloway drove on. He stopped the car outside his cottage, jumped out and waved me over.

'Get in, Grace, quick.'

I got into the front seat beside him.

'Did you see those two men down at the pier?' he said, looking through the back window.

'Yes — were they police?'

'Worse. They're Provos and they were asking all sorts of questions about somebody sounding very like your friend, that Saul fella. Asked if he was travelling with another fella, like the big brute the police showed me. And Jesus, didn't your ma pipe up about your man Saul — said she'd seen somebody like him hanging round the village.'

'But . . . but what's Saul got to do with those men? I don't understand — '

'Face it, girl, he's trouble and he's in trouble by the sound of it. Your ma at least didn't mention he'd been staying here, at least she knew that much, but wasn't I waiting for her to say he'd been down at The Scrog — '

I gasped. 'Oh no! Did she?'

'No, thankfully, and they went on their way, but somebody else will tell them, you mark my words. Look, I tell you what, I'll drive you down to The Scrog and if he's there you can warn him, at least.'

I nodded. The news had sickened me to my stomach. Dalloway started up the car and drove quickly around the bay, constantly checking the road behind in the windscreen mirror. He switched the radio on and searched for a news programme but there was only Saturday afternoon football on every station. George Best was in the process of scoring a hat trick for Manchester United. Despite his urgency, Dalloway became absorbed in the commentary, raising his fist in excitement when Best scored another goal.

'Their lane's up there, Dalloway,' I said, in case he missed it.

He sped up to the lane and turned sharply into it. The car rocked along the dips and potholes.

'I'll wait for you in the car — you run on in,' he said, turning up the volume of the radio.

I jumped out and ran across the yard and up the passageway to Uncle Sean's cottage. At the front, I heard children crying and a man shouting. I hesitated, then ran around to the back. Saul sat on the back doorstep with his head in his hands. I called to him and he looked up with shock already etched on his face.

'Grace! Oh Grace, have you heard?'

'Yes — they were looking for you down at the pier . . . '

He stood up, his eyes wide. 'What? Who?'

Uncle Sean opened the back door and ran over to me. 'Have you seen her? Where is she?'

I looked from Uncle Sean's frantic face to Saul's scared one in total confusion.

'Seen who?' I asked Uncle Sean.

'Ginny — she's gone! Left! Ah God, I thought you'd news,' he half cried, stumbling around the yard, dragging his shirt across his chest. The boys' bewildered eyes peered out from the doorway. Behind them the baby cried.

Saul clutched me by my arms. 'Who's looking for me, Grace?'

'Two IRA men . . . Dalloway said they were asking questions.'

He paled, his eyes stricken.

'I've got to get out of here,' he whispered, turning back towards the door.

'What's going on, Saul?' I asked him.

He turned back to me and looked hard into my eyes. 'Grace, would you come with me?'

I stepped back from him. Uncle Sean had run off into the pig house.

'But . . . wait, where did Ginny go? I can't believe she'd leave the children.'

'She left a note, said she couldn't stick it any more. We don't know if she'd run off with some fella or what. She's been acting strange recently — but Grace, listen — come with me. You've no life here anyway.'

'You wouldn't have come back for me . . . you're only asking me because I'm here — '

'No! There was something I had to do first, then I was coming to see you. Look, we have to make a plan. We don't have much time.'

'But I promised Ginny I'd look out for the baby . . . oh God. She'd this all planned, she must've. Oh listen to that wee thing crying

487

her head off. What's going to become of her?'

'Ginny would've wanted you to come with me. Look, we don't have to be here to make sure the child's looked after. Sean's a good man and we can send him money.'

'I don't know . . . I heard about you and Mrs O'Mahoney's niece . . . '

'What? I only ever spoke to her once, in the shop — whatever you heard is lies.'

He pulled me close to him. 'Grace, I need you with me. Please come.' He leaned his forehead against mine. 'Please.'

I broke free of him and ran into the house, brushing past the boys in the doorway. I picked up the baby from her cot and held her against my jumping heart. She snuggled her hot wet face into the side of my neck and gradually quietened as I rubbed her back. The boys watched me suspiciously.

Saul followed me in, wringing his hands.

'Look, Grace, why don't you go home and think it over, and if you decide you want to come, meet me at the mill tomorrow morning at ten o'clock. I'll get a car between now and then and we'll go. Just promise me you'll think about it.'

The baby gurgled and bobbed her head against my jaw.

'What about the child? And the wee boys even?'

He couldn't hide his distress when he looked at them. Then a thought struck me, and I went out to find Uncle Sean. I met him coming out of the shed, one hand slapped over his mouth.

'Uncle Sean, I know a good girl who could look after the children, until you find Ginny. She'd be very good to them — '

'Huh?'

'Wee Maisie McGuinness from Crumlin. She can't speak or hear properly but she wouldn't take her eyes off them, and she's real smart.'

He rubbed his hand down his chin and on to his throat and took in a jagged breath.

'Aye, I know her da. They're good people.'

'I can ask her tomorrow at Mass. I know she's mad looking a job.'

'I suppose it would do . . . I could go and look for Ginny. I daren't tell her ma — she's a bad heart.'

'That'll do then.'

I handed the baby to him and ran back down the yard, Saul at my heels.

'Grace — will you promise me you'll think about it? We could be happy.'

I promised him I would. But trying to forget my other promise was killing me.

★　★　★

That night I dreamt of my father. He was mowing the lawn and all the neighbours were in the kitchen, eating stew, and everyone had forgotten that he was supposed to be dead, except me. I told them, 'He's alive, alive!' and they laughed. I went to the door and called him in for stew. I put it on to a plate that I'd forgotten to warm and when I turned to set it down on the table in front of him, he had turned into Walter Matthau.

I awoke with my face screwed up and a dull pounding headache. Within seconds Mother came into the room and pulled across the curtains. The sunlight poured straight into my eyes.

'I don't want to be late for Mass,' she said, opening the window wide.

I raised myself on my elbows, blinking.

'What are you going to wear?' she asked, looking in the wardrobe. 'Have you no nice suit?'

I stifled a yawn. 'Just the Donegal tweed one I got at Christmas . . . it's a bit warm — '

'It'll do. Make sure you've a nice white collar underneath it.'

She began to rearrange the books on the corner shelf. I lay waiting for her to go. I hadn't put my nightdress on and I didn't want her to see me in my underwear.

'Frank tells me you'd Willy with you

yesterday,' she said casually.

'Yes. I think he's doing a bit better.'

'Him and Sadie are very forgiving people. There's others who find it harder . . . you got off light.'

She spoke with an air of distraction. I sat up, keeping the blankets over my shoulders.

She turned to the dressing table and began to shake out the lace mats. 'Why haven't you been taking the tablets for your fits?'

I didn't know what to say.

'Well?'

'I . . . they were making me queasy.'

'Why didn't you say so when I told you about going to the hospital?'

'I didn't think.'

'And what if you'd taken another fit and made another show of yourself in front of the people? Don't you care about people talking about you? Sure the whole country thinks you're . . . never mind. We'll just have to get you more tablets.'

'I . . . eh . . . don't think I need any.'

She turned to face me. 'Are you mad? Do you mean to tell me there's nothing wrong with you?'

I wanted to hurl my alarm clock at her face. 'I think I'm better now.'

She turned back to the dressing table and pulled out the side drawer. 'Only for being able to blame the fits, I would not be able to hold my head up among the people.'

I considered making a dash to the back of the door to grab my dressing gown but she spun around, with the Dr White's in her hand.

'How come you haven't used any of these?'

I blushed faintly at the sight of them. 'Oh, I don't need them yet.'

She threw them on to the bed. 'You have your monthly in the first week of the month, don't you? This is the fifteenth of August.'

'It hasn't been regular recently,' I said quickly.

She picked them up and put them back in the drawer.

'Get up. We're going to be late.'

She made no move to go. I put my feet on the floor.

'What's keeping you?'

I stepped quickly over to the door and reached out for the dressing gown. It had snagged on the hook. I held my breath under the weight of her stare, hunching my shoulders to distract from my breasts. She stood watching until I'd freed the dressing gown and put it on, then she left without a word.

I searched frantically for a blouse with a white collar but could only find a round-neck one with a frill on the front, which was too tight in the armpits. I threw it on and pulled on a pair of American Tan tights and the tweedy skirt. The waistband dug into me and the jacket collar itched my neck.

Mother was walking in and out of the bathroom and her bedroom. I got on to my knees and stretched into the back of the wardrobe and took out a lacy underwear set Ginny had given me. I folded it as small as it would go and wrapped it in a new lace handkerchief, then stuffed it in the brown leather handbag which went with the suit. Then I took the envelope with my birth certificate in it from the top of the wardrobe and put it in the bag too.

The clock chimed for 8.30 a.m. I waited for Mother in the kitchen. The birds weren't up yet. She came in spraying a cloud of Lenthéric perfume in front of her and walking into it. Her lemon bouclé suit made mine look like a headmistress's, and when I got into the car, I noticed a ladder in my tights.

She gave me her walking stick to hold and drove quickly to the chapel, even though we were early.

'Did I tell you why they want to see me at the hospital, by the way,' she said, switching off the engine.

'It's a check-up, isn't it?

'It's more than that,' she said, smoothing her eyebrows in the windscreen mirror.

I waited.

'Because of the internal damage, I have to have a complete hysterectomy. They're taking every damn bit out.'

I stared straight ahead at the empty street. She reached out and yanked my face around by the chin.

'I'm losing everything that makes me a woman, do you hear me?' she said in a near whisper.

'I'm sorry . . . sorry.'

'So you should be. It's your fault. All yours and nobody else's. I will have a limp for the rest of my life. It will get worse and the bone will crumble in ten years. I will lose my womb and that will make me old. You did this to me. You.'

'But Mam — Mother, you said if it hadn't been for me, you would've been killed!'

She took her hand off my chin and held her wrist limply. 'It would've been better if I'd died. You have destroyed my life anyway.'

She took the stick and eased herself out of the car. I sat and waited for her to walk ahead, blanking out her words. They didn't matter any more.

I could see the top of the mill beyond the

494

trees in the distance and felt an urge to run towards it. But I had to see Maisie, had to keep my promise to Ginny in some small way. I got out of the car and tried to swivel the cutting waistband around my middle. From the gates I saw Mother under the archway, talking to Nelly Mullen. She had pink lupins for the altar in her arms.

'Pssssst! Grace!'

The voice was coming from the grotto at the top of the graveyard. I walked on slowly. It came again.

Mother had gone into the chapel with Nelly. I looked at my watch. Fifteen minutes to spare before Mass started. I turned and walked across to the grotto. I blessed myself. The high decorative hedge behind the stone frame rustled and a small slender hand crept around the edge.

'Ivy — is that you?'

One dark eye peeped out.

'Get in here would you — I can't be seen.'

I looked around, then darted behind the grotto. Ivy stood half smiling at me. Her hair was growing back in black tufts and the pupil of her left eye was enlarged and off-centre.

'That's the frumpiest get-up I've ever seen,' she whispered, eyeing me up and down. 'Look, I shouldn't be here — '

'Are you all right, Ivy? I've . . . I've sort of

missed you around.'

'Well you're gonna miss me more. I'm out of here and your Frank's coming with me.'

'What? Frank?'

'I told him I didn't think it was right going off without telling you or you'd be worried sick, no matter about your oul' Ma. He's waiting for me now. I . . . I think I could grow to love him, Grace, and you know he's always been in a notion of me.'

'But . . . I — where are you going?'

'New Zealand. Tonight.'

I opened my mouth but no sound came out.

'There's no life for me here, Grace.'

'I can't believe this! What about Frank? He's got the farm and everything . . . '

'He wants you to have it. He's getting far better land out there — he'll make more money. Go to see the solicitor, Grace — Frank signed his inheritance over to you. Don't look so scared. We'll write.' She leaned over and kissed me on the cheek. 'I forgot to thank you for finding me that night. Jesus, I was nearly a goner. Look, I have to go right now.'

She patted my cheek. My mind reeled.

'But . . . why . . . Ivy, wait! Why do you have to run away like this? Sure it's only a seven-day wonder, what happened to you

. . . I can't understand it.'

She made to go, then turned and took me by the arm. 'Grace, I'm pregnant. That's what I was trying to tell you that night. That's why I have to go away.'

'Pregnant? Oh Ivy! Is . . . and Frank's the father?'

'No, but he says he'll look after the baby as if it's his own.'

'But who — is it the soldier?'

'No. I'm three months gone and he used a johnny.'

'Who?'

'It's Saul. Saul's the father, but he doesn't know — so keep it zipped. Sure he's supposed to have been messing with that girl O'Mahoney too. Real bloody Romeo, him. Look, I have to go. Goodbye, Grace — take care of yourself.'

She ducked through a gap in the hedge and disappeared.

I leaned against the grotto until the church bells bonged and woke me out of my stupor. I blundered out from behind the grotto, forgetting to look first. The postmistress and Mrs O'Mahoney gaped at me from the side of the graveyard. I walked past them in a daze and went into the chapel. Mother stood at the back, looking at her watch.

I automatically lifted a Mass sheet from the

collection table. The heading swum before my glazed eyes

Parish of Preacher's Bay.
The Assumption.
15 August 1974.

Mother approached me and gestured towards the aisle. I followed her like a robot. She walked up to the fifth seat from the front and stood back to let me in first. I slid over to the middle and she sat at the end, going over her reading. The Virgin had been garlanded in roses and the sun fell on her beautiful gormless face. I stared at her so hard I thought I saw her blink.

Father O'Loan had everyone on their feet for the Confiteor before I noticed Mass had begun.

'I confess to Almighty God and those before me that I have sinned . . . '

That's when it started.

Hot sweat trickles. I reach up and scratch my burning neck. I smell old wet tea leaves off myself. The hissing in my ears shoots up to full volume. I can hear only the hiss and the sound of my swallow, and my breathing in my nose and my ears. Father O'Loan walks over to the bench, hands joined, and sits down beside the altar boy, a big fluffy white cloud nestling up to a little one.

A woman's heels clack up to the altar. She genuflects and walks up to the pulpit. She is my mother. Her mouth opens and the cacophony starts. I tug at the waistband. She is talking about the arc of the covenant opening in heaven. I can see inside it. A giant prawn in the tabernacle.

'Now a great sign appeared in heaven; a woman, adorned with the sun, standing on the moon, and with twelve stars on her head for a crown.'

How lovely. How beautiful . . .

The woman pauses. She looks down at me with fond sparkly eyes.

'She was pregnant, and in labour, crying aloud in the pangs of childbirth . . . '

The fiery itch spreads from my neck down my chest and into my groin.

The woman's voice is soft. I can barely hear it above the hiss. She is speaking of a huge red dragon with ten horns and seven heads with crowns on them.

'Its tail dragged a third of the stars from the sky and dropped them to the earth, and the dragon stopped in front of the woman as she was having the child, so he could eat it as soon as it was born from its mother. The woman brought a male child into the — '

I heard a scream rip out of my chest. My

legs stood up of their own volition and ran into the aisle. I saw Mother's hands melt into the sides of the pulpit. I closed my eyes and I saw the Charlois bull gore a baby and eat it. I recognised the baby's cry.

'Maisie McGuinness! Maisie McGuiness! Are you there?'

The aisle became very long and massively wide. On the pews sat dolls. I ran to the bottom. No Maisie. I tore back to my seat. Father O'Loan was standing beside the woman in the pulpit.

'Go on! Go on! I know! On your right stands the queen, in garments of gold!'

Hands hold my arms and drag me back into the aisle. I wave goodbye to the prawn in the tabernacle. It has grown little hands and feet, and a big black eye. They turn me around and march me down the aisle. It has shrunk again and there are real people with moon faces in the seats. I smile at them and pat my groin.

'This is my tabernacle,' I tell the men at my sides.

The doors swing open in front of us and I walk into the sun. Then I spin into the black.

19

The east wind sliced in through the tall slim trees on the island and chilled the clearing by the tower. Wild garlic soured the air, made colder by the lack of light. Only faint slivers of early April sunlight filtered through the trees.

Georgina sank her spade into the upturned earth.

'Dalloway, there's no need really. You look tired. I can do it myself.'

'I'm not tired — just old. Digging is no job for a girl. Anyway, I wouldn't mind seeing what these monks left down there. What is it you said you were looking for?'

Georgina sighed. 'Oh, just some coins, or things like the brass pins they used on their cloaks. And I can do this as well as any guy, Dalloway. I used go on digs with the archaeology club at university.'

She spaded soil from the hole.

'They say that round tower dates back to ten and twenty, round the time them big Danes invaded. See the way they've the door built away up high? That's so those boys couldn't get in after them.'

'I know that, Dalloway. It's a watch tower.'

They dug on, falling into an easy rhythm.

'Good soft ground,' Dalloway said. 'I could do with a bag of it for the garden.'

He paused for a moment, leaning on the handle of his spade and loosening his tie.

'You know the *Maid of Antrim* used to stop here on her pleasure cruises. The children loved roaming about the place. Grace and Frank were over here regular when they were small.'

Georgina blew a loose strand of hair away from her face.

'What was Grace like as a child?'

'Ach, she was a good wee girl. Powerful shy. No harm in her.'

'What went wrong with her?'

'That's not for me to say.'

Georgina's spade hit against something hard.

'I've got something — over here, Dalloway. Go carefully now.'

She probed the earth with the side of her spade, gently upturning the moist black soil, and gradually uncovering the unmistakable curve of a human jawbone.

'Fuck!' Georgina shrieked.

Dalloway put the side of his fist to his mouth and stepped back.

'Is that what I think it is?' whispered

Georgina, falling to her knees. She took a deep breath and clawed at the soil until the skull was uncovered.

'Don't think that's one of your monks,' Dalloway said quietly.

His calm fleetingly struck Georgina as odd. She continued to push the soil away with her hands.

'No. It's too recent . . . and this is far too shallow. Can't have been there for more than twenty or thirty years. Could you not give me a hand?'

'I want no part of it,' he said, edging back.

Minutes later the torso lay exposed. Dalloway walked away and blessed himself. Georgina worked carefully until the full skeleton was visible.

'Whoever he is, he had good leather boots on him,' she said, chipping the earth away from the skeleton's feet. Dalloway watched silently from the side of the tower, resting his shoulder against the flaking stone wall.

'Did you ever hear of anyone going missing locally over the years, Dalloway?'

'No, not a one. Not that I can think — '

'Oh! Did you hear that? That's something very hard . . . '

Georgina stood up and tested the surface at the foot of the skeleton with her spade. She began to dig quickly.

'It looks like . . . some kind of . . . toolbox . . . it is — there's the handle,' she said, excitement creeping into her voice. 'I'll dig away round it and you give it a pull.'

Dalloway hesitated, then moved forward and hauled at the handle. The box slid out of the pliant earth with ease.

'I wonder does the deceased there have a key?' he said, scratching his brow. Like many dark men, his eyebrows had stayed black while the hair on his head had turned silver.

Georgina ignored him and kicked the box on to its side, then with all the force she could muster, brought her spade down along the rim.

'You'd be as well to leave that alone,' Dalloway said, moving towards her.

'No! I can do it.'

She held the spade aloft with both hands and slammed down repeatedly on the hinges. Eventually the lid snapped open. She stuck the spade under it and pulled it back, tipping the box on to its side.

'Jesus,' she whispered.

Small clear plastic bags of cash tumbled out on to the ground. Georgina sank to her knees and emptied out the box. 'My God, there must be thousands of pounds there!'

Dalloway looked down at her, a knowing look in his brown eyes. 'You weren't expecting to find oul' brooches down there at all, were you?'

She got down on all fours and began to put the gold back into the toolbox. 'Not really, Dalloway.'

'Well, if you're going to the police, you can count me out.'

Georgina stood up and began to re-cover the skeleton. 'No, I won't be going to the police. Not just yet, anyway. Look, you're going to have to trust me on this one, and keep quiet about this. Grace has a lot of questions to answer.'

'Grace?'

Georgina heard the lack of surprise in the old man's voice and noted how he diverted his eyes from hers. 'Yes. Good wee Grace.'

* * *

She came into my room and asked me straight out.

I knew she'd get there some time, but not nearly as quick. When I didn't answer her, she threatened to go to the police.

'I'm just about fed up with all this secrecy — why won't you talk to me?' she shouted.

I put my hands up against my ears.

'Well, we'll see what the cops have to say about it then.' She went to the door.

505

'I don't think your brothers will be too well pleased.'

The sound of my voice took us both by surprise. I hadn't heard it since I spoke to Dalloway, a week ago. I sounded croaky, and old.

She looked at me with her chin raised, the image of her father.

'Oh! She speaks!'

'I've had nothing to say to you until now. But it's time now, I suppose.' I reached out for the glass on the bedside table. It was empty.

'What do you mean? And what do Ignatius and Bobby have to do with it?'

I pulled myself up against the pillows. 'Can I have a glass of water please?'

She ran up the hall and back again with the water, spilling some of it on to the continental quilt she'd bought for my bed.

I took a sip and put the glass on my locker. She stood looking down at me, her hands on her hips.

'Well?'

'Well, that's their inheritance you'd be messing with.'

'Their inheritance?' she squeaked.

'Yes. I've left it to them, along with a bit of meadow.'

She sank down on the side of the bed. It

was half a minute before she spoke.

'But . . . I . . . whose bones are they beside the money?'

'Oh, it doesn't matter about him.'

'Grace! How can you say that about a person?'

'That person died trying to murder somebody else, and he'd killed plenty more first.'

I drained the glass. She sat staring at me accusingly, shaking her head.

'I tell you what, you're obviously a good snooper, but didn't you think to take a look under my mattress? Was that too obvious? You didn't think I'd keep everything together, did you? I think you'll find your answers down there, middle left.'

She gawked at me for a few seconds, then stood up and stuck her arm in under the mattress. She found the letter right away.

'This is crazy. You don't open your mouth all this time, now all this? Who is this letter from anyway?'

She pulled out the last page.

'Saul?'

'Yes. The one I'm sure you've heard all about, from Molly and Nelly. Not much gets past those two. The letter will tell you what you want to know. Read it out please.'

She held the first pale blue page close to her face.

29 August 1974
'Dear Grace

You don't know how much I wanted you to come with me. I waited all day at the mill for you. But you've made your decision and I have to live with that. I also have to live with the fear of being hunted down, Grace. I couldn't tell you at the time. It was an impossible situation. You deserve to hear the whole story. Please don't think too badly of me when I tell you.'

She paused to straighten the pages, then continued.

'I think you always knew the story I told wasn't true. I could see it in your eyes.

On the night you found me, I'd been out on the lough in a dinghy, with another guy. I can't tell you his name. It was an IRA operation. I'm not proud of it but I got mixed up with them after the Loyalists burned us out of our house. We had been ordered to dig up some funds hidden on Matt's Island and bring them to America to buy guns.

We had trouble locating the spot in the dusk but eventually I found it and began to dig. Then just when I hit on a box, next thing I know this guy is taking a pistol out and pointing it at me. It jammed and we got into a fight. I got the gun and hit him with it around the head and he fell and smashed the back of his head against the round tower. I felt for his pulse but he was gone. I didn't know what I was doing. I buried him where he fell, then I panicked and ran back to the shore.

It was dark and cold, so I decided to stay on the island for the night. I pulled the dinghy in over the stones and lay in it but there was a terrible smell, like something dead, and it began to rain. I took the dinghy back on the water and I was heading towards a pink light in the distance when the air started to go out of her. There was nothing I could do. It was a lightweight thing and it must have got ripped. It completely deflated. I pulled my boots and my bottoms off and swam towards a pink light in the distance. It was so cold, unbelievable for May. I worked out later I was in that water for four hours.'

She turned the page, glancing at me. I closed my eyes.

'I'd get so far, then I'd lose my bearings. I couldn't see the light and I realised I was drifting back towards the island. I was scared to death. I swam out to what I thought was the shore again and I began to go numb. I went down twice. I began to think about weird things, like the boy I sat beside in primary school, silly stuff, and I started to pray but I couldn't remember the words. I slipped under the third time, then I felt something hit against my foot. I don't know where I got the strength from but I managed to pull myself forward. I'd got onto the shallows.

I don't remember a lot after that. I know I lost my shirt getting through that big thorny hedge at the top of the shore bank. I saw a light on at your house and walked across the field towards it but I was falling down with exhaustion and the cold. Then I saw a big round container in the middle of the field — '

She turned another page.

' — and I got into it and fell asleep for a while. There was hay in it. It was still dark when I woke up and I knew I had to get out of the cold or I would die. I pitched myself out of the thing and dragged myself towards your house. I think the worst bit of the whole lot was those sharp stones around the back of the house digging into my bare feet.

So there you go. That's what happened. Do you see why I couldn't tell you? I reckoned I had a little time before they'd come looking because this guy had been planning to go to the States the next morning. If it hadn't been for that gun turning up, things might have been all right. It sank with the dinghy and our unit got wind of it when the police started asking questions.

All that time, Grace, I didn't expect to fall for you. When you saw me at the bonfire, I was doing some fairly risky intelligence-gathering, hoping I could pull something off on my own. But I knew the game was up after the gun turned up and they came looking for me. This is the important part, Grace. Only four people, including me, knew the whereabouts of that stash and one of them is buried on the island. The other two are locked up in Long Kesh and they don't have the map. I've enclosed it for you, Grace. That money could buy you your freedom. If you don't use it to come to me (I'll let Sean know where), then use it to get your freedom, anywhere away from Preacher's Bay.

I hope life treats you well, Grace.

Saul

PS I've sent you my locket. I'd like to think of you wearing it.'

She lowered the pages. She had a glimmer in her eyes. 'Sean?'

'Yes. Your father. He brought me that letter personally, to the home.'

'The home?'

'Purdysburn. The loony bin. I was there for five years after he went. I miscarried my baby there.'

'Jesus, you were pregnant? Nobody said.'

'You don't talk about those sort of things around here. I wouldn't have been a good mother anyway. You learn cruelty, you see, and it becomes the most natural thing in the world.'

She ran her hand through her hair. 'But I heard about him. He got somebody else pregnant.'

'Oh yes. He was a very fertile boy, it seems. But the O'Mahoney child wasn't his, like everybody thought. That turned out to be the butcher's.' I took a sip of water. 'No, Saul's son is alive and well and living with his mother — Ivy — in New Zealand. Frank's with them. He's the only father the child's ever known. They won't come back now. They're happy.'

She sat down the edge of the bed. 'But why didn't you take the money and follow Saul?'

I sank back into my pillows. The fatigue was setting in again. 'Apart from anything else, it was too late by the time I got out of the home.'

She shook her head and as I watched her sitting there, a little unsure of herself, and a little like me, I felt my life force dwindling.

'And what happened to your mother? Nobody would really say.'

It seemed only fair to tell her everything.

'She died having her womb out. She never did get to visit me. I mourned her, despite everything. Everyone said she was the third, that her death would bring the run of bad luck to an end. So much for that. There were three dead already.'

My hand shook as I took another sip of water. I leaned back, exhausted.

'The house was empty when I got home but I had the land, and I grew to love it as much as Daddy did. I built up the farm . . . and I found the real me. I was free.'

She sat down beside me and took my hand in hers. A lone tear dripped off her cheek. 'What happened to Saul?'

'Oh they found him. In England. Brought him back home to the border. They tortured him all night, then shot him in the face.'

'Where is he buried?'

'They put him through a factory meat grinder and fed him to pigs. Actually, he always liked pigs.'

She widened her watery eyes at me.

I yawned. 'Georgina, I'm tired.'

She stood up. 'One last thing, Grace. Why did you pay my school fees?'

'Oh, that. I made a promise to your mother that I'd always look out for you. I had to educate myself with books to keep the other promise she made me make. I knew you'd get better attention at that school if those nunners were being looked after.'

'You were right. They were wonderful.'

'Your mother loved you, you know. I know it mightn't have seemed that way, but she did. If she'd stayed, it would have been worse for you.'

She sighed. 'I think, at the back of it all, that's why I've been drinking. I thought I was to blame for her leaving and that guilt never left me.'

'You are not to blame for anything. Kill your guilt before it kills you. I learned that the hard way.'

She smiled and turned the door handle. I

turned my head on the pillow towards her.

'So aren't you wondering how you've done of out my will?'

'No . . . no, don't be like that.'

I smoothed out the quilt. 'You get the house and the farm. Look after it, won't you?'

She didn't speak for a moment. 'I . . . I don't know what to say . . . '

'Best not say anything then. You won't go to the police now, will you?'

'No.'

'Good. Now, would you go and ask Dalloway to come and see me please? That old cod knew rightly what was on the island. He was the only one I ever told.'

She smiled. 'I thought as much, the way he was acting. I'll run up and tell him now. Need a bit of fresh air.'

She came back to the bed and kissed me on the cheek. Nobody had done that since Ivy. After she'd gone, I lay and watched the sun slide down on to the water and the sky turn peachy. I took Saul's locket from under the neck of my night-dress and held it, and fell asleep thinking of sprickleybacks in a stream.

★   ★   ★

Is that a shadow? It's got very dark all of a sudden.

'Who's there?'

The shadow moves towards me. There's something in front of it.

It doesn't speak. It comes closer. I put out my hand and flick on the lamp . . . there's a pink velvet cushion in front of me.

'Oh . . . what are you doing?'

He presses the cushion into my face and holds it there.

Oh, but there was no need, really . . . it's all sorted out now . . .

I can see the most dazzling azaleas. And I can hear that orchestra.

It's in tune now.

THE END

Other titles published by
The House of Ulverscroft:

THE MEMORY STONES

Kate O'Riordan

Nell Hennessy left rural Ireland at sixteen to have her daughter, Ali. In over thirty years, she has never returned. Now she lives an uncluttered, elegant life in Paris, enjoying her independence, only broken from time to time by her married lover, Henri. Until a phone call shatters the peace of her carefully constructed world . . . Her daughter and granddaughter may be in grave danger and Nell can no longer avoid the inevitable. She must return to her childhood home. But what prevented Nell making that journey before? And how has the unspoken impinged on the lives of four generations of women?